# THE LAST DRUID

## BY TERRY BROOKS

# THE FALL OF SHANNARA

# SHANNARA

## THE LAST DRUID

# TERRY BROOKS

DEL REY

NEW YORK

2021 Del Rey Mass Market Edition

Copyright © 2020 by Terry Brooks
Map copyright © 2012 by Russ Charpentier
Excerpt from *Child of Light* by Terry Brooks
copyright © 2021 by Terry Brooks

Published in the United States by Del Rey, an imprint of Random House,
a division of Penguin Random House LLC, New York.

DEL REY is a registered trademark and the CIRCLE colophon is a
trademark of Penguin Random House LLC.

Originally published in hardcover in the United States
by Del Rey, an imprint of Random House, a division of
Penguin Random House LLC, in 2020.

The map by Russ Charpentier was originally published in
*Wards of Faerie* by Terry Brooks, published in the United States
by Del Rey, an imprint of Random House, a division of
Penguin Random House LLC, in 2012.

This book contains an excerpt from the forthcoming book
*Child of Light* by Terry Brooks. This excerpt has been set for this edition
only and may not reflect the final content of the forthcoming edition.

ISBN 978-0-399-17856-6
Ebook ISBN 978-0-399-17855-9

Printed in the United States of America

randomhousebooks.com

4  6  8  9  7  5  3

Del Rey mass market edition: June 2021

FOR MY READERS:
THOSE WHO STARTED OUT WITH ME,
THOSE WHO CLIMBED ABOARD ALONG THE WAY,
THOSE WHO STAYED TO THE VERY END,
AND ESPECIALLY THOSE WHO MAKE UP
THE SHANNARA COMMUNITY.
THERE ARE NO WORDS TO EXPRESS ADEQUATELY
HOW MUCH YOU HAVE GIVEN ME.

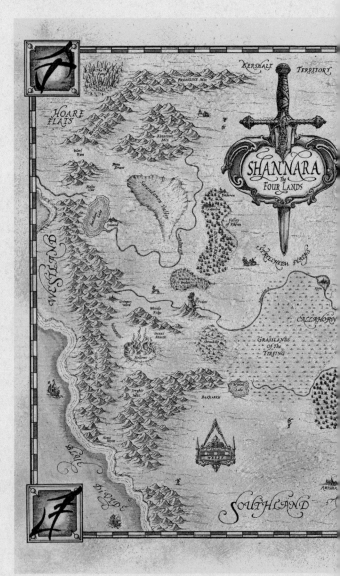

# ONE

◆

TARSHA KAYNIN WAS NOT dead. She should have been, but she was not.

It surprised her when she woke from the blackness into which she had fallen when she had gone over the cliffs of Cleeg Hold and dropped toward the churning waters of the Mermidon several hundred feet below. She could feel sheets of hard rain beating down on her, soaking her clothing and chilling her body. She could hear the sounds of the storm all around her—the staccato slap of raindrops against the stone walls of the Rock Spur cliffs, the howl of the wind, and the thunder of the rain-swollen river as it surged wildly down its narrow channel. She was dangling from something that had snagged her and now held her fast. Yet as the buffeting winds set her swaying back and forth, she was reminded of how precarious her situation was.

Still, she was not dead.

Her aching, throbbing head provided further proof. She must have hit it as she fell. Perhaps the blow was even responsible for saving her. Perhaps it had slowed her just enough, arresting her fall sufficiently to allow the cliffs to catch hold of her. She could not remember, and she would likely never know for certain. But one thing she did know: She could not remain where she was. Sooner or later, the winds would tug her loose and she would begin falling once more.

Her eyes were tightly closed—in part to shut out the fury of the storm, and in part to protect her vision. The rain was falling so hard that each drop stung the skin of her face, and she did not want to chance what it might do to her eyes if she opened them. But the darkness allowed her the space and time to regain herself, to recall the events that had led to this moment. Her memory was momentarily fuzzy—a result not only of the blow to her head, but of something more . . .

*Tavo!*

It all came rushing back in a flurry of terrible images. Drisker, her brother, and herself landing on a rocky shelf high on the cliffs of the Rock Spur at the entrance to Cleeg Hold. Clizia Porse, using her magic to attack them from hiding, striking Tavo so hard he went down in a heap. Drisker rushing to strike back. A gap in time opening as she cradled her brother fearfully, willing him to wake once more. And the storm all around them—the flashes of lightning and the booming of thunder, the darkness and the rain, the overwhelming sense of everything having gone wrong . . .

Then a blow of such force—a strike of dark magic launched by Clizia Porse before either she or Tavo could prepare for it—and she was thrown through the air and over the cliffside into . . .

*Unconsciousness, emptiness, the dark.*

What had happened to her companions? She had no way of knowing.

Carefully, so as not to jar her position, she lifted one hand to shield her eyes from the rain so she could peer upward. She could see the cliff wall behind her and the rocky projection that had caught the collar of her heavy cloak to stop her descent and hold her fast. A one-in-a-million chance of this happening, and yet it had. Again, she recalled Parlindru's words, foretelling her future: *Three times you shall die, but each time you shall come back to life.* Surely, this qualified as one of those times. Was this the last of the three? Tavo had nearly killed her twice, so mustn't it be?

She forced herself to concentrate, to stop the rambling flow of her thoughts, and to study the rain-slickened rock she must somehow climb to safety. She could not see the edge she had tumbled over; it was too far above her and lost in blackness. But it didn't matter. She knew she had to find a way to reach it.

What skill did she possess—what magic—that would allow her to do this? She tried to ignore the aching in her head; the pain made it hard for her to think.

Drisker had helped her to develop a considerable range of talents, and she had taught herself others. Yet she saw no projections on which she could gain any handholds save for the one that had snagged her, and one was not enough. She searched for foliage or vines she might grip, but there was nothing. She could try calling for help, but that would be dangerous. If Clizia was still up there, she might hear—although the sounds of the storm were so furious that she couldn't imagine anyone hearing anything.

Then, as if in response to nothing more than contemplating the possibility, lightning flashed and a dark figure stood at the edge of the cliff, leaning over. Tarsha's glimpse of this apparition was fleeting, but she knew instinctively it was the witch. She kept watching. Looking away now would not help; either she had been seen or she hadn't. So she waited, eyes fixed on the point where she had spied the other woman. Then the lightning flashed again, illuminating the cliff edge, and Clizia Porse was gone.

Tarsha held her breath. Had Clizia seen her dangling against the cliffside? Was she visible from above? She waited, the minutes ticking away in her head. She imagined her death dozens of times over—a drop into the abyss of the canyon, everything brought to an abrupt end. She imagined what it would feel like.

Then she heard a new sound, one she recognized—the whine of power generated from diapson crystals as thrusters engaged and an airship lifted off. The sound heightened then slowly died away as the airship moved farther off. Clizia was gone.

Tarsha waited until she was certain, then cried out for Tavo and Drisker, one after the other, over and over. When there was no response and she realized no help was coming, she knew she was going to have to save herself.

But how could she manage it? Even if there were hand- and footholds to be found on the cliff face, she would have to swing close enough to the rock wall to grab onto them before her cloak tore loose. It was a faint hope at best, but without any way to gain purchase on the cliffside, it was unthinkable.

For a while she just hung there, a steady erosion of any hope breaking down her failing confidence, certain that—with the next gust of wind—she was going to die. She tried to tell herself that she just needed to think it through, that something would occur to her if she did.

But her situation suggested otherwise, and she began to despair.

Then, still running through the list of skills she had acquired while mastering the wishsong's magic, she paused momentarily when she remembered her ability to appear in one place while actually being in another. Like the Skaar almost, but . . .

She caught herself, stumbling over a possibility that seemed so remote and unlikely that she almost dismissed it out of hand. But desperation forced her to consider it further.

If she could make herself appear to be in one place when she was really in another, might it not be possible to actually *move* herself elsewhere? To transport herself, in the flesh? Was it not a logical extension of how the wishsong could make the impossible manifest? Logic and life experience told her otherwise, but her understanding had progressed beyond both of these barriers. If necessity was the mother of invention, then why couldn't her desperation make the impossible real? Just because she had never tried it didn't mean it couldn't be done.

And what other choice did she have now?

She closed her eyes once more and began to hum softly, summoning the magic. She had to be very careful. She had to both free herself from her cloak and place herself in virtual form back atop the rocky shelf. And she had to accomplish this and hold it all in place while she took it one step further and moved her corporeal form into her apparition. She was not even sure how she would do this—only that she must find a way.

Even more daunting, she could not experiment, but must make it happen on the first try.

*Three times you shall die, but each time you shall come back to life.*

*Let it be so.*

She forced herself to relax, then seized hold of her magic and pictured herself on the precipice somewhere above where she dangled and projected the image that would place her there. Then she closed her eyes to the world and pictured herself lifting upward. Through her singing, she projected what she wanted to happen, making it real by force of will alone. She imagined and then caused herself to lift out of her cloak and into the rain-swept emptiness of air and wind—rising, as a shade might, into the storm, the weight of her body becoming that of a feather. She sang herself clear of her garment, sang her way into the void, so insubstantial that not even the wind and rain and cold were a part of her existence. She gave herself over to her magic, disappearing into the impossible in an effort to make it real, closing off any thoughts of falling or of death.

*Believing.*

It seemed to take forever before she felt herself merge with her projected image and allowed herself to become corporeal again. As weight and solidity returned to her form, she was aware of firm ground beneath her feet once more; the hard, rocky surface of the ledge was as real as the shortness of breath that engulfed her the moment her song died away. She stood where she was for long seconds, afraid to look, unwilling to break the spell. It was entirely possible she was only fooling herself and nothing had happened. If she looked, she would know. And if she had deceived herself, she would fall.

She felt as if the world had shifted on its axis—as if something in her life had been upended and nothing would ever be the same again. She opened her eyes . . .

And the truth was there, waiting to welcome her into its arms.

# TWO

FOR LONG MOMENTS, TARSHA stood where she was—soaked to the skin, battered and aching, but alive. She stood on the edge of the precipice she had willed herself to reach, through no more than the magic of her wishsong. She should have died. She should have fallen into the canyon and been lost forever. But death had been denied once more, and she had been given yet another chance at life. And the surge of intense gratitude and happiness she felt as she embraced this unlikely truth filled her with new hope.

When she had convinced herself that the feel of the hard rock beneath her boots was reality and not imagination, she turned back to find Tavo. At first, she didn't see him. The gloom and the rain conspired to wrap everything in a blanket of shadows and shimmering damp. All she could make out—and this only barely—was the dark bulk of the airship that she and her companions had flown in on.

When she finally spied her brother's huddled form sprawled upon the ground, she rushed to him at once, but her heart sank as she neared. He lay so still. She dropped to her knees and pulled him against her, whispering his name, calling him to wake, begging him not to leave her. But she could already tell that he had. The life had gone out of him. She bent to him and cradled him, realizing as she did so that he had been cut nearly in half, discovering, too, that his throat had been slit. Refusing to accept what her eyes were revealing, raging against the unfairness, she used what faltering remains of her wishsong magic she still possessed in an attempt to revive him, filling the air with its sound, wrapping him with its healing power, summoning every last bit of magic she had at her command until there was nothing left to try.

Then she wept as she clutched him to her until there were no more tears left, and those she had shed had mingled with the rain and were lost. That he should have died like this was unthinkable. He had been so strong in his magic; he must have been rendered completely helpless for this to happen.

*Tavo,* she whispered to herself. *Tavo, Tavo.*

He had suffered so much in his short life, and all of it leading to this. He had come back from his madness and begun to regain control of himself. Drisker had helped him believe that he might yet have a purpose to his life, and that he might put that purpose to good use. He had come to realize that his sister loved him— and had always loved him. He had recognized that she was there for him and would always be.

Except, she thought with a bitterness that nearly undid her, she hadn't been there when he needed her the most.

It didn't matter that she couldn't be there, that she was herself in danger of dying. Or that she had done everything possible to protect him from a creature so devoid of any morals or compassion that killing was nothing more than a necessary exercise. The hard truth was still that she had failed him when he needed her, and she would have to live with that the rest of her life.

What she felt about Clizia Porse in the few seconds that she allowed herself to consider it was so incendiary that her rage and pain transformed into unspeakable thoughts of what she would do to the witch once she caught up to her again. Because she would find her. She would hunt Clizia to the ends of the earth and beyond. She would bring her to bay, and then she would destroy her once and for all.

She laid Tavo down again carefully, touched his face gently, and bent to kiss him. The rain was beginning to lessen as the storm moved eastward. She rose and looked about at the bleak emptiness. She needed to find Drisker.

She summoned a werelight the way Drisker had taught her and moved toward the opening into Cleeg Hold through which he had disappeared while giving chase to the witch. The corridor she entered wound ahead for a long way, and there was visual evidence of the battle that had been fought here. Finally she reached a widening in the passageway in which the magic's residue was so thick that the space she was entering stank of it. The floor, walls, and ceiling were scarred with gouges and tears. It was not hard to imagine what had happened. This was where Drisker had caught up to Clizia, and a terrible struggle had ensued. What had happened was unknowable, but two things were certain: Clizia had emerged to kill Tavo, and Drisker was missing.

She took time to search for any sign of the Druid, both at the battle site and in the stretch of corridor beyond, but there was nothing that revealed the details of what had transpired. It was possible that Drisker, like Tavo, was dead, but she could not make herself believe it. Not until she had real proof—and even then she wasn't sure she could accept it. Drisker had survived so much. The slaughter of the Druids at Paranor, his banishment into a limbo existence, the assassination attempts, and more. He was bigger and stronger than any death that might come for him.

Yet he was still missing.

She retraced her steps, trying to decide what to do. She was alone now, and a part of her was whispering that enough was enough. How much could she expect to accomplish on her own? How real was the possibility that she could track down Clizia and dispatch her in revenge for all that had happened? Maybe it was time to step away from all this. What chance did she have without Drisker Arc's leadership and guidance?

She didn't know.

But there was something else to consider. If she walked away now, she would be abandoning Drisker and those who had gone on to Skaarsland to try to save the Four Lands. She would be discarding all of her efforts to make Tavo's life mean something beyond the madness that had seized him and caused him to hurt so many people. It was bad enough that her brother was dead; it would be worse to abandon the fight that had cost him his life. Also, she knew what

Drisker would say if he were there. She had promised to serve him in exchange for the help he had given Tavo. Until she knew definitively that he was gone, she had no right to consider only herself.

She took a deep breath and put aside her doubts. She couldn't quit now. She wouldn't. If she were to do so, she would never recover from the sense of failure she would have to live with.

But what was she to do now? Where was she to go?

She returned through the passageways of Cleeg Hold to where Tavo lay and knelt beside him. The storm had passed now, leaving behind remnants of damp, chilly air, rain-slickened stone, and distant rumbles of thunder. For a long time, she didn't move or even look up at the skies as the clouds separated and marched on in solitary splendor to reveal broad swatches of blue. Sunshine brightened the world anew.

It was then Tarsha made her decision. She needed to find out what had happened to Drisker. If he was still alive, she must find a way to make contact with him. She had done so before—or, more accurately, *he* had contacted *her*. Dreams and visions were a means of communication for Druids removed to other places, so perhaps it would be so here. In the alternative, she must find a magic that would reveal the truth about his fate.

Such capabilities were beyond her, but help might be found in Drisker's books of magic—the ones he had retrieved from the ill-fated forest imp, Flinc. She had saved the books from the fire that had destroyed his home, only to have Flinc pretend that he was the one who had saved them. Drisker had discovered the truth, of course, and then had hidden the books again. As yet, even Clizia had been unable to find them, but Tarsha thought she knew where they were and how they could be retrieved. If she was right, she would have a chance to study them and perhaps learn what she needed to know about Drisker and what her own future required of her.

First, though, she must return to Emberen to discover if she was right.

She broke from her reverie, retrieved a blanket from the airship, wrapped it about her brother, and secured it tightly with ropes she retrieved from a storage bin. With strength she didn't know she possessed, she dragged his body to the craft, lifted it over her shoulders to carry up the short ladder, and laid it inside on the floor. It was the best she could do for now. When she reached Emberen, she would bury her brother there. There was nowhere else she could think to take him. He no longer had a home in Backing Fell, and it saddened her to think of how uprooted and isolated he had made himself, how devoid of family and home he had been when he died alone in this far-off place in the deep Westland. She decided that if he belonged anywhere, it was in Emberen, near the home of the man who had done the most to help him.

It was where Tarsha would hope to end her days, as well, as it was now her only home, too.

She knew she should sleep before departing. She was already exhausted from the day's struggles and nightfall was coming on, the skies east already darkening. But she could not bear to spend another moment in this place. She could at least fly to somewhere less forbidding before stopping for the night and giving herself over to sleep.

Taking a quick look around at the peaks of the Rock Spur and the site of her brother's last moments—thinking of how it might have been Drisker's final moments, as well—she climbed into the airship, powered up the diapson crystals nestled within the confines of their parse tubes, and lifted off into the widening blue of the late-afternoon skies.

She flew out of the Rock Spur and into the foothills that formed the western border of Elven country. Finding a sheltered spot along the Mermidon, she set down, wrapped herself in blankets in the cockpit, and promptly fell asleep. Had she been less tired or more concerned for her safety, she might have taken better precautions against unwelcome intrusion or threats of attack, but by then her exhaustion was complete, her need for rest pressing down on her like a great weight and her ability to think impeded.

Thus she slept without thoughts of safety or care for her fate, and dreamed of Parlindru.

The seer appeared to her as a shade, a ghost, as she stepped from heavy gloom to greet Tarsha with a smile. Her features were clear and so familiar that Tarsha found herself smiling back, but the rest of her was not much more than a gathering of mist and shadows, shifting endlessly as she approached.

*You have suffered much, Tarsha Kaynin,* Parlindru said, speaking the words so that they were no more than thoughts in the girl's mind. *I am sorry. But life deals out unexpected joys and sorrows, and we can but treasure or suffer each. A word, then—after which I will go. You have found my prophecy to be true, have you not?*

Tarsha nodded.

*Do you remember the rule of three? Do you remember what I told you about how it would affect your life?*

Tarsha nodded again. In her mind, she spoke her answer. *Three times shall I love and all three shall be true, but only one will endure. Three times shall I die but each death shall see me rise anew. Three times shall I have a chance to make a difference in the lives of others and three times shall I do so. But one time only shall I change the world.*

*Some of these prophecies have happened. Some have not. Your tale is not ended, and your life is not complete. All of us live under the promises offered by the rule of three. For you, some of this is now evident, but some has yet to be revealed. For that to happen, much will be asked of you. Some of this, you already know. The rest will reveal itself in time. But this much I can tell you. You may not turn aside. You may not forsake what you have been given to do.*

*How will I know what that is? How can I be certain?*

The old woman changed suddenly to one much younger, but clearly the same. *Your heart will whisper to you. Your conscience will guide you. Your truth will reveal itself.*

She slowly reverted again, the age lines and depressions returning, the course of her life revealing itself on her face.

*I am so tired,* Tarsha confessed.

*So you must rest both mind and body before continuing on.*

*But I don't know if that will be enough. I've lost everything. I've lost the people I care about. I've lost the path I thought I knew. I've lost the will to do what I think is expected of me. I am broken, Parlindru. I am weak and unsure and lacking.*

The words were out of her mouth before she could stop them and she broke down in tears, ashamed and at the same time relieved to have shared her terrible sense of failure. Without moving, Parlindru seemed to reach out and stroke her cheek.

*All these will come back to you, Tarsha, so long as you do not lose your faith. Hold it close. Believe in its power.*

She withdrew her hand, whispered farewell, and was gone.

Whereupon Tarsha Kaynin woke to find herself alone.

# THREE

◆

It took Tarsha another two days of hard traveling to cross east out of the foothills below the Rock
Spur Mountains to the Tirfing grasslands, then turn
north along the edges of Drey Wood and the Streleheim past the Rhenn and up to where the village of
Emberen could be found, nestled in the Elven forests
miles above the city of Arborlon. Any weather that
might have required a longer journey had moved off
into the Borderlands and eventually south into the
Anar. So the days were sunny, the skies clear, and flying smooth and uneventful.

It was late in the afternoon of day three of her travels when she sighted her destination, and she set down
on the small airfield that serviced the village's public
and private transport, where the field manager was
waiting. He observed that she seemed "all tuckered
out" and inquired if she needed anything. She asked
for a wagon and horse so that she might transport the
body of someone she loved whom she had brought
home to bury.

"I can help you with that," said the man. She had
found him before to be somewhat surly, but now he

seemed subdued. "In fact, I will drive the wagon myself to wherever you wish to go, and see to it that your loved one is laid to rest."

"That isn't necessary," she demurred. "I can handle it myself."

"Of course you can, young lady. But I made a bargain with your father to help you anytime you might show yourself in the village. He asked that I look after you and aid you in every way I could. He gave me credits to bind our bargain, so please don't make it impossible for me to hold up my end. Let me help."

She objected once more to this extra effort—skipping over his mistaken assumption that Drisker and she were related—but he refused to hear of it. He would leave the airfield temporarily in the care of his eldest son until his return. Her craft would be cleaned and put away safe until she needed it. There was no point in arguing; his mind was made up.

"Your father and I, we weren't friends, really. But we were men who treated each other as worthy. Your father, you know, was a man to be reckoned with and admired."

*My father. Drisker.* She nearly broke down again, tears welling up in her eyes at the idea of it. At how close it was to the truth.

"This is a hard time for you. I understand that. I lost my wife a year ago and am still getting over it. You and I, we may not know each other as well as your father and I did, but we have a community to share and common decency to bind us. Come, now."

She nodded her agreement and began the process of unloading supplies and clothing while waiting for the other to procure a wagon. When he returned, he helped her take Tavo's body from the cockpit of the airship and place it in the wagon bed, surrounded by the rest of what she would take with her. They rode in silence toward the cottage Drisker had arranged to be built for him two months ago, following the destruction of the old one. Tarsha was told she could set up house and await her father's return, happy to have a place that could be hers for as long as she needed it.

As they neared the cottage, she asked her companion to pull his wagon to the side of the road while she walked on ahead alone. He asked for an explanation, but she told him this was something private and that she would only be a minute. She climbed down and walked until she was almost to the cottage, then used her magic to search the house and grounds for any signs of life. It was not unreasonable to wonder if perhaps Clizia—who had taken up residence here before—might have chosen to return. She did not expect her to, but caution was necessary wherever Tarsha might go from now on.

Her search yielded nothing. The cottage was vacant and the land surrounding it empty. She turned away, satisfied, and walked back to the wagon.

Once arrived, and with the field manager providing company, she walked the grounds until she had selected a place filled with sunshine and wildflowers in which Tavo could be laid to rest. Her companion immediately set about digging a grave, insisting he would do the work on his own and she was not to involve herself but to sit with her loved one. She had not told the man who it was she was burying, and he had not asked. So she had forsaken conversation for a final few moments with her brother, sitting close to his wrapped form, lost in her memories.

When the grave was dug, the two picked up Tavo and lowered his blanket-wrapped body, still tightly secured by the ropes, into the ground. The airfield manager then filled in the hole and tamped down the loose earth.

"There now, all done," he said with a final pat of the spade handle. "Laid to rest close at hand, where you can visit him. He'll be at peace now, knowing you'll be watching over him." He paused. "I'll arrange a headstone, if you wish, tomorrow."

"No, let me take care of that," she replied. "I want to craft it myself."

She thanked him profusely and waited until he was gone to kneel in front of her brother's grave and speak softly to him.

"I failed you, Tavo, and I am sorry beyond words. I should have found a way to be with you, to protect you from what happened. I should have done better. All I can do now is tell you that I loved you always. If forgiveness is needed for the acts of madness you committed, I am offering it. You were not responsible for what happened to Mother and Father. How could you be when you did not understand what you were doing? Anyone who had been locked away and mistreated as you were might easily have done the same. Nor can you be held accountable for all the others who suffered at your hands while you were trying to protect yourself. All that *must* be forgiven. Not just by me, but by yourself, as well. Give yourself that forgiveness. Wherever you are now, rest easy."

She was crying again, sobbing hard, so she stopped for a moment to compose herself. Then she began whispering once more.

"Clizia Porse will not escape punishment for what she has done. It may not be me who administers that punishment—or even Drisker—but it will be delivered in full. There shall be no peace in this evil woman's life from this moment forward. She shall be a hunted thing: a creature deserving of no mercy and no forgiveness and no respite. And all that we set out to do together—you and I and Drisker—will be done. I will do my part, just as Drisker and the others will do theirs."

She caught herself, realizing that she was assuming a great deal by including Drisker Arc, who might not even still be alive. But she could not make herself think otherwise if she wished to keep him alive in her heart.

She reached down and smoothed over a rough spot in the earthen fill that covered her brother. She took her time, using her palm. She let herself grieve as she did so, knowing it would not be the last time—that there would be no end to her grieving until the life was gone out of her.

Shards of fading daylight played off her white-blond hair as she sat back quietly, staring down at the grave. It was all so unfair. It was all so final and arbitrary and unacceptable. She would have done anything to change it. Anything.

A moment later, she looked up and found Fade sitting across from her. The big moor cat was as still as stone, and her coming had escaped Tarsha entirely. How could anything so big move so quietly? She wiped away a few tears and smiled. "Well met, Fade."

The cat said nothing, of course, and made no movement.

"Are you here to watch over me? Or just to keep me company?"

Nothing.

Fade held her position a moment longer, then rose and walked back into the trees. Gone for now, it seemed, but Tarsha was certain the cat would not go far.

She rose and stood looking down at the fresh patch of earth. "I want you to remember me, Tavo. I want you to remember that I will always be thinking of you. I will always miss you and love you."

She went back into the house to put away her clothing and supplies, goods and weapons, then made herself dinner. The darkness was complete by the time she sat down to eat, the last of the daylight vanished, and the sky was filled with a scattering of stars above a slender crescent moon just visible through the treetops to the east. She took her time with her meal, not tasting much as she ate, washing it down with several glasses of ale. She was no longer crying, and the food and drink helped ease her hunger and thirst. But she was not sleepy, and the thought of taking to bed right away was not attractive. Too keyed up, too distraught, she needed to fill the time in some other way.

So she wrapped herself in her cloak to stay warm against the night's chill and walked back out to Tavo's grave. Once settled, she simply sat there, listening to the night sounds and looking about for reassurance she was alone. Finally, she began to whisper to her brother, recounting the memories of their life, one after another, describing them in full. She took her time, and let her thoughts wander and her words carry her where they wished. She avoided the harsh and unpleasant recollections and confined herself to the ones that made her smile. She hoped it might ease her mind and her grief—and, to her surprise, it did. She lost herself in those memories, pausing now and again to recall details, her smiles frequent and genuine. She did not cry this time—not once—but simply gave herself over to the recounting of all she remembered about her early years with Tavo and how much he had meant to her.

She spent a long time confessing how she had discovered the wishsong within herself and how uncertain it had left her, the magic a force she could not deny and one she needed to understand and master. She admitted how Tavo's discovery of his own magic had worried her, because by then he was beginning to exhibit signs of instability. But she kept her words soft and light and positive, and did not assign blame or infuse her narrative with negative feelings. She told him how much she had always loved and admired him; told him, too, how she missed him when he was gone and how hard it had been not to be able to see him. If there were holes in their love for each other, they came mostly because of their parents' decision to send him away and keep her at home.

Was it all true? Perhaps. And perhaps not. It didn't

matter. She just needed to talk about it with him. Even if he could not hear her—though she liked thinking he could—the words needed to be spoken if she was ever to find peace.

Somewhere halfway through her effort, Fade appeared again—at first no more than a pair of gleaming eyes that she recognized immediately, then the rest of the big moor cat materializing as she lay down on the other side of Tavo's grave and listened. It was comforting to have Fade there—a reassuring presence in the darkness, an audience of one that would never judge or attempt to interrupt, reassuring in her steadfastness.

When Tarsha had said everything she thought needed saying, she sat silently in the darkness once more, wondering how long she had been speaking, how much of the night was gone. The moon had set and the stars had changed their positions in the sky, but there was no sign of morning yet. She felt at peace from having told her story. Sleep overtook her, and she nodded off.

When she jerked awake, aware suddenly of what was happening, Fade was gone. Yawning, she rose and went into the cottage, and she slept undisturbed for the remainder of the night.

The next morning when she rose, the sun was already climbing the sky toward midday, and the air was warm and welcoming. She washed and dressed, fixed a breakfast of cakes and cured meat on a small, fire-heated griddle, served the cakes and cured meat with sliced apples and cold water, and ate on the porch. She took her time, thinking through what she had decided to do once her meal was consumed.

Then she cleaned her dishes, tidied up the cottage, and went out into the day to keep her promise to craft a headstone for her brother. She found the materials and tools she needed and for several hours worked to craft her marker. Then, deciding she needed a break, she set off on another mission.

She had promised she would go after Clizia in order to settle accounts, and she would. But first she must attempt to find Drisker. Yes, Clizia had the scrye orb, which would allow her contact with the Druid, but gaining possession of the latter required tracking down the former, and she knew from sad experience this might be much harder and require more time than making a different choice. Finding Drisker was more important than settling scores with the witch, and she thought she knew a better way to do this that did not require the orb.

The books of magic would not be far, she told herself. At one time she had thought they might have been hidden in the cottage, but on reflection she realized the cottage was still being built when Drisker had departed for the last time. The site of his former residence was too unlikely, as well. Nothing remained but burned timbers, ashes, and scorched earth. So what did that leave? Would Drisker have given them to someone to keep watch over while he was away? She could think of no one—the airfield manager included—who would be a good choice. Just having such books in your possession was an invitation to an unpleasant end, should those searching discover you had them. No, Drisker would have been far more clever. He would have been careful to choose someone so unlikely, no one would ever expect it.

Someone like Flinc.

Once Drisker had retrieved the stolen books from the forest imp, he might have carried them right back and charged the imp with their care. He might have warned Flinc that they would be sought by enemies and Flinc must find a way to make sure they were sufficiently concealed.

But Flinc was dead. So if her speculation was true, where would he have hidden the books? Could they be somewhere in the forest imp's underground lair? It was a long shot, but it was possible.

She walked into the trees, making her way through to the deeper forest. As she progressed farther in, the light began to darken and the sounds of the forest dwellers began to change. Yet she did not feel intimidated or in danger. By now, she was sufficiently familiar with this patch of woods that she felt certain there was no threat she could not handle. She kept a close watch on her surroundings but pushed steadily on.

There was a chance—well, more than a chance— that she was mistaken about what had become of the books. But this was her first best guess about where they might have been hidden. It was also true that she might be wrong about how they got there. Drisker might not have taken them back; Flinc might have stolen them once again. It was not out of the question. Flinc was a Faerie creature, after all, his behavior mercurial and unpredictable.

But he would have had to steal back the books in

the little time that remained following Drisker's departure for Paranor and Clizia's arrival in Emberen. After that, his days had been numbered.

Thinking of Flinc forever gone made Tarsha sad all over again. So many had died in this struggle with the rogue Druid. So many had given everything, Tavo included.

She wondered suddenly if she might find Clizia Porse waiting, settled down in the forest imp's underground home—having come looking for the books, as well, and having found them.

She slowed her pace at the prospect, but quickly decided that this was so unlikely as to be nearly impossible and picked up her pace once more. She would be careful, nevertheless. She just needed a starting point to begin her search for Drisker, to discover what had happened to him. The books of magic might provide her with a way to obtain this information. If they didn't or if she failed to find and retrieve them, she had no idea what she would do.

As she was nearing Flinc's underground home, she used her magic to seek out other life-forms in the area. She detected the usual small animals and birds and one thing more, but for some reason she could not get a clear read on the nature of this other life-form—neither size nor shape nor species. It was just something that was alive and nearby.

Worried now, she stopped where she was. What if it *was* Clizia? But Clizia believed her dead. And she wouldn't go to this extent to hide herself from anyone else. Nor had she set any wards against intruders, which she surely would have done if she was concerned about being discovered.

No, this was something else.

Tarsha moved ahead once more, albeit more cautiously. When she reached the clearing where the tunnel leading down into Flinc's home was located, she paused for a closer look. All was back as it had been before Clizia's attack; the tunnel entry had been either repaired or replaced.

But who would have done that?

She walked out into the clearing and stood looking at the concealment to the tunnel entry, reaffirming that she was not mistaken, that everything was back to where it had been.

Then she sensed a presence behind her and froze.

"Welcome home, Tarsha of the beautiful eyes," a familiar voice said.

She turned to face the speaker and felt something fall away inside.

# FOUR

---

At first, after Clizia's trap was sprung, Drisker Arc fell into blackness for an endless stretch of time. There was nothing to see—and no sound, no tastes or smells, no feeling, no anything. Drisker folded into a ball and hung on, waiting for something more to reveal itself. He was not at all sure what sort of trap he had stumbled into. He was certain it had been designed to ensnare him, but other than that he couldn't be sure of its purpose. He managed to summon sufficient magic to enclose himself in a protective shield so that he would not be helpless when the falling ended, but other than this single act he could manage nothing.

The end came when his descent slowed and then stopped altogether. He was still cocooned away, still unaware of where he was, still a prisoner with no means available to free himself.

He waited patiently, keeping control over himself with steady and purposeful determination.

Eventually, he realized the blackness was giving way to a semblance of daylight. As his surroundings began to take shape, he saw that he was in a thick patch of woods, its trees old and shaggy and witch-bent, with limbs stretching so far skyward he could not tell where they ended. The ground around him was a mix of brush and grasses, thickly grown but not lush. Rather, everything had a haggard and badly worn air that suggested a place where life had been forced to fight hard for survival. As his senses heightened, he could smell rot and decay. He could see blackened patches on the trees and brush; he could smell and taste the parts that were slowly being eaten away by the corrosion.

He searched for movement in the twilight darkness, but found none. If anything lived here, it was either in hiding or out of view.

He was infuriated he had allowed this to happen. It had been a foolish choice to go after Clizia alone, but he had thought it was best to catch up to the rogue Druid at once. Tarsha and Tavo were both down, but while both were stunned, neither seemed seriously injured and he didn't think it necessary to wait for them to recover. So, impulsively, he had determined he would do what was needed on his own.

Had he not made this choice—which, in retrospect, was likely the most foolish of his entire life—he might have lost Clizia but would not be wherever it was he found himself now. He should have helped his companions and gone after her later. Now everything and everyone was at risk.

He found himself worrying about the fate of his sibling companions. Having disposed of him, Clizia would have gone back either to take them prisoner or to kill them. If she succeeded in doing either, he would have to place the blame squarely on his own shoulders, and he would spend the rest of his life—whatever life he had left—blaming himself for what had happened.

Yet both Kaynins possessed the considerable magic of the wishsong to aid them, and both were resourceful. He had to hope this was sufficient to see them through any confrontation that took place. Tarsha, in particular, was smart enough to find a way to protect them, and would not tend toward rash behavior of the sort he had just exhibited. With Tavo beside her, she should be more than a match for Clizia Porse.

At least, that was what he told himself.

The light had brightened further, and his surroundings were coming into sharper focus. He could see mountains and hills through breaks in the trees. He could just spy the thread of a distant river, flowing sluggishly across a barren plain. What was troubling was that everything was pretty much the same color, wherever he looked—a dismal, flat, ashen gray. Sky, horizon, landmarks, the air itself, all were marked by gloom that . . .

No! It wasn't possible. Even Clizia couldn't do that! He stared into the distance some more, then dropped the magic that shielded him and climbed to his feet to look more closely. He felt his throat tighten. Maybe she couldn't, but somehow she had. With the aid of magic that should have been beyond her command, she had dispatched him to the one place from which he couldn't escape.

*The Forbidding.*

He felt everything drop away—any chance of finding a way out, all possibility of rescue, even the hope of extending his life beyond the short, brutal span that now seemed to be his destiny. Created in the time of Faerie by the creatures of light to imprison those they believed to be servants of the dark, the Forbidding was a place of no return. Once locked away, you were there until you died. Grianne Ohmsford alone had managed to escape, and then only with the help of her nephew, Penderrin. The Druid Histories had recorded it all. Drisker had never thought he would need to know more about it in his lifetime.

Now to find himself imprisoned like this—to find himself trapped in a cage with no door and no lock or key—left him devastated. He sat down slowly, trying to compose his scattered thoughts and rioting emotions.

Trying just to think straight.

He could not expect help from Tarsha Kaynin. She wouldn't know—couldn't know—where he was. Even if she were to somehow discover what had happened, she wouldn't have the faintest idea how to free him. None of those who had gone to Skaarsland could be of any help, either.

Then he remembered something else. When Grianne had first been sent into this prison by means of a powerful magic called a triagenel—and while the power of the Forbidding was still strong and undeniable—something already imprisoned within had to be sent into the Four Lands to take her place. A switch had to be made for the magic to work. So what sort of demon had Clizia released from the Forbidding to make room for him? Whatever had been released, he was in no position to do anything about it. It was all he could do to come to terms with his own situation. He was not yet reconciled to what had been done to him, but he knew enough about the danger he was in to want to settle his mind and focus on determining what he was going to do to stay alive. If nothing had begun hunting him already, it was only a matter of time.

And likely there would be more than one.

If only he knew where everything was and could orient himself. If only he knew which way to go now that he was trapped here.

He knew the landscape of the Forbidding closely mirrored his own world—and aside from an absence of any real color, the terrain would approximate what he knew of the Four Lands. Grianne, according to her entries in the Druid Histories describing her imprisonment, had been taken to a fortress that was situated somewhere in this world close to where Tyrsis would have been in his. She had been taken there to service the whims of the Straken Lord and live out her life as his slave. In the end, that hadn't worked out so well for the demon, which she subsequently escaped and later killed. But going to that fortress might be a reasonable starting point for Drisker.

Then another thought occurred to him, this one the most troubling yet.

Hadn't Grianne Ohmsford been sent back to the Forbidding a second time, and wasn't she still imprisoned here as a result?

The thought was sudden and unexpected, and Drisker found himself thinking back to his initial summoning of Allanon at the Hadeshorn, when Grianne—reverted now to the Ilse Witch—had come to him instead. She had told him she still lived and was still imprisoned and had come to him using the passageways of the dead. If he wanted her help in finding a way to save the Four Lands, she would give it to him, but only if he agreed to free her from the Forbidding. It had occurred to him then that keeping his end of the bargain might mean coming into the demon prison himself—perhaps even exchanging himself for her to keep his word. But now that he was here, he could find her and perhaps they could discover a way to escape together.

He was abruptly energized by the idea. Then, just as quickly, a further thought occurred. What if Clizia had already freed the Ilse Witch? What if she had already accomplished what he had promised, and it was Grianne for whom he had been swapped?

The thought was so chilling that, for a moment, he couldn't breathe. What if it was Clizia's intent that she and the Ilse Witch should be allies, rulers over the Four Lands from atop a new Druid order?

But he immediately decided that this conclusion presumed a lot. In the first place, how was Clizia to know that Grianne Ohmsford was still alive? And even if she were capable of making such a determination, an alliance between them was unlikely. Two such powerful Druids would never accept each other as equals. Neither would ever trust the other.

Drisker leaned against one of the ancient trees while trying to regain his composure. It was not an easy feat to accomplish. In truth, he was still shaken to his core by the raft of possibilities. He had gone from disbelief to belief back to disbelief in minutes, and he still wasn't sure of what to do. Nor was he sure what his betrayer might have already done while he was trapped here. He needed to find out, and he couldn't do it standing around bemoaning his fate.

He had to start moving right away.

Eyes watched the Druid as he departed the patch of woods and set out toward the river that flowed south through the broad grasslands valley. There were more than one pair fixed on him, and they watched with varying degrees of interest. Some saw him as food, some as sport, and some as a puzzle. But all were thinking of finding out more. They hid within the shadows of the land in which they were trapped, all of them sad and angry and bored. But mostly they were skilled at staying alive. They hunted and they fought and they waited for opportunity of any kind.

This newcomer, this human creature, offered just such an opportunity.

One by one—and, in some cases, in pairs and packs—they began to track him.

Drisker walked for hours, and the look of the Forbidding never changed. It remained barren and weather-blasted and hazy gray—a monochromatic ruin of what Drisker knew from the Druid Histories to be nothing more than a dismal approximation of his own world, conjured through the use of Faerie magic thousands of years ago. There was nothing reassuring or pleasing about any of it, and it served only to remind the Druid of the grimness of his situation. Vast stretches and broad heights encircled him, all offering endless opportunities for concealment. That there were things hiding in wait, if not coming after him directly, was certain. The Druid Histories written hundreds of years ago by Grianne Ohmsford had made that clear enough.

So while he preferred not to reveal his presence to those who could detect the use of magic, he saw no way to avoid it. He needed to wrap himself in shielding to protect against attacks and search his surroundings to make sure he was not walking into a perilous situation. It soon proved a worthwhile effort. Right away, he found denizens of the Forbidding hiding close at hand—some large, some small, but all watching. He could not know what sorts of creatures he might encounter, or understand the nature of the threat they posed, but at least he could know they were there. Even from reading the entries in the Histories, he knew there would be dangers unknown to the writer.

He was going to have to be prepared for everything, because it would not be long before he was tested.

And as it happened, the testing began much more quickly than he had expected.

He was just cresting a low rise when he encountered a pack of Furies. He knew what they were instantly. Grianne had nearly lost her life to them, saving herself by assimilating into their pack and assuming their feral behavior, making them think she was one of them while nearly losing her humanity in the process. The pack was perhaps twenty strong—small in size for Furies, who frequently traveled in groups of more than a hundred. Furies were catlike creatures weighing maybe fifty pounds each, lean and rawboned beneath a light covering of hair: an obscene approximation of house pets. Their hunting behavior never varied; they always worked in packs to bring down prey. Or to kill for sport, which they did often.

His first thought was wishful thinking: Perhaps they had not sensed him. Faint hope, for their twisted cat faces looked up immediately, gleaming eyes fixing on him. Their sinewy bodies shifted at once into an attack posture, all turning in unison. Grianne had categorized them as mindless killers. You might stop one or two—more, if you were capable of summoning real magic—but you could not stop them all, because once committed to a battle they would never give up. You couldn't run from them; they were too swift and agile. And if they reached you, there was little hope against their razor-sharp teeth and claws.

Drisker—having already considered the choice of the weapons he could call on before setting out—immediately vanished.

It was the same skill he had used in his lessons with Tarsha, and he had learned not only how to hide himself physically, but also how to mask his scent. He did so now, shifting sideways in order to move farther away while still keeping the Furies in view. He executed this perfectly, and the Furies were left confused and—after a few further curious cat moments—disinterested. But Drisker took no chances. He kept his disguise in place—even though it drained him of strength—until he was well clear.

Then, near exhaustion, he breathed deeply of the fetid air, almost gagging from the taste, before setting off once more. He could not use his magic this way often. If he did, he would soon grow too weary to summon it, and his hunters would have him. Other means of protection were needed if there were many more of these encounters. Plus, soon he would have to stop for the night. It had been a long time since he had last slept, and his struggles had left him exhausted in both body and mind. He was still functioning, if not on a particularly high level.

But there was nowhere he could sleep safely, so he had no choice but to press on, even though the world about him was growing darker and his ability to sense what was out there in the gloom was lessening. He found himself once more regretting his impulsive nature. First there was his rash decision to go back into Paranor once the Skaar had taken control so that he might release the Guardian to destroy them, and now it was his insistence on trying to put an end to Clizia Porse on his own.

He shook his head ruefully, but regrets accomplished nothing at this point. What would save him now was caution and quick thinking.

Still, he could feel his weariness starting to work against him. His mind was wandering. Not enough to cause him to drop his protection or cease scanning the world about him—not yet, anyway—but soon enough it would. The erosion was not so gradual that he couldn't recognize it was happening, but gradual enough that he was finding it harder to recognize the extent to which it diminished him.

He thought about his long-ago decision to leave the Druid order and seek refuge in Emberen. Abandoning his obligations and forsaking the other Druids had been a poor solution to the misbehavior and recalcitrance of those he had been elected to lead. Looking back on it, he imagined it was the beginning of everything bad that had happened in the Four Lands. He could make a good argument that, had he stayed, he would have spied out the traitor Kassen, disposed of him, and blocked the Skaar efforts to breach the walls of Paranor. Everything that had transpired since was born of that failure. The weight of guilt engendered by this knowledge was enough to bury him, if he were foolish enough to dwell on it.

Yet he realized—upon acknowledging this—that it was exactly what he had been doing all along.

Ahead, a broad patch of trees and brush came into view. He turned toward it at once, immediately searching for creatures in hiding. He found a few, but not many. They were not huge in size, though perhaps dangerous for other reasons, but Drisker could no longer afford to be picky about where he spent the night. His choices were few, and what remained of the daylight was slowly leaching away. The trees ahead were going to be the safest place he would find in the time that remained.

As it turned out, the choice was better than he had expected.

He did not think sleeping on the ground was a good idea, and at first glance the trees seemed tall and limbless for the first twenty feet. But he soon discovered one that had been used for a watchtower; handgrips and footholds had been fastened into the trunk to allow for climbing, and there was even a platform. On further investigation, he found a vine studded with razor-sharp thorns that could provide a barrier against anything trying to reach him. So he cut loose the vine, tied a length of cord he carried in his belt around one end, and hauled the vine up behind him as he climbed to his perch. Several yards down from the platform, at a place when the grips and holds ended, he wrapped his thorny protection about the entire trunk, concealing it as best he could within the leafy lower branches. That would be enough to stop anyone or anything from climbing up or over. Any effort to cut their way past the vine or to try to bypass it was almost certain to cause harm, and he would hear it.

It wasn't perfect, but it would do, and Drisker was too exhausted to do more. He was hungry and thirsty as well, but there was no way to find anything until morning. Stumbling about in the darkness was an invitation to disaster.

Wrapped in his cloak against inclement weather and unexpected attacks, he situated himself on the platform with his back braced against the trunk, about thirty feet off the ground, and paused to make certain he was safe.

But staying awake any longer proved impossible, and he was asleep almost at once.

# FIVE

◆

WHEN DRISKER WOKE THE following morning, the dawn light had already begun to cast the world around him in the familiar ominous gray color he remembered from the day before. He had slept poorly, restless and aware of the dangers all around him. The platform on which he had settled himself had proved a poor substitute for a bed, and as a result his body ached everywhere. Had he been anywhere else, he would have been certain he had contracted an illness of some sort, or perhaps a wasting disease.

It took a while for his body to regain feeling in all its various cramped and sore parts, and he spent long minutes stretching and testing before he was satisfied that everything still functioned. As he made whatever adjustments to his body he could to prepare it for what lay ahead, he studied the terrain around him and listened to its sounds. There were several screams from off in the distance and a few grunts and roars, as if animals might be waking, but nothing close. Birds—or an approximation of birds—passed in silent flight overhead: solitary creatures that looked more like rodents with wings.

Already he was telling himself that he had to find a way out of the Forbidding—and soon. But he was also aware that if he failed to find Grianne Ohmsford, he had no way to make that happen and was in danger of finding himself trapped in this wretched twilight prison forever.

When he was sufficiently mobile, he rose and climbed down from his perch to the ground below, keeping close watch as he did so, his senses pricked and his protective magic at the ready. But there seemed to be nothing lingering close by. The gloom was also providing sufficient light by now that he could find his way and spy out the pitfalls of the terrain.

More to the point, it was enough to help him find food and drink, which he needed to do immediately. He was hungry and thirsty beyond belief.

Where he would find sustenance in maybe whatever form it might take was another matter. He had seen no drinkable water yesterday—only gray, rank-smelling pools. The river he was traveling toward might provide something better, but the prospect of catching and eating anything that lived here seemed risky.

Still, for lack of any better options, he began walking south, making for the river. Behind him, mountains that approximated the Dragon's Teeth rose skyward, jagged and threatening. The river, he decided, was the Forbidding's version of the Mermidon. What must this world's approximation of the Rainbow Lake look like—bands of black and gray arching over a murky body of fetid water? The Forbidding's rank smell was ever-present and intrusive. How anything could live here was unimaginable. And yet live here they did.

In the distance, a huge winged creature swept through the skies, its sinewy body covered in scales, its wings leathery and batlike, its jaws filled with razor-sharp teeth. It soared with silent purpose over the land below. Hunting, Drisker supposed. In this land, everything was hunting. He recognized the creature from descriptions he had read in the Histories. A dragon—Dracha, as it was called over here. They came in all shapes and sizes and were a dominant species.

Yet there were other, worse things living in the Forbidding. Much worse.

He walked for perhaps an hour, the world about him unchangingly dismal. The light, such as it was, did not brighten. He sensed the creatures about him as he passed, but none came near enough to offer a threat. Nevertheless, the threat was there, a constant presence. It made him fearful in a way he seldom ever was. With so much magic at his command—with so many weapons—he was not often overmatched or inclined to be afraid of what he might encounter. But that was not so here. In the Forbidding, the sheer number of predators was enough to overwhelm him. And in the Forbidding, everything was not only a predator, but also prey.

He tried to focus on other things, such as the whereabouts of Tarsha and Tavo, but quickly gave it up as pointless when the dark thoughts and the fear returned. He wondered if anyone would ever know what had happened to him. If the Kaynin siblings were both dead, how would anyone know? And even if they were still alive and had somehow escaped the witch, would they have any idea at all what had become of him? How would they find out? There was no one to tell them, no way to track him, no hint of his fate. Even if Tarsha wanted an answer to this question, she lacked the means to find it.

Ahead, the river came into view. And with it, directly in front of him, was a placid, clear pond. He stopped to make sure the pond wasn't a mirage and, after deciding it wasn't, pondered further whether its waters were safe to drink. But his thirst was raging, and the lure of potable water was so strong that he determined he must take the chance. The smell might be bad, and the taste foul, but it would fill a need he could no longer afford to ignore.

He walked to the edge of the pond, knelt, and slowly leaned down to test its water.

"What are you doing?" a voice cried out.

He straightened at once. A spindly, spider-like creature stood to one side of him, its Gnome-like face scrunched in disapproval. Hair sprouted everywhere from its crooked body, bulking up its otherwise scrawny form and giving it a wild, untamed look. A memory tugged at him.

"Do you intend to kill yourself?" the creature demanded. "Is that why you wish to drink toxic water? *These* waters"—he gestured at the pond—"will kill you in five seconds!"

Drisker's memory returned. "You're an Ulk Bog."

"Brilliant. I suppose next you will announce that you have found yourself in the Forbidding and discovered how terrible it is!"

Drisker smiled. "And who are you?"

"I am one who is honored to serve she who was once Grianne of the trees and earth, she who was and remains the Straken Queen. She who I am proud to call my friend. I am Weka Dart!"

Drisker couldn't believe his good fortune. "I know of you!"

The Ulk Bog beamed. "Everyone knows of me. They know of my intelligence and my skills. They know of my clever wits. They know of the value of my services."

It was all coming together. Drisker rose. "You've been following me, haven't you?"

Weka Dart nodded. "But you couldn't tell I was there, could you? I was too clever for you."

"You were. Now tell me, why were you following me? Did Grianne send you?"

"Ah, you are not so dim-witted as you appear. Of course she sent me. I am to make certain you reach her in one piece. That is possible, is it not? You are a Straken, aren't you?"

*Straken.* Witch, in the common language of those imprisoned within the Forbidding. "I am a Druid. Like Grianne Ohmsford, your Straken Queen. She was once a Druid, too. We are alike."

Weka Dart shook his head at once. "No, you are not like her. No one is like her. You aspire to be, perhaps, but you can never hope to compare."

Drisker didn't care to argue the point. "But she sent you to find me. So she knew I was here."

"She knows everything—even your name. Drisker

Arc." He gave Drisker a determined look. "Do you hope she will take you for a mate?"

"What? No! I come for another reason." Drisker changed the subject quickly. "So if you were sent to find me, why did you wait so long to show yourself?"

The Ulk Bog shrugged. "You seemed to be doing fine on your own. You managed to fool the Furies. You were traveling in the right direction and avoiding all the other bad things that might make a meal of you. You found a place to sleep that was safe enough— although I did have to dispatch a tree serpent during the night so it would not find you. But when you bent to drink the water, it was not something I could stand by and watch. My lady would have been very disappointed in me if I had."

"Because I would have been dead."

"Very."

Drisker took a moment to assess the situation, as he now understood it. "Why *did* Grianne send you to find me?"

Weka Dart smiled, showing all of his sharp-pointed teeth. "That is for her to say, not me. We must leave now so you can find out."

They set out at once. The Ulk Bog soon proved annoying beyond reason, chattering away as if it were as necessary as breathing. He never once paused and seemed to have no interest in any response the Druid might care to give. He talked about only one thing: Grianne Ohmsford. He extolled her virtues endlessly, going on and on about her intelligence and consideration for others, about her ability to lead the other creatures in the Forbidding, and about her wondrous accomplishments. Now and then, he also cataloged a few of his own small but valuable contributions to her efforts and the extent to which she relied upon his services.

Drisker put up with it for as long as he could, then stopped him midsentence. "I need to find water," he insisted.

After grumbling about being interrupted, the voluble fellow advised patience and to trust in his intentions to help as soon as help was available. Which meant, Drisker discovered, until they reached the river. Once there, almost an hour later, the Ulk Bog found a stream coming out of the mountains that, while silt-filled and discolored, was drinkable. Drisker swallowed the water greedily and without hesitation, deciding he would have to trust this strange creature, like it or not, because there was no one else to turn to.

"We will eat when we stop for the night," Weka Dart added before Drisker could ask.

"How far are we going?"

His guide scrunched up his features. "Three days' journey. We must cross the length of the Pashanon to Kraal Reach. She waits for us there, in her castle."

"Her castle?"

"She destroyed the Straken Lord. She threw down Tael Riverine when he came into your world with his followers to take it for himself. But when the demons were returned to the Forbidding, she was sent with them. Now she rules the creatures trapped here. She is the Straken Queen."

Drisker knew Grianne was a prisoner in the Forbidding. Having reverted to her identity as the Ilse Witch during her confrontation with Tael Riverine, she had been swept up at the birth of the new Ellcrys and carried away with all the other demons into this limbo prison. When she had appeared to him at the Hadeshorn, she had told Drisker that she was not dead, but alive and well. What she had not said was that she was now ruler over all those imprisoned with her. He supposed it was a logical result of her having destroyed their former ruler, but it troubled him to find her so deeply enmeshed in this world's affairs. If she was not only one of the demons but their leader, what might he expect of her if he found a way to return them both to the Four Lands?

But he had made a bargain with her. He had given his word. She wanted to be free of the Forbidding and returned to the life and the world from which she had been taken. She had said she wanted to die as the creature she had been before: a Faerie creature in service to Mother Tanequil. For that was what she had been, hadn't she? That was what Pen Ohmsford had given her the chance to become at the end of her life.

All this she had lost with the dying of the old Ellcrys and the fall of the Forbidding. And this was what she wanted back. He thought she was being genuine when she said it, and there was no reason to doubt her yet. She had been alive—such as life might be in her present circumstances—for almost a thousand years, but these past two hundred had seen her returned to the terrible creature she had once been and had fought so hard to escape. She was, no doubt, immensely unhappy and desperate to be free.

It might not seem possible now, but he knew he had to try to find a way to give her back what had been stolen from her.

Weka Dart was nattering on, skipping ahead and then back again, always moving—a bundle of energy that would not be contained, and much of it centered on his mouth. Drisker endured it, because to try to stop it would have been both futile and petty, and he needed the Ulk Bog to help him reach Grianne Ohmsford.

Three days of this journey lay ahead of him, and he was dreading every step.

They walked until nightfall, their journey uneventful. Now and then, Weka Dart urged them quickly into hiding, but only once did they actually see what it was that threatened. In that single viewing, Drisker caught sight of a huge, lumbering beast that was crossing an open space in front of them and did not deviate from its path as it went. Had they been seen, he was unsure what would have transpired, but he was just as glad he would never find out. He was grateful in those moments that he had the services of the Ulk Bog to make certain they stayed alive.

When they stopped for the night, his guide told him to stay put, and vanished into the growing dark with no explanation. On his return, he carried the limp body of a small spiky creature that Drisker did not recognize. On closer inspection, the Druid saw it was a bird of some kind.

"Food!" Weka Dart announced, and began plucking out the feathers.

When it was reduced to meat and bones, the Ulk

Bog glanced up, saw that Drisker was frowning at him, and used some of his drinking water to wash the bird clean. Drisker, in an effort to speed things along and overly anxious to eat, summoned flames to his fingertips using Druid magic so they could cook the bird. But the Ulk Bog was already biting into the carcass, and when he glanced over at what Drisker was attempting, he had an immediate fit.

"No, no, no! Do you want to get us killed? Every Fury and Gormie and Dracha and whatever else might be out there hunting will be on top of us in minutes!" He tore off a leg and passed it over. "Use common sense, if you have any. Eat it this way."

"Raw?"

Weka Dart rolled his eyes. "This is how you are *supposed* to eat it, Straken. This is why I *caught* it. Now stop arguing!"

Drisker began gnawing on the leg and found the meat quite good, if a bit gamy. He ate what he was given, and a second helping besides. By the time he was finished, he thought maybe he had never tasted anything quite so good. And when both were sated, they sat together in the dark looking out at the gloom.

"How safe are we here?" Drisker asked after a while.

"Safe enough, so long as one of us keeps watch. I will watch first. Ulk Bogs don't need much sleep. Too risky to sleep when you are smaller and weaker than almost everything else. But you can sleep. I will protect you."

Drisker didn't argue the matter. He had already entrusted his life to this strange creature. He waited perhaps five minutes, then rolled into his frayed and torn travel cloak and was asleep within minutes.

The following day, they crossed the river and angled southwest into a region of the Forbidding that Weka Dart called Huka Flats. It was desolate country—more so, even, than anything they had passed through so far. Much of it was dried-out flatland with dozens upon dozens of holes in the ground. After eyeing the holes for a bit, Drisker asked what they were.

"Homes for Barkies," his companion answered. When the Druid looked at him questioningly, he added, "Burrowing creatures about twice the size of your foot. Very shy—unless you make the mistake of getting too close to the entrances to their homes. Then they come out. Two, maybe three hundred at a time. Enough to pull you down and eat you while you are still alive. Not a pleasant experience. I have seen it happen. But walk where I walk and you'll be safe enough."

They went on, Drisker proceeding more cautiously now, his eyes on the dark burrows surrounding them.

"Why do you call them Barkies?" he asked, trying to steer his thoughts away from the images Weka Dart's descriptive words had generated in his mind.

"They bark at night. Sometimes they bark *all* night. You can hear them for miles. But Barkies feed in the daytime. Like now. They keep quiet when they're hunting. They just lie in wait in their burrows."

Drisker couldn't get out of there soon enough, but it still took them almost an hour to traverse the Barkie burrow village and get clear enough for the Druid to breathe freely again.

The day passed without incident—if you didn't count the times the Ulk Bog either had them hide or simply stand motionless until some form of danger passed by. Ahead, mountains appeared against a misty horizon. This was where they would find Kraal Reach, but it was late in the day and there didn't seem to be any chance of reaching it before darkness.

"You've come to take her away, haven't you?" Weka Dart said suddenly, and Drisker could detect hints of both anger and sadness in his voice. Drisker hesitated, unsure of what to say. "If you've not come to be her mate," the other continued, "then you must be here to take her away. Like before."

*Like before?* Then the Druid recalled that Grianne, when the Ard Rhys of the newly re-formed Druid order of Paranor, had been sent into the Forbidding by the rogue Druid Shadea a'Ru and would still be here if her nephew, Pen Ohmsford, hadn't found a way to take her back to the Four Lands.

"I'm here," he said finally, "because I was sent. Unwillingly, I should add. Just like Grianne, both times she appeared." He paused. "But I won't lie. When I leave, she may choose to come with me."

"You will *take* her!"

A firm accusation. Drisker shook his head. "I don't have that power over her. She spoke to me while I was still in our old world. She told me she wants to come home. It is a part of the reason I am here."

"It is wrong of you to agree with her! She belongs here."

Drisker suddenly wondered if the Ulk Bog would rather lead him into danger than let him get anywhere near his beloved mistress.

"Why don't we wait and see what she has to say about it?" Drisker suggested, then paused. "Or do you intend to rid yourself of me on the way to reach her, in spite of what your queen has asked of you?"

Weka Dart wheeled on him, his monkey-face a mask of fury, his spiky hair bristling everywhere from his head to his toes. "It doesn't matter what I want! I am loyal to my queen! I would never betray her. Not for any reason. She is always to be respected and obeyed. Always!"

He wheeled away again, stomping off.

*Well, that went well,* Drisker thought.

He followed the angry creature because he didn't have any other choice, afraid he had created a divide between them he could not close. For the rest of the day, they walked in silence. The light dimmed swiftly, and the Ulk Bog found shelter for them in a cluster of rocks situated on a rise that allowed them to be protected on three sides.

"We stay here tonight," he declared without looking at Drisker. "It is the best we can do. You have magic. Maybe you can use it to protect us if we are threatened. Or is that too much to ask?"

Then he was gone into the darkness to find dinner for them, returning almost immediately with something new and equally unfamiliar as last night's offering. Whatever it was, he skinned and cleaned it, and they devoured it raw and in silence. The grayness of the day grew darker with nightfall. The sky clouded over, the air grew misty, and the world was blanketed in gloom and a sense of inevitable decay. Drisker stared out at it from their shelter and wondered how anything could manage to live here. Listening to Weka Dart speak of the Forbidding as if it were a real home—a place he chose to be and believed Grianne Ohmsford belonged in—was hard to accept. But then he hadn't been born to it and lived in it all his life.

They had finished their meal and were sitting together, still looking out at the night, when the Ulk Bog finally spoke again. "I was wrong to be so harsh," he said in his rough voice. "I was being selfish."

Drisker nodded. "You want her to stay. I understand."

"If she leaves here, she will leave me behind. She did so before. She said I could not come with her, that I must stay where I belonged. But there is nothing here for me without her."

"Maybe things won't turn out the way you think."

"They will. I can tell. She will leave me."

"If she thinks she needs to go, maybe you have to let her. You wouldn't deny her that, would you? Don't you care enough about her to want her to be where she chooses?"

The Ulk Bog shook his head. "I don't know."

Drisker wanted to find something to say that might dispel the sense of inevitability the other was struggling with. "There is a good chance no one will be leaving," he said at last. "I have no way of getting back, and if history is any judge, neither does she. We are both trapped in this world, and we may both have to stay here. So nothing is settled."

Weka Dart gave a slow nod but did not otherwise respond. He simply sat there, stubbornly silent, his gaze fixed on the darkness.

Drisker felt very sleepy and decided to roll himself into his travel cloak and stretch out. Once he closed his eyes, he was asleep at once.

When he woke the following morning, the world was awash in rain and gloom so thick it approximated night. The air had gone cold and the world silent, and it seemed as if everything surrounding him had died while he slept. He was aware of Weka Dart snoring close beside him, but the sound of the rain drowned out everything else.

He was also suddenly in possession of a raging sore throat, a fever so hot he was sweating, and a body aching with such pain that he could not make himself rise. He tried to sit up and failed; he was so weak he could not move. He stared into the mistiness and rainfall and wondered how this had happened.

He was sick, and his Druid instincts told him it was not a sickness he could do anything about.

Seconds later, he tried again to rise, failed, and collapsed back into the folds of his travel cloak, unconscious.

# SIX

STANDING TRANSFIXED IN THE shady, quiet clearing, Tarsha Kaynin found herself face-to-face with the impossible.

Not ten feet away stood the forest imp, Flinc.

"Is it really you?" she managed, after she had recovered her wits.

The little creature made a show of looking down at himself and running his hands over his body. "It appears so."

"But you were dead! Clizia Porse had you trapped in your home and you stayed behind to let me escape . . ." She trailed off helplessly. "I don't understand!"

The forest imp smiled. "There is nothing much to understand. I stayed to keep the witch from following you, and I was successful in my efforts. The witch and your brother trapped me in my home, so I used a little of the magic with which all forest imps are blessed and made her think I was dead. It was the easiest solution. There, Tarsha of the beautiful eyes. Are those tears I see?"

Impulsively, Tarsha knelt down and hugged him. "I'm so happy to see you!"

"Then I am happy, as well."

"But you didn't try to let me know you were still alive? You didn't communicate this with Drisker? You didn't come looking for us?"

Flinc shook his grizzled head, and his old man's face took on a forlorn cast. "How could I? Drisker was trapped in Paranor, as I recall. And you left Emberen and the Westland. It seemed best to just wait until one of you returned. My kind doesn't travel far beyond the borders of our forestland."

Tarsha's face grew grave. "Things are very bad, Flinc. The boy who was with Clizia? My brother? She killed him." Unbidden tears filled her eyes. "She tried to kill me, too. She believes me dead. And she did something to Drisker. He's disappeared."

"Oh, I wouldn't worry about him. If the *chil'haen russ'hai* is alive, disappeared or no, all will be well. And what of your companions? The highlander with the black blade and the Elf? What of them?"

"They have left the Four Lands to try to stop the Skaar invasion. I am completely on my own. I came here for help, but I did not think to find you; that is something I never could have imagined!"

She hugged him anew and was buried under a wave of relief and gratitude as she did so.

"Stop, please," the imp protested, struggling to free himself. "It was nothing special for me to fool the witch. She is not nearly so clever as she thinks. She thought it my intent to kill myself and take her and your brother with me, but for the Faerie reality is not a constant. It shifts and moves like the wind, and we ride its currents and turn them to our purposes." He paused, eyes bright and questioning. "I could show you more, if you were to decide to stay with me. I have rebuilt my home and put it back the way it was. You would be safe there."

Tarsha shook her head in disbelief. As if she would risk another kidnapping, well intended or not. "You never change, do you, Flinc? I cannot stay with you. I must find Drisker and help him. And Clizia Porse has to be stopped." She gave him a wry smile. "My kind is not so much inclined to be homebodies as your kind are. I am happy you are alive and well, but I have my own path to follow. Will you help me?"

"Have you any doubt? Have I ever not helped you—or at least tried my best? You need only ask."

"All right." She brushed back the strands of white-blond hair that had fallen over her face and wiped her eyes. "Here is what I need. I have to find Drisker, and I don't know how to do that. I thought maybe if I found Drisker's books of magic—the ones you took from me—I might find something in them that would help me. I know Drisker took them back from you, but where are they now?"

Flinc seemed surprised. "This is all the help you require? Such an easy task! Come with me."

He turned toward his tunnel entry and invited her to follow. The trapdoor was back in place and the tunnel lighted and clean. When they reached the entry to his underground lair, she found the heavy door there as before, looking very much as if it had never been damaged. Once inside, she found almost everything put back exactly the way it had been. There was no sign of the damage inflicted by Clizia, and no evidence of whatever had happened in the ensuing struggle.

Tarsha moved over to the little table and sat in one of the two chairs. "This is real magic," she offered, gesturing to his rehabilitated home.

Flinc looked pleased. "I like keeping everything neat and tidy. I lost a few treasures, but most I was able to save. Would you like a cup of tea?"

She gave him a look. "That depends on what you intend to put in the tea. I wouldn't like to think you hadn't learned your lesson."

"Oh, no, it will be ordinary tea. You have my promise, lovely Tarsha. Only tea, and nothing more."

So she accepted the offer, and while he brewed the tea, she sat pondering the fact of his continued existence. She had been so sure his life had been snuffed out, and yet here he was, much as he always had been. It gave her hope that not all of Clizia's schemes were successful. That, under the right circumstances, Clizia could be defeated.

When the tea was ready, Flinc brought it to the table with two cups and poured it in front of her, making a point of tasting it first so that she would not be worried about his intentions.

"I am sorry for what I did," he said quietly, taking his seat. "I apologize. I do not want you to hate me. I value your friendship."

"You have it," she replied. "We will always be friends." She sipped her tea and let the warmth settle inside her. "So you can help me find Drisker? You have a way?"

"Perhaps."

He finished his tea and carefully poured himself another cup. When he gave her a questioning look, she nodded her acquiescence and he refilled hers, as well. Then he sat back and looked at the ceiling for a moment.

"I was very bad a while back. I brought you here under false pretenses because I wanted to keep you for my own. There is no kinder way of putting it. No, don't say anything just yet." He motioned for her to stop as she tried to object to his characterization of what he had done. "Just let me finish. I helped to save you after you fled the Druid's burning home to hide in the deep woods, but then I made several bad decisions. I took you for myself and hid you from the *russ'hai*. After lying to him—to my friend who trusted me—about your fate, I returned his books of magic to him and claimed it was I who had saved them. But he is a Druid, and Druids are not easily fooled. He saw through me and had me bring him here and return you safely. He told me in no uncertain terms what would happen if I ever attempted such trickery again."

He paused. "And then he did something extraordinary. He came back the following day carrying the books of magic and asked if I would look out for them. He said he was going to go away and did not know for how long. He was worried that something would happen to the books if they were left unprotected. This was before his house was attacked and burned, before all the trouble with the witch began. But Druids are often prescient, and it was so here, because eventually the witch did come looking for the books."

"But she didn't find them."

He shook his head. "She did not."

"And you still have them?"

"Indeed. Would you like to see them?"

She gave him a relieved smile. "Very much."

They spent the remainder of the day poring over the books, each taking one as both were able to read the old Elfish language in which they were written. For the forest imp, it was just another language of the people of his time, and so entirely familiar. For Tarsha, reading the language was possible because of her wishsong magic, which allowed for an immediate translation of any written language into her own.

Still, it was slow going. The language was archaic and filled with words that lacked any meaningful translation, so she was forced to constantly ask Flinc for help. As well, each book was long, and the writing was small and cramped. Much of it could be skipped over, but not too hastily, because small references to the relevant magics could be missed.

By day's end, they were halfway through, and Tarsha accepted the forest imp's invitation to spend the night so they could finish their work on the following day. She was gradually growing less concerned that he might try to keep her there permanently. All of his efforts seemed directed solely toward helping her find a way to either reach out to Drisker, wherever he was, or at least discover his location. She remembered Drisker's ability to appear to her as an astral projection when he was trapped in Paranor, and she kept hoping she might find a way to make that happen here. But she had no way of knowing how Drisker had managed it so that she might go to him.

Flinc offered her his bed, but she refused. She would not take advantage of his hospitality that way, she told him. She would sleep on the floor instead, rolled up in blankets that he provided her. What she did not say was that the very thought of being back in that bed sent shivers up her spine. Maybe it was the memories of him having kept her in it before, when he had drugged her. Better that she avoid reliving them even if they were only memories now and safely in the past.

They worked all through the next morning on the books, and they were more than halfway through when the forest imp suggested they go for a walk to clear their heads. Tarsha was quick to agree, anxious for a break from all the reading and ready for a little sunlight. She was troubled by the fact they had not yet found anything useful in their search, and she wanted to postpone the prospect of having failed for as long as possible.

To her surprise, the day was indeed filled with sunshine and the woods were alive with birdsong and late-winter flowers growing in small, bright patches. They made their way along trails and now and then off them, for Flinc was entirely familiar with the forest and in no danger of getting lost. Tarsha found herself thinking of her brother as she walked, remembering their times in the forests of Backing Fell, working with the magic of the wishsong, attempting to discover what it could do. She had done so alone at first, the magic still a closely held secret. But later, when Tavo had discovered it existed in himself as well, she had worked to help him master it.

She wondered if she had helped or hurt him by doing so. The magic had never worked in the right way for him, and he had never learned how to manage it as she did. She experienced a deep uncertainty as she remembered. How much responsibility did she bear for what had happened to her brother? Perhaps she should have seen the inevitable result even then. Perhaps she could have divined how it would all end and done something more to prevent it from happening. She didn't like to think so, but she had been a realist for so much of her life that she couldn't deny the possibility.

"Have we walked long enough?" she asked, suddenly impatient with her lack of progress. "I think we should get back to work."

Without a word, Flinc swung off the settled path and took them through the forest in a different direction. Tarsha didn't have the least idea of where they were or where they were going, but the forest imp seemed to know his way instinctively.

"Something occurs to me," Flinc said abruptly. "I noticed several places in the *russ'hai*'s book where he made marginal notes—references to something he called the Druid Histories. Does this mean something to you?"

Indeed, it did. "What it means is that I might have to go to Paranor. I had forgotten the Druid Histories. Each High Druid recorded, in his or her own time, information about the events and magics involved in their service. So things that were not particular to

Drisker's books might appear in the more comprehensive Histories."

"I will show you when we are back at my home," the imp offered, looking pleased.

Tarsha nodded. The trouble was, if she had to go to Paranor, she did not know how to get inside. You had to be a Druid or be invited in by a Druid in order to enter. The Guardian of the Keep waited for those who lacked proper status, and she had no wish to encounter that particular creature. Clizia Porse had discovered what could happen if you contravened this rule—and she *was* a Druid.

Tarsha could think of no reason she would be allowed in, or allowed to find the Druid Histories, which were locked away—let alone be able to understand them sufficiently to find the help she was looking for.

Once back at Flinc's home, they settled side by side at the table while he paged through the book he had been studying to show her the writings in the margins. Tarsha remembered seeing similar notes in her book as well, but hers was the newer of the two and possessed fewer entries—a consequence, she thought, of all the earliest recordings having been entered in Flinc's older copy.

As Flint had said, there were passing references to the Druid Histories in both books, but none that gave her any further information.

Nor was there anything that specifically referred to a magic that could help her find someone who was missing. Or at least, not anything new. There was mention of the scrye waters and the scrye orbs—both of which she was familiar with—but nothing else.

She thought at first, when considering the possibility of returning to Paranor, that she could locate Drisker by using the scrye waters. But then she recalled that it only showed uses of magic within the Four Lands, not the identity of those who used it, so she didn't see much chance of any help there.

What she really needed was a scrye orb of the sort both Drisker and Clizia possessed. Then, perhaps, she could summon Drisker and speak with him as he had done with Clizia. But to obtain a scrye orb, she had to find Clizia and take or steal hers away. Her hatred of the witch was sufficient to drive her to try, but reason suggested she should think twice. Clizia had bested her and Tavo and Drisker together, so how would she manage such a feat alone? And if she failed, what would become of Drisker then? No one but Tarsha and Clizia knew what had happened to him. And even Tarsha wasn't sure. If she died, the only person who wished to restore him to the Four Lands would be gone.

The urge to act on any of these possibilities was maddeningly tantalizing, but none of them offered a reasonable path to finding the Druid. Enraged as she was at what Clizia Porse had done to Tavo, she knew she could not abandon the Druid. She had to help him before she could think of revenge on the witch.

Tarsha and Flinc went back to studying their respective books, and the hours passed away and the day with it. By nightfall, they were just finishing the final pages when the forest imp—apparently paging ahead in expectation of finishing and wanting to see how much was left—gave a puzzled grunt.

"What in *haist*'s name is this?" he muttered, almost to himself.

Tarsha set down her book and moved to the other side of the table to peer over his shoulder. She was surprised, when she bent down, to find how small he seemed. Earlier, she had thought him much larger. But you couldn't just grow and shrink at will.

Or could you, if you were a Faerie creature?

"See?" he asked, pointing to the margin of the page he was reading.

This time, it wasn't writing he had discovered; it was a drawing. It was right at the end of the book and didn't seem to refer to anything on the page. It appeared to be a sort of box with a series of small circles at its center, several dozen in number. Most of the circles were blank, but eight of them had numbers written inside, going from one to eight in random fashion. She stared at it in confusion, in part because there was something familiar about it. She read through the writing on the page, but it was something about nature's secrets and concealments, and she could not make a connection.

"What is it?" Flinc asked her.

"Don't know," she replied. "But there is something . . ."

She continued to ponder, but she couldn't make the connection. After a time, they went back to work. It took them less than an hour to finish, and the end result was discouraging. Two long days of reading Drisker's books had yielded nothing of use.

So they put the books aside and made themselves a dinner of cold meat, cheeses, bread, and root vegetables and ate at the little table, adding glasses of ale because Flinc thought they deserved it. Neither said much while they ate, disappointed and tired.

"What will you do now?" the forest imp asked at one point, but Tarsha only shook her head, too discouraged to do anything more. All her hopes and expectations were exhausted. *What will you do now?* She had no idea.

Halfway through the meal, she began to cry as she was thinking of all those she had lost, especially Tavo. Her crying was silent and evidenced only by the tears that rolled down her cheeks. Flinc said nothing, but politely kept his head lowered and continued to eat. She was grateful for this. She was disinterested in expressions of sadness and comfort, and disdainful of sympathy. She was stronger than this.

She wiped her eyes and put on her best stone-faced expression.

"I'm tired, Flinc," she said, rising. "I'm going to sleep. Thank you for helping me read through the books. We'll talk about it tomorrow. Maybe we can find another way."

She found her blankets, spread them out, lay down and rolled herself up, and was asleep almost at once.

But she was awake again sometime after midnight.

She had been dreaming fitfully, but she remembered nothing of the dream on waking. She sat up abruptly, a different memory crowding to the forefront of her mind. It was so urgent, so demanding, that she found its source instantly and was rolling out of her blankets even as she called for Flinc.

The forest imp was beside her while she was still struggling to free herself from her wrappings, crying, "What's wrong, what's happened? Are you all right?"

"The drawing in the book!" she gasped. "The one with all the little circles and numbers—I know what it is! I've seen it before. Down in the hidden passageway that leads underground from outside the walls of the Keep to its cellars. It's part of a border of bolts that fastens the doors in place to the rock walls. But it's more than that, too. It's the way into the Keep. If the tips of the bolts on the correct plate are touched in the numbered order, the doors will open."

"You're sure about this?" Flinc looked doubtful. "It's easy to confuse such things . . ."

"No! I was there. I saw Drisker open the doors. I watched him. I paid enough attention to know which plate he was using. I didn't remember the sequence, but now I have it!"

She was so excited she was practically vibrating. Flinc watched her for a moment, then slowly sat on the floor and rubbed his bristled head with both hands. His hair, which was always poking straight up or out, didn't look any different for his having slept. He stared at her for a moment, then nodded slowly.

"So you're going there. To Paranor."

She nodded at once. "I'll leave in the morning. I could leave right now, as awake as I am, but I want to make the journey in the daylight."

"A wise decision. Will you go alone?"

"Unless you'd rather go with me . . ."

Flinc smiled. "I think you know the answer. A homebody doesn't care for travel."

"Then I'll go alone. I'll copy the drawing and leave the books with you. Just be careful while I'm gone. Clizia Porse is still out there."

His smile brightened further. "So, I think, is Drisker Arc."

She nodded in agreement and fervently hoped he was right.

# SEVEN

WHEN DRISKER ARC WOKE again, his surroundings were unchanged. Barren, blasted, empty countryside for as far as the eye could see—which wasn't far. Heavy rain fell with such force it formed a curtain that effectively obscured everything beyond a stone's throw. The sound of the downpour was a thunderous hammering as sheets of rain impacted against rocks and earth. The gloom persisted, and even after only a few days in the Forbidding, the Druid knew that time had already lost purpose. It could be either day or night, the difference so minimal as to render one indistinguishable from the other.

Weka Dart was hovering over him, the anxiety impossible to mistake. "Straken?" he asked tentatively. "Can you hear me?"

Drisker nodded, finding the question an odd one. Then the heat of his fever reasserted itself as if a furnace had been ignited inside him, and the aching and waves of nausea returned. He remembered waking earlier, so sick he could not manage more than a few moments of awareness before he was unconscious again. Now he was awake once more, but for how long?

"What's wrong with me?" he whispered.

The Ulk Bog was suddenly frantic. "I don't know! I can't tell! I have no healing skills, and I haven't seen anyone sick like this before. You are all spotted! Like an Isgrint! The spots are everywhere on your body. Has this happened before?"

Drisker shook his head. "Do you have something to help with the aching and the nausea? Any medicine at all?"

"Nothing. I carry no medicines or ointments. I don't get sick. Ulk Bogs are very healthy."

*Good for you,* Drisker thought wearily, ready to go back to sleep. But he forced himself to remain awake. *An Isgrint? What is an Isgrint?* His mind spun with confusion as waves of raw stomach-churning revolt threatened to overwhelm him. But he held fast to his determination not to give in.

"You have to get me to your mistress," he whispered. "She will know how to heal me, if anyone does. We have to leave. Now."

But Weka Dart held him down the minute he tried to rise, and he was so drained of strength he could not break free. "Straken, you are too weak to go anywhere. We have at least a day's journey ahead of us, and the rain makes the walking harder and the way more dangerous."

Drisker knew he was right; there was nothing he could do to help them against any sort of threat. Even if he could get to his feet and somehow manage to stumble through the treacherous terrain, he probably wouldn't last for more than a couple of miles. Even fighting to get free of the hands holding him down caused his head to spin and his gorge to rise anew.

He closed his eyes. "Then you have to go alone. You have to get word to your mistress so she can come for me. Can you do that?"

The Ulk Bog shook his head at once. "Do not ask it of me, I beg you. I cannot leave you alone. You cannot defend yourself while you are this sick. You would have no protection without me."

"I can manage. I have a Straken's magic, Weka Dart. I need you to go. If you don't, I may die of this sickness. Don't argue with me. Pick up what you need and go. Now!"

Weka Dart released his grip on Drisker and climbed to his feet. "If something happens to you, my mistress will never forgive me." He shook his grizzled head, his distress evident. "I cannot believe I am doing this! I know I shouldn't. Something terrible will happen to you if I go. Probably before I am a mile away."

The Druid swallowed hard. "Your concerns are unnecessary. Just leave me your food and water; I won't be able to find anything on my own. Then go. No more arguing. I'll be all right."

He had no way of knowing how this could possibly be true, but he felt certain he could not recover from his sickness without a Healer. Grianne Ohmsford had those skills, and even as the Ilse Witch she would know how to employ them. He watched in silence as Weka Dart stripped off his waterskin and food sack and set them next to him.

Then, without another word, the Ulk Bog rushed

out into the curtains of rain and was swallowed from view.

Drisker stared after him, as if by doing so he could hasten his efforts to bring help. But soon enough he felt the weariness and aching return, and saw the need for taking protective measures before he lapsed into unconsciousness again. Doing nothing was not an option if he wanted to avoid being eaten while he slept. He must use magic to protect himself as best he could. He was already much too weak to be as effective with his defenses as he would have liked. But he had enough strength and sufficient skill to create at least a small barrier between himself and the world surrounding him.

He dragged himself into a sitting position, facing out into the rain. He was tucked back into his concave shelter in the jumble of rocks, with enough of a covering over his head that it kept the rain off, as certain as he could be that any attack would have to come from the front. If he could manage to form a shield that stretched from left to right and from the ground up to the top of the shelter, he would be completely enclosed. In fact, he would be sealed in, which meant he would be trapped. But he tried not to think of it that way. What mattered was that, for anything to get at him, it would have to scratch and claw its way through a screen of magic.

Braced against the rocks, he summoned the magic that would form his shield. It required a tremendous effort even to bring it alive. He didn't stop to rest; he simply pressed on, afraid if he hesitated he would not be able to continue. Calling out words in the Ancient

Elfish language from which the magic was created, and making accompanying gestures that enabled and strengthened it, he began construction of his shield and stretched it across his shelter's opening. Twice, his grip on the edges slipped and he was forced to start over. Once, he almost lost the entire shield to a powerful gust of wind. Protection of the magnitude he required demanded substance as well as presence, and the weight of it bore down on him as he fought to set it in place.

The minutes passed. An hour slipped by, and still he worked. Sweat was pouring off him, and the aching of his body no longer had definable limits. Worse still, he was fighting hard not to pass out. Black spots had begun to appear before his eyes, and the world was shifting around him. He knew he was losing the battle to stay conscious. If he didn't finish quickly, he wouldn't finish at all—and there was every reason to believe the entire shield would collapse and everything he had tried to do would be irretrievably lost.

But he couldn't manage it. He was too tired and too hampered by his sickness to construct what was needed. He had tried his best, but for once his best was not going to be enough. He thought about Grianne and her hopes of escaping the Forbidding. He thought about Tarsha and Tavo, wondering if they were alive and if they could bring Clizia Porse to bay without him. And he worried about those who had gone to Skaarsland, and how everyone in the Four Lands would be caught up in a cataclysmic war between nations if they were not successful.

He might have blacked out for a moment. He was

never sure afterward. But when the moment was finished, so was the protective shield he had thought beyond his reach. He stared at its shimmer against the curtain of rain. He traced its outlines along the edges of the rocks and across the ground in front of him—solid everywhere with no gaps, no signs of loosening, and no indication of any flaws.

He leaned back against the rocks and tightened his cloak around him. Beyond his shelter, the rain continued. There were no signs of it ceasing and no indication of any breaks in the weather.

He closed his eyes in exhaustion and went to sleep sitting up.

Far to the south, beyond the lower borders of the Pashanon and nearing the last stretch of country before arriving at Kraal Reach, Weka Dart smiled to himself, pleased he had gotten this far so fast. He had run most of the way, heedless of weather and terrain, of dangers seen and hidden. He had covered the distance in half the time another would, driven by his commitment to see the stricken man he had left behind rescued before one of the larger predators could get to him. His mistress would be pleased that he had come so quickly. She would be proud of his efforts and come at once to this man she had asked him to find and bring back.

He fought to see through the continuing downpour, every inch of his journey a sodden mist-and-rain-clogged nightmare. He was soaked through by now, but steady movement kept him warm enough and he was energized by his progress. His thoughts of his mistress—of the Straken Queen, Grianne Ohmsford—drove him on. He wondered momentarily if the Druid had been right about her need to leave and return to the world from which she had been snatched. Could he blame her for wanting to be herself again, for wanting to become Grianne Ohmsford once more? As the Ilse Witch, she was no longer physically attractive or completely in control of her emotions. Her unwarranted outbursts and uncontrollable rages were becoming more frequent, and there was no one who hadn't felt her wrath of late. Himself included.

Worse, there were rumors of an impending effort to remove her as Straken Queen.

Permanently.

Scrunching up his wizened features at the thought of losing her for whatever cause, he ran on.

Drisker Arc was dreaming. He had fallen asleep and had not woken even once in the hours that followed. It was night again by now, and the darkness helped comfort him. The rains still fell, but not with the same intensity as earlier. The heavy weather was passing, with a hint of clearing skies evident to the west. By morning, everything would be as it had been before the storm—if you discounted all the standing water and muddy flats and runoffs. But that was all hours away yet, and the Druid was aware of none of it.

In his dream, he was seated at a small fire across from Tarsha Kaynin. He had no idea how this had happened—how they had somehow found each other—but he knew she was alive, and that gave him hope. He stared at her raptly, but even though she was talking he could not manage to hear what she was saying. He tried hard to listen, watching the movement of her mouth and noting her gestures, but he remained in a soundless vacuum.

He tried to speak to her instead. He managed a few ragged words, but she showed no understanding. She just stared at him, and then shrugged, pointing at her ears and shaking her head.

She couldn't hear him at all. Suddenly he understood: They could see each other, but not communicate verbally.

She pointed to him and shrugged, then slowly mouthed something. He could not quite decipher the words, but her gestures made it clearer: *Where?*

How to tell her? He pointed at his surroundings, and she gave him a questioning look.

In response, he mouthed a single word. *Forbidding.*

*Forbidding!* She pointed at him with a horrified look and repeated the word, mouthing it slowly. *Forbidding?*

He nodded.

The look on her face turned desperate. She pointed to him and then made a beckoning gesture. He understood. She was asking if he could escape. Could he manage to get back to her?

He shook his head. *No,* he mouthed.

Pointing at herself, then gesturing to her surroundings, she mouthed two words. He understood the first word—*Druids*—but was unsure of the second.

*Tavo?* He mouthed the name carefully.

*Tavo,* she repeated. She made a slicing movement across her throat and began to cry. Then, all at once, she became very excited. *Flinc!* She made an exaggerated expression and some wild motions. *Alive!*

He smiled in spite of himself. The little forest imp was nothing if not resourceful. Dead one minute, alive the next. Drisker was happy for the news. But he was frustrated by the lack of any verbal communication at all with Tarsha. That he could reach out to her and see her and know she was well was a great relief. But not being able to discover her circumstances or plans for Clizia or any of the rest of what was hidden from him was maddening. Mouthing words could accomplish only so much.

She was trying to tell him something, mouthing and gesturing frantically, but the words were unclear and she never finished. Blackness enfolded her, and she was gone.

And at the moment she disappeared, Drisker's dreaming ended abruptly.

Tarsha had been dreaming, too. She was camped on the Streleheim, two days into her journey to Paranor, with the night deep and still about her. She had rolled into her blankets inside her two-man airship and gone to sleep several hours earlier. She had made no conscious effort to reach out to Drisker, not knowing how he had managed to do so while still trapped inside Paranor. She simply fell asleep, and suddenly he was there in her dreams.

When he first appeared, sitting across a campfire from her, she had been stunned and then elated. She immediately launched into a recitation of everything that had befallen her, but eventually noticed that he didn't seem to be listening. Desperate for him to hear her and respond, she began shouting her words, pleading with him to answer.

Until finally it became apparent he couldn't hear her. Nor, apparently, could she hear him. She mouthed a few words and gestured to clarify what was happening. They exchanged a few gestures and mouthings of words, but for the most part neither could understand the other. And then—just like that—he was gone again, as if he had never been there in the first place. As if he were nothing more than a figment of her imagination. He disappeared just as she was trying to figure out how to ask him about entering Paranor and gaining access to the Druid Histories. She had the drawing from his private books that showed her how to get past the door at the end of the underground tunnel that opened into the Keep, but she had no way of knowing what to do if the Guardian of the Keep surfaced.

And now he was trapped in the Forbidding—the Forbidding! Was she right in her understanding of what he was trying to tell her? Was there any way Clizia Porse could send him into the Forbidding when he wasn't a demon? Or was this all just a dream, one conjured by weariness and exhaustion and desperation . . .

She came awake then, jarred out of her sleep by something she had forgotten and was finally remembering.

At the Hadeshorn, where she had gone with Drisker to meet with the Shade of Allanon, something had transpired that she had not understood and her companion had not explained. At Allanon's urging, Drisker had dipped his fingers into the waters of the Hadeshorn and placed them against her forehead. He had held them there while murmuring words of Ancient Elfish. Then later, when they were departing the Valley of Shale and she had pressed him to tell her what that was all about, he had demurred. He had said she must be patient and he would tell her later.

But he never had explained. He had instead been snatched away and trapped inside the Forbidding before he could do so.

Yet as she sat up within her aircraft, the darkened sky pinpricked with stars and the chill of the night air sharp against her skin, she thought she might know anyway. She stared into the distance without seeing, thinking it through—remembering how the touching and the speaking of the words had come about, and remembering his reticence both to complete the act and then to talk about it afterward.

One of the last exchanges between Drisker and Allanon before he had done the shade's urging was about her destiny. One or the other had clearly related what she had been told by the seer Parlindru. That she would make three choices, and that one of those choices would change the world. Then the shade had said to Drisker, "Ordain her."

For what reason? To ordain her as what?

As a Druid, she realized. Nothing else made sense. He was marking her as a Druid—or at least as a student of the lore and a Druid-in-training. He was giving her that designation, and he was reluctant to do so.

She folded in on herself, drawing the blankets closer. Why would he do that? In case something happened to him, so she could carry on? As a precaution? Or as an anointment? But was this what Druids did for one another? She couldn't know, of course, but it seemed unlikely that every Druid would be hauled off to the Hadeshorn to make their Druid tenure official.

So why her?

Because he sensed she might be the last? Because the Shade of Allanon sensed it, too?

Drisker had said she was not a Druid, and he did not intend that she should be. The training he had given her was merely meant to enable her to master the wishsong, not to turn her into a Druid. But in some way, for some purpose—and at Allanon's insistence—he had done something of that very sort in the little ceremony at the edge of the Hadeshorn.

What she wondered now was if that act had in some way given her access to Paranor and its secrets. If so, she should be able to enter without fear of retaliation from the Guardian of the Keep. She should be able to gain access to the Druid Histories and to the archives and the talismans of magic they contained.

And there was only one way to find out if she was right.

It was still late at night—too early to rise and set out if she wanted to sleep, which she did—so she rolled back up in her blankets and lay down once more. She was awake enough she did not expect to fall asleep again easily, so of course she did exactly that. This time she did not dream.

Awake again with the sunrise, she ate a little from the stores she had brought and allowed herself a small portion of ale. The day was bright and clear, a pleasant change from the storms she had endured in the Rock Spur, and she found that the sun warmed her even in the chilly air. She flew east toward Paranor, and by late afternoon she had arrived and set down her small craft some distance away from the Keep but close to the entrance to the underground tunnel.

She remembered the way and the location, and carrying the drawing she had made of the entry key she found her way in and started ahead into the darkness. She was able to make a flame at her fingertips to help guide her—a skill she had learned from Drisker—so the journey was short and uneventful. It was musty and dry and silent in the passageway, and she could hear herself breathe. When she reached the huge iron door that barred entry, she gathered her courage, then pulled out the drawing.

But as she stood there, staring from drawing to door, her doubts about what she was attempting gnawed at her with a rat's persistence. Drisker had not resurfaced in her dreams or come to her while awake, so she was left only with the small but important revelation that he was now trapped within the Forbidding and that Clizia had engineered it. It felt as if Drisker was always being trapped somewhere other than where she was, which worried her deeply. How was she to accomplish anything if he was never here? How was she to know what she could and couldn't do safely?

There was no good reason to think she was right

in her conclusion that Drisker had endowed her with Druid status so that she could enter the Keep. She might believe it was true, but she had no real confirmation—and with Drisker locked away, she was not likely to receive that confirmation before she had to go inside.

She wondered if she should wait until the following morning before attempting to unlock the door and enter, just to see if he might resurface in her dreams, knowing he would come if he could manage it to complete their truncated conversation. How they had connected while she slept remained a mystery—both when he was trapped inside Paranor and now. Yet it had felt real enough; it felt as if he were actually there, trying to reveal what he knew she wanted to know, just as she had tried to do for him.

But eventually she decided that such a delay would be a foolish waste of time, and instead boldly triggered the locks. The door gave smoothly and silently, opening before her.

She entered the cellars of Paranor as if become a shade herself—drifting into the cavernous chambers with their connecting corridors, all of it devoid of any sign of life. She made her way through and along the passageways' snaking lengths, searching for a stairway leading up. From here, she would have to find her way to the Druid Histories, which she knew could be found on the third floor, in the offices of the High Druid. It would take time to find those offices, but once she had done so, she would use the wishsong to search for what was hidden in their walls.

It was a reasonable plan. She believed she was safe now. The Guardian of the Keep had not revealed its presence. Even without help from Drisker, she could do this.

And then she heard the hissing.

# EIGHT

◆

NOW AND AGAIN, TIME stops. It happens often when one is caught off guard and shocked into inactivity—when one becomes so afraid that the ability to think and move vanishes. Then everything seems to go still and sometimes to disappear entirely.

It was so for Tarsha Kaynin as she heard the sibilant hiss echo through the corridors and chambers of the Keep's shadowed cellars. The hiss was raw and inhuman, a deep and rumbling warning, and she knew at once what had caused it. Even without ever having heard it before, she knew. There could be only one source of such a sound in this vast and empty Druid fortress.

It was the Guardian of the Keep.

And it was coming for her.

She had thought she'd managed to keep it at bay—that it had recognized her as either a Druid-in-training or bestowed with the protective mantle of her Druid mentor. She had been so sure. But now all of her certainty was shattered, leaving her defenseless. She closed her eyes and fought to control her fear and indecision. She managed to momentarily subdue both, but she remained where she was, standing alone in the center of a seemingly endless dark. She would not turn back; she would not flee. Her knowledge of what was needed and of the rightness of her cause held her fast. The Guardian might be coming for her, but she could not give in to it. She would simply have to find a way to turn it aside. She was there doing a Druid's work, and she had presence of mind enough to know if she gave in now, she was defeated forever.

So she stood where she was, waiting. The hissing increased in volume and the air before her began to take on a nasty greenish tint. This would be an excellent time, she thought, for Drisker to appear and tell her what to do. But she knew he would not—and, in truth, could not—so she would have to handle matters on her own.

She summoned the wishsong magic and held it before her like a shield. What she would do when the Guardian reached her was beyond imagining. The Guardian of the Keep was a creature of mist and deep magic that lacked both substance and form, but was capable of wielding immense power nevertheless. It might be able to penetrate her defenses simply by infusing itself into them and passing through unharmed.

She took an involuntary step back as the cavernous hallway ahead filled floor-to-ceiling and wall-to-wall with thick, roiling brume—a sensory mix of what one found in a swamp, laden with toxins and rife with the stench of death. She fought down her revulsion and held fast to her convictions, and in her mind whispered, over and over, *I belong here; I am one of the Druids.*

She stared in dismay as the mist rose up, completely filling the passageway before her, consuming everything in its greenish wave. It formed a wall to block her—a wall that threatened to descend, enfolding and swallowing her whole. It hung in the air before her, generating an urge to flee that was almost overpowering, yet still she held her ground. The mist began to swirl with hypnotic intent, its threat plain and its intention undeniable. She increased the power of her wishsong and brought it forward until it was set flat against the mist to bar its advance. She could feel it pressing against her shields, and sensed that it could break through whenever it chose.

She felt her strength failing. She could sense her courage begin to give way to the terrible threat it fought to hold back.

The hissing increased in volume until it approached the roar of a waterfall—a huge, monstrous release of pressure so deafening she felt engulfed by it. It seemed to force her backward, pushing up against her as she stood unprotected before its immense power. Her mind spun, and her common sense told her she had to get out of there, that this creature of magic was too much for her and she would surely be destroyed. What made her think it would accept her as anything more than another intruder? She had been a fool, deluded into hoping there could be any sort of recognition of her purpose.

This was the end, and she had brought it on herself.

But it was too late to change her mind. It was too late to do anything but stand there and accept whatever would happen.

She abruptly straightened, facing it full-on, her head lifted defiantly. "I have a right to be here!" she cried out. "I am a Druid and share the right to enter!"

Nothing. She might as well have been shouting down a well.

Then the Guardian tightened its mist-infused self to form a featureless, amorphous shape, elongated and sinuous, with only the suggestion of a head on a body—and the head inclined toward her ever so slowly, in a gesture that could not be mistaken for anything other than what it was.

It was bowing to her.

No words passed between them. No other action was taken. The acknowledgment was made, then the mist dissipated in a scattering of brume and darkness. The light returned, and the Guardian of the Keep was gone.

Silence wrapped the empty space left behind, filling Paranor's chambers and corridors, leaving a ringing in Tarsha's ears and a spinning in her mind that threatened to topple her.

*It recognized me! It knew who or at least what I am. It respected my Druid connection or my magic or something equally persuasive, and it chose to let me continue.*

She remained where she was for long minutes after, waiting for the beating of her heart to slow and her breathing to steady. She was overcome with relief and gratitude. Everything had changed so quickly she could barely give credence to it. She had stood on the threshold of her own death and been given a reprieve.

It was a miracle. It was another instance of how thin the line was between life and death.

*Parlindru!* she thought suddenly. Was this another instance of the rule of three? Was this another escape from death of the sort to which the rule might apply?

She didn't know. There were so many instances in her life since encountering the seer where Parlindru's prophecy might apply. It was pointless to speculate on which ones mattered.

When she felt ready, she started ahead once more. She continued down the corridors and through the chambers until she found a stairway leading up, then began to climb. She went all the way to the third floor before she broke down. The tears came unbidden, her legs gave out, and she collapsed against the wall, burying her face in her hands.

*Thank you, thank you!* She whispered it so quietly she wasn't sure she had actually spoken the words.

She did not know exactly to whom she was whispering her thanks. To Drisker or the Guardian or the fates that watched over her, or all of them together. She said it in a relieved rush, and she cast it out there to whoever deserved it. Then she pulled herself together again, climbed to her feet, and continued moving down the hallway once more.

It took her almost two hours to find the room she was looking for. All of the doors she passed bore insignias she did not recognize. The insignias were clearly meant to serve as identifications, but that didn't help someone who didn't know what any of them meant. She opened the doors that were not locked to try to make sense of each room, but nothing looked right.

Undaunted, she kept on searching, traversing the entire length of the corridor, moving from side to side with each new door she reached.

"This is ridiculous!" she announced aloud in frustration at one point.

When she finally found the offices of the High Druid, she did so for the least likely reason she would have expected: She recognized the insignia carved into a plaque on the door. It was the insignia that belonged exclusively to Paranor's High Druids, and Drisker's books of magic had it embossed on their covers. There it was before her now, so she did not hesitate to enter.

Inside she found a reception room with chairs and a desk, and beyond an office with shelves and files for storage. She walked the entirety of the room once and then began her search, opening drawers and pulling books and folders. But she quickly determined that none of this was what she was looking for. The Druid Histories were elsewhere, undoubtedly hidden from view and not accessible to those who did not know how to find them.

Much like herself.

She seated herself in one of the more comfortable chairs to think things over. She knew that entries in the Druid Histories had been made by various Druids over the years—most of them High Druids at the time of the chronicling. Beyond that, she knew almost nothing, so it didn't take long for her to accept that, without help, she was lost. She slumped in the chair, more tired than she had realized, pondering what to do. Her thoughts returned momentarily to her encounter with the Guardian of the Keep, and a chill ran through her body as she relived the experience. Once more, she heard the terrible hissing, felt the monstrous presence, saw the greenish mist closing in about her, and she wasn't past remembering how insignificant and vulnerable it had made her feel.

Maybe she never would be.

She looked around the chamber and wished she could leave. Just being inside this mausoleum left her feeling trapped, like she should be looking for a way out. The feeling that she had overstayed her allotted time—whatever it was—persisted, and her thoughts spun anew. Why would anyone want to be a member of the Druid order if it meant this stone-and-iron prison would be your home? How could you ever accept the cold emptiness and deep silence? How could you stay sane housed within such a soulless construction? Certainly, this must have contributed to Drisker Arc's decision to abandon his position as Ard Rhys when he felt everyone had turned against him and he was accomplishing nothing. How could it not?

But she couldn't allow herself to think about leaving just yet. Not until she found the Druid Histories and read them through. She thought of Tavo and Drisker and those who had gone to Skaarsland. Whatever happened here—whatever she accomplished or failed to accomplish—would in all likelihood impact them. With Tavo, the matter was already settled. He was gone forever, his life given to save hers, his transgressions redeemed by his sacrifice.

As she attempted to stiffen her resolve, staring down at her clasped hands, a sudden weariness came over her—perhaps from the stress of encountering and facing down the Guardian, perhaps simply from the exertion she had expended in getting this far. Thinking to rest for a moment or two before she continued her search for the Histories, she leaned back in the padded chair and closed her eyes.

She was asleep almost instantly.

Drisker Arc had lapsed back into unconsciousness midway through his encounter with Tarsha. Falling into a black hole into which no dreams could reach, he lost all contact with the real world. When he woke again, it was daylight but he had no sense of how much time had passed. The light in the Forbidding was diffuse and directionless, with no indication of its origin or its location, and so offered him little help. Here the world functioned on a different level entirely, and long ago Grianne Ohmsford, upon her rescue and return to the Four Lands, had written in the Druid Histories that she believed time passed at a different rate in the Forbidding. She had arrived at this conclusion from speaking with Pen and others in her family afterward, when she was already planning to resign her station as Ard Rhys of the Third Druid Order and enter the service of Mother Tanequil.

So it was now with Drisker, who, without being able to explain why, sensed that the movement of time in the Forbidding was different from what he remembered when he was still within the Four Lands.

What this meant was that he could not be certain how long ago it was that his connection with Tarsha Kaynin had been broken. It was astonishing that they had been able to reach each other at all, given the nature of the barrier that enclosed the Forbidding. Yet apparently while they could make contact visually, they could not speak to each other. Was this always to be so? Was this perhaps a function of the misaligned time flows? Or was this barrier a onetime event only? Now that he was awake again, he must try to find out.

To do so, he employed the same magic he had used to project himself beyond the walls of Paranor while it was still in limbo and return to the Four Lands. He was still weak, still wrapped in his sickness, aching and nauseous, limited in his use of his Druid magic, and altogether uncertain whether he could make a connection. Yet projecting his image was easier than he had expected, his reach by astral projection still strong enough to enable him to appear to her in recognizable form.

But he failed to find her.

"Tarsha!" he cried, calling out to her, seeking to bring her to him.

But still nothing happened. She did not respond.

He continued to try, over and over. He used every skill and trick of magic he knew to make a connection, but she failed to appear. Eventually, his strength was sapped, and he gave up. Apparently the time before had been a quirk of fate. He could not reach her now. Their chance at connecting had come and gone, and he would have to let her continue on with her efforts back in the Four Lands as best she could. It was galling to him, but there was only so much he could do.

Nevertheless, after resting a bit, he tried again. But again he could not manage to find her. Frustration and anger filled him in equal parts, and he felt his chance of helping her in any way fading. Exhausted, he lay back. There was nothing more he could do but wait on Weka Dart. Perhaps Grianne Ohmsford would have a suggestion of what he might do.

If, of course, he deemed it a good idea to confide in her. He was not sure yet of how much he should allow her to know.

He fell asleep pondering the matter.

Tarsha was still asleep and dreaming when Drisker Arc appeared out of the ether. But something woke her, something that warned her of his presence. Her head snapped up at once, and when she saw him, she sprang to her feet. "Drisker! What happened to you? You just disappeared midsentence. Are you all right now? Will you disappear like that again?"

But she was dreaming, she realized, and remembered that no words could be exchanged when they communicated in dreams. She quit talking and pointed at him, mouthing, *Okay?*

He nodded back, pointed at her, and said, *Paranor?*

She nodded, gesturing at her surroundings, walking from one wall to the other, letting him see the room. Then she shrugged, parodied reading, swept the room with her hands, and mouthed, *Histories?*

He seemed to understand. He pointed to the wall she was standing before. She looked around, but there was nothing there. She turned back again and shrugged that she didn't understand. He shrugged in turn and shook his head questioningly.

She was instantly infuriated. How was she supposed to explain her purpose here? What was his problem? She mimed reading, turning pages, then jabbed a finger at him angrily and gestured back to her and Paranor.

But Drisker frowned and shook his head.

Now she was really incensed, and found herself falling into speech. "I'm trying to help you! I came all the way to Paranor to find a way to do that! I read your books on magic and found a drawing of the key to the tunnel door and used it to enter. Then the Guardian appeared and I thought I was dead. I thought it was going to destroy me, but it didn't. It bowed to me. It bowed as if it knew me and was offering itself or . . . I don't know! Anyway, I need to read the Histories!"

She was speaking so fast the words were tumbling over one another. She forced herself to speak more slowly. "There might be something in the Histories about how Grianne Ohmsford got back from the Forbidding. If I search hard enough, perhaps . . ."

But of course he couldn't hear her, she realized. All that shouting and gesturing and anger and frustration had been wasted. She shook her head at him in dismay and gestured again at the wall and again mimed reading books.

To her surprise, he nodded this time and gestured back. *Go.*

She did as he requested, everything moving about as it does in dreams so that now she was facing the wall and four paintings, all of them of Paranor, hanging in a row with Drisker now standing right in front of them. She looked at him questioningly. He gestured for her to move over to the second picture, mimicked lifting his hands and placing one on either side of the picture, palms flat and fingers spread, and leaning into the wall. Then he stepped back and motioned for her to do the same.

She did. Nothing happened. Then she looked at him. He was moving up behind her. She could feel his presence pressing into her. He gestured for her to place her fingers on top of his. When she did, they disappeared. She almost screamed in shock, but realized nothing had happened otherwise. She looked at him, and he mouthed a single word.

*Press.*

He waited then, giving her a chance to repeat the word. When she did, he nodded. Then he was gone again.

When she woke again, it was morning. Immediately she rose from her chair and walked to the wall and its four pictures. Remembering Drisker's instructions, she stood before the second and placed her hands and fingers where he had told her. She was helped by the fact that there were faint smudges where the tips of his fingers and hers, conjoined in her dream, had rested—no doubt a legacy of all the High Druids throughout the years doing this very thing—then waited. Nothing happened. Finally she felt the substance of the wall changing as it began to melt, and she stepped away quickly.

A smile lit her countenance. Shelves lined every wall of the chamber beyond, filled with the Druid Histories.

# NINE

TARSHA PULLED THE FIRST several books from
their places on the shelves, took a seat at the heavy
wooden table that dominated the center of the room,
and began reading. She had already decided to concentrate her efforts on the events surrounding Grianne Ohmsford's imprisonment and rescue, thinking
it likely that anything of use would be found there.
In particular, she wanted to find the specifics of how
Grianne's nephew, Pen, had managed to get into the
Forbidding and bring his aunt out again. Some sort
of potent magic must have been at play to allow this
to happen, and Tarsha needed to know if it could be
used again.

To her dismay, the Histories ran to over a hundred
volumes, and her initial search was simply to find
which of them contained any record of Grianne's
rescue. She presumed there would be at least one,
but it took a long time to find what she was looking
for. Tarsha knew the history of the order in general
terms, but she did not know exactly where—within
a several-hundred-year range—the chronicles of Grianne's service as Ard Rhys could be found. That alone

took several hours, and when she finally found it, she discovered it comprised the better part of two entire books.

Undaunted, she began the arduous task of reading both books in their entirety, beginning with Grianne's time as Ard Rhys. This required the rest of the day. She noted the passage of time from the way the light through the windows of the offices began to dim with the arrival of sunset. The day had gone by more quickly than she had imagined, and still she hadn't found anything useful. Smokeless lamps within the chamber housing the Druid Histories ignited automatically—triggered by her presence—so at least she was able to see well enough as she continued her reading.

It was shortly after nightfall when she found the first mention of the black staff. It was in a section of the second book written by Grianne, which detailed how Penderrin Ohmsford, her brave and determined young nephew, had journeyed deep within the wilderness of the Charnal Mountains. There he had located a magical being that took the form of a tree called a tanequil and discovered it was sentient and he could communicate with it. After great effort, he was able to persuade the tanequil to give him one of her branches so he could fashion it into a rune-marked staff that would breach the walls of the Forbidding and allow him to rescue his aunt.

It was a compelling and almost unbelievable story, and it told her everything she needed to know about Pen Ohmsford. His willingness to risk himself for Grianne demonstrated a courage that exceeded anything she had ever known. But at its end, and upon Grianne's return, there was a gap in the written record. Several pages following the account had been left blank—as if Grianne had intended to write more but had never followed through. She wrote of her return with Penderrin, and how the staff had saved them both from the Forbidding, but after that came a chronicle of the fates of Shadea a'Ru and the other rogue Druids who had helped imprison Grianne. There was no further mention of the staff.

Then Tarsha noticed something she had missed before. Just before the blank pages, there was evidence of several pages having been carefully excised—as if Grianne had written something and then decided she didn't want it there after all, but had left room for something else to be written another time, should there be a reason. But why had she removed the pages, if indeed it was she who had done so? And why had she decided she might want to make a different entry later?

Tarsha skipped ahead, bypassing entries from Druid scribes who had reported Grianne's disappearance and the beginning of a new order, but found nothing more about the staff. She skimmed all the way to the end of the book, but still there was no mention. And by then, she was another hundred years into the history of the Druids and Grianne had dropped away entirely.

So Tarsha went back to the point where Pen had rescued his aunt and reread the entire recording of events to see if she had missed anything. She had not. What had become of the black staff following Grianne's return was never mentioned. Its fate remained a mystery.

But the staff looked to offer the best possibility for helping Drisker, and she had to find out what had become of it. Perhaps there were other writings, other histories that had recorded the parts missing from these books—family histories, personal writings about Grianne and her fate. Wouldn't Pen have kept something like this after returning? Wouldn't he have written it all down, if only for himself and his descendants?

If so, she had no idea where those writings could be found. There hadn't been any Ohmsfords in the Four Lands for years. Only the appearance of Shea Ohmsford, who had gone to Skaarsland on the *Behemoth*—and her own and Tavo's use of the wishsong—suggested there might be any of the family remaining. Shea appeared clueless about his heritage and even his name, and whatever Ohmsfords had been in her family tree were long lost to history.

So where else should she be looking?

She was left with no choice but to keep reading all the remaining Histories, in an effort to see if something more wasn't contained in them that would help. At one point, too tired to continue, she put her head down on the reading table that dominated the center of the library and went to sleep. She had no idea how long she slept, but when she came awake again she found herself at least marginally refreshed, if stiff and sore from using the table and chair as a makeshift bed. She also realized that Drisker hadn't come to her in her dreams.

She briefly considered leaving the room and curling up in one of those more comfortable chairs and sleeping longer, but a little food and drink seemed more important. She had found a nearby storeroom earlier, which still contained edible food, and returned there now to gather some and fill a pitcher with water before returning to the table and her studies, in an effort to discover if there was anything more to solve the mystery of the black staff.

When she saw the daylight filtering through the exterior windows of the adjoining room, heralding the arrival of the sunrise, she leaned back in her chair and sighed. She really did need to sleep before continuing. She blinked away her weariness and bent over the book she was perusing. She finished the page she was on and was turning it to read the next when the wall that had vanished to admit her earlier reappeared, reforming into a solid barrier. She stared at it in surprise for a moment, then rose and walked over to touch it. Wood-paneled stone barred her way. She tried placing her hands against the wall as she had done from the outside, pushing against the wood. She tried shifting her hands. Everything failed. The wall remained firmly in place.

She stepped back and stared at it with a mix of rage, frustration, and fear.

How could this be happening?

She was trapped.

Drisker Arc, unaware of what was happening to Tarsha, slept on and off after breaking contact, his mind and body exhausted, his sickness all-consuming. Everything continued to ache, his muscles and joints throbbing. His nausea was so severe he woke repeatedly, retching and gasping for breath, and his intense fever left his skin covered in a sheen of sweat. Even his dreams were dark and meaningless, his thoughts scattered and incoherent. He was in serious trouble and he knew it. But even his vaunted magic, when he tried to use it for healing, could not seem to lessen his suffering for more than a few moments.

Then, on his last wakening, he found things had suddenly gotten much worse.

Just beyond the shield he had created to protect him from predators, a monstrous insect was watching him. It wasn't an insect the likes of which the Druid had ever encountered—even discounting its size—but looked instead like something cobbled together from parts of other bugs. It had six legs, hairy and crooked, on which its body rested. Its head was small and bent over, connected to a very long neck. Its body was bulbous and seemed to be secreting some sort of liquid.

Drisker went very still, hoping it might not have seen him or be interested in him as food, but then it began to paw at the shield. The Druid wished he had been strong enough when he built the shield to have installed a poison or acid component, but all he could do at this point was hope the creature would lose interest and move on.

Instead, it pushed harder, using considerable force to try to break through. Clearly it had made up its mind about whether or not Drisker was edible. Testing the shield at various points while its eyes remained fixed on the Druid, the creature finally found a place where the barrier yielded to its touch, ever so slightly. It pushed harder, and the shield gave a little more.

Drisker waited, his magic summoned to his fingertips, ready to strike. There was nothing else he could do. When the shield gave, he would probably have only a single moment in which to damage the creature enough that it would back off. And he would have to hope that, in spite of the limitations placed on him by his sickness, it would be enough.

Then, abruptly, the entire world beyond his shield seemed to explode in a burst of dazzling white light, followed by ash-filled smoke gathering in a lingering haze. A second explosion followed, and by now the Druid was hiding his eyes so as not to be blinded. He huddled against the wall behind the already failing shield, his body racked with pain and weakness, and waited helplessly for whatever would happen.

When the smoke cleared, fading into the gloom, the monstrous insect was gone and Grianne Ohmsford stood in its place. She regarded Drisker for a moment, her expression unreadable, then reached out and swept his protective shield aside as if it were spiderwebbing.

"I thought you were supposed to rescue me," she growled, snarly and disdainful as she stared down at him with distaste. She took a step closer and wrinkled her nose. "You smell like something the cat dragged in."

The Druid supposed she was right.

Still locked away in the library in Paranor, Tarsha had been reading for what must have been hours, taking time off to nap twice when her eyes grew too heavy to continue, before she finally found what she was searching for. It was further on in that second book, and she might not have found it at all if she hadn't decided that, if anything existed about the disappearance of the black staff, it would be there. Why? Because no one else but those who were alive in the time of Grianne Ohmsford would know anything about it. She had already gone forward another four books and was looking at having to read over twenty more when she came to this conclusion.

She went back to the only book she had found with any mention of the black staff and began searching for hidden sleeves or resewn patches of liner. Maybe here, she thought, was where the notes she needed would be hidden. But she could find nothing—no sleeves, no hidden pockets, and no evidence of tampering with the covers. So she turned back to where she had read about the staff and read through those passages again. When she came to the blank pages without finding anything new, she stopped and stared at the empty whiteness of the paper.

Maybe she was looking at this all wrong.

What if Grianne had torn out those pages not because she didn't like what she had written but because she didn't want just anyone to be able to read it—Druids included? What if she had rewritten them on the blank pages in an ink that would reappear if the right magic was summoned?

But why would Grianne do that? What could be so important that she wanted to keep it secret from virtually everyone?

Tarsha tried to think of something, but could not come up with a scenario in which the fate of the black staff mattered sufficiently that no one should be allowed to know of it besides Grianne.

And there it was, right in front of her face. For whatever reason, Grianne Ohmsford had decided, as Ard Rhys, only *she should know* what had become of the black staff. No one but she should be able to find it again.

Because . . .

Tarsha's mind went blank at this point. She backed away from thinking about it further, satisfied for the moment that she knew—or at least thought she knew—the explanation for the blank pages. But she would have to test her theory. If she could find a way to make the entry she assumed was there appear, she might find the answer to everything else.

She returned to the blank pages, opening the book so the first two were revealed. Then she laid the book down in front of her, with the blank pages staring back at her. All she had to work with was the magic of the wishsong.

*Wish for it, sing for it, and it will happen.*

Those were Drisker's words to her once upon a time, when he was explaining why it was such a powerful magic and why only those with Ohmsford blood could make use of it. This was a magic that was inherited, not learned, and while you could refine and improve your usage if you possessed it, you could never acquire it any other way.

She hadn't really stopped to think about this before; she had simply reacted to whichever danger threatened or whatever need surfaced, knowing that the magic would come to her aid. Long years of living with the wishsong had taught her the process, and she had quit worrying that whatever help she required might not be given.

But this time she paused.

If Grianne Ohmsford had sealed the page by turning the ink invisible, she was likely aware that at some point another magic user might think to defeat her efforts. So wouldn't she have installed some sort of preventive device to make sure only she could reveal the words? Of course she would. This was Grianne Ohmsford she was talking about.

There could be no room for mistakes if she attempted this. A mistake might cause the pages to self-destruct.

Tarsha leaned back in her chair, distancing herself from the book. She was exhausted all over again by now, and she needed to rest before attempting anything that involved using magic. Especially magic trying to unlock the puzzle of the blank pages.

So she laid her head down on the table, using her crossed arms as a cushion, and she slept.

Drisker Arc stared back at the wraithlike figure before him, his sickness sufficiently progressed he could no longer see clearly enough to be certain who he was looking at. But when she came closer and knelt beside him, he realized Weka Dart had brought the help he had been sent to find.

"I wasn't sure you would come," he managed to gasp, his throat constricting with a mix of emotions.

"I come because I need your help. As apparently you need mine. Neither of us will find it without the other. Let me see your face and hands."

He pulled back his cowl to better reveal his face and held out his hands. She took hold—her own hands rough and scabrous—then peered closely at his face.

"Excrement poisoning, by my reading, Ard-Rhys-that-was," she whispered. "From eating food of the sort you shouldn't have. I will have a word with the Ulk Bog on our return. You will live, but for a while you will wish you hadn't."

"I already wish that." He coughed as his throat tightened anew. "You made short work of the insect that was coming for me. What was it?"

"A thorax-major species. Lots of them in the world of the Jarka Ruus. No threat to me, but plenty to you. It would have made a quick meal of you had your shield not held. Impressive work for such a sick man. Now lie still."

She summoned a magic he did not recognize and layered it over his body. It had a suffocating feel, and he tried to break free.

"Lie still," she repeated sternly, holding him down. "Let it work."

He forced himself to accept what was being done, feeling the magic penetrate his body. When it had infused itself sufficiently that she was satisfied, she summoned another magic—this one forming a potion that coalesced tightly in the air before him, then streamed into his mouth and ran down his throat, burning all the way. He gasped and tried to spit it out, but could not manage it.

"There now," the Ilse Witch said quietly. "The healing will begin. Much of it will be peaceful, and you should sleep whenever you can. Just remember, in the end you will be yourself again. Or, with luck, there might even be a noticeable improvement."

She chuckled and rose, calling over her shoulder. A pair of slouched and craggy-faced demons came forward, their elongated arms reaching down to gather him up. He did not resist. What was the point? In his present state, he was all but helpless.

"Don't . . . be too hard on . . . Weka Dart," he called over as he was being carried away. "He . . . did what . . . I asked of him. He . . . saved me."

She moved over to walk next to him. Ahead, he saw a carriage made of bones tied with ligaments and chains. A pair of creatures that resembled oxen crossed with bears were harnessed to it.

*A rolling death cart,* he thought to himself. *A coffin on wheels.*

"I will have to let him be for now," she advised, smiling mostly to herself. "An Oric Clawling was lying in wait just outside our gates, and he missed seeing it. It was very nearly the end of him, but my guards managed to pull him free. Well, most of him, anyway. He might have to learn to get by with just one arm until the other regrows."

She turned away. "But that's enough talking. Rest now. We have a day's journey ahead of us."

Drisker closed his eyes and was asleep again immediately.

Exhausted and drugged, he gave no thought to Tarsha Kaynin.

Tarsha woke hungry and thirsty with no way to do anything about either. As of yesterday, she had eaten all her stores of food and drunk everything left in the pitcher. She tried repeatedly to make the wall open again—using everything from words of power in Ancient Elfish to arcane gestures, singly and in combination—but nothing helped. Then, when she could think of nothing more to try, she abandoned her efforts and went back to the Druid History with the blank pages.

What was the key to making the contents of the page reveal themselves? What was the key to releasing the locks she had grown increasingly certain Grianne Ohmsford had placed on them? It had to be something a non-Druid would not know to do. The more she thought about it, the more convinced she became that it was a voice command. Writing on the pages would be destructive, and gestures were too easily misinterpreted. But words or phrases voiced—there could be no mistaking those when spoken clearly.

So maybe a name? Someone or something most would not know about? Not something that was written in the books or commonly known from the history of the Four Lands, but something peculiar to Grianne and her time? She must have expected it would need to be accessed one day—although not necessarily by her—so, in her absence, who would she choose?

Not necessarily a Druid, not after what had happened with Shadea and her allies. Could her own name be the key? Could Grianne possibly know she would be the one to come looking?

"Tarsha Kaynin," she said, although the moment the words left her mouth she felt foolish. It seemed impossible that Grianne Ohmsford would have been able to predict the future with that much accuracy.

When nothing happened, her suspicion was confirmed.

She ran through a litany of other possible names, including all those from the Ohmsford family and friends, but nothing worked.

*Wait a minute.*

Who would think this worth the effort? It wouldn't be just anyone. It would be someone searching for exactly what Tarsha was searching for. And that someone would almost certainly be making this effort for the same reason she was: to find a way into the Forbidding. Because the staff didn't appear to have any other useful purpose.

Something about her reasoning still felt slightly off, but overall it seemed solid. So she had to think about it the way Grianne would have and settle on what words would work to unlock the hidden writings of the blank pages.

*Keep it simple.* That's what Grianne would have done. Because she had already determined at that point of her life to join the aeriads that served Mother Tanequil and would know she would not, in all likelihood, be the one to need access to her writings. But she'd want to restrict access to the right one.

Tarsha knew almost before she finished asking the question. She had known all along, even if she hadn't made the connection. Whoever used it would need to be an Ohmsford descendant.

And have use of the wishsong.

Tarsha pressed the book flat against the table in front of her, placed her hands on the pages, summoned just enough of the wishsong to reveal her heritage as an Ohmsford, and began to hum softly. After a few moments, she shifted the hum into a song, one that required only four notes, singing in Ancient Elfish, "Show me the words."

The pages beneath her hands rippled in response, a kind of shimmer of recognition. But still they remained blank.

*Almost,* she thought, and felt a surge of excitement. Immediately she repeated the process with one small change, pouring a bit more of her magic into the process.

"Show me the words. Reveal what is written."

And all at once, the pages were filled with words—everything that had been written all those years ago. In line after line, they appeared to Tarsha, traveling down the front page and moving on to those that followed until all the blank pages were full.

Tarsha Kaynin leaned back momentarily, her face alight with immense satisfaction. She had been right. The writings on the excised pages were not destroyed, but rewritten in a way that allowed them to be concealed from all but the one whom they were intended for. All her work at puzzling it through had been rewarded. All that remained was for her to discover what was hidden there.

She took a deep breath to steady herself, then leaned forward and began to read.

# TEN

------------------------------◆------------------------------

**THIRD DRUID ORDER, ENTRY 108/987—
ARD RHYS GRIANNE OHMSFORD,
CHRONICLER:**

*My time of service is drawing to a close. As of this
writing, my difficult and demanding tenure as Ard
Rhys is almost finished. I have returned to the Four
Lands. The rebellion has been quelled; the rebels are
no more. Paranor is safely in the hands of those loyal
Druids who have loved and cared for her. The relevant
events are recorded on the preceding pages in full, and
we are all looking forward to a new and better era in
the years ahead.*

*Yet a few final words need to be added before I can
put down my pen and close this book for the last time.
Not everyone will be able to read or even find what I
am about to write. This entry may never again need to
be seen, and I can only hope this is how events unfold.
So much of what we have endured as Druids within
the Four Lands has been above and beyond our darkest expectations. Still, most of what has transpired*

*has been laid to rest for good and our hope is for a better future.*

*I have been at the very heart of this discord. It is difficult for me to admit, because I have tried so hard to overcome my past and to prove my worth. Even though I was a child when I was taken and made into the creature that was loathed and feared by so many, I sought to prove that I had earned forgiveness for my transgressions and had become the person I would have been even were I not subverted by an unspeakable evil. But no explanations will suffice; no wishful thinking will help. The reality is what matters, and the reality is that, for some transgressions, there can never be forgiveness. We are all victims of our lives, and we cannot change what we do in the aftermath; we can only try to make up for it. Nor can we change the minds of all those who have come to see us as they wrongly believe us to be. Some can never forget. Some beliefs are fixed in stone.*

*So it is for me. I was the Ilse Witch for years, and even though I have been Ard Rhys of the Third Druid Order and demonstrated a careful and well-intentioned stewardship of my office and tried my level best to act as caretaker to all the peoples of the Four Lands, I am condemned by too many to be forever what I once was. No one can alter how they are perceived or regarded in the minds of those who doubt and fear. I have learned this. I have seen the results within my own Druid family, and I must accept that the rebellion of those Druids who wished me gone was entirely my own fault.*

*Why do I say this? I presumed too much. I believed*

I could bring everyone back to me with friendship and caring. I believed I could be forgiven. I was wrong. From some journeys, there can be no return.

Enough. I go on too long. I wanted to put these thoughts down somewhere so that perhaps one day my ancestors might read them and convey my thoughts to others. By then, all those alive now will be gone, and I will be a memory. A new beginning might be possible. Perhaps this, at least, will survive me and serve as an explanation for how I lived my life.

But there is another reason for this writing, as well.

I was saved from the Forbidding by my nephew, Penderrin Ohmsford, the son of my brother and only sibling, Bek, with the aid of a black staff procured from a sentient tree called the tanequil. Pen traveled to find this tree and communicated his need to help me. He persuaded the tanequil to give him a branch on which he then formed the symbols that would enable the staff to find me and bring me back. The staff was called a darkwand, and it responded only to Pen. It cost him two of his fingers and an unforgettable memory of his defiling. It took courage and perseverance beyond anything I have ever known for Pen to endure this and to come for me and bring me back, and I owe him my life and whatever future remains to me.

You have already read of my final encounter with Shadea a'Ru and her rebel companions. But there was another resolution needed to bring this terrible episode to an end. By trapping me through use of triagenel magic and sending me into the Forbidding, the rebel Druids allowed one of the prison's resident demons to be sent to the Four Lands in my place. A *switching of bodies is always required for triagenel magic to work. Thus a creature called the Moric was dispatched out of the Forbidding and into my old world to take my place. This demon presented a huge threat, and it needed to be sent back. For this to happen, the darkwand was employed once more.*

*It was Penderrin who summoned the necessary magic, and with his father and mother and a handful of others went to a meeting with the Moric, which was disguised as the Federation Prime Minister, Sen Dunsidan. But they knew him for what he was, and they convinced him the darkwand was a gift of magic. Because there was a lure to it that few could resist, the Moric seized the staff and was transported, along with it, back into the Forbidding. But this time there was no way for the demon to come out again, since the staff would not answer to anyone who was not an Ohmsford. So while the staff would transport the Moric back into the Forbidding at Penderrin Ohmsford's bidding, it would not allow the demon a chance for another escape.*

*Yet I believe that if it still exists, it possesses the magic with which it was imbued. While Penderrin asked it to go dark for the demon, the residual magic will still respond to him or any Ohmsford descendant who tries to wield it. It is in the nature of how such magic works, from the Sword of Shannara on down. When such a magic is given, a blood bond is formed— and once formed will serve any who carry the blood of the gifted. But I said nothing to my nephew of this. Pen will never return to the Forbidding, and nor will I. But one can never see the future clearly, and so I have determined to write down these words so that the truth of the darkwand's magic will not be lost entirely. I cannot envision how or even if this will ever prove useful, but I have done what I think I must.*

*As a precaution, I write this in ink that will only appear to another of my blood—to an Ohmsford and no other. It is our heritage and is of use to no one else. If it is lost, that is fate's decision. If it is needed, these words will be uncovered and the truth revealed.*

*In closing, I have discovered something about myself. Perhaps as a result of the time I spent within the Forbidding, or as a consequence of the extreme expenditure of magic I was required to suffer, my precognitive abilities have become greatly enhanced. And what were once small visions have now become so strong that they threaten my sanity. One showed my return to the Forbidding—a prospect that terrifies me.*

*I try my best to shut out these visions, yet memories of my time as the Ilse Witch haunt me regularly. My decision to seek relief by serving as an aeriad for Mother Tanequil may help prevent any further visions. I am hopeful. I am in need of peace. Penderrin will fly me to where Mother Tanequil roots, and I will seek entry into her order. I will offer to replace the girl Pen loved—who gave herself for me—thus repaying them both. He does not know this, yet. He will discover the truth when I am gone.*

*And now I am done, and this writing is complete.*

*Peace and better times await me, and I go to find them,*

*Grianne Ohmsford*

Tarsha was stunned. At first she thought she must have read it wrong, so she went back and read it a second time. But she had not been mistaken.

Grianne Ohmsford had meant this for her—even without knowing who she might be or when she might read it. But Tarsha had been mistaken about where the black staff could be found. It wasn't somewhere in the Four Lands. It was back inside the Forbidding where she couldn't get at it, and it had been there for hundreds of years.

Only Grianne—along with a handful of those others who were dead and gone—would ever have known this. Drisker hadn't known; perhaps he hadn't even known there was a black staff in the first place. But what mattered was that, like herself, he didn't know it was inside the Forbidding.

Which prompted an interesting question. What difference did it make to Drisker's situation? She had hoped the staff might offer him a means of escape. But if it only responded to one who possessed Ohmsford blood, how would it help him even if he found and recovered it?

And if the staff was still inside the Forbidding and Grianne Ohmsford knew about it, why hadn't she recovered it herself? Why had she asked for Drisker's help? Why had she made the bargain with him to help him with his efforts in the Four Lands in exchange for helping to free her from the Forbidding?

Why hadn't she claimed the staff and made her escape?

# ELEVEN

◆

BELLADRIN RISH WAS YOUNG, reasonably attractive, and very, very clever—and she knew how to play to these strengths. You could have asked Ketter Vause, had he still been alive, or Kol'Dre—even though he had not even known she was Skaar before she killed him—and they would have been forced to admit she possessed all of these attributes and had fooled them both right up to the end.

In the wake of Ketter Vause's death, she had reported his assassination to his guards and attendants and asked that the commanders of his army report to the Prime Minister's quarters for an important briefing. She did this swiftly and efficiently, then saw to the removal of the bodies of the Prime Minister and his assassin, first swearing all who were involved in this effort to silence. No word of what had happened was to be leaked to anyone in the camp, no matter who or why, and violation of this command was to be considered treason.

She had given no details. Explanations were never needed for those not in command.

By force of personality and her recognized position

as the Prime Minister's personal assistant, she was able to turn aside any questions from those who aided her. Instead, they wrapped the dead and carried them away for burial, and pledged to do exactly as she had ordered.

When they were gone, she took time to clean the blood off herself, discard her sleeping garb, and dress in fresh clothes for the confrontation ahead. And it would be a confrontation. Then she waited for the commanders of the Federation army to arrive while reflecting on what she had brought about and what she was expecting to do next.

She was sorry about Kol'Dre, but he had sealed his own fate by relying too heavily on his friendship with Ajin d'Amphere and on his long years of service to the crown. Neither was ever protection enough when you crossed a king—which the Penetrator had done when he had sought to conceal Ajin's transgressions and disobedience. Belladrin had not known Kol'Dre personally, but he was well known to most of the other Skaar Penetrators, his exploits chronicled in stories that celebrated his daring and his success. Belladrin had admired him and respected his abilities enough to be especially cautious when Cor d'Amphere had ordered her to kill him. Because the Skaar king had made clear that any mistakes would earn her a trip to the netherworld in his place.

And there was good reason for this warning. Her job description required both that she be successful and that she avoid being caught. So Kol'Dre's death was not undertaken out of spite or ambition, but out of necessity and with a larger purpose in view. The

Penetrator had overstepped himself and needed to be removed, but even dead he would still serve a useful purpose. Belladrin Rish was exactly the right person to see that both results were achieved, and her king and benefactor had entrusted her with the responsibility for doing so.

So she had been careful and thorough, and Kol'Dre was no more. And while she had admired him, she had also felt a certain amount of resentment. Kol'Dre had lived his life in full view of his people, an iconic figure whose accomplishments were reported and acknowledged and respected. She would never have any of that. She would always be forced to remain in the shadows, all but invisible. She would always be a ghost.

She, too, was a Penetrator, and every bit as good as Kol'Dre was. The difference between them was that she was always kept in the background—right from the very first day that Cor d'Amphere had tapped her to serve him personally. He had made the nature of what he expected from her very clear. He wanted someone who would work only for him and always be a secret to everyone else. He had used her over and over, instructing her to ingratiate herself into the households and lives of various members of enemy nations, so that conquering them could be more easily achieved. She looked nothing like who or what she was, but rather exactly like what she pretended to be: a young woman more clever than her years would suggest, and more able to assist and advise those she purportedly served than they expected.

For her assignment to the Four Lands, the Skaar

king had sent her ahead shortly after the report came back that Kol'Dre had found a new home for their people. Her job was to discover the most dangerous of their potential enemies, infiltrate them, serve in a position of responsibility, then report back everything that might be of use. She was accomplished at learning new languages and manipulating people, so she was perfectly suited for the job. And it had been so much easier to insinuate herself into the hierarchy of the Federation than it had been with other governments on other assignments, for Ketter Vause had been a vain and overconfident man who saw himself as far from ordinary and liked to be acknowledged as such by those surrounding him. And she had been his eager audience of one, who at the same time could not only advise him on but also help to implement the solutions.

She harbored no regrets about his demise, as she did about Kol'Dre's. She cared nothing for Ketter Vause. His death had been necessary—as much for the confusion it would create as for the opportunities it would present. The witch, Clizia Porse, had provided the blueprint, but it was Belladrin Rish who was tasked with carrying it out.

She scrunched her face into a frown, thinking of how fully she had allowed herself to become submerged in her present circumstances and how much she missed the life she had enjoyed before becoming a Penetrator and a slave. Belladrin Rish wasn't even her name, and it certainly hadn't been her name the last time she had engaged in an infiltration, or the time before that . . . or even the time before that. Her real

name was Eris'Sin, but she hadn't used it since she
had entered Cor d'Amphere's service in exchange for
the king agreeing to spare her father's life. And her
mother's, as well, she had assumed from the beginning, although the king had never directly made the
threat. But when one fell out of favor—or was caught
with his hand in the king's pocket, as her father had
been—it was usually a death sentence for both. And
often for their children, too.

If there was mercy to be found in the monarchy of
the Skaar—a people committed to a warlike existence
of exploring and conquering—she had never seen it.
So it was fortunate that she was as smart and intuitive
as she was. It was a blessing that she had been granted
an interview with the king so that she could plead for
her family's safety and persuade him—while letting
him think it was his idea—that she could be an asset
to him as his personal facilitator and attendant. She
would be willing to take an oath to serve him as such
and pledged never to mislead or betray him. Things
he could not do for himself, she promised, she would
do for him.

Somewhat to her surprise, he had agreed to her
suggestion. Of course, he saw things somewhat differently than she did, but her goal had been achieved. He
had agreed to spare the lives of herself and her parents
so long as she served him ably. Only later, when she
realized the nature of the imprisonment to which she
had sentenced herself, did she realize what he had in
mind. Her unique position as King's Personal Penetrator had been invented especially for her, and carried
with it a countless number of unpleasant duties.

So here she was, some eight years later, carrying out yet another assignment that would end in the downfall of yet another country. It had never bothered her before, but she had to admit it was bothering her now. Mostly, she had managed to distance herself from those she pretended to serve and admire. Mostly, she had felt so little for them that, when they were betrayed and destroyed, she was more than ready to move on to a new pretend life. But not this time. This time it was different.

A part of it was a growing fear that her time was running out. She had never thought this way before, but Cor d'Amphere's willingness to dispatch his most efficient and productive Penetrator with such callous indifference made her own position feel a lot more tenuous. One day, on little more than a whim, he might find himself tired or suspicious of her. To her way of thinking, Kol'Dre's allegiance to Ajin was not a betrayal; it was a quality that should have been praised and admired. Kol'Dre had not actively schemed against his king in any way. He had not worked to betray him. For years and years, he had performed his duties as Penetrator loyally and with great success. There was more to be gained by letting Kol'Dre live and continue to carry out his function as Penetrator than there was by simply dispatching him.

Yet Cor d'Amphere had chosen the latter.

Couldn't he just as easily reach the same conclusion about her at some point?

She was also dismayed at how killing Kol'Dre had made her feel. It wasn't the first time she had been asked to kill someone. But before, she had mostly been able to delegate such tasks to others. She had remained in the background, manipulating lives and conveying useful information, avoiding engaging in violence. But not this time, and it had left her feeling haunted. She could not shake off how loathsome and dirty it had left her—how sick at heart and somehow diminished. She hated Cor d'Amphere for making her do it, for making her speak those words to Kol as he was dying, and for leaving her to deal with the emotional consequences of what she had done. She knew he believed it would not trouble her, that she would not suffer for it. And she knew he would feel free to ask it of her again.

And there was a further problem—one that centered on the Four Lands. Yes, she had found Ketter Vause and many of the ministers of the Federation's Coalition Council vain, self-centered, and consumed by a lust for power. But leaders are not always the best representatives of their people, and she was aware that what she disliked about them was not uniformly true of all Southlanders or members of other Races in other parts of the Four Lands. In fact, she knew it to be exactly the opposite, as she had found many people she had come to like and admire. She had been living in the Four Lands for three years, and in spite of her intentions not to do so, she had grown fond of this country.

But it was the Dwarves Battenhyle and Lakodan who had brought home to her how much she had come to care about this place. These were men she very much admired and genuinely liked. No-nonsense, bluff, and real, filled with concern for others—they were just the kind she most desired to befriend. How else could she explain her dismay at the way in which Ketter Vause had lied to and betrayed them once they had agreed to his bargain? How else to explain why she had resolved to do as much as she could to persuade Vause to honor his agreement? To involve herself so thoroughly in helping them was not something she had ever risked before, and it made her question the direction of her life.

These were only musings, though. After all, what could she do that would free her from her servitude to the king without risking the lives of her family? She could care and ponder as much as she liked, but it always came back to the same thing. If she stepped out of line or attempted to break free of her commitment, her family would suffer the consequences.

A rustle of canvas caused her to turn. The tent flaps widened sufficiently to admit the lean, slouched figure of Choten Benz. He slipped inside silently, and as he approached his hatchet face lifted out of shadow so that she could see the brightness of his eyes. Right away, she knew this was to be a different kind of confrontation.

"Belladrin," he said. "Is it true that the Prime Minister is dead?"

The almost dismissive way he asked it suggested how little he cared. She shifted back into character at once, showing him an expression of grief and bewilderment. "Assassinated by one of our own soldiers."

"Can you explain to me how this happened?"

She nodded, tears running down her cheeks. It was why he was here ahead of the others. She had sent for him first, wanting this time with him alone, sensing she might find in this enigmatic man a much-needed ally. "To your satisfaction, Commander Benz? To the satisfaction of others? I doubt it. But here are the details anyway."

She told him the story she had concocted, not bothering to wait for the others. This was the man she needed to stand with her. She had seen how even the most senior commanders of the Federation army behaved in his presence. They avoided him. They kept their distance. They were clearly intimidated. While he lacked seniority, he possessed experience and skills far beyond their own. He had killed men in hand-to-hand combat. He had survived the worst possible situations time after time. He possessed an independence and self-confidence that suggested he would never be one of them, but would always be the Prime Minister's favorite because of those abilities.

Vause had assigned him to her, but he had done so without thinking it through. Vause believed Choten Benz to be his man, but Belladrin Rish was certain she had won him over in Crackenrood and claimed him for herself.

"So there you are, in a few words," she said as she finished up her explanation. "This soldier managed to gain entry to the camp and these quarters, getting past not only the guards but myself as I slept on the floor of the anteroom, and killed the Prime Minister. But by singular good fortune I woke just as he was about to make his escape, caught him by surprise, and put an end to him."

She allowed some of her genuine distress over causing Kol'Dre's death to show, knowing it would bolster her charade.

Benz nodded, one corner of his mouth quirking. "Bold work. You are to be congratulated for your bravery. Not many would have taken the risk. Lucky."

"Not luck," she corrected him at once. "Determination. I was furious and terrified all at once, make no mistake. But there was no one else but me to stop him. He was absorbed in his work and did not sense my approach until he turned and found my dagger in his chest. So he died knowing I had killed him, but not quite believing I had managed it."

Choten Benz nodded slowly and then looked around the room. "So now you will tell this tale to the commanders. You will inform them of their leader's regrettable demise, confront them with the reality of needing an immediate change of leadership, and do . . . what else?"

"What I know the Prime Minister would have wanted me to do. Speak my mind. Provide advice for what to do next. Offer what information I have at my disposal, if asked. Suggest a course of action they might choose to embrace."

She made it sound as if this was something she could make happen with little effort, and she saw the mix of surprise and curiosity in his eyes. In that moment, she decided she might have overdone it.

"Well, then," he said, "I think perhaps you could use a man like me to stand beside you during this meeting."

Pleased by his response, she let her expression bubble over into a convincing display of gratitude. "That would be much appreciated. I am not one of them. I am an outsider, and it would greatly help if you were there to support me. I will be very much alone otherwise. But until a new Prime Minster can be chosen, I know Ketter Vause would have wanted us to hold the course. And I am best positioned to do that, having been his confidante for so long. At least, I hope I am."

Benz shook his head. "Don't underestimate yourself. Look what you've accomplished since you arrived. You are the one who kept your head and saved the entire army when their leaders panicked as the Skaar attacked them. And now you've managed to kill the Prime Minister's assassin—and not without great risk to yourself. You also ventured into Dwarf country and charmed the pants off Battenhyle and Lakodan, and I can assure you those two are not easily persuaded. No, I think maybe you will have the respect you seek. But there are some hungry wolves among all the sheep, and there will be an attempt to establish a claim to the leadership by at least one or two of them. What if they try to brush you aside?"

"Oh, they will. But I will convince them it would be unwise to underestimate me."

He stared, disbelief evident in his eyes. "Will you? How?"

"Because I still speak with the former Prime Minister's voice." She smiled. "Are you prepared to stand at my side?"

"As opposed to standing by sheep and wolves who detest and mistrust me? I think I'll risk choosing you."

He smiled back for an instant, and then something cold crept into his expression. "But let me be clear about one thing, Belladrin. For now, I am willing to support you, but I am not sure how far I can trust you, as you seem far more competent than someone with your degree of experience should be. This will work to your advantage, because many will underestimate you, but be advised that I don't intend to allow you to sabotage my own interests. Don't think to make me your dupe."

She went cold with fear as he finished. He knew. Somehow, he knew who and what she was. That put her in his power, and she saw everything falling apart in front of her.

This time, she held herself perfectly still. "What do you mean by that, Commander Benz?" she managed.

"I mean that you are nothing like what you pretend to be—or at least what others might think you to be. You are smart and efficient and you know how to ma-nipulate people. You are ambitious, and you want real power. I think you will come to possess it one day, and I wouldn't mind being there when you do, but I know the truth about you. You served the Prime Minister ably—served him much better than he deserved—but you didn't like him. I knew that from the first. Admit-tedly, you had reason not to like him; he was a fool-ish, self-absorbed, overconfident pretender who made poor use of his position. Neither of us cares that he is dead. In fact, best that he is. It affords you an op-portunity to advance yourself and that is fine, in my opinion. And if I am wrong about this and have of-fended you, I will leave now and not return. Just tell me to do so."

He paused, waiting. There was a calmness about

him that was disturbing. But she had been mistaken about what he knew, she realized, with no small measure of relief. He did not know that she was a Skaar and a spy. What he meant was that he saw her as someone looking to improve her situation, and what he sought from her was an understanding that he would not allow her to gain power over him. He would always keep her at arm's remove.

She almost permitted herself a smile.

"Commander Benz," she replied, "I have the utmost respect for you. You have helped me on more than one occasion, and I do not intend to forget that. I give you my word that if we agree to become allies, I will never deceive you about my intentions or take you for a fool. Is that assurance sufficient?"

He nodded slowly. "For the moment. In return for what you offer, I promise I will be honest with you—assuming you will be the same with me. We are very much alike, you know. We both prefer to avoid those who see themselves as better than others, but are incapable of rising to the level to which they pretend."

"Agreed. And you are right; I did not care much about the Prime Minister," she admitted. "But I did what I could to make him follow the right course. I couldn't save him from his fate, but I can see to it that the Federation and perhaps the people of the Four Lands are saved as a result of his sacrifice."

"His unintentional sacrifice," Benz corrected gently.

She smiled and reached out her hand. "I welcome your help, Commander. I value your service as my friend and ally."

The other did not take her hand. "I am your ally, agreed. I will have to wait a bit longer before believing we can also be friends."

"Fair enough. Friendship must be earned. Simply follow my lead when the other commanders arrive and support me where you can."

Benz nodded. "Agreed."

They stood staring at each other in the half-light of the smokeless lamps, each taking the measure of the other, lost in thoughts that were deeply personal. It was enough for now, Belladrin decided. Enough to see her through what waited.

Then, as if in response, the tent flaps parted once more, and the commanders of the Federation army trooped in one by one, impatient to hear the details of the Prime Minister's demise.

Belladrin had guessed wrong on how long it would take at least one of the commanders she had summoned to question whether she could speak for the now deceased Ketter Vause. She had thought she would at least get through her prepared remarks and a brief explanation about what happened to the Prime Minister, but she had assumed too much.

"So he's dead—assassinated while you slept nearby—but you still act as if you have his permission to address us with his authority."

Drusten Aarcobin was a senior officer among those gathered, and a full commander in the Federation army. He was also a man who had long since exceeded his ability to live up to the expectations of his title and position.

She smiled sweetly in response. "How close to him were you, Commander? Close enough that he divulged his intentions for dealing with the Skaar invaders? Close enough that he confided in you how he planned to end this standoff?" She paused. "Close enough that he invited *you* to sleep where you might be able to protect him? If so, I will step aside and you can conduct this meeting."

Aarcobin turned beet red. "You are nothing but a girl who assisted him by acting as his scribe. You were never intended to be anything more. You have no experience or special abilities to call upon. Do not pretend . . ."

"Excuse me, Commander," Choten Benz interrupted from one side, where he was standing apart from the others, "but it was Belladrin whom the Prime Minister expressly asked to travel to Crackenrood to secure the Reveals from the Dwarves. And who succeeded in carrying out his orders, allowing us all to stand here with our heads still attached to our shoulders."

"That doesn't mean . . ."

"I might remind you, as well, that it was Belladrin who took charge during the Skaar surprise attack on our rear lines while our air fleet and our Prime Minister were elsewhere so that we could repel our enemy."

There was a muttering of agreement among the other commanders that Aarcobin could not miss. "He trusted both her *and* her advice," Benz continued with a quick glance at Belladrin. "I witnessed it myself on more than one occasion. She knows exactly what he intended, and if you give her a chance, she might reveal it to you."

Aarcobin stared at him balefully, but then gave a short nod.

"Commander Benz is right," Belladrin affirmed. "The Prime Minister had a very definite plan in mind for how to handle our situation with the Skaar. He knew an attack was inevitable if nothing was done to forestall it. He felt such an attack would cost us many lives and resolve nothing. The Skaar are experienced, skilled soldiers with a huge number of conquests behind them."

She was embellishing now, trying to set the stage for what Benz and the other commanders believed Vause had confided in her.

"The Prime Minister felt an accord needed to be reached if at all possible. His first meeting suggested there might be no chance of such an agreement, but things are different now. And not because of his death, although that changes things as well. But just before he was assassinated, he received a message from the Skaar king, Cor d'Amphere. I have that message here in my pocket."

She reached in and pulled out a piece of paper, but Aarcobin quickly stepped forward. "How did you come by this? Did you steal it from him?"

Belladrin held her ground but pulled the document out of his reach. "Manners please, Commander. Of course I did not steal it! Why ever would I bother? He showed it to me, and we talked about it. Then he put it in his drawer. I retrieved it so it would not be lost, and now I intend to share its contents. Let me read it to you."

She waited for him to step back again, ignoring the expression of frustration on his face, before bringing the letter back in front of her. In a clear, steady voice, she read the contents to those assembled.

To the Honorable Prime Minister Ketter Vause:

I have reviewed my position and demands regarding any settlement of our current occupation of the lands north of the Mermidon River and any claims to lands of the Federation to which we might feel entitled. A prolonged stand-off and eventual war between our peoples will satisfy no one and settle nothing. My daughter overstepped the authority she was granted, and by doing so unfortunately created the impasse that now exists.

Permitting our occupation of the lands to the north is more than sufficient to satisfy our needs, and no other claims will be pursued. Mutual respect and accord between our peoples is what we seek to achieve.

I ask you to engage in a discussion with me, one-on-one, at your earliest convenience, so that we might achieve that goal.

With respect,
Cor d'Amphere, King of Skaarsland
and Eurodia

She handed the letter to Aarcobin, who quickly scanned its contents and handed it to the others. "Why would we do this?" he snapped.

*Progress,* Belladrin thought. *I have him asking my opinion now.*

"Why not, Commander? What have we to lose by engaging in a discussion? We might actually be able to achieve something without bloodshed. We might find a solution to our impasse, even with the Prime Minister gone."

Audin Messit, another full commander, cleared his throat. "This man sent an assassin to kill our Prime Minister and the attempt succeeded, in spite of your heroics. Why should we agree to do anything he asks?"

"Well, for one thing," she replied, "the blame for the Prime Minister's assassination is not his."

Heads turned, all looking at one another in disbelief. "Nonsense!" Aarcobin exclaimed at once. "Who else could be responsible?"

"Why not us? Why not a disgruntled member of the military? How else could he have gotten close enough to kill the Prime Minister if he was not one of us? He bypassed half a dozen guards without being noticed. And I will tell you something more—something I have held back until now. The assassin was wearing a Federation uniform. And his skin was dark, not fair like the Skaar. So it seems far more likely that he was a soldier, if the uniform and his appearance are any indication."

She paused to let that sink in as the assembled commanders frowned and muttered among themselves, then said, "Ask yourselves this. If Cor d'Amphere intended to assassinate Ketter Vause, why bother with this request for a meeting? Again, what would be the point?"

Fresh muttering rose among the assembled Federation officers, but again Messit took the floor. "I think we have to postpone any action until the Coalition Council chooses a new Prime Minister. We need new leadership before we make a decision of this magnitude."

But now a few of the younger officers were looking at him as if he were insane. "Postpone *any* action?" Lieutenant Commander Carrison Oberion asked incredulously. "We cannot afford to do that! The Skaar will realize something is wrong with our command structure if we delay when he has offered a chance for a truce. Our country is threatened, Commander Messit. The whole of the Four Lands is in danger. We cannot abrogate our responsibility to protect them by doing *nothing*!"

Messit tried to argue the point, but the majority of the commanders shouted him down. "Young woman!" Oberion called over to Belladrin. "You said you had a plan for dealing with this situation. Why don't you tell us what it is?"

Belladrin had them where she wanted them now. "We have an offer of negotiation in the form of a letter from the Skaar king. Let's take advantage of it. Let's arrange a meeting and talk to him."

"But Ketter Vause is dead!" Aarcobin shouted angrily. "Who will do the negotiating, if not our Prime Minister?"

Belladrin had already caught Choten Benz watching her, and she gave him a small nod. Benz, no stranger to intrigue and manipulation, knew at once what she wanted and nodded back with approval.

"Fellow Commanders," he bellowed, interrupting a renewed round of arguing, and the weight of his voice silenced the room. "We no longer have our Prime Minister and may not have a new one for months, given the speed with which the Coalition Council addresses such matters. Constant bickering, debate, secret negotiation, and other forms of maneuvering are sure to be the order of the day. But while we do not have Ketter Vause, we do have someone who filled his shoes quite ably in negotiating with the Dwarves—someone who knew his mind and was privy to his thoughts." He paused for effect. "We have Belladrin."

"No!" screamed Aarcobin.

"That is ridiculous!" echoed Messit.

"It makes perfect sense," Benz insisted. "Why do you keep trying to denigrate or ignore her many accomplishments? This young woman had the Prime Minister's ear and acted ably on whatever task she was given."

He wheeled back to Belladrin. "Would you act for us now?" he demanded.

"I would if I had the blessing of all present," she replied. "But I would want a few of you to accompany me, were I to accept. I do not pretend to be a skilled negotiator, and I would welcome guidance. Also, I will step aside, should you ask, once matters get under way. Commander Aarcobin, I would desire your presence particularly. And you, Commander Benz. And you, Commander Messit. Will you agree to this?"

She knew the answer to the question before she asked it, and was rewarded with an uneasy round of muttering that told her she was right. It was a difficult decision for them to make, but they saw no better solution to the problem. Belladrin had given them an easy way out by suggesting that others should take responsibility for any possible consequences. It was an old story with the military: kick the matter upstairs and let someone else deal with it.

Most had decided immediately that the suggestion Belladrin Rish had offered made good sense—even if she hadn't been the one to propose it. The attendant guilt she experienced at having won them over was something she would have to live with, because the charade she was orchestrating would see them all dead. Every last one of them.

At the moment, her suggestion of a way to move forward seemed a choice they could live with. Only later would they understand that this decision would mean the exact opposite.

# TWELVE

ONCE SHE HAD THEIR reluctant permission to act on the Skaar king's offer of a truce, Belladrin gave them no time to change their minds. She did not want to risk anyone rethinking their agreement to her plan and trying to persuade the others to back out, so she immediately dispatched a messenger with a handwritten note for Cor d'Amphere, requesting a meeting at the Skaar encampment by sunset that very day. She claimed she was writing him at the Prime Minister's behest because he had fallen ill, and so she, as his personal aide, would attend in his place. Three senior Federation commanders, all of whom were invested with the authority to act on his behalf, would accompany her. The message ended by asking for a written promise of safe passage for the negotiators.

On the surface, the contents seemed straightforward enough, but in reality they conveyed much more than what they revealed on the surface. They told Cor d'Amphere that Ketter Vause was dead. They did not reveal Kol'Dre's fate, but that would come later. They let the Skaar king know Belladrin had succeeded in the plan he had devised for ridding him of any further serious threat from the Federation. Most important, they assured him everything he sought to achieve was going the way he had hoped.

Again, her sense of guilt surfaced, but she tamped it down. It grew more difficult each time to do this, but she understood her situation and what it required of her. Duty sometimes required restraint. It was necessarily so here.

She promised the messenger before he departed that no harm would befall him by going into the Skaar encampment, and ordered him to wait for the Skaar king to provide him with a written reply.

But she was not out of the woods yet. Aarcobin and a few others demanded to be shown the body of the dead assassin, just to verify that what she had told them was accurate. Substitute *true* for *accurate*, and you understood their intentions. To avoid suspicion, she took them to where Kol'Dre had been wrapped for burial, along with Ketter Vause, and ordered the bodies unwrapped for viewing. What they saw was what she hoped they would see. Ketter Vause wore his death mask and the marks of his killing. His assassin was darkly complected, his hair was brown rather than blond, his eyes a cinnamon shade rather than blue, and his overall appearance nothing like that of the Skaar they had found among the dead attackers. He was also wearing a Federation uniform, as she had said. A cursory glance was all it took to persuade them that she had told the truth. To all appearances, the assassin did not appear to be a Skaar, and whether he was a Southlander and a soldier in the Federation army or someone else entirely was strictly a matter of conjecture.

It made her smile to hear their muttered responses and see the shaking of their heads as they trooped away. People were so easily fooled. All you had to do was give them a reason to believe something and they would almost always do so. It was the result she had been working toward right from the beginning, but it had required a complex and fluid combination of maneuvers only she could manage.

At least, that was how she saw it. Because that was the way she had managed to stay alive this long.

From the moment she had first appeared before Ketter Vause to apply for the position of personal assistant, she had known she could manipulate him. She was young and pretty, and he was clearly drawn to her. She was also confident and intelligent and willing to work hard and do what she was told. She had embellished her false story with just enough eagerness to learn at the feet of a master of leadership and success. She included a dab of flattery and a blushing dismissal of her own abilities as being anywhere near as significant as his. She provided a quick and assured reply to a hypothetical question about how she might handle a difficult situation to cap things off.

She projected a pleasant personality.

She offered the promise of being a loyal follower.

She gave evidence of the depth of her commitment.

She flattered him by insisting only he could teach her to be anything close to the politician he was.

It was what she did best—and was exactly what she had shown Cor d'Amphere she could do when she sought to save her father's life eight years earlier. Her assignment to act as the king's personal Penetrator would have placed her at odds with his daughter and Kol'Dre, but she was not required to encounter them directly and risk exposing herself, nor would she be asked to do so. She was there to provide the Skaar king with his own, separate source of information, and she would never be asked to report to anyone else.

And now, any concerns she might have harbored over a chance encounter with either one were over. Ajin was banished and Kol'Dre was dead at her hands. Besides, she was too deeply involved in the king's scheme to bother with any of that.

"Are you sure you know what you are doing?" Choten Benz asked her once the others had gone.

She gave him a look. "You seemed ready enough to support me. Have you changed your mind?"

The other's hard features tightened, but he shook his head. "Unless I discover I was mistaken. Don't let that happen."

"Just do what you promised," she snapped. "Stand with me. Watch my back. Give me your support against these stiff-necked fools."

She had almost wandered over a border that she wouldn't have been able to cross back from, so she gave him a smile. "Nothing is going to happen that you don't already know. We will speak with the Skaar king. We will listen to what he has to say. Then we will discuss it and make a decision. If he says the right things, and we can sign an agreement to that effect, we should be fine. After all, the attacks launched against us were provoked, weren't they? Didn't we go after them first?"

"I'm not so sure about that. We might never know. But I agree with the rest. Just know that if you are playing a game, I will drop you as fast as the others."

She smiled. "Oh, I know that much about you. But I won't give you cause."

"Best not, Belladrin. I am not the forgiving type." Then he turned and went out with the others.

She had decided right away she would have to watch him and perhaps even eliminate him entirely if he proved to be too troublesome. Or if he somehow guessed the real truth about her, which up to now he hadn't.

An uneasiness crept into her thoughts. Things weren't the same anymore. With Ketter Vause dead, everything was changing. She wasn't the same. Having killed one man, she was already thinking she might have to kill another, and she was fully prepared to do so. But not without strong doubts. The guilt was overwhelming already, and she was not sure she could handle any more. She felt an anger toward Cor d'Amphere for bringing her to this. She knew she had to share responsibility; she had offered to serve him. But the Skaar king had manipulated her until she felt used up. She remembered herself as a girl and wondered how she had managed to discard so much of who she once was. Rationally, she understood it. Emotionally, she was beginning to wonder what would become of her.

But there wasn't much time to think about it or much reason to bother. She was stuck in a situation of her own making and she had to deal with how matters were, not how she would like them to be.

The messenger she had dispatched returned unharmed and with a response from the Skaar king, inviting her and her three companions to attend him as requested at sunset. In the hours before departing, she arranged for the burial of both Ketter Vause and Kol'Dre. There was griping about tradition and proper treatment for a Prime Minister, but she was quick to brush it off by pointing out that Vause was being buried in the field, like any other fallen soldier.

Aarcobin and Messit, who came with a few others in tow, suggested that flying Ketter Vause home and allowing him to be buried there would be more honorable and more in keeping with tradition.

"He was not a common soldier," Aarcobin argued. "He was a Prime Minister of the Federation and a great statesman. He deserves to be carried back to his family and laid in state in his coffin and given full honors. You deny him all of that by hauling him away to some hole in the woods!"

Belladrin almost laughed out loud. This was the same man who could barely stand to be in the same room with Vause—who had thought him an incompetent statesman and an idiot. There had been little love lost between the two, and claims of affront on a pretense of respect were ridiculous.

"Consider this," she replied calmly. "Someone would have to accompany him home and act as spokesman for the rest of us. This would mean facing the Coalition Council with the news that, while accomplishing nothing in the field other than fighting a battle and losing a great number of men, we have allowed our Prime Minister to be assassinated. But if we return home with an agreement for a truce, we can offer some good news that will help mitigate the bad."

"He could be kept with us until then," Messit chimed in.

She looked at him coldly. "We could be here for days, Commander. What do you think the body would smell like after a week?"

So the matter had been dropped and the hours had passed, and as the sun dropped toward the jagged, mountainous line of the horizon, the four negotiators set forth. There was clear tension among them—in part because the senior commanders did not much care for either Benz or Belladrin, and in part because all four of them were flying right into the lion's den. There was no guarantee that Cor d'Amphere would honor the promise of safe passage and allow them to fly out again, so the risk they were taking was clear.

Except for Belladrin, who risked nothing. She already knew exactly what was going to happen, so for her there was no uncertainty. By the time this day was ended, the fates of the three with her—and the remainder of the Federation army advance force— would have been settled.

And with them, in all likelihood, the fates of all the peoples of the Four Lands.

No one talked during the flight until they had almost arrived. At that point, with the enemy camp in sight, Aarcobin reminded the others of his senior status in the Federation army and announced that he would be handling the negotiation. It would be best if the others made it a point to agree with him, as a strong show of support would give them the best chance of succeeding in their efforts.

Belladrin said nothing. She had encountered this sort of behavior from Lieutenant Fillian when she traveled to the Dwarf village of Crackenrood. Such blowhards could always be undone in the moment, and there was no point in saying anything now. Plus, she already knew how things were going to proceed, so there was no reason to argue. He would discover the truth for himself quickly enough.

Still wrapped in silence and wariness, they landed their airship on a designated open space near the foothills of the Dragon's Teeth, where they disembarked to be met by a handful of Skaar soldiers and relieved of their weapons.

"You will need to be blindfolded, as well," the leader of the escort advised.

"Isn't this supposed to be a peaceful meeting?" Aarcobin demanded at once.

The soldier smiled. "Your previous visit was a surprise attack on our camp, Commander. You would have seen us wiped out to the last man. I think you might understand our precautions, given your past behavior."

Aarcobin glowered but said nothing more as he and his companions were blindfolded. With a soldier positioned to guide each of them safely, they were marched a rather long distance over rough terrain and into what was easily discerned as a shaded woods, to a place where the blindfolds were removed and they were permitted to see again. What they discovered was a tented camp too small in size to be of service to more than a few dozen Skaar. They stood around for a few moments in the company of their escorts, then Cor d'Amphere abruptly emerged from one of the tents and walked over.

He glanced from one face to another. "Belladrin Rish?" he addressed her.

"Your Majesty," she replied.

"Who are your companions?"

She introduced them in turn, but none deigned to address the king formally or offer any sort of verbal recognition. Even Benz stood frozen in place, his expression unreadable, his posture rigid.

The Skaar king looked them over when she had finished and nodded to himself. "Commanders," he said, "your presence is welcome, but I think I will limit any discussion to your Prime Minister's personal aide. When I am done with her, she will tell you what I am asking and then you can consider the matter in depth. Until then, this negotiation will be kept to the two of us."

The three Federation commanders looked at one another. Aarcobin opened his mouth to speak, but the Skaar king silenced him with a gesture and a look.

"Spare yourself the trouble of objecting, Commander," he said softly. "This is not a point of negotiation. It will be done as I have said, and if you do not approve, you will be taken back to your airship and sent home without any discussion at all."

"Your Majesty," Messit began, then faltered when the king's gaze shifted to him.

"The matter is settled," Cor d'Amphere stated. "Would Ketter Vause allow you to be present in any discussion if he were here? I think not. He showed no inclination to do so in the past, so we will continue that practice now." He beckoned for Belladrin to follow and turned back toward the tent. "Come this way, if you please."

She glanced at her three companions and shrugged. "I will be back to tell you everything. No agreement will be offered until you have heard whatever I have been told. So be patient."

Then she hurried after the king, leaving the commanders to stew. That, at least, was overwhelmingly satisfying. She had known all along she would end up alone with Cor d'Amphere, and there would be no discussion of an agreement. The king would want to discuss any adjustments she might need to make to the plan he had already settled on.

Still, her stomach churned unpleasantly as she followed the king into his tent. For the Federation, this was the beginning of the end.

Once inside the tent, Cor d'Amphere beckoned her to a chair and then seated himself across from her. "Congratulations. You seem to have won the day."

"For now."

"Details, please."

"There's not much to tell, Your Majesty. I slept in the tent as we planned. Kol'Dre appeared as expected. I saw him enter, but he did not realize I was watching him. So he proceeded into the sleeping chambers of the Prime Minister and killed him. I was waiting for him on his way out. It was over quickly."

"You gave him my message? You whispered it in his ear as he was dying? Word for word, as I asked you to?"

*"Cor d'Amphere thanks you for your service and bids me tell you it will no longer be required.* Did I get it right?"

The king clapped his hands softly. "I wish I could have been there to see it! That self-deluded pretender to the throne. As if he could ever be king! As if I would ever allow him to wed my daughter! What a fool." He looked closely at her. "But you are not happy about any of this, are you? Your expression gives you away."

She shook her head. "It is not my place to judge or to question your decisions, my lord."

He nodded slowly. "You are so tactful, Belladrin. I respect you for that. But you are wise, too. I cannot imagine how either one of us would succeed in this world without the other."

Belladrin masked a surge of rage, but managed to say placidly enough, "You would be fine on your own, Your Majesty."

The king gave her a long look. "Indeed. Well, to business, then. We will spend some time playing at negotiation so those fools out there will think we are discussing the terms of the truce they expect. What we must do, however, is review where matters will go from here."

"What do you want me to say?" she asked.

"Tell them what we agreed to before: that we are signing a truce stating we are laying claim to the territory they refer to as the Northland, which then becomes our responsibility. We agree not to venture into the other three lands to lay claim to any part of them, or to attempt to build settlements or homesteads. Any travel we do will be confined to trade. We will bring our people over from their homeland in small groups until we are settled, and we will permit regular visits from a Southland delegation to show we are in compliance."

He paused. "We will agree to respect their territories as long as they agree to respect ours. The same will be true in our dealings with the other lands and their inhabitants. There will be no encroachment and no overt acts of war so long as we are left alone. Any violations of this agreement will be referred to the appropriate Skaar and Federation authorities to be dealt with accordingly."

He paused again. "Is that everything?"

She nodded. "I think so."

"The proposed agreement of truce is already prepared." He rose and retrieved a multi-page document from a nearby table and handed it to her. "You should read it. Just to be sure. We have time."

She did as he asked, not rushing the effort. They had to be inside this tent long enough so no one would question that they were actually doing anything. Reading the truce was boring, but it was better than wasting time with small talk. She read it carefully, taking the better part of an hour, then handed it back to him. He shook his head and refused it.

"Take it with you. Show it to them. Have them

read it. I've added a few bits I know they will disagree with, just to give them something to negotiate, but assure them any reasonable changes they request will be made within a few days and we should have a final draft to carry back to Arishaig for signing."

"So you want me to stay with them?"

"For now. We need your eyes and ears inside their camp. We need you to observe and report back. There are still things to be learned, preparations to be made, and plans to be laid out. You will be a key part of that effort. But it won't take long. The end will come quickly enough."

How well she knew. And it did not make her feel any better. "So you are decided on this, Your Majesty?"

"Would you have me do something else?"

It was a risk, but she felt compelled to ask it anyway. "I was merely wondering if the truce was not sufficient. Perhaps their promise will be enough to keep them in line. Do they really present such a danger?"

He sighed. "You are still so young in some ways, Belladrin. Any conquering force knows that the greatest threat must be eliminated from the beginning. You have seen already how eager they were to cross the river and destroy us. What makes you think such treachery will vanish with the death of one man? These people may not have our skills and talents, but they share our lust for control. And—sooner or later—they will turn against us."

She nodded, rose, and took the document from him. "As you say."

"Are there some you favor?" he pressed. "A handful you would wish me to spare?"

He was searching for a weakness, and she knew better than to reveal one. "No. None."

He nodded and smiled. "Then we will kill them all."

# THIRTEEN

◆

FAR TO THE EAST, across the vast expanse of the Tiderace where the islands of the Nambizi could be found, the crew of the *Behemoth* faced a difficult choice. It had been three days since the attack by the bat-riding pirates that hunted these islands, and two days since the effort to find and retrieve Dar Leah and Ajin d'Amphere had been undertaken in the aftermath. Brecon Elessedil had insisted on it at once, and Rocan had been quick to support him.

But after long hours of searching with no result, the Rover crew seemed impatient to acknowledge what now seemed likely: that their missing comrades were dead. Even two dangerous night searches had revealed nothing. There had been not only no sign of the missing comrades or their vessel, but also no indication of what had happened to them. Only this morning there had been a meeting between Rocan and his family to discuss the matter, and Shea Ohmsford had positioned himself where he could hear most of it.

"None of us wants to abandon them, Rocan," his cousin Sartren insisted, "but it is dangerous for us to delay longer. Those pirates are likely to have friends and comrades who will attack again once they discover we are still here."

"They will think twice before they try that!" Rocan snapped in reply.

"Maybe so. But once they do, they will see we are vulnerable, stuck on the ground as we are."

"What more are we supposed to do?" demanded another man. "We have searched for two days straight and there is no sign of them anywhere!"

"Even your creature hasn't been able to find a sign that would lead us to them," another said, gesturing toward Seelah, who was lounging against the ship's railing a few yards away.

All eyes shifted to the young shape-shifter, now in her most glamorous form, who met their gazes and then casually looked away. She hadn't been seen in days, choosing to remain below with Rocan in his cabin. Until yesterday, when she had finally emerged to help with the search.

"Wouldn't she have found them by now if they were alive?" the man added.

It was true, Shea knew. Seelah had abilities the rest of them lacked, and yet even she had been unable to find a trace of the missing pair. The airship's company had gone out the past two days at sunrise and remained out most of the night, all to no avail. They still had no idea what had become of Dar and Ajin. It was a painful admission to have to make, but the boy was nothing if not practical after a lifetime spent on the streets of Varfleet.

"They've gone into the ocean, Rocan," said a third. "You said as much yourself. If they hadn't, they would have returned. Or at least they would have found a way to signal us as we searched the coastline."

"So you would quit on them, would you?" Suddenly Rocan sounded dangerous. "Perhaps you would like to discuss it with the Elven prince? I'm sure he would have an interesting response to such a plan."

Even in hiding, safely tucked away, Shea felt a shiver go up his spine at the suggestion.

"Don't be like that," Sartren interjected quickly. "No one wants to quit, and you know it. But we need a deadline. We need to give it no more than another day or two before admitting the worst. You know that as well as I do."

A long silence followed, and Shea waited for someone to speak. Then Rocan said, quietly and firmly, "We will look for another *three* days. After that, we leave and go on."

The meeting broke up and the men dispersed, with Rocan and Seelah retreating below once more. Shea waited, thinking about what had been decided. Three days was longer than he would have expected; it seemed Rocan Arneas was determined to give the Blade and the Skaar princess every chance of being found alive. But he was in a difficult position. As leader of the expedition, he had to decide when to continue on. As a friend to those missing, he had to reconcile his decision with his conscience. If left to his own devices and free of the constraints of the mission that had brought them all to this point in time, he would have stayed for as long as it took.

But he could not do that here.

Shea settled himself back in the shadows, thinking.

What about that boy he had encountered in the valley beyond their beach camp? What was his name? Borshawk? Maybe he would know something about what had become of Ajin and Dar. Or maybe he would be able to help in finding them. He was a resident of the valley and acquainted with its creatures and likely much of the rest of the island. There was a chance, wasn't there?

Shea rose and slipped back into the camp, already thinking of how he would go about it. If he told Rocan what he intended, the Rover would forbid it on the spot. Either that, or he would insist that someone accompany Shea, and then Borshawk might not show. No, he needed to go alone, but that would give Rocan someone else to worry about besides Dar and Ajin. So either way, there would be a problem.

Still, it was not a difficult decision. He was going, and he had known it from the moment he came up with the idea. He could not sit around and do nothing when there was a possibility he might be able to help. He wouldn't be missed until sundown, so he had all day to make contact with Borshawk and see if he had any information. But still he needed an excuse for being absent.

He chose to go to Sartren. He found the young Rover working on repairing the mast rigging and sat down beside him. "How's it looking?"

Sartren glanced up. "Well enough. We should be able to replace most of the lines. The spars are another matter. A couple of them were broken in half. We'll need to fashion new ones."

"So you'll need the wood to do so?"

"We will."

"What if I could get it for you?"

Sartren stopped what he was doing and stared at him. "What are you up to, Shea?"

"Nothing. But there are trees not far down the coast that would do the job. What if I were to cut down a few to be dragged back here?"

Sartren hesitated.

"What else do I have to do? I could work on the rigging with you, but I don't really know where all the ropes go. I would be more useful foraging. I don't have to go far. I'll stay out of trouble. I promise."

"It worries me when you feel the need to promise." Sartren sighed. "All right, then, but be back before dark, young Shea. If not, I'll have your hide. And that's only after Rocan has finished with it!"

Trying to be casual, Shea rose and walked away. It was early morning, the sun still low on the eastern horizon. Shadow layered the beach, allowing him to slide in and out of view of anyone looking in his direction. He took advantage and angled toward the forests inland and the entrance to the valley. He made sure he was out of sight before quickly doubling back and using the foliage of the grasses and trees of the verge to remain hidden, then made his way to the opening in the foothills fronting the mountains beyond.

He went as swiftly as he could, but it still took him over an hour to reach the valley entrance and make his way through to the interior. The passage was narrow and heavily overgrown with grasses and brush, and the giant hardwoods leaned out from the roots as if ready to topple. Shadows enveloped him as he passed through. The darkness felt oppressive.

But on the far side where the valley opened up before him, sunlight broke through patchy clouds and a feeling of well-being returned. Ahead, the whole of the valley sprawled out before him, its thick green canopy catching the sunlight as an all-weather cloak might catch the rainfall. He scanned the valley for a time, searching for signs of life, but there was no one to be seen and nothing further he could do without help.

Cupping his hands to his mouth, he called as loudly as he could, "Borshawk! Borshawk!"

He listened to his voice echoing across the valley, reverberating back to him in steadily dwindling clarity.

Nothing happened.

He tried again. And then once more. Still nothing.

Unwilling to start wandering about without any idea of where he might be going or what might be lying in wait, he sat down to think. The minutes slipped away, and still Borshawk didn't show. He looked for some sign of movement in the trees—something that would signal the approach of that huge monster over whom the boy seemed to possess at least limited control—but he saw nothing. Like Rocan, he knew he had to limit his endeavors. He'd give it another hour, then go back.

When he felt the tap on his shoulder it caught him so unprepared he jumped up and whirled about.

"Friend!" Borshawk greeted him with a smile.

"Borshawk!" Shea's response was a mix of shock and relief. He wanted to say something about sneaking up on people, but his communication abilities with the other boy were still too limited.

Borshawk held his hand out and Shea accepted it in a firm grip. He noted that the other boy was more simply dressed than before, his attire less ornate and colorful. He still wore face paint—three white stripes on each cheek and another on his forehead, the former applied horizontally and the latter vertically, so that it ran down his nose. He also wore a pair of knives strapped about his waist and carried a short spear, which ended in another of those long iron blades.

Shea gestured for Borshawk to sit, and the other boy did so. Shea thought about how he could tell him what he needed. Pointing to himself and holding up two fingers, he tried to indicate two other people, gesturing back toward the coast and showing them walking into the valley and being chased out again by something big. Borshawk nodded, seeming to understand. Shea then indicated a flying object with men wearing face paint and sashes and carrying weapons—the pirates that had attacked them and been driven off.

Again, Borshawk nodded.

Shea paused. How should he explain the rest?

"Friends," he said, using the one word the other boy might understand. Then indicated with two fingers the ones who had come into the valley.

Borshawk nodded once more. *"Ashtas."*

Shea spoke once more, using his hands to make explanatory gestures. "These two"—holding up two fingers—"friends. *Ashtas.* They chased the pirates off." He showed a series of fingers with a single finger coming after them. Then he pointed down the coast toward where Ajin and Dar had disappeared. "But they didn't come back." He made a shrug followed by a gesture to show the finger disappearing.

Then he drew a line in the dirt and marked one side with wavy lines and the other with pointed triangles. "Water," he said, pointing to the first. "Mountains," he said, pointing to the second. Then he pointed to each again, gestured with the finger used to represent their airship, showing it going into the water with a shrug and then into the mountains with another shrug.

Borshawk stared at him for a moment and then launched into a whole raft of words that Shea could not understand. After a few moments of being overwhelmed by the verbiage, Shea held up his hands in a warding motion and shook his head to demonstrate his confusion.

Borshawk looked extremely frustrated, but he gave a curt nod and began redrawing Shea's effort at depicting the valley. First a line—but this one was more crooked with protrusions and indentations. Then he showed the waving lines and pointed toward the ocean. Then he drew a series of valleys, each one very different from the ones before. There were seven of them in all. He pointed to the one closest to him and in that valley drew two dots and pointed to Shea and himself, then at the valley around them.

Shea nodded. "This valley, you and me." Pointing first to Borshawk and then to himself. "Friends. *Ashtas*," he said.

The other boy nodded. Then he pointed at the other valleys and shrugged. And pointed at the water and indicated a major indentation about four valleys down. He mimicked the flying motion and dotted the waters.

Was he saying this was where the raiders had come from? Did he know this for a fact? Shea wasn't sure, but he nodded anyway.

Finally, Borshawk pointed at Shea and himself and then at each of the valleys and made another flying motion. He repeated this several times, each time indicating the two of them and then making the flying motion. Shea shook his head. Was he saying they should fly to these valleys and that this was where Ajin and Dar could be found?

Finally, Borshawk got to his feet, beckoned Shea to stand with him, and turned to look down the length of their valley. Taking a deep breath, he let out a series of whistles that were so shrill and sharp, they must have reverberated down the whole length of this valley—a staccato sequence that shattered the silence. When he was finished, he made a silencing motion to Shea. Long minutes passed without anything happening. Shea waited patiently, thinking that perhaps Borshawk was summoning that huge beast again, even without knowing why he would do so. At one point he started to ask, but the other boy hushed him at once.

After a time, Shea found himself wondering if his efforts were actually leading to anything. He wasn't the sort to quit when there was a chance of succeeding. And he was not lacking in confidence or hope; he possessed plenty of both. But he was practical, too. And when you reached a certain point in any endeavor without realizing your goal, you backed off and started over. So perhaps he was mistaken here. Perhaps Borshawk would not be able to help him after all.

Then, from far off, a fresh series of whistles sounded, a shrill response to Borshawk's. The whistles went on for a time, then the valley was silent again, but the boy turned to Shea with a broad smile. *"Ashtas,"* he said. "Friends." And he pointed in the direction of the whistles.

"You've found them?" Shea asked, forgetting the language barrier.

Borshawk dropped to one knee next to the drawing he had made, beckoning Shea down beside him, and pointed to the fourth valley over, the one directly opposite the bay where he had drawn the pirate ships.

*"Ashtas,"* he said, nodding. Then he pointed to Shea and himself and made the flying motion once more, ending with a quizzical look.

Shea nodded at once. "Yes. We go find them?" He repeated the other boy's gestures, indicating them and then the fourth valley. Then he shook his head. "How?"

He knew it would take days on foot. He knew if he did this, he would have to go back and tell Rocan, and then convince the Rover to let Shea and Borshawk conduct the necessary search. But Borshawk would never show himself to the others, so it appeared he would have to go without telling Rocan anything.

But as sometimes happens with such decisions, this one was made for him. Borshawk turned away again to give a further sharp whistle, undulating and lengthy but still a single long note. Shea—as usual by now— had no idea what the other boy was doing, but was more than willing to wait and see. Again, long minutes passed. Overhead, the clouds had dispersed and the sky had cleared to allow the sun to flood the valley with golden light and a freshness that was bracing and welcome. Shea looked up into its blue depths and felt a surge of fresh hope.

Then a dot appeared on the horizon, tiny at first and far off in the distance, but increasing in size as it came nearer. Soon Shea could make out wings and realized he was watching the approach of a large bird. Abruptly, it gave a shrill cry, and immediately Borshawk whistled back in response. So clearly the other boy had summoned it. But what could a bird . . .

Then it doubled in size, then tripled, and Shea gasped. Whatever its species, this bird was enormous. And as with that horned creature from before, Borshawk could control it.

So this was how they would get to the fourth valley—and there would be no going back to tell Rocan what had happened.

Then a soft touch on his shoulder caused him to turn, and he found himself face-to-face with Seelah.

# FOURTEEN

◆

ONCE AGAIN, AJIN D'AMPHERE'S airship was falling out of the sky. Only this time she wasn't with men who were her guards, one of whom wanted her dead. This time she was with Dar Leah.

"Ajin!" he screamed at her from his station at the flash rip mounted on the rear of their small craft.

Just her name, nothing more. It was enough. She knew why he was calling to her, of course, and why the call was so desperate. She was at the controls of their small craft, and she was the only one who could save them.

"Stay where you are!" she shouted back, worried that if he released his safety line or tried to move about, he could be thrown from the airship and lost over the side. If he was to die, she wanted it to be with her.

A wild, crazy thought and yet there it was, nudging at her.

She shoved the starboard thrusters full-on once more, trying to reignite them, but the failure of the diapson crystals was total and there was no help to be had. The Skaar princess was an expert flier, and she had done everything she could to regain the power she needed to slow their descent. Her earlier efforts had almost saved them. For a few brief moments, the crystals had responded, and it looked as if the plummeting craft could be saved. But then they failed for good, and at this point she wasn't left with many options. She tried powering up and down in a series of bucking stops and starts, but it wasn't enough. The result was a somewhat slower spiral down into the jungles below, though still too fast to save them. In the absence of something coming to their aid, there was nothing to keep them from slamming into the mountains encircling the valley below.

They had perhaps a minute left. Likely less.

*Judgment,* she thought. *That's all I have to work with.*

"Hold tight!" she shouted over her shoulder.

With one hand on the port thruster and one on the rudder, she increased power. At once the craft picked up speed, spiraling faster toward the ground but still pulling to the right. *Have to time it just right,* she thought. She peered over the side at what lay below. Foliage and lots of it. Some attached to huge trunks that would smash them to pieces, but there were some spaces in between that were more open and welcoming.

She powered back and watched the ground rise to meet her. *Got to spiral away from those mountains at just the right moment,* she told herself. She pulled back on the wing lifts. *A little, not too much.* The ground was close now—a green carpet riddled with trunks and stumps on one side, and a forty-degree stone cliff face on the other. When she came around on the latter again, she reduced their power to almost nothing, and the airship dropped down in response.

The ground was right there beneath them.

The craft struck with such force it threw Ajin a full foot in spite of the safety lines and belts, slamming against the rugged terrain, bouncing repeatedly, then slamming down for good and skewing sideways. It struck something hard, and the front half of their craft shattered. Ajin was thrown into the controls once more, but her safety lines kept her from being thrown clear.

Behind her, Dar gave a grunt of pain and went still.

No time to look back. She still had the controls working and she reversed power on the port thrusters. It spun them about for an instant, but then she cut the power once more. They were still moving, sliding now through grasses and brush, leaping and falling over hillocks and rutted earth with ferocious force. But now they were turned about, and she was forced to look over her shoulder to see where they were going. She glimpsed Dar slumped in his seat, clearly unconscious. Beyond him and coming up fast was a large body of water—a lake! She fought to use the lifts and rudder to slow their slide, but they failed to provide the help she needed, and seconds later the two-man was plunging into water and shadows.

Ajin had enough sense to hold her breath as they struck and sank, thinking she had to help Dar. But when she began releasing her restraining ties, the one about her waist refused to come free. She worked at it in every way she could think of, finally reaching for her knives and finding one missing and the other trapped behind her where she couldn't free it.

She had a moment to realize what was going to happen, and then everything was spotting before her eyes and she could feel herself blacking out. She was going to die with Dar, after all.

*Be careful what you wish for,* she thought before losing consciousness entirely.

Time must have passed, because the next thing she knew she was lying facedown in a field with pressure being applied to her back and shoulders by strong hands, and water was spilling from her mouth and lungs in what felt like a torrent. She gasped and choked as the liquid she had swallowed was forced from her lungs. Shocked to discover she was still alive, she turned her head just enough to look up into the Blade's stern features.

"I knew you'd save me," she whispered, her voice a rough and ragged shadow of itself.

"No, you didn't."

She managed a smirk. "All right, I didn't. I was planning to save *you.*"

He pulled a face. "Next time we crash-land, I'll give you the chance. Are you all right now?"

She pulled herself up into a sitting position, nodding. "You?"

"A bump on the head that will ache for a week and a few bruises."

"But we're alive, aren't we? I thought maybe we were finished this time. That was a bad landing."

He smiled and pulled her against him, giving her an impulsive hug that made her feel like almost dying was worth it. "That was a *great* landing. I don't know anyone else who could have managed it. Including me."

She backed away and looked him in the eyes. "No, you could have managed it, too. You are I are too much alike for it to be any other way." Then she kissed him hard on the lips and held him there for a long time before letting him go. "You must see it by now."

He gave her a resigned look. "Maybe. Want to find if there is a way out of here?"

They climbed to their feet and looked around. They were far down the length of the valley, but closer to the ocean than the interior. This valley, like the other, was heavily overgrown with foliage, brush, and trees. The mountains towered over it on three sides, and a quick scan revealed no easily identifiable path leading out. The lake into which they had plunged was oddly shaped and apparently quite deep, given what Dar described as his efforts to free Ajin and pull her to the surface.

"We went pretty far in," he told her. "I remember hitting my head during the fall, but nothing after that until the shock of the water. I was able to get my own straps unhooked and then crawl over to cut yours off. I started for the surface, pulling you behind me. But it was hard to move by that time, so we must have been deep under. I almost gave out; I think another ten feet would have been too much. But here we are—still alive."

Ajin took a deep breath as she looked around again. "Those walls look too steep to climb. I don't see a way out."

"There has to be."

"Then we'd better start searching. We don't have any food or water, and it will be dark in a few hours. I don't know about you, but I don't care to run into another of those horned monsters we stumbled across in that other valley."

Without another word, she struck out. She had already determined that it made more sense to go toward the ocean than deeper into the island. If anyone from the *Behemoth* was searching for them, it would be along the shoreline, so maybe Dar and she could find help there. Or maybe when it got dark, they could start a fire to signal any rescuers. Whatever it required, they would find a way.

Suddenly she was aware that something was wrong with her left arm. A pain that hadn't been there before had surfaced, sharp and angry. She glanced down and saw that blood was seeping through a long tear in her sleeve. She drew to a halt. Further inspection revealed a deep gash in her upper arm, near the shoulder. The flesh around the injury was purple and blood-bruised. Something jagged had cut her badly.

Dar came up to see what she was doing, and saw the arm. "Let me see. Looks like a jagged piece of metal did that. Must have happened during the crash, when the airship broke apart. In any case, we can't leave it like that."

He took hold of her arm carefully, examining it from several different angles, then led her over to a patch of grass and sat her down. "We need to wash and bind it." He grinned. "You are one tough princess." He looked around, then rose to his feet. "Wait here and don't move."

He tore off the sleeves of his tunic and walked back to the edge of the lake, where he dipped one of them in the water. When he returned, he used the wet sleeve to wash out the wound. She managed to remain still while he worked, although the pain was considerable. But she refused to give in to the nausea and the urge to cry out. She had suffered injuries before, so this was nothing new. She sat there without moving while he finished cleaning off the blood and bound the wound with the dry sleeve so that it was protected. It should not come open again before it had a chance to heal.

When he was done, he leaned forward and kissed her nose. "Best we can do for now. Try to keep from bumping into anything. I'll help you when you need it."

She exhaled sharply as the pain diminished a tad. "So, you have training as a Healer, too?"

"A little. Enough to fix this sort of injury. Are you all right otherwise? We haven't missed anything, have we?"

"You winced when you got up a moment ago. Let's take a look at your ribs."

He undid his tunic and pulled it open. His right side was discolored, and her touch caused him to wince. "Cracked ribs, maybe," she announced. "But most likely just badly bruised. We need to bind them just in case. Tear off my sleeves. We can use them to form a compress."

He did so, knotting them together to form a wrap.

"If we keep this up," he said with a grunt, "we'll end up without any clothes on at all."

Then, realizing what he had said, he turned red. "I didn't mean to suggest . . ."

She put a finger to his lips. "Why, Dar Leah, you're blushing!"

She helped him wrap the makeshift compress around his waist so that a smooth, wide piece of cloth was tight against the damaged area, then fastened his tunic back in place. Neither spoke, but the tension between them was palpable.

Then they were on their way again, walking toward the end of the valley and the ocean beyond.

Ajin, in spite of the pain from her arm and the uncertainty from being marooned and essentially lost, was feeling good. What she wanted most in the world was for Dar Leah to be with her, and now she had him. His attentions were sweet and genuine, and she sensed they had turned a corner since that first confrontation outside the walls of Paranor. Always before, there had been that sense of separation between two people who were enemies by circumstance and need. She had been attracted to him at once, even though the feeling wasn't mutual, but fate and circumstance had drawn them together over and over until at last they were made shipmates on the *Behemoth* and now made more dependent on each other by shared misfortune.

The Blade might have thought she was delusional when she told him they were meant to be together, but she could tell he was coming around. He hadn't said so, admittedly, but his actions supported it.

Now, though, she found herself wondering what

they would do with this mutual recognition once it was far enough out in the open to be unavoidable.

The matter was not to be decided that day, however. Or anytime soon, as it turned out. Nor would they get out of the valley as easily as they had expected. They walked until it was too dark to continue, and Ajin kept looking for some sign that suggested they were making progress. But no matter how long they walked, their destination did not seem to get any closer. Finally, they had to take shelter, which they did by climbing into a cluster of rocks and then settling themselves into the most uncomfortable positions Ajin could ever remember enduring. Dar tried to help her, but there was little that he could do about his ribs. They took turns keeping watch, but in spite of their diligence and consideration for each other, no sleep was to be had. In the end, when they spied the first glimmer of sunrise on the horizon, they climbed out of their haven in disgust and started walking again.

The second day was more disheartening than the first. Progress went well enough until midday when they reached the shores of an enormous lake that cut right across their path and seemed to stretch for miles in either direction. They chose a path for skirting the lake's shores and walked for hours without finding an end. At one point, Ajin considered trying to swim across but quickly abandoned the idea. With the injuries to her arm and his ribs, too many things could go wrong—not the least of which was the possibility of predators lurking in the lake's depths. While walking, they had witnessed some large splashes out in the deeper regions, and that was enough to discourage any further thoughts about swimming. At least on shore they had a chance of seeing anything that came for them.

By sunset, they still hadn't reached the end of the lake or even appeared to have gotten closer to any part of the valley walls. They slept this night a bit more comfortably, choosing a grassy stretch among a cluster of large spruce that offered their shaggy boughs as a protective shelter. They agreed to take turns keeping watch, but Dar let her sleep far too long and she was not pleased when he woke her.

"I can see dawn light to the east, Dar Leah," she said groggily as she pushed herself into a sitting position. "You let me sleep most of the night."

"You need the rest more than I do, Ajin. I only need a couple of hours. Wake me when I've had them."

He was asleep within minutes. She was irritated at first at his high-handed behavior; her army life as a woman among men had been built around an expectation of equality. But realizing how much better she felt after almost a full night's sleep, she eventually softened to his act of kindness. After all, she wasn't a soldier anymore or even a part of an army. Neither of them was, and their relationship was much different from that of comrades-in-arms. She sat next to him, looking down at his face, thinking that— whatever else happened in her life—she could not lose him. She had already lost almost everything she held dear—her father, her soldiers, her rank and standing in the Skaar army; one day soon, perhaps, she would even lose her life. She found herself thinking about what waited for her back home in Skaarsland, and it was not reassuring.

At one point she allowed herself to run her fingers along his cheek, the pressure so gentle she was barely touching him. She fingered his long hair and the material of his tunic, then slipped her hand inside the fabric to feel his chest. He stirred and she took her hand away, but not too quickly. She could still feel the heat of his body on her fingertips. She could still feel the beating of his pulse where she had placed her fingertips.

*Darcon Leah.* She spoke his name in her mind. *Can't you see we are meant to be together? Can't you feel how right it is?*

After she woke him as he had asked, they set out once more. They found the end of the lake by midmorning and had circled around to the other side by midday to continue west toward the ocean.

The lake, while they had circled it, had at least provided them with water, but they had still found no food, and hunger was beginning to take its toll. And Ajin found herself worrying about where they would find water again now that the lake was behind them.

It was impossible to be certain about their choice of direction, even with the sun to help guide them. No other point of reference offered itself, and they had not been entirely sure of their directions even after setting out. But there was no help for it, and nothing to do but to keep walking.

Twice that day, they came across creatures that were possible predators, but turned out to be vegetarians. One was a six-foot horned lizard the color of mud that hissed at them in warning before it moved away. The other was a lumbering four-legged beast much bigger than the lizard but likewise with no real interest in them; it seemed much more intent on the odd-looking fruits it was busy devouring. But at least sampling what fruit it left when it wandered off didn't seem to harm them—though what remained was pitifully scarce.

Otherwise, there was little to be found.

That night was spent in a shelter formed by an embankment bracketed by boulders that mostly blocked the way into their nest and would allow Dar and Ajin to defend themselves better than if they were out in the open. They had only the ground and some fir boughs with which to find comfort, but they used both to curl up against each other and find warmth and a sense of safety. For this night, at least, they slept soundly and were not disturbed.

On waking, they began walking again. To Ajin's relief, they found a small stream trickling down from one of the distant walls through the green carpet of the valley floor, and after tasting the water they decided it was drinkable. They swallowed as much as they could hold comfortably and then moved on again, lacking any reasonable way of carrying more water with them. The best they could hope for was that they would find another such stream along the way—though Ajin found herself missing the vast lake.

Food remained a problem. They had not come across any more of those fruits—or anything else they were sure was edible. "Another day or so, and our definition of what is and isn't edible is likely to change," Ajin muttered bleakly.

They pushed on, trying not to think about hunger. They were in their fourth day of travel, and had eaten no more than a handful of fruit. It was beginning to take a toll on both of them. Neither had the energy they'd had on starting out on this trek. After finding water, they were now desperate to find something more to eat.

But by day's end, they had found nothing—not even fruit or greens that looked recognizable. What they did find was a lean-to: a small structure constructed of lengths of wood from tree limbs tied together with pieces of vine. It sat back in a grove of hardwoods, situated so that it was both protected and concealed. Finding it was a complete accident. They walked up and stood staring at it for long minutes before speaking.

"Someone lives in this valley," Dar said finally.

The shelter was well constructed and relatively new. Whoever built it knew what they were doing. "We haven't seen anyone," Ajin replied.

"We might want to pay more attention from here on." The Blade took a moment to consider. "Still, it seems like a good place to spend the night."

So they did, cutting conifer bows from other trees nearby to carpet the ground and snuggling into the lean-to together, using each other for warmth. It wasn't particularly cold at night in this valley, but without blankets or any other form of covering, the extra warmth was welcome. In any event, it was Ajin's favorite part of the day. She welcomed the feel of Dar against her, the warmth and reassurance of his presence, but mostly the dreams it fueled of a life together. It was silly to be so smitten, she knew, but it felt like so much more, and she clung to it.

She was sound asleep, deep in the night, when Dar jiggled her shoulders softly from where he lay behind her, waking her. "Ajin," he whispered.

Ajin opened her eyes to find their shelter surrounded by a dozen pairs of eyes looking in at them. Their owners wore ragged clothing and carried spears, which possessed the largest blades she had ever seen— each consisting of a sharpened iron point inserted and bound into a split cut into the end of a rough wooden haft. Knives were strapped about their waists, and their faces and chests were painted with black stripes across their cheeks and foreheads.

*Jutes,* she realized. But what were they doing on these islands? The Jute nations were Eurodian-based, situated far to the north. These men were a long way from home. She could feel Dar reaching for his sword, and she quickly seized his arm. "No, wait. I speak a little of their language. I've been in their country, where I picked up a few words. Let me try talking to them first."

Without waiting for him to agree, she sat up to face the men gathered in front of her. "*Cesh'ay Tou'ranzi . . . aboq mou? Jutes fo'zen?*"

"*Reshe,*" one responded. Then he pointed to her with his spear. "*Skaar?*"

"*Nosh Skaar. Vos coup'kip ahn?*"

Without glancing at Dar she said, "They think I'm a Skaar. We conquered their nation years ago and they hate us. I told him we were from a land to the far west, another continent. If he finds out the truth, I'm dead."

She turned back to the man and asked him in his own language why they were so far from home. They were looking at one another, clearly surprised this young woman knew their tongue, but they were not threatening, so Ajin risked a quick smile. No one smiled back.

"*Pouk sanz arn peesh,*" one said. "We are a hunting party," she translated for Dar.

But they clearly weren't. They were hundreds of miles from Eurodia, and the lack of any real game on this island was apparent. She grew wary. Something wasn't right.

"*Pouk ast fren?*"

The same man was still talking. He was asking now if they were part of a larger group and if their friends were looking for them. Ajin gave Dar a look that didn't require translating. *Watch out.* "*Reshe. Isht,*" she replied. Yes and yes.

"*Cush'ta resen irrit'la quaes?*" he asked. Would you like something to eat and drink while waiting?

This time when she translated to Dar, she made herself smile the entire time. "They are offering us food and water, but I don't think we should eat or drink anything."

"Why are they out here at this time of night?" Dar asked. "What would they be hunting?"

"Us, maybe?"

"Then we ought to settle matters here and now."

"No. Too risky. Too many of them, and we're barely awake. Let them think we believe them to be friends and are willing to share their hospitality. They will be off guard if we agree to go with them. If they turn on us, we can fight our way clear."

"Won't they just track us if we do that, Ajin?"

"Not if they're all dead." Her look was stony. "If you want, we can try to end it here. But I think we ought to be sure."

Dar nodded. Ajin turned to the speaker. *"Aqu'un jemja westay tak ek orianta."* Thank you for offering your help. We would be happy to go with you.

They rose, stretched, and started out, Jutes all around them. It made Ajin feel claustrophobic to be so surrounded, but she clamped down on the scowl that threatened to break free and tucked away her feelings of doubt. She was still wondering why these men would bother to lure them into their camp rather than kill them while they slept. But whatever was going on, it was nothing she wanted any part of, and she studied them closely as they walked, waiting for the flash of a blade or a sudden threatening movement.

After less than five minutes of walking, Darcon Leah bent close. "Pretend I am saying something funny and laugh as hard as you can. When you do, watch for them to laugh with you."

Dar made an offhand remark, and she laughed as directed. As she did, some of those closest laughed with her. When they did, she caught glimpses of white teeth.

The teeth were filed to a point. All of them. She exchanged a quick look with Dar. *Cannibals.*

# FIFTEEN

◆

THE JUTES HAD WALKED Ajin and Dar for less than thirty minutes when the whistling started—shrill and quite close. Immediately their escort started looking around, clearly startled and perhaps, from the way they crouched and wheeled this way and that, frightened. But there was no way of telling where the whistling was coming from or what it meant. It lasted only a short span of seconds, and then the silence was back.

Dar glanced at Ajin, who looked perplexed. *What is that?* she mouthed. But he only shook his head.

More time passed, and then a shrieking sounded, this time decidedly closer, high and piercing, splitting the silence with shocking power that stopped the procession in its tracks.

The natives formed a tight circle about their guests and looked out into the night. Whatever was happening, they seemed to be expecting trouble. But after a long wait with none appearing, their leader beckoned them ahead. Ajin tried asking in the Jute tongue what the whistling meant, but she was pointedly ignored.

After a moment, though, Dar bent close. "That whistling was of the same sort that boy gave to calm his horned friend when we encountered them in the valley," he confided in a whisper. "The shrieking was something else. I think the two were signaling." He took a quick glance around. "From the way our escort reacted, I think they recognized both. It might be they've met before. And not as friends."

She nodded. "But who would they be signaling?"

"Not sure. But we should think about what we're going to do if it means trouble. We'd better have a plan for escaping this bunch."

"Oh, I'm way ahead of you on that. Just be ready when I signal."

*Great. Just wait for her to let him know whether to run or fight. The princess rules.* "How about you be ready for when I signal?" he whispered back.

She laughed softly. "That way we can both be ready."

Their journey ended at a camp that was little more than a series of half-wall shelters and weapons racks. A fire was burning, and they were invited to sit down and rest. Their hosts were speaking in their native tongue, having established that Ajin understood enough to be able to translate. The princess nodded and beckoned Dar to join her. They sat shoulder-to-shoulder, turned slightly away from each other so that they could see everything around them. Neither was about to risk letting any of the Jutes get behind them unawares. Food was prepared and some sort of drink offered, but they declined both with smiles. Dar pretended to be full, rubbing his stomach and exhaling sharply. But the Nambizi did not appear fooled and looked at them with suspicion.

"If you have any ideas, now might be a good time to tell me," Dar said.

He did a quick head count and found that two more men had appeared to join the party—men who had apparently stayed behind to watch their camp while the others were out. That meant there were sixteen of them altogether—more than he wanted to fight at once, even with Ajin to help him. But it was looking more and more as if it might be inevitable.

*Cannibals,* he kept thinking.

"We have to escape right now," he whispered. "They won't wait much longer if they intend to make a meal of us."

She shook her head. "We'll stall until daybreak if we can. We don't know which way to run. In the dark, we won't stand a chance."

"We might not stand a chance anyway, if they can track us. And it seems likely to me they know the country." He sighed. "But it might be easier in the daylight than now."

"For them, too." Then she sighed, clearly unhappy with their choices. "But I don't much care to end up as someone's meal. Let me try something else first."

She rose and went over to the leader, speaking to him quietly. The conversation lasted only a short time and then she was back, resuming her seat next to Dar. "I suggested we should leave, that our friends would be looking for us. He said it was too dangerous. He said there were enemies and predators lying in wait, and we were safer here. I agreed."

"You *agreed*?"

"Better to let him think we are under his control,

relying on him. He made it plain that he didn't want us leaving, so we might as well let him think we'll comply. We can still make a break if we need to, but they don't seem to be in any hurry to do anything to us just yet. For the moment, they seem more concerned with the whistling. A few of them wandered off, probably scouting for the source. What do *you* want to do?"

He shook his head. "Sit tight until we see a chance to either slip away or make a run for it. But I don't think we can wait very long."

"Coming with them was a bad idea."

"It wasn't as if we had a choice, with a dozen spears surrounding us. What I don't understand is why we're still alive."

"Maybe they think they can get their hands on the friends we told them were looking for us, too?"

"Maybe."

Time passed. The Jutes continued to be restless and alert, pairs of them coming and going, the rest huddled together in small groups. They had their weapons out and ready by now—bows and arrows and those odd-shaped spears with long blades fastened into short hafts. They seemed to have forgotten about Dar and Ajin for the moment, and the pair sat quietly, waiting for something to happen.

When something finally did, it caught them completely by surprise. The shriek sounded as if it were right on top of them—a shrill howl that caused the Jutes to rush to the perimeter of their camp, closest to where the sound seemed to have originated, with weapons held protectively before them. A black shadow charged through the camp, low and swift, down on all fours, and the Jutes scattered in all directions.

Seconds later the shadow was gone again. By then, Dar and Ajin were on their feet by unspoken consent, racing in the opposite direction into the darkness. There was enough light from the moon and stars to see a little of each other and where they were going, so they could keep from being separated. Dar took the lead, but Ajin—smaller, lighter, and quicker—passed him by almost immediately. Neither looked back as they ran, ignoring whatever was happening behind them, seeking only to put distance between themselves and those who might be giving chase. Through trees and brush, over logs and ruts, down gullies and across streams they raced, the sounds behind them quickly disappearing.

"Are they following?" Ajin called back to Dar at one point.

The Blade risked a quick glance around. "Can't see them, if they are."

They ran for a long time without saying anything further, having no better plan than to get so far away the Jutes would lose interest in the chase. They listened for the whistling, but it did not come again. The night around them was deep and still, and the only sounds were the ones they made in their determination to keep running.

When at last they had run themselves out, they drew to a halt on a rise amid the heavy forest and stood breathing heavily. Overhead, a half-moon passed in descent toward the horizon, but they could not tell much from that. The stars were of no help, either. Their alignment in this part of the world was unfamiliar.

"When the sun rises, maybe we can tell which direction we should be going," Ajin suggested. "But we should keep walking."

They started out again, moving at a slower pace, regaining their strength while still making progress. Dar was worried that, in the absence of a visible landmark, they might be traveling in a circle without realizing it. But moving in any direction still felt better than the alternative, and so far there had been no further signs of pursuit. They didn't talk, both aware of how far voices carried.

Neither doubted pursuit was coming. Neither believed their flight was over.

And they were not wrong. They had gone back to running after a time—a slow jog rather than a fast sprint. But they were tiring, and there was still no indication of a chase. It might have been an hour or two since they fled the camp; there was no way of telling.

Suddenly Ajin caught his arm, whispering in a ragged voice, "I have to rest a moment."

Dar had been thinking the same, his legs aching, his breathing heavy, and his lungs on fire. He slowed and stopped, nodding in agreement, wondering how much longer they could keep going. They were standing in a clearing surrounded by forest, the sky open and clear above. There were stars everywhere, but their identity remained a mystery.

Then, as they moved toward the concealment of the trees, two of the Jutes stepped into view in front of them.

Both pairs were caught by surprise. Both were quick to react.

The man closest to Dar thrust his spear at him instantly—a clear indication that any pretense at friendship was over. Dar sidestepped, seized the man, and threw him to the ground. Out came the Sword of Leah as the second man came at him from the side, but Ajin was already attacking, knife in hand. In seconds, both attackers lay dead.

"We better run!" Ajin exclaimed.

Then matters got completely out of hand.

The pair had just resumed fleeing again when they ran right into another group of pursuers. This time there were five, and all came at them at once. Dar called up his blade's magic, and it burned with fiery brightness in response, causing their attackers to back away in shock and fear, unsure what they were facing. *"Daebo!"* screamed one, and the others took up the cry. Demon, demon! Ajin shouted it back at them, but they held their ground, and when Dar did nothing more than back away, they decided maybe he wasn't a demon after all and came at them. Ajin responded, bold as ever, never afraid of combat. She was quick and fluid, and two of their attackers lay lifeless on the ground in only seconds. Though aware that his sword could not work its magic against non-magical creatures, Dar could still use it as a weapon and rushed at the other three. But they refused to give ground, their sharp-bladed spears thrusting as they feinted and lunged.

Then another pair appeared at their backs, these two armed with bows and arrows. Staying safely out of reach, they fitted their arrows in place and drew back the strings. Ajin took down one with a throwing knife, but the second put an arrow in Dar's shoulder.

An instant later more Jutes appeared, and matters took a bleaker turn. There were too many of them now, and they ringed their prey. Dar knew he and Ajin were finished. Their only option was to attack and hope they could break through to safety or bring down a sufficient number that the others would choose to flee.

Abruptly a shriek rent the darkness overhead, and the same creature that had attacked the Jutes in their camp appeared once more, launching out of nowhere, claws extended. Several of its victims were torn apart as it charged through, claws ripping and tearing, screams rising up as bodies fell. This was enough for the rest, who turned at once and fled back into the trees.

Their attacker did not attempt to follow. Instead, it turned to Dar and Ajin where they were crouching in anticipation of a fresh attack from this new enemy. Then slowly the shadow began to change shape, reforming until it was recognizable.

Seelah.

The Blade and the princess straightened, but before either of them could speak, another shriek broke the spell—this one coming from overhead. A giant winged predator hove into view, its great wings spread wide, its jaws opening as it screamed again. A shrike, but the biggest Dar had ever seen. They shrank from it as it drew closer, unsure of what was happening.

But when the bird settled down right in front of

them, folding its wings against its body, Dar saw Shea Ohmsford sitting astride its shoulders, calling out in greeting. Behind him was another boy, this one a native, facial features and clothing suggesting he was from an Afrique tribe.

Shea slid down the giant bird's back and rushed over. "Found you!" he exclaimed, clasping Dar's hand in greeting. "And just in time! That was close, wasn't it?"

The Blade could not quite believe it was the boy. "Where did you come from? What are you doing on this bird?"

"Oh, that's a kind of shrike. Huge, isn't it? I don't know its name, but Borshawk does." He pointed to his companion. "That's Borshawk. We're friends. We met a few nights back in the valley."

"But how did you find us?"

Seelah had moved over to Shea and was licking his ear. The boy shoved her away. "Stop that!" He turned back to Dar. "Borshawk's people live on this island, and in most of these valleys. Not this one, though. They stay out of this one—except for one or two scouts to keep an eye on things. Borshawk is one of them."

Then he proceeded to tell them all about his first encounter with the other boy and his subsequent search to find him again so he might try to help find Dar and Ajin before the pirates returned.

"Those were cannibals!" he exclaimed, wide-eyed. "Outcasts from some other part of the world. Don't know how they ended up here, but they would have eaten you!"

Ajin laughed. "We figured it out in time. They invited us to dinner, but we didn't want to end up as the main course."

"So you and Seelah and this boy came looking and found us?" He still couldn't quite believe it.

"It didn't happen exactly like that." Seelah was nudging him, and again Shea pushed her away. "I found Borshawk, then Seelah found us both. I planned to come alone, but she must have followed me. I couldn't get rid of her. I tried to send her back to tell Rocan about where I was, but she just wouldn't move. Then the bird flew in, and so we all came together. Anyway, we searched for you the rest of the day and night. Did you hear us signaling you? That was Borshawk and the shrike. Anyway, when we found you, Seelah jumped right off and attacked those men. Then we all followed after you—Borshawk and I flying, Seelah tracking you on the ground. But what about you? Everyone thought you were dead. How did you end up here?"

Now it was Ajin's turn to explain—which she quickly did, telling him about their crash, their efforts to walk out of the valley, and finally their encounter with the cannibals. While she was talking, Borshawk climbed down from his bird and walked over to them.

"*Untak equit perrintat,*" he said, gesturing in the direction of the fleeing Jutes.

To Shea's obvious surprise, Ajin answered him back in his own tongue. They talked between themselves for a few minutes, then she turned back again.

"The boy says we have to go. Those natives will be back, and this time there will be more of them. He says the ones we were captured by were only a small band. These men are exiles and are very dangerous. I think I got most of that right. We don't speak exactly the same form of his language, but it's close enough that we can understand each other."

Dar glanced around. The darkness was beginning to fade, the dawn finally arriving. But it was still hazy and the sky was a gray overcast. "How do we get out of here?"

"Apparently by riding the bird. I don't think it belongs to him, but he has some sort of connection with these giant animals, some ability to communicate with them."

"He can talk to them," Shea interjected. "They listen to him and do what he asks. Like with that horned beast you ran into."

"His people are an offshoot of the Nambizi nation—rather like the Wing Riders are of the Westland Elves. Anyway, they have scouts in all these valleys to keep track of those Jute cannibals. I guess there are quite a few, in exile from their homeland for eating human flesh. Mostly they stay where they belong, but not always."

"But the animals and this bird . . . ?" Dar started to ask.

"No idea. Aberrations that survived the Great Wars and now live on this island and maybe on other islands, too? I couldn't make out that part of what he said. But what matters is getting out of here."

Dar agreed. Riding atop a giant bird didn't seem like a great idea, but now Borshawk was speaking to Ajin.

"He says the bird will fly us out—you, me, Shea,

and Seelah—but he will stay behind and walk out. He says the bird can't carry more."

Shea shook his head at once. "I won't leave him! I'll walk out with him."

Ajin said something to the other boy, who shook his head firmly. "Not a chance," she translated. "You go with us. Right now."

"I won't do it!" Shea insisted. "He saved you. He helped me find you! I'm not running away now."

Borshawk came over and placed his hands on Shea's shoulders, looking him in the face. He said a few words and pointed to the bird.

Ajin nodded. "He understands," she translated. "He says you are a warrior, but you can't help him. He can manage on his own. You have to fly out with us."

The other boy said something else, then stepped back.

"He said you would dishonor him if you refused."

Shea looked trapped and unhappy, and at first Dar thought he would continue to resist. But then he simply nodded, hugged the other boy for a moment, then turned away. "You tell him he better stay safe or I will be back!" he shouted over his shoulder.

Borshawk waited for them to climb onto the giant bird and settle themselves in place. Then he called to the shrike, which dipped its head immediately. The boy whispered to him—words or simply sounds, it was hard to tell—before stepping away again.

"Friend!" he called out to Shea. *"Byshan teh!"*

Two fingers dipped into a pouch at his waist and emerged with the tips covered in white paint, which he swept across Shea's forehead and cheeks to create the familiar stripes.

"Borshawk!" Shea shouted back and held up two of his own fingers, drawing them across his own forehead and cheeks.

Then the shrike lifted off and they were flying. The clouds were breaking up, and the sunrise revealed a dazzling brightness in the east that cast its light earthward in streamers. Dar watched Shea sitting forward, looking down at Borshawk as he dwindled in size. He waved once more, and once more Borshawk waved back.

A second later, a group of Jutes flooded out of the woods. Borshawk was running now—not directly away, but cutting a path across to the south, his small figure flying across the clearing and disappearing into the trees. A few minutes passed and suddenly there were screams and shouts from where the boy had disappeared—and then silence.

Shea wheeled around. "We have to go back for him!" he yelled at Dar.

The Blade shook his head. "Do you know how to make this bird do that? Because I don't."

Shea stared at him helplessly, then at Ajin and Seelah, and turned away, defeated.

They flew on, out of the valley to the waters of the Tiderace and along the coast toward the *Behemoth* and their companions. All the while the sky was clearing, the sun brightening, and the air warming. It was a fine day for either flying or sailing. The smell of the ocean and the coastline below rose up to greet them, pungent and welcoming, but Shea ignored it. He just sat there, staring ahead, refusing to talk, and Dar and Ajin let him be.

Around midday, the shrike let them off just down the coast from their friends and the airship, as if somehow it knew what was expected of it. Once they had dismounted—and without waiting longer—it lifted off again and disappeared back into the valley. The three passengers watched it go, then hurried to reunite with those they had left behind. There were exclamations of surprise and gleeful backslapping and more than a few words of mingled chastisement and relief. But through it all Shea Ohmsford had little to say and nothing to contribute. Rocan pressed him for more until Dar explained what had happened.

"We may have lost the other boy. Shea didn't want to leave him behind, and now he thinks he is paying the price for doing what he was told. Just let him be a bit."

So Rocan did, and the others gave him space as well as they prepared to set sail once more for Skaarsland. In the day since Shea had been gone, the *Behemoth* had been repaired and made fully operational once more, so there was no need to linger. Most were anxious to resume their journey and reach their destination— Shea being the notable exception. The only one who had any luck reasoning with him was the old man, Tindall, who sat beside him in silence for a long time on the aft deck before he started talking. No one could hear what he was saying, but the boy was responding.

They were a mile or so up the coast, heading northward, when a shout rose from the forward deck and everyone rushed to the railing. Shea was brooding midship with Seelah, who was doing her best to comfort him in her inimitable Seelah way, one arm draped about his shoulders while she occasionally nuzzled him, but none of her efforts seemed to be achieving much. The boy glanced after the others curiously when they charged off, but remained where he was, too despondent to care what drew them. Dar, who had been keeping watch nearby, went along for a look, then quickly returned. "Come with me," he ordered, practically yanking the boy out of Seelah's possessive grip. "Right now. Hurry!"

When they found an open space on the starboard railing, the Blade pointed. "Look up there, Shea Ohmsford."

The boy did, unresponsive for a moment, then lunged for a better look, his body rigid. A giant bird was circling the sky ahead of them, a familiar dark figure seated atop its feathered body. An arm lifted, waving farewell to the airship.

Shea was smiling and laughing as he waved back. When he stepped away from the railing, he paused long enough to face Dar. "I knew he would be all right," he said to the Blade with a casual shrug. "I was never really worried."

Dar Leah had to work hard not to roll his eyes.

# SIXTEEN

◆

DRISKER ARC CAME AWAKE slowly, rising up from blackness and lethargy to a shadowy, cold world of gray stone. At first, he had no idea where he was or what he was doing there. Everything felt disconnected and unreal. He knew he had been unconscious for some time and that it was due to a misfortune that had befallen him . . . a sickness, he decided after a few moments' thought. He was weak and disoriented, but he was also hungry and thirsty, which was a good sign.

Then he remembered the source of his problem. He had eaten food he shouldn't have. So while food poisoning was bad, he would recover from it. And it seemed to him now, lying in his blanketed bed, that he had already begun the healing process. But it was so cold! He rose up enough to see that the fireplace contained nothing but ashes and shadows. No fire burned; no wood waited to be lit. A glance around revealed no food or water, either. A pair of windows opened through a pitted wall to one side, but they were barred and shuttered.

So, he concluded with a touch of wryness, this was

not an establishment that placed much emphasis on creature comforts.

Then, as more pieces of his memory returned, he realized he had been brought here by the Straken Queen and was in her fortress castle at Kraal Reach.

After that, he lay back in his bed and waited for his memory to straighten itself out. Weka Dart must have reached her and told her he lay poisoned and disabled. She must have arrived just in time to save him, because there had been that creature . . . He closed his eyes tightly against the image that formed and then opened them again. There had been that creature that he had managed to keep at bay with his magic just long enough for the queen of this horrific world to appear and destroy it.

He recalled the flash and fire, the power she wielded to dismiss the threat when his own magic had begun to fail, the fire she had summoned to burn the creature to ash. Then she had brought Drisker out of his place of concealment and into a carriage. Yes, and back here to Kraal Reach to recover from his sickness.

How long had he slept? How long since he had been saved . . .

If saved he was.

Good not to assume too much just yet. No doubt the Straken Queen wanted to escape the Forbidding as much as he did, but he needed to be careful. Just because they shared a similar goal did not mean they were allies. Because each had separate and very distinct reasons for wanting release.

*Tarsha,* he remembered suddenly. *What became of her?*

He lay quietly after that for a long time, thinking things through. He had reached her while dreaming through astral projection and found her inside Paranor. He had helped her get inside the chambers that housed the Druid Histories, where she seemed intent on doing some research to help him escape the Forbidding. But he had never gotten back to her—or she to him. How long ago had that been? How many days had passed?

He knew at once he had to reach her right away, yet how was he to manage that? The only way they had been able to communicate so far had been in dreams while both were asleep. To reach her was more coincidence than intention. And even then, even if he did find her in his dreams, their communication could not include spoken words. But he had to try something. He had to harden himself against his weakness and uncertainty and find a way. There was too much at stake to delay.

He took a series of slow, deep breaths, then tested himself by moving his limbs and body beneath the covers.

Then he forced himself to sit up.

It went more smoothly than he had expected, and he swung his legs from under the covers and out over the side of the bed. But when he had managed to sit up all the way, he abruptly realized he wasn't alone. The Straken Queen sat off to one side in the shadows, bent and worn, her ancient features haggard and her eyes as hard as iron. She was watching him closely, but he did not think she could tell what he was thinking. Even she did not possess such power.

He met her gaze squarely. "How long have I been sleeping?"

"A full day."

Her voice was harsh and ragged, like a hasp torn from its seating. He gave her a nod. "I must have been much sicker than I thought."

She shrugged. "It was the medicine I gave you and the magic I employed. Both were very powerful. But you seem to be on the mend."

He nodded. "What of Weka Dart?"

"The Ulk Bog? What of him?"

"You said he reached you and brought you to me. But I remember there was something more, wasn't there?"

"Oh, that. Well, in this world, Drisker Arc, we pay a price for our ineptitude and our carelessness. He was warned to protect you from the things that might harm you in the Forbidding—of which there are many—and it was a charge he was not to take lightly. Yet he fed you food you could not tolerate, and to cover his mistake, he rushed back to find me to seek help. But he forgot to exercise the necessary precautions. He was almost to the gates when he aroused the interest of an Oric Clawling—vicious little beasties—that decided it was dinnertime. Only the quick action of my guards saved him. And then not quite all of him."

"His arm, wasn't it?"

"Yes, he lost his arm from the elbow down. But the Clawling lost its life, so the trade should be considered a fair one. Besides, the arm should grow back. His species tends to regenerate."

Drisker stared at her, reminded anew of the horrors of this place and the hard, unforgiving lives of its denizens. Yet of them all, she was by far the worst. Much worse, he expected, than the creature whose place she had taken. Tael Riverine, the Straken Lord, had been no match for her. Nor, apparently, had any other demonkind since.

"How have you survived for so long?" he asked her impulsively. "Surely it can't have been easy."

"Easy?" She laughed outright, her tone derisive. "Nothing here is easy. I fight every day of my hopeless, wretched existence to survive. I do so because my hatred of what has been done to me is too great to allow me to die and be done with it all. Do you know my story, Druid? Do you know why I am here? Wrongfully imprisoned. Unfairly trapped!"

"A little, perhaps. You were caught up in the rebirth of the Ellcrys. When the old tree died, a new one was born—and the Forbidding, which had gone down with the old Ellcrys's death, went back up again. And all the creatures that had escaped were caught up and swept back into their prison."

She grimaced, her features knotting. "And I along with them—I, who did not belong. I was taken—wrongfully, shamefully, and completely unnecessarily. I was no demon from the Forbidding. I was stolen away, but I survived this as I have survived everything."

She paused. "That Ohmsford boy—Railing was his name, as I recall—tore me from my sanctuary with his begging and pleading to Mother Tanequil. He ripped me away from the small sense of belonging I had found, from my life as an aeriad, so that I might serve *his* interests. In the process, Grianne Ohmsford was lost and I was reborn as the Ilse Witch. Because, you see, the witch's power was the power I needed to survive. But as a result, I became one of the demon-kind and the Forbidding took me."

Drisker remembered some of it and knew the rest to be true as well, although not entirely as she claimed. But it did no good to argue specifics at this point. What mattered was escape.

"Magic was used to send me here, just as it took you," he said. "A once-Druid, now an exile, named Clizia Porse, trapped me in a triagenel and sent me here. Something from inside the Forbidding must have been sent back in my place, as the magic of release always requires an exchange of one being for another. Do you know of this?"

"I know of the rule, but it is not absolute. And I know nothing of any exchange. What I do know is that there are other ways to find release. There are exceptions. But being exiled here yourself suggests perhaps I was wrong to think you had come simply to save me, as was our bargain. Is that so, Drisker Arc?"

He stared at her, thinking of what answer he should give.

She gestured dismissively. "Never mind. You are here no matter the means, and you will honor our bargain. For now, I will leave you to heal as best you are able. I will come again when you are better. Then we will talk further."

She backed away from him, almost as if afraid to look away, her eyes never leaving his, her face a mask contorted by the long drain on her life and the pitiless vagaries of her misfortunes. "Do not attempt to leave here, Druid. There are worse fates than the loss suffered by my little Ulk Bog, and I am familiar with them all. You will wait here on my pleasure."

Then she was through the door, closing it behind her, the lock clicking into place.

He was suddenly very tired. He sat on the edge of his bed, noticing suddenly that there was food and drink at his bedside. The witch must have supplied it on entering, while he was still asleep. He picked up a glass, poured water into it, and drank. Marginally tolerable, but much needed. He ate a few bites of food he did not recognize, but did not question. If she wanted him dead, it would be easy enough to arrange without bothering to poison him. For now, he believed, she would help him in his recovery, and he would tell her that when she returned.

With Grianne gone, however, his thoughts returned to Tarsha. He would try to sleep some more. If he concentrated hard enough, perhaps he would be able to reach Tarsha. It was a faint hope, but it was all he had to work with.

He tried to sleep, but sleep would not come. At first, his thoughts were directed toward Tarsha and himself and their respective situations. But eventually he began to think of other things, his mind wandering, his interest in sleeping forgotten. And in the way these things sometimes work, it was then he fell asleep.

Quickly enough, he was dreaming. He was back in Paranor, in the Druid's Keep, in the chamber that housed the Druid Histories. And there was Tarsha, slumped over the old wooden table with the Histories scattered all around her, sleeping with her head on her folded arms. She was right where he had left her, only now she was slumped in her chair, her expression worn and depleted, not focusing on much of anything.

When she became aware of him, she rose, blinking rapidly. *Drisker?*

He couldn't hear her, of course, but he could read his name on her lips as she spoke it. She had a frantic look and mouthed something wildly that he could not understand.

Seeing his incomprehension, she then pointed toward the entry wall, and he saw it was closed. It must have happened while she was working, and now she was trapped in the room with no way to escape. But for how many days? Her cheeks looked hollow and her lips were cracked and parched, so he knew he had to get her out immediately.

He nodded his understanding and patted the air with both hands in an effort to offer reassurance. Then he moved to the wall that had imprisoned her and placed his hands just so. He let her take a long look and then stepped back. The imprints from his fingertips were clearly visible. He motioned for her to put her fingertips where his had been and watched her do so. Nothing happened, and she looked back at him in dismay. Again he patted the air and mimed shoving.

She did what he indicated. This time the wall quickly disappeared and she was free.

She stood where she was for a moment, a look of shock and relief mirrored on her young face. Then she returned to the table, snatched up one of the books, and left the chamber, moving over to the easy chair she had occupied earlier, where she collapsed.

Drisker felt something sieze up inside at the thought of what she was going through. She was all alone now, her allies dispersed and her brother dead, while he was trapped within the Forbidding. She was taking on so much, and she was still only a girl. She had matured, but the weight of what she faced might still end up crushing her.

A moment later, she beckoned him close and pulled out a sheet of paper on which she had printed out: *A magic called a darkwand is inside the Forbidding. Anyone with Ohmsford blood can use it to get free. Would Grianne help you?*

Tarsha reached out to him, as if momentarily forgetting he was nothing more than a projection of himself. Then she drew her hand back quickly when she realized the futility of what she was attempting and dropped her gaze. But he was still pondering her message. A darkwand? He did not recall this magic. How he had missed learning about it while reading the Druid Histories was difficult to understand, but Tarsha had found it and was telling him it was a way out.

Or was it? If so, why hadn't Grianne used it a long time ago? If it was there, why hadn't she found it and escaped? Why had she come to him at the Hadeshorn to ask him to find a way to help free her? There was too much he didn't know, too much he still needed to find out. Too many questions and too few answers.

Answers that perhaps only the Straken Queen could give him.

Then, abruptly, he realized he had failed to warn

Tarsha of another danger—one he had dismissed earlier and which she knew nothing about. Clizia had transported him by use of a triagenel into the Forbidding, but for that to happen, something within the prison—a demon of some sort—must have been released in exchange. It was likely Clizia would have appropriated it for her own usage immediately, and it was entirely possible that Tarsha knew nothing of this. But if Clizia found out she was still alive, she might well use this demon to hunt her.

He scrambled about, searching for paper and writing tools, saw them a few feet away on a desk, and reached for them.

Instantly, his dream began to go soft and vague around the edges. *No!* he screamed in dismay. But before he could do anything to stop it, he had disappeared back into sleep.

# SEVENTEEN

AFTER DRISKER ARC'S IMAGE was gone and the dream finished, Tarsha continued to sleep for a time. When she woke, she was shocked to discover she was still trapped within the chamber housing the Druid Histories and not outside as she had been in her dreams. She rose and walked to the sealed-over wall, finding with no small amount of relief the faint trace of fingerprints from years of Druids past that she had missed before. Feeling rather foolish, she placed her own fingertips over the imprints, pushed hard, and the wall disappeared. Relief flooded through her as she stumbled back outside again. Tucked in her tunic was the paper with the brief sentences she had shown Drisker. She had to hope he understood what she was trying to tell him. She had to hope it would give him a way to get free and come back to her.

She left the offices of the High Druid behind and went searching for food and drink. Down the hall a short distance away was the pantry she had taken advantage of earlier. Her choices were limited, but sufficient to satisfy her need for nourishment. She sat at a small dining table to eat and drink, trying hard not to rush. Nothing had ever tasted better. She took her time consuming enough not only to regain her strength, but to sustain her for the journey that lay ahead. Then she rose, pulled her cloak about her, and departed Paranor. She had done all she could here. She had to hope it would be enough.

She went downstairs to the cellars and the underground tunnel that would take her back outside the walls of the Keep. The Guardian did not reappear; nor did she hear or see any sign of it. The hallways echoed hollowly with her footsteps and breathing, but were silent otherwise. Paranor's Druids were all gone. If Drisker failed to return, no more would come. Unless he meant for her . . .

She could not finish the thought. But the image was there, firmly fixed in her mind. She was standing at the edge of the waters of the Hadeshorn with the Shade of Allanon looking on as Drisker whispered words of magic and touched her forehead with waters from the black lake.

She pushed the image aside. She had other matters to consider—matters more immediately pressing than her future prospects.

She could not decide where to go next. Back to Emberen was the logical choice—back to her safehold where Flinc and Fade could keep her safe. But Drisker would want her to warn those who needed warning that Clizia Porse was still out there, still as dangerous as ever. And she wanted to find Clizia in any case and settle matters once and for all. But she did not know where the witch was and she did know how to find Ketter Vause. It seemed to her it might be best to find the Federation Prime Minister first, but she knew she would have to do so carefully. Drisker had departed with Tavo and her under something of a cloud, and Vause had definitely blamed him for Clizia's escape. Now Tarsha would have to find a way to make Ketter Vause put all that aside. Of course, it was possible that Vause might not even agree to see her, once she presented herself, but she could not permit that to happen. It was far too important that he listen to what she had to say.

She would have to travel to the Federation encampment to speak with Vause, and that meant a long flight from Paranor over the mountains of the Dragon's Teeth, down into the hill country beyond where the Skaar had last been encamped, and across the Mermidon. It would take hours to accomplish this, but she was reasonably well rested by now and thought she could manage it.

She walked through the tunnel after locking the doors to the cellars and the Keep, exited the trapdoor and locked it as well, then walked back to where she had left her airship. The sun was starting to set by the time she arrived, and she had no idea how many days had passed since she had found herself locked in the chamber housing the Druid Histories. It felt strange so much time might have passed without her experiencing any of it. But her life since going to Drisker's cottage had taken on a surreal aspect, and her disconnection from anything that was happening elsewhere had become the norm. Too often subjected to the whims of a fate that seemed to have no consideration for either her well-being or her peace of mind, she felt constantly adrift.

She walked around her airship, examining the protections she had employed to alert her to intruders, and found them all intact. By now she was realizing that her earlier assessment of her ability to fly Drisker's two-man all the way to the south bank of the Mermidon was overly ambitious. She already was feeling the need to sleep again. Since it was dark and the sky was clouded over, screening away moon and stars and their attendant light, making a decision about what to do was easy.

She climbed into her aircraft, curled up on the passenger's bench with a blanket wrapped about her, and went to sleep.

When the sunrise woke her, she felt sufficiently rested and fresh again. Waiting until daylight had been the right decision. She rummaged around the storage compartments and found some dried foodstuffs and water and made a meal of them. She was already thinking ahead to how she needed to handle her meeting with Ketter Vause, given her concerns about the reception she was going to receive. She decided she should tell him only just enough to persuade him of the danger he was in and let the rest reveal itself later. After all, what mattered most was that he be made to understand the peril and take steps to act on it. Beyond that, the rest of what she knew—about Drisker's fate and her own rather desperate situation—would be of little help.

She set out as soon as her meal was finished, flying south toward the jagged peaks of the Dragon's

Teeth, angling toward the Kennon Pass. She reached it in several hours, passing through its twisting length at a low height to help avoid detection, and then continuing on toward the Mermidon. By midafternoon, she was crossing the river and turning south for the Federation camp. It was only a short time later that she had reached the perimeter and swung about for the airfield.

She landed smoothly, by now sufficiently familiar with how her craft handled to feel comfortable. No sooner had she landed than sentries approached, with the airfield manager following hard on their heels. She told them she was a companion of the Druid, Drisker Arc, and had come to give a report to the Prime Minister.

"Miss," the airfield manager addressed her with a concerned look, "I suppose you haven't heard, but Ketter Vause was assassinated two weeks ago. Apparently by a disgruntled soldier, but no one seems exactly sure."

This was news she wasn't prepared for. She wondered momentarily if Clizia might have returned and dispatched him. "Did anyone see it happen?"

"He was killed in his sleep," said another man. "As unlikely as it might seem, Belladrin Rish caught the assassin trying to escape and killed him. She's someone to be reckoned with, that young woman."

So not Clizia, apparently, and she was still in time. Tarsha remembered Belladrin, though they had not spoken more than once or twice. A young woman serving as a personal assistant to the Prime Minister, she recalled, and she had seemed capable enough in that capacity. But as a protector able to dispatch an assassin? Like the soldier, she found it hard to believe.

"So who is in charge of the army now?" she asked. "Whom can I speak to? Has a new Prime Minister been appointed?"

The airfield manager chuckled. "A new Prime Minister appointed so quickly? Unlikely; that process will drag on for weeks. There are commanders of the army, certainly, but you might do better speaking with Miss Rish herself. She seems to have been given control over organizational matters."

"The fact is," yet another soldier jumped in quickly, "she took control the moment we learned that the Prime Minister was dead. She even traveled into the Skaar encampment with several of our commanders to negotiate a truce with the Skaar king. Brave girl, to manage that! Once all the details have been finalized and the treaty has been ratified in Arishaig, we'll be breaking camp and heading home. Well, most of us. A small force will remain behind to ward against a breach of the truce."

"A truce?" Tarsha repeated in disbelief.

"Come with me, miss," the soldier told her. "I'll take you to Miss Rish, and you can speak with her yourself."

Tarsha felt her head spin as she passed into the encampment. So Ketter Vause was dead, but a truce had been reached anyway? And what Drisker had believed to be the danger of a war between the Federation and the Skaar was no longer immediate? So how much danger was there of Clizia doing anything more to stir the pot now that the Prime Minister was dead and the armies of both Federation and Skaar were standing down?

But Clizia might not know any of this yet; she'd have to come here to find out, much as Tarsha had. And when she did, Tarsha would be waiting.

She was taken into what had formerly been the quarters of the Prime Minister to meet with Belladrin Rish. It made sense, of course, but at the same time it was troubling. For a personal assistant—however competent and well informed she might be—to have gained such power virtually overnight was highly unusual, to say the least. That the commanders of the army had allowed her to negotiate a truce with the Skaar king—and especially that she had succeeded in doing so when so many other efforts had apparently failed—was likewise impossible to understand. There was clearly more to all this than Tarsha knew, but she imagined she would get at least some answers when she and Belladrin spoke.

Her guide made her wait in the tent's antechamber while one of the soldiers on guard went inside to inform Miss Rish—as he, too, called her—of Tarsha's presence. He was gone only a moment, and then Belladrin herself burst through the opening and rushed to embrace Tarsha.

"Thank the fates you are safe!" she exclaimed, stepping back with a broad smile. Her dark hair was unexpectedly short-cropped, and her face had taken on a less youthful cast, giving her a more mature, seasoned look. "You've heard, I imagine? The Prime Minister is gone, struck down in his sleep. We are all devastated! But come inside. Can I offer you a glass of ale? Have you come far? What of Drisker Arc and your brother?"

With questions flying, she pulled Tarsha into the inner chambers and sat her down on a bench, then poured ale from a decanter into two glasses and handed one to Tarsha. "Now, tell me everything!"

Her reception was a clear invitation to gossip, but Tarsha remembered to keep her head. Belladrin Rish wasn't that much older than she was, but she was clearly not lacking in self-confidence. And Tarsha had been schooled well enough by Drisker in the value of never revealing more than was needed—by personal example as much as by verbal instruction—so she knew to step carefully.

"Drisker remains behind with my brother," she said, praying she managed to hide the spear of grief that went through her at the words. "He is engaged in other matters. We'll see him again soon enough." *I hope.* "However, he dispatched me to advise you of what we believe to be a serious threat from Clizia Porse. Although it now appears you have negated that threat, in part through your own capable efforts at securing a truce with the Skaar."

Belladrin blushed. "It is not all it might seem, and my role has been greatly exaggerated. The Prime Minister made the necessary arrangements for a meeting with the Skaar king before his death, and I simply followed through because he would have wanted it that way. He trusted me to bring the Dwarves of Crackenrood with their Reveals when they were needed, so this was just one last service I could perform."

Tarsha took a long drink of ale and brushed back a few bothersome strands of her white-blond hair. Like Belladrin, she had cut it short. She had done so during her last visit to the Federation camp; she was young enough that she thought it prudent to avoid unwanted attention from overeager soldiers. But her cut was less military in its look than Belladrin's; the other young woman now looked almost masculine.

"You've done well," Tarsha said, putting her thoughts about the other's appearance aside. "That the commanders would accept this—or you, for that matter!—speaks to your persuasive powers. So is the war truly at an end? Will you actually go home to Arishaig soon, as the airfield manager said?"

"Well, as soon as the treaty is ratified, but we will not be abandoning our post entirely," Belladrin assured her. "We leave a watch, to be certain the Skaar attempt nothing untoward."

"And what of you? Will you continue to serve?"

There was a momentary hesitation. "If I am needed; I am but a civil servant. And the Coalition Council must choose a new Prime Minister, who may prefer a very different aide. Tell me, what sort of threat are we facing from Clizia Porse?"

Tarsha took another drink of ale and leaned forward. "Now? Perhaps nothing. But I think she might still seek Vause's death, and thus might come here as I did, not knowing that he is dead already. And she remains dangerous."

Belladrin Rish considered. "I beg to differ. Her main target is already gone, and those of us left are well beneath her notice. Plus, we have dozens of guards stationed everywhere since the assassination, so Clizia will have trouble even getting into the camp." She paused. "But what about yourself? How much danger are you in? Haven't you placed yourself in a situation in which Clizia could be perilous to you as well?"

Tarsha smiled reassuringly. "More than you know! But I have magic, too; I was trained to use it by Drisker. I am not without protections I can call upon." A bit of bravado there, but she didn't want Belladrin to see her as weak in any way.

"Even so, Clizia is hunting you, isn't she?"

"Not at the moment. Clizia thinks me dead, so she will not be looking for me. Best to worry about your own safety and that of your companions. It is Clizia's intention to reestablish the Druid order with herself at its helm, so she will do whatever she thinks necessary to make this happen. Even if she is not an immediate threat, we still have to find a way to stop her."

"I understand. I can promise you if she comes here, we will see her imprisoned. And if we decide that she is responsible for what happened to Ketter Vause, then she will be executed. You do think she arranged to have the Prime Minister killed, don't you? It sounds that way to me."

Tarsha hesitated. "I'm not sure."

"Well, it is enough that she tried to kill him once before, whether she was successful or not. That alone is cause enough for eliminating her. The decision might not be mine, but I will do what I can to encourage it."

Belladrin paused, looking thoughtful. "I have an idea. Since you seem so certain Clizia Porse is coming here to kill the Prime Minister, why don't you stay with us for a time and see if she does? That way you would be here to help us. If she has magic, as you say, then your own magic might be more of a match for her than anything the Federation can use to stop her."

Tarsha liked the idea immediately. She had nowhere else to look for Clizia, and waiting for the witch to come to her made sense. At least it was worth a try. She could always change her mind later.

"Thank you," she said. "I appreciate the offer. If you can find room for me, I'll give it a try. I do think she is coming."

After all, they were both seeking to achieve the same result.

Once Tarsha Kaynin had been escorted to private quarters in a tent nearby, Belladrin sat thinking through what she had just learned and how it might impact her own situation. Clizia Porse was a problem she did not need. The rogue Druid might well return, seeking to kill Ketter Vause, but once she discovered Vause was already dead, where would she turn next?

Belladrin realized, of course, that Tarsha was also a potential threat. If she found out who Belladrin really was and what she and Cor d'Amphere were planning, she would try to prevent it from happening. But this was a threat more easily dealt with. Her suggestion that Tarsha stay was made mostly in the interests of self-preservation. Keep those who offered a potential threat close enough at hand that you could stop them from interfering.

She wondered suddenly if she should send warning to Cor d'Amphere of the danger he was facing if Clizia arrived, so he could have adequate time to decide how much danger she presented both to him and to his plans for the Federation. If she was seeking an alliance once again, Belladrin could only hope that the king would remember how those other alliances had ended. Perhaps she could suggest that it might be in his best interests to avoid any sort of new agreement with this dangerous and unpredictable woman.

But then she hesitated. Trying to tell Cor d'Amphere what to do in any situation—no matter how tactful or careful she was—was tricky. Best to not even consider that option.

Besides, she was beginning to question the whole plan to remove the Federation as a threat to the Skaar. She had questioned it privately from the beginning and then in an oblique fashion to the king. But it was clear he had made up his mind. Fine for him—but not so fine for her. She was sick of living with her guilt— first for what she had done for so many years, and now for what she was about to do. She was riddled with questions about where her life was going, and she wanted out of this trap. She wanted to be free of Cor d'Amphere and his demands.

Maybe now she was being shown a path to achieve this.

And maybe she should take it.

# EIGHTEEN

AFTER LEAVING TARSHA AND Paranor, Drisker Arc woke to find himself back in his bedchamber in the dungeon-like depths of Kraal Reach, alone and exhausted anew. Reaching out to his young student—even in a dream—had drained him of the last of his newly regained strength. How long he'd slept was anyone's guess, but his dream had left him troubled. His memory of it was vague, tugging at him in that nonspecific way the remnants of dreams do while leaving him unsure of the particulars. He was left lethargic and confused when his sleep finally relinquished its hold on him. Gradually, he became aware of the by-now-familiar smell of the fortress interior, the touch of chill in the air in his unheated quarters, and the absence of sound from anywhere in the surrounding rooms beyond his sight.

He lay where he was for a long time, waiting to wake fully, replaying in his still-sluggish mind memories of the events he had witnessed while in Paranor—of Tarsha trapped in the chamber that housed the Druid Histories, of helping her escape, and of her attempt to relate by handwritten note what she could not convey by speaking. She had discovered in the Histories something she believed might help him escape the Forbidding and return to the Four Lands.

The black staff called the darkwand.

Despite the fact that he himself could not wield it, it still seemed to be his best hope. But he wondered what she must surely be wondering, too: If Grianne knew the staff was here in the Forbidding, why hadn't she found it and escaped centuries ago? Why did she need *him* to help her?

It was at this moment that he became aware of another presence—someone or something not within his view but waiting at his back, silent and patient. Who it was would remain a mystery until he turned over to look, but he was not ready to do that yet. Nor did he finally decide, after some debate, if he was even willing to look.

"Why don't you come around to the other side of the bed so I can see who you are?" he asked quietly.

No response.

"I present no danger, so why would you hide yourself now that I am awake?" he continued. "Is there a reason you choose to remain unseen?"

A shuffling of feet answered him, and a small, gnarled figure slowly materialized from out of the pervasive gloom. Hunched over and wrapped in ragged clothing, it took its time appearing, leaving Drisker uncertain of its identity until it was standing directly in front of him, not three feet away.

"Weka Dart," Drisker greeted the creature, raising himself on one elbow. He took in the damaged face and the absence of a large part of the Ulk Bog's left arm. "I am very sorry for what happened to you. You saved my life, and I am sad it cost you an arm."

The Ulk Bog's eyes glistened with tears, and his head dropped into shadow. "I am fine. My arm will grow back." He seemed to require a moment to master himself. "I made a promise to my mistress and I kept it. I know the value of honor in a world where there is little. Do you know this now, too, Straken?"

*Where is this going?* "Honor has value in any world and in all lives. It defines who and what we are, be it human or Ulk Bog."

"Then you will demonstrate your gratitude for what I have done for you, and honor my sacrifice, by promising you will not take my mistress away with you when you go."

"You would have my word on this?"

"I would. She is everything to me! I am nothing without her!"

Drisker sat up so that the two—the seven-foot-tall Druid seated and the considerably shorter Ulk Bog standing—were face-to-face. A few moments passed as the former considered his response.

"I will give you the only promise I know I can keep," Drisker said finally. "I must find a way back into the Four Lands—into my homeland—but I do not require your Straken Queen to accompany me when I do. But she is her own person and entitled to her own decision. She will make whatever choice she feels she must, Weka Dart, and nothing I say is likely to change that."

"You can try. You can persuade her. You are a

Straken, just as she is. She will value whatever you tell her. She will listen to you."

"You overestimate my influence. There is no reason for her to listen to me about anything."

"She talks about you as if you are important. I think she will listen to you. You just don't want to help."

He was sounding petulant now. Drisker shook his head. "I mean what I told you. She has no reason to listen to me."

The Ulk Bog's face crumpled. "Will you do nothing, then?"

Drisker sighed. "Understand something, Weka Dart. She came to *me* in the Four Lands and asked for my help. I did not offer it first. This idea of returning is hers, not mine."

"I don't believe you!"

"Perhaps you should consider her interests before your own. What if she thinks she might be better off returning to the Four Lands? What if she really wants to leave?"

"But she left once and came back, didn't she? She could have stayed where she was, but they didn't want her there. Why would she go back again to people who do not want her?"

"It's difficult to explain. Maybe some who live in the Four Lands don't want her back, but she might want to go back for herself. For her own reasons that have nothing to do with anyone else." Drisker was sinking under the weight of this pointless argument. "Maybe the demons of the Forbidding don't want her, either. Maybe she knows that. Even if you want her here, maybe others don't."

"Don't say that!" Weka Dart exclaimed in a burst of anger. "Everyone loves her!"

*Doubtful,* Drisker thought. "No one is loved by everyone. You just want her to stay because you are her friend. But sometimes you have to let go of the people you care about. Sometimes you have to understand what they want and need."

"That's enough!" a familiar voice growled from the doorway, and Grianne Ohmsford walked into the room. "Weka Dart. There shall be no more of this talk. The Druid is right: I am the only one who decides what is best for me. You know this. You also know I am not without my share of enemies. There are many who would be delighted to see me gone. Now get out!"

The little Ulk Bog shrank from her and scurried from the room without looking back.

"He tries," the Straken Queen murmured. "And he does care. But in this world, neither is sufficient."

Once Weka had gone, Grianne Ohmsford stepped all the way into the chamber and walked over to Drisker's bed. "You seem rested enough, so it's time we talked."

Drisker nodded. "Let me guess: I owe you for saving my life. I gave you my word I would help you escape the Forbidding if you helped me try to prevent the Skaar invasion. You kept your promise; now I have to find a way to keep mine. Does that sound about right?"

"Drisker, Drisker," she murmured, in an almost teasing way. "Yes, such are indeed the terms of our bargain, but we must promise each other something.

We must promise to be completely honest with the other. It will be hard, but we must persevere. No deceptions, no holding back, no half-truths, and no lies. For we have larger concerns that demand our attention now, and I cannot have you hiding things from me, as you are doing now."

"Hiding things? Hiding what?"

She gave him a look. "Please do not play games with me. I know when magic is being used in my own home. Even if it is happening while you sleep."

He realized at once what he had missed. "You know I have been in contact with someone."

He made it a statement of fact, and she nodded slowly. "I know you wish to find a way out of here, now that you are as trapped as I am. I can only hope you are keeping your word and trying to find a way out for me as well. If you know someone you think can help us, someone back in the Four Lands, tell me who it is."

There was no point in dissembling. "A young woman named Tarsha Kaynin. My student."

"Tell me what she told you. Has she been able to help you? Did she find something useful?"

So Drisker told her everything about Tarsha's visit to the Keep and her search of the Druid records. Or almost everything. He did not reveal what he had learned about Tarsha during his encounter with the Shade of Allanon, who had demanded Drisker ordain the girl as his successor. That, he kept to himself as information Grianne did not need. Already, he was breaking his promise to her by omitting something he knew that she did not, but then there were limits to everything—even the extent to which one could keep one's word.

He had just reached the crux of what Tarsha had uncovered when she stopped him in midsentence. "This girl, Tarsha. I remember her from when I came to you at the Hadeshorn. She was born with the wishsong. She must have real magic for you to take such an interest in her, and you clearly have great faith in her abilities. So what is it about her that you are not telling me? Is there something special that you see in her, beyond her magic?"

He smiled in spite of himself. There was little that could be kept from this woman. "There might be. I am not yet sure."

"But you suspect?"

He shook his head. "None of it impacts the rest of what I have to tell you. In fact, letting me finish will allow you to better understand why she is so important to both of us. Did I already mention she was an Ohmsford descendant?"

He knew he had not, but she must have guessed as much from knowing she had the use of the wishsong.

"This has a bearing on what you are telling me? This will provide us with a way . . ." Then she stopped and smiled. "Ah. She has uncovered my hidden writings in the Histories, hasn't she? She knows about the darkwand."

She moved over to the side of the bed and sat down next to Drisker, almost as if they were companions now, as if they shared something so private and sacred that all barriers between them had been removed. "Clever girl. What does she know? Tell me."

He shook his head. "I'm not sure what she knows other than what I told you. We are only able to reach each other in dreams, and even then we can't seem to communicate by speaking. When we try to talk, neither of us can hear the other. We can see each other and use gestures and such, but it limits us. She managed to tell me where she was and what she was trying to do, so I was able to help her gain access to the Druid Histories. She also held up a note she wrote, letting me know the darkwand was inside the Forbidding and that you can use it because you have Ohmsford blood."

He paused, drawing a deep breath. "If we can locate this talisman and if you really can use it, then perhaps we have a way to escape this prison."

She nodded slowly. "Perhaps."

"Then why haven't you searched for it yourself? You knew it was still here, inside the Forbidding, and—as an Ohmsford—you have the power to wield it."

"Presumably. But Penderrin was the only one to ever make use of it, so I can't be sure. And finding the wand has thus far proved impossible—at least for me."

She leaned in, her ancient face a map of crevices and crosshatching—the map of her long, hard, vicious life—but also a reflection of something more that glittered from beneath her brows. Drisker was struck by what he saw: a mix of softness and deep regret, of kindness once prevalent and now reduced to almost nothing. There was a humanity deep within her that had been all but stripped away by her trials.

"I forgot about the darkwand," she confessed quietly. "Truly forgot, in the days of tranquility and peace I found with Mother Tanequil during my life as an aeriad. There was no reason to remember! The part of me that had been the Ilse Witch had vanished during my days with the other aeriads, while in service to our mistress. There had been so much pain and regret in my life until then, and I welcomed a chance to let it all fall away from me. I did not want to hold on to it, and so I made the decision not to."

She gave a deep, weight-releasing sort of sigh. "When I was returned to the Forbidding—even though I had been dragged back into service as the Ilse Witch so that I might face and destroy the Straken Lord— I still gave no thought to the darkwand. Not at first. I was consumed by grief and regret and rage at being sent back to a place I despised. I was forced to discover anew the struggle required to survive in this demon-infested spot. I was one of them, after all. I suppose I still am, but a small part of me remembers what I was before and wants it back."

"But the darkwand? How long did it take you to remember?"

"It did not happen as you might expect. I had been here for years before my attention was drawn to the staff once more—and maybe longer; time flows strangely in this world. But here, Drisker Arc, as in our own land, there are machinations and scheming on an epic scale. More than one demon would like my title, and more than I care to think about would like to see me dead. Enemies on all sides beset me. Now and then, they act against me, and I cast them down with-out remorse—because I have resolved to survive and

I am still stronger than them all. But new candidates always arise, and new power centers form. So the struggle to see me ousted and dispatched continues."

She paused, her eyes shifting away to focus on something he could not see, consumed by memories that clearly haunted her.

"There is a new species of demon in the Forbidding," she said at last. "They are called the Chule. In this place, evolution happens much more swiftly, and with less regard for the laws of nature, than in the Four Lands. The Chule are bipeds—a form of humanoid, but strong and savage beyond anything of similar breeding in our world. They have existed for about a hundred of our years. Their present lord is Vendra Trax, and he has long coveted my place. He would make himself Straken King in an instant, if he could, but he still lacks my strength and my skill with magic. He lacks my cunning, as well. But he grows stronger as I grow weaker, so one day soon he will have his way."

She shrugged, her face a mask of dark resolve. "Not that I much care at this point. I tire of this life, this world, and the injustices I have suffered. I want only to be allowed to die in my old world, in the arms of Mother Tanequil—in the only place I was ever happy."

Her focus drifted again, and Drisker gave her the space she sought, saying nothing. "But we were discussing the darkwand," she continued after a few moments. "When I was first banished into the Forbidding, a demon called the Moric changed places with me, entering the Four Lands, where he came to disguise himself as the Federation Prime Minister. After Penderrin brought me out, he had to redress the balance and send the Moric back, for which purpose he used the dark-wand again. The Moric was transported—carrying with him the darkwand—back into the Forbidding, where he belonged. But a dragon was waiting, and the darkwand offered the Moric no protection; he was consumed. I am not sure precisely what happened to the staff after that—though I have searched high and low—but through circumstances to which I am not privy, it was ultimately brought to the Chule and Ansa Trax, Vendra's granduncle, in the mistaken belief he would understand it and be able to make use of it. But Ansa could do neither, because only an Ohmsford can summon and employ its magic."

Drisker interrupted. "So how did you find out about it?"

She sneered at his rudeness. "First, you must understand this was a long time ago. I was informed of the darkwand's reappearance by one of my spies. I have them everywhere, of course; I would not be alive if I did not. So I went to Ansa Trax and asked for the staff's return. He refused me. If I wanted it this badly, he reasoned, it must hold value for him, too. He would keep the staff until I was willing to give up my position as Straken Queen and accept him as my lord and master."

She paused. "Then I made a mistake. I told him the staff was useless to anyone but me—that only I could summon the magic—but that just gave him further reason to keep it from me. I even promised him I would leave the Forbidding and he would be free to become Straken King, but he refused to believe me and remained intractable.

"When I finally departed his fortress, the Iron Crèche, I did so determined that somehow I would return and take the darkwand back. I used spies to try to find it, but they failed. My patience was at an end, so I went into his fortress myself a second time—at Ansa's open invitation—and searched for it. Nothing. Shortly afterward, Ansa Trax died, suddenly and mysteriously. His son became king. Pule Trax claimed he knew nothing of the staff's whereabouts, so I stormed the Iron Crèche, found him, forced him to talk, and then killed him. But all my tortures revealed nothing, and the staff remained missing.

"After his nephew, Vendra Trax, eliminated all other claimants to the throne, family and friends alike, he made himself king of the Chule. Under Vendra, the Chule grew stronger, and his power grew alongside. When I demanded the staff back, he claimed it had been stolen before his time and he knew nothing about its whereabouts. I knew he lied. Storming the Iron Crèche a second time felt pointless. Wherever the darkwand was hidden, I would not find it that way. If I could have gotten Vendra here, to Kraal Reach, I would have had my answer soon enough. I would have broken him like I broke Pule. He would have begged me to let him tell me where the darkwand was concealed!"

She shook her head. "So I chose, once again, to use spies. They tried to locate the darkwand for decades, but still could not find it. Eventually I realized I was becoming fixated on its recovery—crazed by my frustration, consumed by the wrong I had suffered to the detriment of everything else. So I abandoned my efforts to reclaim it. I let go of this madness as I let go of so much else in my life, and ceased to think about it."

"But now I've reminded you again?"

She smiled enigmatically. "More or less. It is enough to say that now you are involved, things are different. I firmly believe that, this time, you and I working together can find where Trax has hidden it."

Drisker shook his head doubtfully. "I don't see why you think I will make a difference . . ."

Grianne Ohmsford's lips twisted. "What is wrong with you? Are you so in need of creating obstacles that you are compelled to seek them out? No wonder you didn't have a way of dealing with the Skaar and the Federation! There are always obstacles to the things we want most, Drisker Arc, but we don't need to dwell on them. We need to make them disappear!"

"But we also need to be cognizant of our limitations," Drisker countered. "And I am still not sure why you are so convinced the two of us can retrieve the darkwand from Vendra Trax and the Chule if you've already tried twice and failed. What makes this attempt any different?"

"Because you are here. Or so I once thought," she said, her voice filled with a heavy contempt. "But you are making me less certain by the minute."

She glared at him, and Drisker knew his perpetual doubts were responsible. Worse, she was right.

"Grianne," he said quietly, "forgive me. I *am* prone to finding obstacles everywhere, but I will try hard not to do so here. I leave leadership on this matter entirely to you. I am here to help in any way I can, but this is not my world, and I am not familiar with it. I promise to put my trust in you."

"You have no choice, Druid. You have no Ohmsford blood. You cannot make the staff's magic respond to you. You say you have reminded me of the darkwand's existence, so maybe that was all you were meant to do. I asked you to find a way to help me escape the Forbidding. Maybe you have. Maybe this time I will find the talisman and make that escape. Without you!"

She lurched from the bed and stood looking down at him. Then she was out the door and gone, the locks clicking into place behind her.

Drisker stared at the closed door and felt a sinking feeling in the pit of his stomach. What if she did as she had threatened? Could she escape and just strand him here? She was bitter, quick to anger, and unpredictable. After a lifetime of harsh treatment, why should she be any other way?

There was nothing he could do for now but wait and see what she decided. He was at her mercy, when it came right down to it. And if she did not allow him to help, to escape with her, he would be trapped here forever.

Unless, perhaps, when the darkwand was back in the Four Lands, Tarsha could take it from Grianne and come into the Forbidding to free him, much as Pen had done for Grianne all those years back. The girl was an Ohmsford, after all . . .

And then he felt wretched for even thinking it. How much could he put one person through, for his own selfish ends? No, he would return to the Four Lands with Grianne, or never return at all.

He lay back on the bed to sleep, but sleep was a long time coming.

Grianne Ohmsford stood just outside the door for a long time after leaving Drisker's bedroom, thinking through the bitter exchange she had just left. She regretted her anger, but not the reason behind it. She knew she needed the Druid in order to find the dark-wand; that he would be the catalyst that would reveal its location. She had learned it from her visions of the future. His presence was necessary if it were to be found, and that was why she had come to him in the Hadeshorn—and why she had made her bargain with him in the first place.

But she had not told him everything, because she was afraid if he knew all he would give way to the weight of it and be unable to do anything. He had touched on this, and she had responded accordingly—almost before she could think to stop herself. And so her anger had flared up in the face of his recalcitrance, and she had come very close to revealing a truth she must not.

A truth she must hide at all costs.

# NINETEEN

◆

CLIZIA PORSE WAS SUFFERING. She was suffering so
badly she could barely make herself get out of bed
long enough to eat and drink. She was so exhausted
that a deep ache had settled into her ancient bones,
and her muscles were sore enough that she cringed
and cried out every time she tried to move. A fever also
had her in its grip: cycles of extreme heat and cold
that came and went with a persistent regularity she
could not seem to shake. She lost count of the hours
and days, the affairs of the world beyond, her schemes
and intentions, and even the presence of the Jachyra,
when it wasn't out hunting. Nothing seemed to help.

Clizia Porse had noticed, after leaving Cleeg Hold
and the Rock Spur—in the wake of destroying Drisker
Arc and the Kaynin siblings—that all was not right.
Back aboard her airship, she was beset with a feeling
of weakness almost immediately. At first, she attrib-
uted it to the effects of the battle she had fought to
survive, and then to a sickness she had somehow contracted earlier but which had lain dormant until now.
Eventually she came to recognize it as a severe side effect of using her magic, because she had been beset by

similar symptoms after killing the Elven king Gerrendren Elessedil and fleeing Arborlon. She had thought herself protected by putting aside the very dangerous Stiehl, forgoing further use of its magic, which she knew to be extremely powerful. Yet it appeared to her now that *any* use of magic was draining her far more quickly than it had in the past, and even abstaining from using the Stiehl was not going to be enough. She was very old by now, and more susceptible to the side effects of calling up powerful magic such as the triagenel she had used to banish Drisker.

What she would need to do from here on out was to husband her strength and use her magic more wisely and cautiously, so as not to deplete herself.

Even so, she wondered if her conclusion was flawed. In other cases in which she had employed her magic against her enemies, she had not experienced this weakness. It had not happened in the Federation encampment when she had been trapped by Drisker Arc and managed to escape by using magic. It had not been true at Paranor when she had fled the Guardian of the Keep. So why should it be true now, when the causes seemed so similar? And yet the longer she examined the problem, the more certain she became that it was.

She was housed in a cottage at the edge of the village of Winstrom, a forested community of traders situated on the eastern border of the Tirfing where it abutted Federation territory some miles above Arishaig. She had taken two days to reach this safe house, a destination she had used before when hiding from the world—a small house owned by an old ally who cared nothing for her machinations but only for her coin and her willingness to spend it freely—and by then she was deep in the throes of whatever illness had beset her. Still uncertain of its origins, she was aware it had surfaced her first night away from Cleeg Hold while she slept within her airship, disturbing her sleep and ending any sense of well-being. By the time she reached the cottage, she was shaking and sweating. Her throat was raw, and her exhaustion so debilitating she almost didn't make it to her bed that night.

While she struggled to weather her illness, she was aware of certain things happening around her. The Jachyra came and went as it chose. What could she do to stop it? She knew it was hunting because it returned with blood on its jaws and savage delight in its eyes. It was a strange, filthy beast that she tolerated only because of its talent for killing and its willingness to accede to her dictates. She knew little of its habits or its predilections; it was its reputation that drew her. It was a Jachyra that had killed Allanon all those centuries ago. It was a Jachyra that had fought the fabled Weapons Master, Garet Jax, to a standstill on the heights of Heaven's Well at the edge of the Maelmord in that same year. They might even have killed each other, although the Druid Histories were not clear.

She had chosen it for its usefulness as a weapon—a thing that killed indiscriminately and without compunction. It was no more than a tool that would serve her purposes in the days ahead—a reasonable exchange for a troublesome Druid, but not an altogether reliable companion. It was fairly obedient, if she didn't demand too much of it, but it was no sort of companion. It stank to high heaven—whether from bodily excretions or something more directly related to its killings—and its habits would have shamed a pig in mud. It brought itself dirtied and bloodied and stinking into her presence over and over, and several times she had gagged and vomited in spite of her resolve. Mostly, it kept to itself in a shed out back—a choice for which she would forever be grateful.

A week passed—or maybe a bit more—but no one came to see her; no one but the owner of the cottage would even know to come, and he was not the sort willing to take that risk. If there were neighbors, she had not seen them. Perhaps the Jachyra had eaten them all. She hoped it was eating farm stock and wild animals instead, but she had no way of knowing. She seldom left her bed, drifting in and out of a coherent state of wakefulness. The world around her was reduced to her bedroom with occasional trips to the privy or kitchen. Everything else ceased to exist.

Then, one day, she woke feeling better.

She was so much better that she felt compelled to get up and walk about the cottage for a time, just to make sure she wasn't mistaken. But her strength appeared to have returned. She washed, dressed, and walked outside for the first time in days, thinking to take a short walk in the surrounding woods, wanting to feel as if she was a part of the larger world again.

She had walked only a short distance before she found the ravaged and mostly consumed carcass of a sizable dog. She studied it a moment, then walked on. Another carcass lay off the path a bit farther on. This one appeared to be a wild animal, but it was hard to tell. She was growing angry by now; the Jachyra had failed to use even a modicum of common sense, leaving its kills too close to the cottage.

She found the old man another three hundred yards farther on. She wouldn't have seen him at all except that she caught a glimpse of blue amid all the greenery of the moss and grass that grew between the dark trunks of the old growth, nestled in where it didn't seem to belong, and so she discovered the body. This one was only partially eaten, so she guessed the Jachyra had made this kill recently and planned on coming back later to consume the rest.

This last discovery was the most disturbing. It was one thing for an animal to go missing, and another for a member of someone's family to disappear. A search would be organized—a search that would eventually reach here and uncover the body. And that, in turn, would lead directly to her doorstep.

She tramped back to the cottage seething with rage and frustration. She had thought the acquisition of the Jachyra a good idea, but now it was beginning to look like a big mistake. This demon monster killed whenever it felt the urge and did nothing to hide its actions. Worse, it killed indiscriminately, paying no attention to the probable consequences. To allow it to run loose was foolhardy, yet what was she supposed to do to stop it? She could barely control its behavior as it was, and if she interfered with its eating habits, she would have a genuine fight on her hands.

Back inside the cottage, she sat down to think things through. Now that she was on the mend and feeling stronger, she needed to decide what to do next about reestablishing the Druid order at Paranor. With Drisker gone, she was the last of the Druids and thus entitled to the position of Ard Rhys. The Guardian had kept her out before, but it would be unable to do so if she declared her intention to form a new order. For the new order to ever consist of more than herself, though, she needed support, and all of her ties had been severed with the Federation, the Elves, and the Skaar. So now she needed to repair at least two out of three. The Federation was most likely to consider an alliance, but only if Ketter Vause was out of the way.

Which brought her back to the reason she had chosen to bring the Jachyra out of the Forbidding. She could send it into the Federation camp—a monster no one had ever seen before and would never see again after it had killed the Prime Minister. She could just give it instructions and turn it loose.

Then she shook her head, knowing that plan was futile. The Jachyra was a savage, feral demon with only the barest capacity for understanding. It would never be able to distinguish Vause from anyone else unless she was there to point him out, which sort of defeated the whole idea of letting the demon do the work for her. So if she already had to go into the Federation camp, she might as well kill the Prime Minister herself. Even if she had to avoid risking harm to herself by sticking with her promise not to use the Stiehl.

Yet whatever inconvenience the Jachyra presented, it was still capable of inciting confusion and fear. So that might be valuable in itself. But what would she do with her pet in the meantime? What could she do with it while she was off dispatching Ketter Vause?

The Jachyra returned before she could reach a decision, and she berated it for its foolish decision to haul its kills back to where they could be traced to her. It slouched to a halt before her, assuming a posture that was meant to suggest shame and regret but failed to demonstrate either. Its body hunched like that of a submissive, yet betrayed itself with knots of muscles and cords of sinew. Its paws flexed and relaxed, and its claws flashed and vanished. Its cruel muzzle lifted to reveal the teeth hiding within its maw, and its nostrils flared. It was listening, but this wasn't a creature that cared what anyone else thought about it. It was a monster, and a monster only understood the basics: survival and pleasure, predators and prey. Nothing else mattered.

No, she was wasting time, she decided. She was almost certain the creature either didn't understand what she was communicating or didn't care, and in the end she settled for ordering it to hide every last trace of the carcasses and the killings. She wasn't even sure it understood that much, but it gave the demon something to do and got it out of the way while she went back to sleep once more.

In the morning, she would fly east until she reached the Mermidon and the Federation camp and deal with Ketter Vause at last. And just hope the Jachyra did not get into too much additional trouble while she was away.

She slept late, and it was nearing midday when she finally departed, ordering the Jachyra to stay in the cottage until she returned. She doubted it would remain there for long, but it was the best she could do at the moment. And to demonstrate anew who was in charge, she summoned a fiery magic that burned about her hands and licked out at the beast. While the Jachyra showed no fear or even any concern, it moved at once to do her bidding and hide itself.

For the moment, at least, her place as leader was reestablished. But she didn't fool herself into thinking this settled their relationship in any way. The Jachyra's memory was inferior to its predatory instincts and uncontrollable urges, and she would have to repeat the process the minute she returned. It might remember that she had brought it out of the Forbidding and into a world of light and substantial prey, but any loyalty to her was likely fleeting. She would have to be wary.

She arrived at the perimeter of the Federation camp on the third day in the late afternoon. The shadows of the tents and the figures moving about within their canvas maze were lengthening as she approached the first of the sentries. She had applied a glamour to make herself look like a Federation messenger and asked to be directed to Ketter Vause. Her plan was simple enough. She would be taken to the Prime Minister, and when she had him alone she would kill him at once and leave before anyone was the wiser. Then, with Vause out of the way, she could bide her time until it was safe to return and offer her services to the new Prime Minister or whoever was in charge at that point. Once a new alliance was in place, she could move on to the next step in her ascension to the position of Ard Rhys.

A fine plan . . . until the sentry told her that Ketter

Vause was already dead, assassinated by a disgruntled Federation soldier.

It caught her by complete surprise and required a moment to recover. What she had thought to accomplish was already done, meaning she could immediately look into creating a new alliance with the Federation. She almost laughed out loud at the irony of it.

She maintained the glamour. "When did this happen?" she asked. "How many days ago?"

The sentry told her, and she did a silent calculation. Vause had been killed while she and Drisker were maneuvering for a confrontation out in the wilderness of the Rock Spur Mountains. So who then had brought about the Prime Minister's demise? She didn't believe the rogue soldier story for a second.

"So whom should I deliver my message to?" she asked. "Who acts for the Prime Minister now?"

The sentry shrugged. "The commanders run the army, give the orders, and assign duties, same as always. Otherwise, it is Miss Rish who acts as the Prime Minister's official spokeswoman. You could deliver your message to her, I suppose."

She recognized hints of disarray. No new Prime Minister for now—or perhaps anytime soon, knowing the machinations of the Coalition Council—so things had been left in other hands for the time being.

"Can you take me to Miss Rish?" she asked.

"This way," said the sentry.

Belladrin Rish was finalizing the last of the treaty details; on the morrow, the treaty would be conveyed to

Arishaig, along with news of Vause's death. Then it was just a waiting game, to see if the Coalition Council would ratify it and how long it would take them. Belladrin's bet was at least two weeks of dickering; it was too good a deal for them to refuse outright. Once the treaty was ratified, the army could start moving out—and Cor d'Amphere's plans could at last come to fruition.

She sat back and rubbed her eyes, then ran her fingers through her dark hair, feeling the strain of being Belladrin Rish manifest in a pounding headache. She was sick of the whole business. She had resolved that, after the deaths of Ketter Vause and Kol'Dre, this would be the end of it. It no longer mattered what Cor d'Amphere had planned for her or what threats he had made against her family. As soon as she was back in Skaarsland, she would gather them up and spirit them away to somewhere they would never be found. She could do it; she had the resources and the means.

But she would never go back to . . . *this*.

She mentally swept together all the years of deceit, treachery, and betrayal in which she had been engaged as a spy and facilitator for the Skaar and cast them away. This was not how she would end her days. This was not how she wished to live out the rest of her life. She was lucky she hadn't been found out this time; not everyone accepted her story about what had happened to Vause and his assailant. Suspicions lingered. She knew for a fact that Choten Benz did not believe her—or at least was convinced she was hiding something. He had spoken to her a number of times since the killings, and each time he made small comments that suggested he knew she was hiding something.

It was also hard to say what her future would be if she returned to Arishaig. Her service and accomplishments might win her a position of high standing in the council, but it was equally possible they would see her as a fraud and have her executed. She could probably help facilitate the former and avoid the latter, but at what cost to herself and others?

Another few weeks at most, and she would be done with this nonsense.

When she heard the tent flaps part behind her, she continued to work while waiting for someone to speak. When no one did, she turned to face one of the camp sentries who was standing just inside the opening.

"Yes, what is it?" she said, more crossly than she had intended.

"A messenger has arrived from the Coalition Council, Miss Rish," the sentry advised her. "Shall I send her in?"

"Please do. Then return to your post."

She looked down to finish the last of her notations, wondering if she could just dispatch the treaty with this messenger instead of sending one of her commanders, and when she heard the tent flaps rustle once more she got to her feet and turned to face the messenger.

"What word do you . . . ?"

Then she trailed off in confusion, because there was no messenger to be found, only an old woman—weathered and gray, hunched and hawk-eyed, dressed in a black robe that hung from her skeletal figure like a shroud. Belladrin managed to stand her ground in spite of the danger she sensed she might be in; she knew who the old woman was. Tarsha Kaynin had been right to believe she would return. But Belladrin had no weapons with which to defend herself, and there was no one else in the tent besides the two of them. She started to call for help, then stopped. What was the point? She would be dead before anyone could save her, if her death was what the old woman intended.

"You're Clizia Porse," she said, trying to keep her voice steady.

The old woman nodded. "I've come to talk."

"That would be a welcome change."

A foolish comment, but it was out before she could stop herself.

Fortunately, Clizia Porse did not rise to the bait. "A much-needed change, perhaps?" Clizia gestured at a chair. "May I? I haven't been well, and I need to sit. What is your name, young woman?"

"Belladrin Rish. And why would you want to speak to me?"

The old woman brushed back strands of her gray hair and shrugged. "I am given to understand that Ketter Vause is dead. You might be more willing than he was to listen to what I have to say."

"I am not much more than a scribe and former assistant to a dead Prime Minister. I doubt there is much I can do for you."

"Shall we find out? And let's not dissemble. When I asked with whom I might speak, the sentry was quick to give your name as the person in charge. I believe you were Ketter Vause's protégée, were you not? You are young to hold such a favorable position, but you seem very mature. He must have valued your skills rather highly."

Belladrin already did not like where this was going. "Perhaps you could tell me why you've returned? You were fleeing Drisker Arc the last time you departed this camp." She walked to a second chair and drew it over to sit next to Clizia. "Aren't you worried you might be in danger, returning like this?"

Clizia chuckled—a deep, throaty sound that ended in a cough. "Forgive me. It is just the irony of your comment. Belladrin—may I call you by your given name?—believe me when I say I am *always* in danger. As for Drisker and his two young companions, I am afraid we've seen the last of them. So, for the moment at least, we should be able to talk undisturbed."

Belladrin marveled. Speaking of irony! Clizia thought Tarsha Kaynin dead, while Belladrin knew otherwise. Here was a piece of knowledge that might prove useful later on. Somewhat emboldened, she filed what she knew away immediately.

"What is it you seek by returning now?"

Clizia smiled, and it reminded Belladrin of the predatory looks she had seen on the faces of those whose main desire was for power. It reminded her of Cor d'Amphere when he had told her which nation he intended to crush next and what part she was to play in bringing it about.

"I desire help from the Federation in reestablishing a Druid presence at Paranor," the old woman said, "and in helping to protect them. The Skaar made easy work of the last batch because they were corrupt and ineffective caregivers to the Four Lands and to the magic they had sworn to protect, so they allowed themselves to be betrayed and annihilated through gross ineptitude. But it is to the Federation's advantage to have a strong Druid presence aligned with them. After all, how far would the Skaar have gotten in their conquest of the Northland if the Druids had been doing their duties? How effective would their ability to vanish have been against the power of Druids under a stronger leadership? Now that the Federation has had a taste of what the Skaar can do, they cannot help but want something done to remove that threat."

Belladrin decided she wanted to see where this was going. "Are you aware there is a truce now between the Skaar and the Federation?"

"A truce?" Clizia sneered in disgust. "And you think that will last? With a people that have conquered every land they have ever come to and now have an eye on ours? This truce, my dear Belladrin, will last precisely as long as the Skaar want it to, and then everything will come crashing down."

*How true,* the younger woman thought. *Truer than you know.* The thought made her sick. "So you would remove this threat in a more permanent way?" she asked.

"Not I alone. But with a rebuilt Druid order and a concerted effort by its members, using magic the Skaar do not have and cannot stand against? Yes, they can be eradicated. Do you believe me?"

"What I believe is that, as matters stand, no one

in all the Four Lands wants to help you—least of all the Federation. Some think you are directly responsible for the death of Ketter Vause. Most think you betrayed the Druids at Paranor. No one who matters likes you or trusts you, so what has changed to make them see you differently?"

Clizia gave her an assessing glance. "You are blunt, aren't you?"

"You said no dissembling."

"So I did. Well, then. You serve a government in disarray, with no Prime Minister and no reliable leadership. This truce on which the Federation is relying is a sham. It will not prevent the Skaar from taking what they want, no matter what the agreement provides. So perhaps you should listen to me."

She leaned forward, her aged face intense and suddenly angry. "I have disposed of the last member of the old Druid order and his two young followers, and rid the Four Lands of their troublesome presence. But in addition, I have found an ally of a different sort. I have conjured up a beast you do not want to challenge and will not survive if you do. I can send my pet to kill Cor d'Amphere, and without his leadership, you can chase his army from the Four Lands for good!"

Belladrin tamped down the sudden surge of hope inside her that perhaps spelled a way out of the impossible mess she now found herself in, and forced herself into a studied calm. "You can conjure demons?"

"Would you like to see? Watch!"

Belladrin did *not* want to see, but before she could stop Clizia, the old woman began to speak in nearly inaudible tones while her hands wove the air. The light inside the tent dimmed as if night had descended, and the air grew chill and stale. Shadows danced, cast by invisible beings, and a grotesque shape emerged from their midst, rising in bits and pieces to coalesce.

The creature, when it appeared fully formed, was so loathsome that Belladrin shrank from it involuntarily. It was not real, she knew, but merely an image. Even so, it was frightening to look upon, and she could not imagine herself ever being in close proximity with the real thing. It appeared to be a cross between a huge cat and a wolf, with suggestions of other predatory creatures thrown in for good measure. Its huge jaws opened to expose rows of teeth, and its sinewy body rippled with muscle.

Then, just as abruptly as it had appeared, it was gone again.

"This is what I offer you," Clizia Porse said. "It is called a Jachyra, and it is a killing machine. Once it is dispatched, there is no escaping it. It will serve well enough to bring down the Skaar king."

Belladrin swallowed hard. "And you can summon more of these creatures? These demons? From where?"

Clizia shook her head. "That is for me to know. All I require is that someone give me leave to act. Allow me to rebuild the Druid order and see to it that no one interferes with me while I am doing so."

Belladrin was not sure how much of all this she believed, but she knew one thing for sure. Clizia Porse was half crazed and extremely dangerous, but this could be the chance she was looking for, the chance to reclaim her own life. No one knew about her connection with Cor. So if Cor were dead . . .

"I lack the authority to agree to anything," she said quickly, trying to calm her pounding heart. "Only the Coalition Council and a new Prime Minister can make the sort of agreement you seek. Surely you must know that?"

Clizia sighed. "Spare me. I am aware of how things work. I have bargained with the Federation before. But now they must listen, and you must make them do so. They are in extreme danger from this invader, and they do not have the means to protect themselves. So you must speak with them. You must speak for me. You must be the one to convince them that what I say is true."

"I can't promise that. Why should they listen to me? I have no real standing now that Ketter Vause is dead. I have no way of persuading them they should do as you ask."

The old woman shook her head and was silent for a moment. "So are you telling me that you are of no value at all? That you cannot even talk to the members of the Coalition Council? That even though you are on record as having done so much to assist Ketter Vause and his army—this army that now looks to you for counsel and organization—you will be ignored? I had thought better of you, Belladrin Rish. Apparently I thought wrong."

Belladrin went cold to the bone. She had gone too far with her disclaimers. If Clizia believed her unable to help, the hope she had unwittingly offered was gone.

"Wait!" she said, her mind racing. "I am not saying I cannot do anything. I can speak to the Federation on your behalf. But in order to help you, I need something to persuade them of your usefulness. They won't take my word without evidence of your value. They need you to prove you can do what you promise. Can you really arrange for your creature to kill Cor d'Amphere? That would rid them of their most dangerous enemy. Then they would be much more willing to pay attention to what you might be asking for. They would, in fact, be eager to help you."

More important, it would set her free of her obligations to the king and give her a clear path to a new life.

Clizia studied her carefully, her eyes bright with barely concealed suspicion. "That was a quick change of mind. Are you playing games with me?"

"I am telling you how I can help. This is no game. I will prove it. I will tell you something you don't know—something you will very much want to know. Tarsha Kaynin is still alive."

The old woman frowned. "You're lying. I saw her go over a cliff and fall hundreds of feet to the rocks below. She is quite dead."

Belladrin held her ground. "So it was her ghost who came to see me not two days ago?"

"You saw her?"

"And spoke with her. She told me you tried to kill her, but failed. She warned me to look out for you. And I assure you, she was looking very much alive."

Clizia flushed a deep red. She immediately regretted leaving the Stiehl behind. "Where is she now?"

Belladrin shook her head. "Before I tell you that, I need to know we have an agreement. You will kill Cor d'Amphere, and I will help you with my superiors. What you do with Tarsha Kaynin is up to you. Do we have an agreement?"

"We do." The old woman climbed to her feet. "How irritating to find the girl is still alive! Well, I suppose I will just have to kill her again. Where is she?"

Belladrin pointed. "Two tents down. Look for the green emblem. She is waiting for you to appear so she can kill you first. But you might want to wait until dark before attempting anything. And even then, the quicker and quieter you can be, the better. I don't want you attracting a lot of attention with this personal vendetta. That would also invalidate our agreement."

"You might want to leave my business to me and concentrate on your own," the witch snapped, clearly irritated. "How soon will you be able to speak to those who can help me directly? I want no delays."

"Anything I say to the Coalition Council about an alliance must wait until you keep your end of the bargain. Once that's over and done, we can speak further. At that point, a clear demonstration of your ability to change the dynamics between the Federation and the Skaar will be most persuasive."

"Persuasive?" A long, very chilling pause. "Very well," the old woman said softly. "I will take you at your word. If I do as I say, you will provide support for me in this matter and will present me with a chance to meet with the new Prime Minister. Do you understand?"

Belladrin exhaled slowly, as if even the sound of her breathing might bring about something terrible. "I will do what I can."

The old woman moved toward the tent flaps, already changing shape and appearance. "No, you will do what I tell you. No excuses."

Belladrin watched her go without saying more, frozen in place. Inside, she was shaking. She had managed to hold herself together in the presence of an evil so dark and unpredictable she had been sure it was going to strike her down. Belladrin believed she was capable enough of standing up to anyone, but she knew instinctively she was no match for this old woman.

She rose, letting her breathing steady and her emotions calm. She had only barely avoided a swift but certain end. And she had done so by making a choice. Better to give up Tarsha Kaynin—who was perhaps a better match for Clizia—than to risk herself further. Tarsha had the use of magic, after all; she had said so. Plus, she had stood up to Clizia Porse once and survived the encounter. Meaning her chances of doing so again were better than Belladrin's own. And while that might not work in Belladrin's favor as surely as the death of Cor d'Amphere, it would at least rid her of another potential problem.

It was not as complete a solution as she would like, perhaps, but in this world you had to grab what was offered you and not moan about what more you wanted. If there were any possibility at all of ridding herself of the Skaar king, she had to take advantage of it. She had to make sure she embraced this chance—the one she had been looking for to turn her life around.

But she must protect herself, too. An image of the

monster that Clizia had conjured flashed in her mind, leaving her shaking.

She moved over to a sideboard with a pitcher of ale sitting on it, poured herself a tankard, and drank it down, letting the sharp-tasting liquid fill her with its chilling presence.

# TWENTY

DAYS HAD PASSED. AT least, Drisker Arc supposed it was days; it was hard to tell inside the Forbidding. He slept mostly, still recovering from his ordeal. It occurred to him that he might have been drugged. Perhaps it was the drink the Straken Queen had provided, or perhaps it was the food. Perhaps she sought to control him by keeping him lethargic and unable to offer any threat. He stopped eating and drinking when he woke the second time, but nothing seemed to help. Save for brief waking moments, he slept constantly and, for the most part, deeply.

During his last period of sleep, before Grianne came to him again, he dreamed. But this dream was not like all the others. In this dream he was walking through a forest. He was aware of a silence so deep and pervasive, it seemed to cocoon him. Something had happened—something so momentous that it would change his life forever—but he could not determine what it was. Where he was walking to or even why was a mystery. He walked because that was what he had to do, and for reasons unknown he knew he must continue.

When the forest ended, he stood on a grassy knoll. Before him lay thousands upon thousands of the dead, their bodies stretched out lifelessly for as far as the eye could see. He stopped and stared, appalled at the carnage and stunned by the numbers. It took him a moment to realize he could not see any evidence of wounds—even on those so close he could reach down and touch them. He recognized no one, and whatever had killed them was nowhere to be seen. The bodies of the dead were unmarked and their cause of death unknown.

After a pause to take the measure of their numbers, he walked on. He strode into their midst—there was a path for him to do so, almost as if it had been created to provide him with passage. He searched the horizon for an indication of what he was walking toward, but nothing was clear. The distance was hazy and unformed, a thick brume that hid whatever waited. The silence of the forest traveled with him, an insistent companion that wrapped about him like a blanket. It was oddly comforting.

*Drisker! Come back!*

A voice called out. He thought to stop and turn, wanting to respond to it in some way, but could not manage to do so.

*Drisker! Do not go!*

He knew this voice. It belonged to Tarsha Kaynin. He had heard it often enough to know. *Tarsha,* he called back, but his voice had no power and the name echoed only in the silence of his thoughts.

*Drisker. We need you.*

Yes, he understood this. He knew they needed him,

and he understood he should return. But his feet kept moving forward, as if he were not attached to them, and they were taking him where they wanted him. He no longer had control of himself; something much stronger now dictated the course of his travels. He listened to Tarsha calling to him over and over, and the helplessness he felt at not being able to respond was almost more than he could bear. But Tarsha could no longer depend on him. She would have to rely on herself and others who cared about her. Although he wanted to offer the help her cries begged for, he could not.

Then Tavo Kaynin was before him, standing there alive in the fields of the dead, his face a mask of confusion and anger.

*Drisker, no!* Tarsha was calling still, her voice suddenly turned frantic, growing stronger even though he was farther away than before.

*Drisker!*

"Drisker," another voice hissed as a hand shook his shoulder and he woke from his dream and his sleep. He blinked and looked up into the cold eyes of the Straken Queen. "Do you plan to sleep the rest of your life away?"

His mind was foggy, his thoughts deadened by the power of the dream, and his response was unguarded. "You drugged me."

She stared at him expressionlessly, then shook her head. "I provided you with a mix of healing magic and medicine. The combination had the effect of making you sleep more deeply. Clearly your body needed it. But now it is time to get up."

He gathered his thoughts and his strength and pushed himself into a sitting position, long legs dangling over the side of the bed. The room was the same as before: cold, gray, and tomblike. There was still no fire in the hearth. All signs of food and drink were gone. Though he listened closely, he could hear no sounds from beyond his room. The Forbidding was unmistakable, and his situation was unchanged.

"What do you intend to do to me?" he asked, remembering now how they had left things.

She moved across to the room's sole chair and seated herself, looking speculative as she faced him. "Make use of you. You are here for a reason, so I would be a fool not to give that reason a chance to reveal itself."

"What do you mean, I am here for a reason? Does this have something to do with whether or not I can help you get free of the Forbidding?"

"Just listen. As you may remember, my dreams often show me the future, and they have done so with you. They show you holding the darkwand and handing it to me."

"And how long have you known this?"

She smiled. "From before I approached you through the Hadeshorn. That is why I came to you then, why I offered you my bargain. Somehow—though I know nothing of the details—you are the key to my escape."

"So the future tells you nothing more?"

"The future reveals what it chooses. Your future is somehow tied to mine; of that I am certain. I knew as much from earlier visions. Other, newer visions intruded while you slept. They were clear on this much:

Our lives share a parallel course. You are needed to find the darkwand, if it can be found at all; I am needed to guide you to it."

"Is my life safe with you, then? Or only safe until you get what you want and then forfeit?"

She laughed. "You are bold, aren't you? You must be getting better to talk to me this way. Yes, your life is your own once more. I do not intend you harm so long as you do not cross me. Just accept that I am meant to lead us in this quest and you are meant to follow. Any attempt to change that would be a mistake. Do you understand?"

He nodded. "I expected nothing less. My goal is the same as your own: to find a way out of the Forbidding and get back to the Four Lands."

"Then we have an accord. And if you honor our bargain and help to free me from this place, I promise to take you with me when I go, if it is at all within my powers." She rose. "So, today we journey back to the Iron Crèche, the fortress of Vendra Trax, where I hope that our combined forces will at last uncover the hiding place of the darkwand. I have chosen a handful of demonkind to accompany us, as we may have need of their services. One is a moench, a burrowing creature that has knowledge of a way through Brockenthrog Weir and into Vendra Trax's fortress. The others have been chosen for protective services. But we are the ones who must think our way past whatever obstacles we encounter. Rise and dress. Drink and food will be provided, and you must eat it. There is no reason to think I would drug you now. All our wits will be needed, Drisker Arc. I hope yours are sufficiently sharpened to meet whatever challenges might come."

She rose from her seat and walked to the door. When she reached it, she paused and looked over her shoulder at him. "I think I will take Weka Dart with us, too. For luck, if nothing else. He seems able to survive almost anything he encounters, and we could use a little of that."

Then she went through the door, closing it securely behind her.

On the same night that Belladrin Rish had made her bargain with Clizia Porse, she was studying maps and deployment records related to the upcoming decampment of the Federation advance force. In the days before that bargain, she had needed to make sure she was involved in this process, so she had suggested to the commanders that her organizational skills could be of use to them in this matter—which was normally under the direct supervision of the Prime Minister.

Mention of his name and of her current position as his official surrogate was all it took for Commander Aarcobin to provide her with everything she requested. No one wanted to be seen causing difficulties for Belladrin Rish, or obstructing her efforts to carry out the last of whatever instructions she might have received from the deceased.

It made her smile, but only for a moment.

The truth of the matter was that, if her bargain with Clizia held, then this would be the end of her service to Cor d'Amphere. She had given him enough of her life and her sanity; she had risked herself for him sufficiently. So many lives had been snuffed out because of her. True, they were mostly the lives of people she had not known or would ever come to know. True also, they were members of communities and nations that were enemies of the Skaar people. She owed them nothing. In all probability, they would have done the same things to her, had they been given the chance.

But all that ignored the terrible impact of killing people and destroying lives. Though gone from the earth, they were not gone from her conscience. They became ghosts that haunted her in an endless parade.

They would be with her forever, and she could do nothing about it. Nothing, that is, about those who were gone, but she could at least stop adding to their numbers. If Clizia Porse followed through on their bargain, Cor d'Amphere would soon be dead, and her problem of breaking away from him before she had any more deaths on her conscience would be solved. And maybe she could help the Federation army actually depart instead of leading them all to slaughter.

She rose and walked to the tent opening, listening for the sounds of the aides and guards she knew were right outside. It was night now, so most had gone to bed. But a few remained, working out there just as she was working in here. She was never alone anymore, it seemed. She was never *allowed* to be alone. Not because she was mistrusted, but because she had made herself so valuable they could not afford to let anything happen to her. The irony was striking. They were protecting the very person who would be responsible for destroying them.

Unless Clizia kept her bargain.

The witch had never been the most stable of allies, but Belladrin needed her now—with an almost fanatical desperation. She hadn't always been like this. When the Skaar king had recruited her, she was only a girl—angry with her father, bitter at her fate, devastated by what the remainder of her life would be like. So she had swallowed it all and focused on the need to protect her family. Survival was all that mattered. But no longer. Her life had lost all meaning, and she no longer valued herself. She was nothing more than a facilitator now.

A valuable slave.

How had she let this happen?

She turned and walked back to her desk, sitting down once more, trying to force herself to concentrate on work.

Seconds later a violent explosion shattered the silence, shouts and screams blossomed from beyond her tent walls, and the entire camp was engulfed in bedlam.

Clizia Porse had allowed just enough time to pass for darkness to fall before reentering the Federation camp to do what she had thought she had done many days ago—kill Tarsha Kaynin. To find out the girl was still alive when she had believed her safely out of the way was galling beyond words. How she had survived her fall off the cliffs of Cleeg Hold was difficult to imagine, but apparently she had. So matters had to be set right immediately. Tarsha was far too dangerous to be allowed to wander about, mixing in Clizia's affairs and generally stirring up trouble. A quick finish to this complication was necessary.

She had thought to implement it immediately upon leaving Belladrin Rish's quarters, but the warning Belladrin had given about how this matter should be handled was not without merit. Clizia's instincts were to go to Tarsha's tent and kill her on the spot, daylight or no. But if anything went wrong—which, given all the potential witnesses, seemed likely—her chance might be lost for good. So waiting for nightfall and cover of darkness persuaded her to delay for several hours.

But now the time was up, and Stiehl or no Stiehl, she was going to eliminate Tarsha once and for all.

She did not reveal herself this time when she passed through the camp, but cloaked herself in magic to hide entirely. Using a powerful glamour, she became invisible as she walked through the darkness unseen. She did not hesitate in her approach to the tent marked by the green emblem. No guards blocked entry; no barriers had been set in place to keep her out. There were wards to signal her arrival, obviously applied by the girl in an effort to warn her of a surprise attack, but the wards were child's play for a practitioner of Clizia's skills, and she disarmed them with barely any effort at all.

She paused then before the tent flaps, thinking through what she would do after she entered and revealed herself. She would have to act quickly; there would be no time for hesitation. She would have to react to whatever situation presented itself.

She scanned the inside of the tent, seeking the girl. Nothing. She cast off her protections and summoned a killing spell before gently easing the tent flaps aside. The light within was dim, its illumination restricted to the corner where it hung. She peered into the shadows and saw nothing, so she moved farther in, turning her attention to the lighted area—encompassing a chair and a small table. Still nothing. She stepped all the way in. The tent was empty.

An awful sense of loss filled Clizia Porse and she stood where she was, just inside the entry, debating what to do next. She allowed her killing spell to dwindle and her magic to cool. There was no sign of Tarsha. Somehow, she had missed her. Somehow, she had let her slip away. She would have to . . .

*Wham!*

The blow sent her reeling, her defensive magic slow and barely sufficient to blunt its full force. Invisible chains began to wrap around her, tightening with frightening force. She stumbled as her legs were bound, and she fought to break free of the chains and regain her balance. Out of the corner of her eye she saw Tarsha Kaynin step into view, face intense, arms extended, hands working fresh magic. She had anticipated Clizia's arrival—perhaps sensed it. Her poorly formed wards were merely a ruse to lure her enemy into a false sense of security. She had hidden herself from both human sight and any countermagic that might unveil her, leaving Clizia deceived and vulnerable to attack.

But she was Clizia Porse, and she was never helpless—no matter how extreme her situation. She broke the chains and righted herself just in time to fend off a further attack, dropping into a crouch and tangling Tarsha's legs in chains of her own. Then she threw out a fiery counterattack and summoned anew her strongest killing spell.

The killing spell rocketed toward Tarsha, who could not manage to dodge it and so turned it aside and sent it caroming through the top of the tent in a fiery streamer of crimson fire that lit up the night sky and caught the attention of everyone within a mile.

The exchange of magic and countermagic between the two combatants continued unabated. There was no thought to stopping, no consideration for calling a truce, and no expectation of quarter to be given. Each wanted the other dead, and each fully expected their battle could not end any other way. The ferocity and intensity of their struggle could be imagined by those standing without—most of them cringing away in fear and dismay, and all of them certain they were witnessing an event of terrible proportions. Even without knowing exactly what was happening, they could feel the fury in the effort and power being expended.

Clizia was beginning to feel a drain on her strength the longer the battle continued, and she was growing frantic. She was more skilled and experienced than Tarsha Kaynin, but the girl was strong and determined. And young—so much younger. Her stamina was immense, making her more than a match for Clizia. It would perhaps prove a difference-maker. Clizia knew she had to find a way past the defenses and attacks being employed against her—just once, enough to let her throw Tarsha down and finish her. As the battle raged, she searched for a way.

And found it.

In the midst of a flurry of fiery exchanges, she threw out an image of Tavo Kaynin, alive and well. At the sight of her brother, Tarsha lost all focus—just for an instant, but long enough to distract her. Clizia was ready, anticipating the distraction, knowing it would leave her enemy vulnerable, if only for that single moment. With a snake's quickness, she struck, an iron hand born of her worst magic penetrating the girl's defenses, tearing into her chest and seizing her heart.

She watched in satisfaction as Tarsha convulsed, her slender body contorting, the terrible expression on her face revealing the excruciating pain the magic was causing her. Such a small thing she was, Clizia thought. So fragile. She squeezed harder. Now Tarsha screamed, but she did something else as well. With a flailing of arms and a twisting of her body, she severed the killing grip as if with a blade, thrusting away the tattered remnants and counterattacking with a flurry of both defensive and offensive spells.

Too late, Clizia realized the danger. Her attack fell apart and her defenses were shattered as she was enveloped by the barrage and sent tumbling. A firestorm of explosions rocketed every which way—the girl's massive response to what had almost been done to her. Clizia had a momentary sense of her own doom. Would nothing kill this girl? Was there no way to overcome this arrogant, willful child?

Bolts of magic ripped through the tent that still hid the combatants, fiery spears that sent everyone seeking fresh shelter. The Federation encampment was engulfed in cries and the pounding of booted feet. The tent caught fire, burning from the top down.

Within, Clizia and Tarsha were surrounded in smoke and bits of burning fabric, and momentarily lost sight of each other. Clizia dragged herself to the entry flaps and used what small strength she retained to turn herself invisible. Whatever might have become of Tarsha Kaynin, she had to get herself clear of the soldiers outside. She needed to flee and recover from tonight's debacle. Her insides seemed to have turned to poisonous jelly, and her muscles ached so badly she could barely move. One arm hung limp; her hearing was diminished. She could deal with most of it, but her weakness was profound—worse than it had ever been after an expenditure of magic. She could not worry further about the girl. She had to hope she might have succeeded in her attempt to kill her—might even have inflicted a mortal wound. But there was no way she could take time to find out now. Even if Tarsha still lived, she would not be recovering from the damage Clizia had done to her anytime soon.

Five seconds later, smoke and ash and fire mingling with residual bits of magic and a wild cacophony of screams and shouts, she was through the entry and gone into the night.

Belladrin Rish had arrived on the scene by then, unaware that the witch was passing right next to her but fully aware of what must have happened. Yes, Clizia had waited for nightfall to attempt to kill Tarsha, but she had not done so quietly. In fact, she realized as a pair of soldiers carried the girl from the remnants of the burning tent—an ash-covered, struggling figure flailing about as if she might launch another attack even on those who were trying to save her—Clizia might have failed entirely.

And what might this mean for her own bargain with Clizia?

Feeling sick, Belladrin rushed over and bent close. "Tarsha?" she said. "Can you hear me?"

The young face turned slightly and her eyes opened, but she did not seem to see Belladrin. In truth, she seemed not to see anything. Her lips moved, but no sound came out.

"Take her to the Healers," Belladrin ordered, aware that Lieutenant Commander Oberion had come up behind her, his own expression dark.

"What's happened?" he asked, but she only shook her head in response.

"Make sure they check for burns and internal injuries," she ordered. "Keep her warm, and keep her quiet. And place a heavy guard on her quarters." She waited for Tarsha to be carried away before turning back to Oberion. "Come to my quarters and I will explain everything. Quickly."

She would have to come up with some plausible story if she did not want to reveal her personal bargain with Clizia. But what? As for Tarsha Kaynin, she did not care to speculate on what would happen now. Either she would live or she would die. All anyone could do was wait and see which path she chose.

And all Belladrin could do was to hope that Clizia's insane feud with the girl had not blighted their bargain—the fulfillment of which she now depended on more than ever.

# TWENTY-ONE

No sooner had Grianne left than Drisker sensed another presence in his bedroom. On looking around, he found Weka Dart standing in a darkened corner like some sort of misshapen wraith. He studied the Ulk Bog in surprise; Weka was so still he might have been a statue.

As the Druid rose to his feet, the little fellow detached himself from the shadows and walked forward. "My mistress told you to ready yourself. Soon you will meet with the others. I've been ordered to take you to them." He paused hesitantly. "I will wait for you in the hall."

Then out the door he went, closing it softly behind him. Drisker watched him go. Had the Ulk Bog's arm gotten longer?

Leaving that mystery for later, Drisker went to splash water on his face, dress, and gather himself mentally for what lay ahead. The journey to Vendra Trax's fortress was apparently at hand, and those who would accompany the Straken Queen had arrived. He thought about what lay ahead but did not dwell on it.

There was no point in looking too closely at the dark possibilities that waited.

He left the room and found Weka Dart just outside the door as promised. The Ulk Bog's gnarled countenance brightened marginally, and an unexpected smile revealed a copious number of teeth. "Are you ready, Straken Lord? The poison seems to have left you. You look fit again."

The Druid nodded. "And your arm is healing?" He pointed.

"Oh, yes. You can tell, can't you? It grows back. Ulk Bogs are very blessed with abilities others lack. It will be just as it was quite soon. As you already are. Do you wish something to eat and drink?"

Drisker was not entirely sure how to answer this, having been poisoned once already by the Ulk Bog. But he was both hungry and thirsty, and he would need his strength in the days ahead. He had to assume the last poisoning was unintentional, and that Grianne Ohmsford had taken steps to prevent anything like that from happening again.

He nodded his agreement.

"This way," Weka Dart directed, and started walking.

They proceeded to what appeared to be a kitchen, although one cobbled together more than artfully designed. There were fire grates and ovens, flat surfaces for food preparation, bins and cold storage for perishables and drinks, and a pair of small tables where one could eat. The Ulk Bog had Drisker sit at one of the tables and went about gathering items on a plate. He poured a liquid from a pitcher on the counter into a tankard that bubbled up and spilled over the sides, added a pinch of something, then carried it all to the table and set it in front of him.

"Eat, please," he said, in a tone that approximated encouragement.

Drisker did so and found everything surprisingly tasty. Even the odd liquid had a bracing effect, and as he consumed his meal he could feel himself growing stronger. "Very good," he complimented.

Weka Dart beamed. "I was a cook once," he said. "I have many skills."

"Tell me about our plans."

A wary look appeared on the wizened face. "Oh, she does not tell me. I know nothing."

"You know everything," Drisker corrected gently. "That is how you manage to stay alive when others don't. Am I not right? Tell me the truth. What will transpire when we leave Kraal Reach?"

The Ulk Bog thought it over for a moment, then gave a reluctant nod. "You will get me in trouble if she finds out . . ."

"Then I will see to it that she doesn't. What are her plans for me?"

"She remains convinced the darkwand is hidden within the Iron Crèche. She will lead a company of her followers from Kraal Reach into Brockenthrog Weir and enter her enemy's fortress lair by means of an underground passage the Chule know nothing about. A moench will show her the way." He paused, a disgusted look on his wizened face. "A waste of time, if you ask me. But she cares nothing for my opinion."

"What is a moench?" He remembered Grianne speaking the name, but nothing of the particulars.

"A cousin to the Ulk Bogs: a burrowing creature somewhat larger and less dependable. Inferior in intelligence. Prone to unwarranted acts of disobedience and retaliation against those it pretends to befriend." He spit to one side. "Loathsome little demons, those. This one, in particular. Its name is Styrik. I would not trust it to carry my boots across a room, but *she* thinks it can be useful. *She* thinks it is so frightened of her, it will not dare to cross her. But I wonder."

"And we have no other choice?"

The Ulk Bog was sulking now, hunched over and glowering, eyes on the floor. "She thinks not."

"And she is the one who decides?"

"Always, Straken Lord." He looked up suddenly. "Do not make the mistake of thinking otherwise."

"Not for a minute. Who else goes with us?"

"A slint and a clawrake. One is a form of shapeshifter, the other a berserker. She controls them both, but if she loses control of either you had best hope there is a large iron door between you and it."

"Names?"

"Neither has a name—or deserves one. And they won't talk to you anyway. Even if they choose to say something, they speak in tongues you wouldn't understand. Stay clear of them."

He said it with such emphasis that Drisker thought he had better do what the Ulk Bog suggested and try not to have anything to do with the pair. Or with the moench, either, for that matter. Best to talk only with

Grianne Ohmsford and Weka Dart, if talk he must. But not talking might be an even better idea.

He tried hard not to think about his chances for survival in the company of these demons but was left with an unmistakable truth. Any protection he was likely to find at this point must come either from the Straken Queen or from his own combination of watchfulness and self-defense. Reliance on anything save those was likely to prove fatal.

"What do we do once we are inside this fortress?"

"The Iron Crèche," Weka repeated. "Ansa Trax named it himself after he had it built."

"The Iron Crèche, then. What do we do once inside?"

"We search out the darkwand. Once we find it, we take it and get out as fast as we can."

He made it sound as if this was all pointless, which Drisker found odd. Then he wondered if the Ulk Bog might be right. "It was my understanding that no one knows where the staff is hidden. How do we know all of a sudden where it is now? How are we supposed to find it?"

Weka Dart looked exasperated. "I am not told anything other than what you now know! Maybe we sniff it out? Styrik is up to the task; his nose is larger than his brain. Or maybe we find a seer with a crystal ball, or we can capture Trax and torture him until he tells us where he's stashed it."

Abruptly, he threw up his hands, his exasperation turning to rage. "Let me be! I have no idea what she expects us to do or even why we are doing it. Maybe you should try to talk her out of it. Maybe she would listen to you. This is your fault, after all, coming here bearing false stories and offering false hopes! I was satisfied with the way things were, but now my mistress undertakes this hazardous quest, and what is to become of me? I will not live another day if she abandons me!"

Drisker held his temper. "I told you already, the choice to return to the Four Lands is not mine to make; it is hers. I have never once suggested it to her. I did not come here willingly. I was brought here in much the same way she was the first time. I was trapped and sent here by magic. If I could go back right now, I would."

"You say this, but I think you lie. You are a Straken, and all Strakens lie. You say what you want me to hear, but you hide the truth. You scheme, and you deceive."

"Yet you think she does not?"

"It is not the same. I understand her! She is different. She is kind to me. She gives me a place in a world that would otherwise devour me. Ulk Bogs are nothing to the other demons. We are less than the dirt they walk on. My mistress knows this. She values my loyalty."

Drisker shook his head helplessly. "So maybe she will choose to stay when this is over."

"I don't trust you."

"But you are coming with us to Brockenthrog Weir. You were there when she said she wants you to come."

The Ulk Bog lowered his eyes and turned away. "I will do whatever my mistress asks of me. I am her servant, and so I serve."

Then he left the kitchen, sulking, not waiting for the Druid. Drisker hesitated a moment, then followed.

They passed down a dozen hallways and went deep into the fortress's interior. It was a cold, damp, dismally gray structure where patches of fog huddled against the ceiling and light was not welcome. Everywhere they went, shadows intruded. There were windows for a while, and then none at all. Torches scattered here and there offered just enough light to suggest a path forward but not enough to reveal much detail. The silence was stifling and omnipresent. It hid things that crept through the shadows, revealing themselves in small flashes of movement. Drisker caught glimpses now and then, but only for an instant. He had no idea what they were or why they were there.

He tried to imagine what it must be like for Grianne Ohmsford to live in this place. She was, at her core, a human being, stolen from a land of light and color, and cast into a place where everything was different. She had been forced to assimilate, knowing it was the only way to endure. How she came to this decision instead of just giving in to a quick death was hard to understand. He was not sure he could have done the same—or even that he would have wanted to. Had he not had a hope of escaping this prison, he might not have been able to stay sane.

And Grianne had been here for centuries, kept alive by the rules that governed the Forbidding and its denizens. She was living out the last years of her life in a netherworld of hate and despair, just another predator fighting to stay alive.

But were his transgressions any less than hers? He

had not killed as willingly as she had when she had been the Ilse Witch, but he had let others die by abandoning them—by abandoning his responsibilities and selfishly seeking peace in his life alone. All of his fellow Druids, slaughtered in Paranor—what were they if not sacrifices for his freedom? How could he think of their deaths as anything else? He had given them up when he might have saved them, so perhaps his fate now, trapped with Grianne inside the Forbidding, was meant to be his punishment. And his redemption likewise required that he suffer as she had, endure as she did, and never leave.

"We are here," Weka Dart announced, breaking into his thoughts.

They stood before a heavy ironbound door fully ten feet in height. Drisker stared at it. What reason could there be for a door to be this high? What sort of creature required such an opening? He found himself hoping he would not have to find out.

But he was doomed to disappointment.

The Ulk Bog stepped forward and, in quick succession, touched a series of iron knobs on a metal plate. When the door opened, he beckoned Drisker inside.

"I have him," he announced to whoever waited within.

The room was massive, the ceiling fully fifty feet high. The few windows were placed so far up on the walls that only small patches of illumination reached down to where their thin light mattered. The walls were constructed of stone blocks, the floors of stone paving, and the ceiling could have been anything, invisible as it was. Even on entering, Drisker could hear the echo of his footfalls in the vast emptiness. For there was nothing in the room but a huge pile of cloth scraps bound with ropes and settled against the wall to one side. But then abruptly there was unexpected movement off to the other side—shadows that shifted in endless patterns through the gloom with no indication of their source or identity.

Ahead, Grianne Ohmsford materialized, turning to face him, giving him a glimpse of a squat, wiry form that pressed up against her, as if seeking to wrap itself about her. Red eyes peered over at him, their gaze deep and unpleasant. A hiss escaped the creature's nearly invisible lips, and it crouched so low it seemed to be hugging the floor.

"*Moench*," Weka Dart sneered softly. He stepped toward it, screaming in fury. "Get away from her!"

The creature shuddered and fell back instantly, then faded into the shadows bit by bit, its hateful eyes and a flash of teeth the last parts of it to disappear.

"Are you ready to travel?" the Straken Queen asked Drisker, her smile unexpectedly welcoming.

"Rested and ready both. Thank you for allowing me time to heal."

"You will need to be at full strength if you are to survive what is coming." She turned to Weka Dart and gestured to where the moench had last been seen. "Tch, you frightened him with your yelling. So jealous, aren't you, little imp?"

"He should not be touching you," the Ulk Bog snarled. "He is not fit even to come near you."

She gave him a considering look and turned away. "Now that we are all gathered . . ."

She broke off on seeing Drisker looking around curiously. To all appearances, the room seemed empty. With even the moench gone, there were only the three of them left—Grianne, Weka Dart, and himself.

"Oh, the others are here, Druid; they simply don't choose to reveal themselves. But they should show better manners—if they had any, of course. Allow me."

She brought a strange metal object to her lips and blew hard. It shrieked as if it were a banshee's cry, so shrill and piercing it felt to Drisker like it might be cutting through his skin. Even the shadows seemed to quiver in the wake of its heart-stopping shriek.

Weka Dart dropped to the floor, hands over his ears, his face scrunched up like crumpled paper. Drisker took a step back, a protective magic already in place to mute the force of the sound.

Sudden movement surfaced all too close to where he stood.

Almost right in front of him, the moench reappeared, spidery arms wrapped around its body, face a grimacing mask of pain. Not far away—perhaps a dozen feet at most—another creature materialized, shadowy and unformed: a shape-shifter that was rapidly changing from one thing to another as if refusing to offer any clear image of itself.

The last of the trio responded more slowly.

Drisker noticed it only when what he had thought to be the collection of rope-bound cloth began to move, unfurling until it was twice the height of the Druid and much wider. It heaved and grunted with a deep, dissatisfied bellow that shook the very stones of the fortress. Squaring up to where Drisker was standing, it started toward him. Drisker braced himself, his magic already summoned in a protective shield.

But Grianne simply stepped between them, her voice ringing out above the grunting emanating from what Drisker knew by now must be the clawrake.

"Hold, *ca'shi'taw insit'an*! Would you run us all down with your lurching? Stand where you are!"

The movement of the cloths and ropes ceased, and a low moaning sounded from within.

"Such a baby," the Straken Queen muttered, shaking her head. "Show yourself, *ish'taw*."

Ancient Elfish, Drisker recognized, but the clawrake seemed to understand it. Without hesitating, it ceased moving forward and threw off its coverings. "*Caiton'osh'dei, Majes'tin.*"

A huge, bowlegged mass of hair—with arms the size of a large man's torso—got down on one knee and lowered its massive head. Gimlet eyes glanced up, then quickly looked away. Its arms stretched toward her and its great hands opened in an acknowledgment of fealty, and the Druid could see now how the clawrake had gotten its name. All six digits on either hand ended in claws big enough to tear down fortress walls.

But not here. Not in this place. Here the Straken Queen ruled, and clearly all the demons she had gathered had long since accepted her dominion. Coming here as an outsider all those years ago, she nonetheless had found a way to rule them, and they had no wish to challenge her. The shape-shifter had materialized, as well, and all three of them bowed their heads and stood awaiting her pleasure.

Drisker was beyond impressed. He walked over to

stand beside her. "How long did it take you to accomplish this?" he asked softly.

She did not look at him. "Years. It was a slow process. They were reluctant to accept me, as you might imagine. Even though I had cast down their king, they did not fear me sufficiently. And fear is what rules in the Forbidding. A few sought to test me, to see if I could be made to disappear. When it was they who disappeared, others started to come around. Then circumstances beyond my control forced me to crush an uprising of Crustlings in the Pashanon and make an example of their leaders, and things changed for good. The strongest within the Forbidding are violent, predatory creatures that only know one way of life. Reason, common sense, peaceful coexistence? Such things hold no sway over them. But they respect strength and power, and I was able to demonstrate I had both—as well as magic beyond anything they had ever encountered. As I said, it took time and patience and more than a few object lessons, but you see the results."

"So now you rule unopposed?"

She snorted. "Hardly. There are always those who will challenge the status quo. There are always potential new rulers waiting in the wings, eager for their turn."

She turned to look at him now. "Someday—maybe sooner than I would like—one of them will find a way to dispose of me and take my place. Vendra Trax is foremost among them—a good reason for you to protect me on our quest to find the darkwand. You would not like what would happen to you if Trax became the new Straken King."

Drisker imagined not. "It wouldn't be so good for you and your followers, either, I'd guess. Tell me how you plan to get us all inside the Chule's fortress."

She shrugged. "Weka Dart has already advised you on my intentions, hasn't he? We are a company with talents and strengths sufficient to overcome whatever obstacles we might encounter. We share a common purpose, and now we have you to help us see it realized. We have a way to get inside if the moench speaks the truth, and he would not dare do otherwise."

She glanced over at the red-eyed demon, which was now allowing its gaze to fix on Drisker. "I find him somewhat unpredictable, but only when he has not been provided with directions to hold him fast to his task." She brushed back her thick gray hair and sighed. "He has his uses."

She made a gesture of dismissal and the moench, clawrake, and slint all broke away and disappeared through the entry door. Weka Dart remained, crouching off to one side, keeping his distance.

"But how do we know the darkwand is hidden inside the Iron Crèche?" he pressed her. "It wasn't there when you searched for it before."

"It may have been, Drisker. I simply couldn't find it then. But this time I will."

"This feels wrong," he replied with a frown. "Too much of it seems left to chance."

"We face formidable obstacles; I won't deny it." She had lowered her voice and seemed to be taking him into her confidence, but he resolved to remain wary. "Brockenthrog Weir is composed of swamp and quicksand, with intermittent islands of cut-blade grasses and willowy boughs. Poisonous creatures of all sorts lie in wait. Predators live out their lives hunting anything that moves. There will be fifty ways to die for every mile we walk—and walk we must. My carriage will help us with the first part of our approach, but it cannot navigate the swamps. So we must proceed on foot, and we will be at our most vulnerable then."

"You cannot expect a group of this size to remain undetected," he pointed out. "Perhaps we would do better going alone, just the two of us."

She gave him a look. "What did I tell you earlier? Which of us leads this expedition, Drisker? Are we unclear about that?"

"You lead," he acknowledged. "I was just asking."

She shook her head. "It did not sound that way. But believe me, the Chule would not hesitate to kill us all, if they found us. As savages go, they are at the top of the food chain."

"You have made preparations to prevent this from happening?"

"Those I chose to accompany us possess skills and capabilities that will enable us to repel whatever comes against us. And I include you in this assessment, Drisker Arc. The dreams say you must be there; the dreams show you handing me the darkwand. And the dreams do not lie."

Drisker wondered. He had less faith in dreams than she did, and he was surprised to see her so wedded to prophecy when she seemed so practical otherwise. Why should his presence make any difference in how things turned out? He had not tested his magic fully since his imprisonment inside the Forbidding, and he was not sure how effective it might be against the myriad creatures that dwelled here. There would be different challenges than had been present in the Four Lands. But if Grianne Ohmsford was convinced he had something to offer, he would be foolish not to agree.

"I will do the best I can," he promised.

"That would be a wise decision. Your life will probably depend on it at some point or other." She paused. "As for the rest of your questions, answers will be provided after we are on our way."

*I hope so,* he thought. He was troubled by the lack of details on how the recovery of the darkwand was going to be accomplished, and he did not like being kept in the dark like this. Especially when their lives were at stake.

He looked around the chilly, gray overcast of the room, taking in its size and scope one final time. "How long do I have before we leave?"

Her laughter was hard and quick. "Such a foolish question, Drisker Arc. We leave immediately."

# TWENTY-TWO

THE *BEHEMOTH* WAS ONLY a day or two away from Skaarsland when its crew and passengers first noticed the change in temperature.

They had been tracking steadily north off the coast of Afrique, traveling a thousand feet above the calm waters of the Tiderace, their flying assisted by southerly winds that helped them recover from the weeks lost after being blown so far off course. But on the day the temperature started to drop, the skies grew overcast and a lower cloud ceiling required them to drop considerably in order to stay in sight of the ocean and the islands off the Skaarsland coast. The cold deepened steadily, and they donned the heavy-weather cloaks and fur-lined hoods they had packed to protect themselves. Even so, the cold penetrated, and any warmth was quickly a distant memory.

Seelah, who had been more in evidence of late—appearing on deck regularly to climb the masts and maneuver her way through the rigging, perhaps to shame the rest of them for their lack of athletic ability—had returned to lurking below.

On the following day, the winds quickened with a

biting chill, and their continuous bursts were strong enough to cause the transport to lurch and buck. Everything had to be tied down, from barrels to sheeting to the crew and passengers themselves. It was not a regular storm they had encountered; that would have passed. After eight hours, they knew it for a weather front that likely spanned the waters and reached beyond the shoreline for as much as several hundred miles.

"Skaarsland," Ajin said suddenly to Rocan Arneas and Dar Leah, with whom she was standing.

She pointed to a distant shoreline, where a mass of rugged cliffs formed a barrier against the surging ocean. Froth capped the waves, and spray filled the air with a glistening sheen. The booming of the waters as they hammered against the rocks was unmistakable.

"No wonder the Skaar want to leave this place," Rocan muttered at one point, causing Dar—who was beside him watching the landmass off the starboard bow pass in and out of heavy shore mists—to smile with undisguised amusement.

"You didn't think we had a good reason?" Ajin asked.

The Rover shook his head. "I know what you said, but I didn't expect it to be this bad."

Ajin did not respond. Typical of late, Dar thought. She had become increasingly withdrawn the farther they had journeyed from the Nambizi islands. She had been counting the days, observing the land they passed, and most certainly calculating the time remaining. At night, when they were alone together, he asked her about it, offering her a chance to voice her concerns. But Ajin d'Amphere was nothing if not strong-willed, and it soon became apparent that she had no intention of speaking about anything that might be troubling her until they had reached their destination.

And maybe not even then, given her habit of locking everything she was feeling away—save for her endless declarations on how she felt about him, that was, because her insistence that they had a future together had not changed. She stroked him and held him and told him she loved him and would continue to love him as long as she lived. To his way of thinking, he hadn't done a thing to deserve her devotion, but he knew by now that nothing he said would change her mind. He also knew that, in spite of his private resolve not to let her persistence affect him, he was slowly beginning to come around. He was spending every night with her already, finding that he enjoyed being with her, and was increasingly wondering if maybe she wasn't right.

There was so much about her that drew him, and even the enmity of their peoples and differences in their lives were not enough to outweigh that. They shared a dry sense of humor and a strong moral code. They saw each other as equals. And she made him feel so good when he was with her—a feeling he had not experienced since his time with Zia Amarodian, and maybe not even then. It was hard to remember Zia anymore. She was long dead in the Charnal Mountains, killed by Ajin and her soldiers. That Ajin had caused her death did trouble him, but he had come to accept that it was not personal but simply a consequence of a reckless confrontation. It had taken him time to come to terms with Ajin's direct involvement, but eventually he had.

Still, other barriers remained, and he kept thinking he should pay heed to them. But why bother? Everything in his life had changed. The Druids at Paranor had been annihilated. The Four Lands had been ravaged by war; thousands had died, and the future for those who still lived looked bleak. The fates of Drisker Arc and Tavo and Tarsha Kaynin were unknown. It was almost a relief to have a distraction that helped him put all that aside. It had become a burden to be stored away for when it mattered again: one so big and so unmanageable he had no answers for its many questions and no solutions for its many problems. Had he not found a way to slip past it and look ahead, the weight of it might already have crushed him.

Yet Ajin offered love, companionship, and healing. She was there for him, and she wanted him. She did not attempt to explain anything or persuade him that the obstacles they both faced could be overcome. She simply told him she loved him, and that was enough.

Standing next to Rocan Arneas, who was signaling his lookouts to come down from their crow's nests, Dar felt oddly hopeful. They were almost at the end of their journey. In the days to come they would determine if Annabelle was capable of overcoming the winter that was threatening to drive the Skaar from their homeland. And if so, they might find a way to forestall the war that was threatening to rip the Four Lands apart. It did no one any good to dwell on how difficult this might be. Difficulties were best overcome by not letting them overwhelm you—and by persistence.

"We have to light the stoves and watch for ice," the Rover was saying. "It's close to freezing. Moisture will build on the surfaces of whatever it touches. And rain, at this point, would be disastrous."

"I'll take care of it," Dar offered, and walked back to light the dozen or so metal stoves that dotted the decking.

Ajin had warned them. The cold was bitter, ice was everywhere, and fire was the only weapon anyone had to fight back. So Rocan had equipped their transport with sufficient stoves that he could create a somewhat warmer atmosphere on deck, which would ascend into the rigging and help protect the airship. Already, Dar could see a sheen of ice glistening on the higher spars and yardarms, so he mobilized the crew members to get the fires lit and start feeding them with wood for fuel.

While he worked, he glanced at the forbidding shoreline, distressed by what he saw. What a grim place! The rock walls of the cliffs, the massive gray splash of the crashing waves, and the mists clinging in streamers to the heights of the cliffs, were all oppressive.

He was walking back to rejoin Rocan and Ajin when Shea Ohmsford caught up with him. "Hold up a minute!" the boy shouted above the howl of the wind.

Dar stopped and turned. "Where's your coat?"

To his shock, the boy was not wearing it. "Too bulky," Shea replied. "I can barely move around in it.

Besides, I don't need a big coat. I'm warm enough in my regular cloak. And I have gloves on."

Dar seized him by his arm and force-marched him back to the partial shelter offered by the forward wall of the pilot box. There he sat him down and faced him, his anger apparent. "I know you think you are invulnerable and can survive anything; most boys your age do. But on an airship, you obey the orders of your captain, whether you agree with them or not. Did you not hear him order you to put on your winter coat early this morning, when we were all gathered?"

Shea nodded. "But I told you . . ."

"Where is it?"

"In my locker."

"Go put it on. And when you have it on, come back."

"But I . . ."

Then, seeing the look in Dar's eyes, he stopped and quickly left.

Still, "Doesn't mean I need it!" he shouted defiantly over his shoulder as he disappeared down the hatchway to their sleeping quarters.

Dar shook his head. Stubborn men and stubborn boys. What was to be done? Stubborn women, too, he amended, thinking of Ajin. Even though she had not shared her plans for what she intended once they reached the capital city, he knew well enough what she would do. She would first go to her mother. Then, at some point, she would go after the *pretender* and likely kill her. He had tried to persuade her that there was nothing to be gained from this, but Ajin had simply dismissed him. This was her way of handling things she felt were her personal business—things she did not care to see him involved with, or which she believed he would never understand. And perhaps she was right, but he did not like being shut out. It was the one area of disagreement they could not seem to resolve.

When Shea returned, he was wearing his coat, which was every bit as confining and bulky as the boy had indicated. Dar paid no attention.

"You can freeze to death in weather like this in a matter of minutes. It can burn your lungs from the inside out, just from breathing the air. You need to preserve your body heat, Shea. So you will wear the coat the rest of the time we are here. Now, what was it you wanted?"

"Tindall," said the boy. "I can't find him. I've searched everywhere."

The Blade nodded. "Very well. Let's you and I have another look."

He sent Shea belowdecks to search the storage areas to see if the old man might be checking on his chemicals and fuels, all of which were secured in one of the centermost chambers where they could be protected from most types of damage. He stayed topside and began a sweeping search of the decking from bow to stern, pausing to look carefully in every nook and cranny while questioning crew and passengers as he went.

Brecon Elessedil caught up with him as he was nearing the platform on which Annabelle rested, heavily wrapped in canvas and insulated batting to protect her against the weather.

"What are you looking for?" The Elven prince had to shout to be heard above the wind. It was getting worse, Dar noted, increasing in force and bitterness. Flakes of snow had appeared, whipping wildly about them in a whirlwind of whiteness.

"Tindall has disappeared!" he shouted back.

Brecon shook his head. "No, he hasn't. He's back there!"

He grabbed Dar, pulling him along until they had reached Annabelle. Then the Elf released him and led the way to the rear of the machine, where Dar noted a gap in the wrappings. "In there?" he asked.

"Said he wanted to be sure she was all right." Brecon shrugged. "I told him he should be belowdecks in this weather, but he ignored me."

Dar nodded his thanks and slipped through the gap. Wedged between a pair of Annabelle's iron struts and against a narrow plating lay Tindall, curled up sound asleep.

The highlander stared. The old man was not wearing his coat, either.

Dar exhaled sharply. *What is wrong with these people?* He reached down and shook Tindall awake, worried for a moment when he did not respond that he had frozen himself. But finally the old man stirred and opened his eyes.

"Just resting. What's wrong?"

Dar helped him sit up. "What are you doing back here in the first place?"

"Making sure Annabelle is safe and sound." He sounded defensive and irritated. "Some of her components can be damaged when it's this cold, you

know. I had to wrap them in protective insulation."
He grinned. "Worried about me, were you?"

"I shouldn't have to be! You should be worrying
about yourself. Where's your coat?"

"I took it off and left it near the canvas opening. It
was too hard to work in, too confining. The work is
very precise, very unforgiving."

"Unforgiving, is it? You and Shea Ohmsford are
too much alike. Old or young, you are objective proof
that it's possible to be foolish at any age." He reached
down and pulled Tindall to his feet. "Get your coat
back on and go down the hatch to your quarters."

The old man yanked himself free. "I don't want to
go inside! I need to go back to work. Let me be!"

"It is well below freezing out here, and the wind is
blowing with enough force to send you over the side.
If something breaks the ties that bind your machine
to the decking, it could fall and crush you. So either
you go down on your own right now or I will carry
you down."

For a moment they were nose-to-nose. Then Tindall nodded. "I'm going. But I'm coming back!"

He moved past Dar, grabbed his coat, shrugged
into it, and was passing through the gap in the canvas when the Blade called after him. "You come back
when I tell you it is safe and not before. Otherwise, I
will have you bound and gagged!"

Tindall stomped away through the snow and cold.
Dar gave him a moment before following. Once outside, he watched until the hunched form reached the
hatchway, fighting hard with every step against the
force of the wind and the rocking of the huge trans-

port. *Stubborn old nut*. Dar began searching for Shea, half expecting to see him coatless again, but instead he found the boy forward with Brecon, standing inside the pilot box, his coat securely fastened. The pair were huddled against the back wall, staying well out of the way of the two Rovers who were wrestling with the thruster controls and steering. He climbed the steps to join them, brushing snow from his coat and stomping his boots to warm his feet. Both crewmates gave him a curt nod without breaking off their efforts to manage the airship. He nodded back and took a place beside the boy and the Elf.

"Tindall wasn't below, but when I came to tell you, Brecon said you'd found him," Shea announced, a bit defensively.

"Did you get the old man out?" Brecon interrupted.

"All the way out and safely belowdecks, although he's threatened to come back up again." He gave Shea a stern look. "Old fool had his coat off, too, trying to work on his machine. Wonder who taught him that?"

Brecon was staring at Shea, too.

"All right, I know not to do it again," the boy muttered grudgingly. "But Tindall has reason to be worried. Some of what makes Annabelle work is very fragile; the controls and measuring devices need to be calibrated to just the right levels. The cold could throw all that off!"

Dar brushed the snow out of his hair. "I understand. But he also does no one any good by freezing himself or catching a sickness that might kill him. He needs to be careful, and you need to help with this, Shea. You have to watch out for him—even if he doesn't choose to watch out for himself."

He turned to Brecon. "We must be getting close to where we need to set down. Have you used the Elf-stones yet today to determine exactly where we are?"

The Elven prince laughed. "I don't have to. The princess knows the way. She has been guiding us ever since we first sighted land. This is her country, and she needs no help from me. But you might want to go forward and ask her what she plans now that we're here. She's more likely to open up to you than she is to the rest of us. I know it's unlikely, but even in weather like this we might be spotted from the ground. So no need to risk showing ourselves if we can avoid it."

Dar agreed. "Give me a minute to get warm and I'll have a word with her."

Brecon laughed. "Why bother getting warm? As soon as you go outside you'll get cold all over again!"

Dar shook his head and went back out into the weather. *Pointless to argue with reasoning like that.*

He stumbled and lurched his way forward to the bow, where Rocan and Ajin were deep in conversation. Even though their words were lost in the wind's howl and the ocean's deep roar, he could tell by their animated hand movements and intense expressions that they were arguing about something.

"The princess wants to hug the shoreline and turn up a river channel to reach her home city," said Rocan angrily as Dar approached. "But I think going inland is too risky if it takes us that close to the Skaar and their weapons. Don't they have airships?"

Dar had to agree. "Why not find a cove along the shoreline and take flits inland?" he asked Ajin.

"Too dangerous." The way she said it suggested she was not exaggerating. "Look at this ocean. Even an inlet or cove would offer little protection against weather like this. The ocean is unforgiving, as I know too well. Staying out on the coast is far riskier than anything we might encounter going farther inland. What we need to do is just what I suggested: follow the river toward the capital city."

"Just sail inland, right up to their docks?" Rocan was growing exasperated. "And you think they won't notice?"

"I didn't say anything about sailing up to their docks. If we enter the river channel, either sailing or flying in, we can put into any number of natural ports along the way. The city is a hundred miles upriver, so Skaar soldiers don't guard the entrance; they don't need to. The river is a mass of riptides and shallows, with rocks that will tear out the bottom of your hull if you don't know where to go. But I do know. I can get us close enough to walk in. I also know where to shelter the *Behemoth* so no one will see us after we're anchored. Doesn't that sound safer to you?"

Dar looked at Rocan. "I think she's right. It will be night by the time we start in. And in this weather, even if we fly above the cliffs, we won't be seen unless the skies clear. And that doesn't look like it's going to happen."

"It hasn't happened for more than a dozen days a year in four years," Ajin affirmed. "It won't happen tonight, either."

"So we anchor where the *Behemoth* can't be seen and go from there. And no one will stumble over the ship once we're at anchor?"

Ajin shrugged. "I won't say there isn't *any* chance, but it won't be any greater than what we would face by anchoring on the coastline. And it will be safer." She paused. "But it's your decision, Captain Arneas."

"Let's consider what we plan to do," Dar said quickly, intervening. "We need to test Annabelle to see if she can effect a change in the weather. That is the first and most important reason we're here, isn't it?"

Rocan nodded. "And we need to get started on that right away."

"Other than that . . ." Dar looked expectantly at the Skaar princess. "What do you intend to do, Ajin?"

She gave him a long look, her blue eyes narrowing. "I think you already know. I will go into the city to find my mother. I need to determine if she is still safe from the *pretender.*"

"Will you come back to the airship afterward?"

Suddenly she was angry, her face flushed and twisted. "I will do whatever I have to do, Dar Leah! I don't have to answer to anyone here. I will do what I must, and it will be my choice. If I don't come back, you can feel free to leave me behind when you go."

"But you will help us in the meantime?" Dar kept his voice calm and steady. He was pressing things, but he needed to know exactly what they could expect of her. "We might need your services."

Ajin shook her head. "I got you here and I will get you safely anchored. But I owe you nothing more."

"I think maybe you do," Rocan interrupted. "We

gave you free passage home. We helped you escape your father and your enemies in the Four Lands. You owe us for that, and doing nothing more than helping us anchor is not sufficient."

She gave him a furious look, then glanced at Dar. He nodded slightly. She exhaled sharply and looked away, her lips tightening. "I am a Skaar princess. I owe nothing to anybody who is inferior in station!"

Dar almost laughed at such a wild proclamation, but he understood the cause. She had been stripped of everything, so she was clinging to the small claim she still had on the Skaar hierarchy. She was frustrated, and she was worried. Her mother was in danger, and she felt compelled to act.

"You are an *exiled* Skaar princess," Rocan pointed out quietly. "And while you are aboard my airship, you are beneath *me* in station. This is my command, not yours. But perhaps we might both be satisfied if we continue doing whatever the situation calls for. I will not hold you to more than your promise to help us in any way you can. Fair enough?"

She glared at him a moment, then nodded. "Well said. I lost my temper. I will help you so long as it does not prevent me from going to my mother."

Dar gave her a smile, but she barely glanced at him.

"We need some sort of map to find our way into and about the city, in case you do not return," Rocan said. "Will you provide us with one?"

"I will draw you one," she promised.

And then she stopped speaking entirely except to give them instructions on where to fly to reach safety.

They flew north for the remainder of that day and far into the next, hugging the coastline without putting the *Behemoth* in danger of being dashed into the cliffs. The wind continued to blow steadily with occasional sharp gusts, the temperature continued to fall, and the snow increased. By the time night arrived, they were engulfed in a virtual whiteout. But Ajin d'Amphere continued to guide them, clearly confident in her knowledge of where to go and how to get there. Even when Dar and Rocan could see nothing, Ajin's instincts and experience seemed unerring, so they let her take command. She kept them flying, dismissing a suggestion from Rocan, who said—once and only once—that it might be safer to seek anchorage until morning.

"It would not be safer to anchor out here. It would be safer to get past all this weather and inland to where we can anchor and sleep. Surely you know your crew is exhausted, Captain. Once at our anchorage, the winds will diminish to almost nothing. And while the cold and the snow remain, we should be able to sleep. Keep flying, please."

So they did, pushing on until Ajin took them through a pair of towering cliffs that bracketed a broad river, flying into the river's mouth at five hundred feet and then ascending to one thousand and a bit more when the cliffs heightened and the passageway narrowed. She had suggested that staying aloft would be safer than attempting a water landing and navigating the treacherous river when visibility was so poor. So they stayed airborne as they traveled, and before long she took them down into a spacious bay that was well inland and surrounded by heavy forest.

Once landed on the bay's much quieter waters, they put out their anchors and secured their vessel. A watch was set while the rest of the passengers and crew went to sleep.

Dar watched Ajin start away without him, reconciling himself to a night of sleeping alone, but then she turned around and came back, taking his hand in hers and towing him after her. He did not resist. They went below to her cabin, where they had slept during the entire voyage to Skaarsland, and she led him inside and closed the door behind them.

"Do not try to pin me down like that ever again," she said softly when they were inside.

"I apologize," he said at once, aware by now of his misstep. "I shouldn't have done that."

She studied his face intently, almost as if trying to find or understand something that was hidden. He stood quietly in front of her, the smokeless lamp at the doorway providing the only light available, playing off her exquisite features as her eyes locked on his.

"My concern is for your safety," he said finally. "Do you not know me well enough by now to see this?"

She smiled suddenly, warm and promising as she stepped close. "I think I will need the rest of my life to know you as well as I want to," she whispered. Then she squeezed his hand and pulled on it gently. "Come to bed."

# TWENTY-THREE

AJIN D'AMPHERE ROSE BEFORE the sky was light and dressed in the darkness of her cabin. She was careful to make no sound, so as not to awaken Dar. She had already determined that she was going into the city alone. He had told her he wanted to accompany her the previous night, and she understood why he felt compelled to offer his protection. Dar meant well, and she knew that he loved her by now—as much as she loved him—but Ajin was still her own person and quite able to handle whatever came her way. And she had no interest in being watched over—not even by him.

So even though she had known how right they would be together and how much she wanted him at her side for the rest of her life, she also knew she needed to maintain her independence. She had relied on herself for too long, careful to keep a measured distance from everyone else—her various lovers, comrades, and friends included. Loving someone meant giving them their independence to whatever degree they required it. She didn't think Dar understood that yet, but she hadn't survived her harsh life as the daughter of a man who had cast both his wife and her aside by clinging to others for help. She had made her own way in the world, and she intended to keep doing so.

By loving Dar as much as she did and letting him know it, she had given up more than she had before. She had let him get closer than anyone save her mother, but she could only go so far before she had to draw a line. So she was drawing that line here. Going to her mother was something she would do alone.

The fire in the little stove had been reduced to ashes, and the cabin was very cold. Once dressed, she grabbed her weapons and a backpack of supplies she had gathered up the night before, and went out the door silently. She did so without making even the slightest sound. She left her boots off until she was outside and well down the hallway. Once at the steps leading up to the hatchway, she slipped the boots on and went topside.

It was snowing again. She watched the heavy flakes fall in a broad curtain of white, breathing in the crisp night air. The sky was overcast, and there was no sign of moon or stars. Ambient light from the distant city and a quartet of muted watch fires fore and aft on the *Behemoth*'s decking provided enough light to let her see where she was going. She moved over to the watch and told him she was leaving for the city, should anyone ask, but would be back in a day or so. And would he be willing to convey her to shore in one of the flits so she could begin her journey?

He agreed, of course. She knew how to ask, and she knew how he would respond. She knew how she affected men. She was Ajin d'Amphere, after all, and she was seldom denied anything she wanted.

She told the Rover sentry that no one was to follow her, but she was thinking primarily of Dar Leah. He would be irritated, but he would come to understand. She would walk the ten miles to where the city was nestled on a bluff along the riverbanks and go in from there. She would find her mother and then decide what else needed doing.

She boarded the flit with the sentry sitting at the controls, and they lifted away from the transport and turned toward the distant shoreline. The waters on which the *Behemoth* rested were black and depthless. White snowflakes tumbled out of the sky, landed on their surface, and disappeared. Of wind, there wasn't a trace, but the air was still and bitter where it touched the skin of her face. She wore her heavy winter coat and gloves, but she was cold nevertheless. That would change once she started walking; her body heat would protect her. The ten miles would pass quickly enough, and she knew the journey would be easy. She was used to walking. She had marched the length and breadth of countless countries in Eurodia.

Memories of childhood came back to her, and for a moment she thought she might cry. But the moment passed and her eyes stayed dry. It took a lot to make her cry these days, and it had for a long time now. She thought about the child she had been and the woman she was, and found herself astonished to think how far she had come in her short life. But how you grew and what you became were not always choices you had control over. They were as much the result of fate and chance as they were of free choice, because all too frequently you had to adapt to what life threw at you.

When the flit landed, she thanked the sentry and started walking into the trees. She did not turn to watch as the flit lifted off for the return flight, her thoughts of what she intended already racing ahead of her. It had seemed the matter was settled. She would find her mother, prepare her for leaving the city, then kill the *pretender*. That she could accomplish both was not something she had questioned, but now she was wondering if the latter was needed. As much as she despised her father's new wife and queen, she no longer felt a white-hot urge to destroy her. In part, it was because she was in love with Dar and saw a future for herself that she had never seen before. In part, it was because she simply no longer cared about the woman. Her father had made the choice to cast off her mother and herself in favor of this scheming, ambitious witch, so maybe he should be left to live with the consequences.

As she walked, the sun rose above the horizon—an invisible presence behind the heavy blanket of clouds covering the sky—lightening the darkness and giving the new day a brighter cast. She tromped through snow that was only a foot deep and feather-light—a recent covering that offered little resistance to her passage. Her breath plumed the air before her as she exhaled, and she felt her body heat expanding beneath the heavy coat. She studied the familiar landscape; she had passed this way hundreds of times before. The trees surrounding her were coated with a mix of ice and moisture, and they had the look of soldiers after a long march and a battle. Everything was dying in this country, she thought suddenly. The world she had known as a child was gone, and what was left was going to disappear if nothing changed.

She wondered if there was any chance for rebirth. After years of this endless winter, *could* other seasons come again to Skaarsland? Would that machine the old man created be able to reverse the effects of this bitter cold and bring back new life to her homeland? Or was it all wishful thinking—a desperate but doomed attempt at recovering what was already irretrievably lost?

She wished she had the answer. She wished she had something positive to tell her mother, something hopeful to offer. But all she had was the knowledge of her own sad condition—of her fall from grace and her dismissal, of her forced return and her determination to save them both from the *pretender*. She had Dar Leah now and she could speak to her mother of him, but she didn't know that she should. Dar was not who her mother would have wished for her. Had circumstances been different, he was not who Ajin would have been looking for, either. But life gave you what it chose—a random and often unexpected series of selections that sometimes turned out to be better than what you would have chosen for yourself.

For her, this was Darcon Leah.

Still, look at what she had been reduced to. She was a princess in name only. She was a soldier without an army. She was the daughter of a king who only wanted to use her for his own purposes. She had been cast adrift. The future she had envisioned had been stolen.

All she had were her determination and her courage, and they would have to be enough to see her through.

She reached the edge of her home city by mid-morning, its snowcapped parapets and towers stark against the gray sky. Once so beautiful, it had become a shadow of its former self. Smoke rose from chimneys and watch fires, and sentries patrolled the walls, but the silence was unnerving. So many of its people were dead or dying. There was so little joy or hope remaining. The lack of laughter or raised voices was distressing. She remembered when it had been otherwise, but ten years of winter—fostering sickness and hunger, loss and despair—had sapped it all away.

The strongest among them had gone west with her father to find a new homeland. Those who remained did so because there was nowhere else for them to go. All of Eurodia suffered the fate of Skaarsland, and no place within its considerable collection of countries and cities offered an escape from the cold. Any hope of a better life waited in the Four Lands, and it was there that those who remained of her people would eventually have to travel.

She shifted her thoughts away from memories and speculation and refocused on what she had come to do.

She would not pass through the main gates; she did not want to announce her coming just yet. She would enter another way and slip unnoticed through the streets until she reached her home and her mother. After they were reunited, she would decide what to do next.

First, of course, she had to figure out how to get

inside the city walls. She approached from the west, choosing to avoid the main gates in the south wall. There was little trade these days, so not all the gates were opened. But there were refugees from all over the island, and more arrived every day as food and clothing ran out and shelters succumbed to the wintry cold. She should be able to find a way in with them, if she was quick enough.

She made her way to the edge of the trees and stood waiting for the better part of an hour for the arrival of a band of refugees. When one finally appeared, it came from the north and looked to have made a long journey. Those on foot were all but staggering. Flatbeds that had seen better days were piled high with furniture, small children, and old men and women. The wagons rumbled along unevenly, wheels creaking, pulled by oxen. She waited until they were at the gates, where they offered various forms of identification or, in some instances, simply gave their names and hometowns. The process moved along quickly, the sentries no longer turning away anyone who looked as if they needed help.

By the time the procession was starting to pass through the gates, Ajin had already pulled up her hood and wrapped her coat tightly about her. As a final touch, she reached down for a handful of loose soil and rubbed it on her face and hands. No one was likely to recognize her now, and she joined the crowd of refugees all but unnoticed. She moved to the back of the line, sidling into their midst, and stayed close until she was safely inside. Then she peeled off to one side and ducked into the shadows.

Traversing the city was second nature for her by now, but it still required effort to avoid discovery. She had to work hard at finding ways to stay hidden. It pained her to have to do so—to have to hide from her own people—but she did not know whom she could trust.

She stood where she was then, thinking about how to go on. She knew how to reach her destination, but she didn't want to make a mistake by being overconfident. To reach her mother's home, she would have to work harder than she ever had at not being seen by anyone who was in league with the *pretender.*

The snow was falling again, more heavily now than before, and the skies were darkening, building up new cloudbanks that were heavy with moisture. She had to get moving. She was cold and tired, and she wanted to see to her mother.

She glanced around, but no one was paying any attention to her, though sentries stood at the gates and patrolled the streets. Before she had departed for the Four Lands, there was already a marked increase in break-ins, looting, and any sort of thuggery you could imagine, and now it appeared that nothing had changed. That would explain the increased presence of soldiers and the hunched and beaten look of the people who passed by.

But much worse was evident. Beggars were everywhere, huddled in corners of buildings and doorways, wrapped in blankets in narrow alleyways, and, if drunk or ill, staggering through the main thoroughfares in search of anything that would relieve their suffering. Children, too. Abandoned, lost, cast off, or runaway; there were dozens to be seen.

She couldn't wait any longer; she had waited too long already. Someone would approach her if she kept standing there.

Taking a deep, steadying breath, she began walking along the building walls, keeping to one side and staying out of the center of the road. When she reached the street she was looking for, she followed it to its far end before shifting to a less busy road to continue in the same direction. Several times beggars approached her, and each time she made a sharp, dismissive gesture. Her heavy coat and the shadowed look of her face within the hood projected the look of someone you did not want to challenge.

Her journey took her no more than thirty minutes, and then she was standing across the roadway from her mother's home. It was situated among a grouping of six, bracketing a narrow lane that dead-ended at the south city wall. These were homes provided by the crown for those personages who had fallen from favor but did not warrant exile. The homes were small but well kept. Their windows revealed interiors that were mostly dark—either because their residents were gone or because it was only midday.

She stared at the third cottage on the left—her mother's home.

Boards were nailed crosswise over the doors and windows. Warning signs suggested that trying to get inside would be a mistake. The building had an unmistakably empty look.

Every fear she had harbored about her mother's

safety surged to the fore, followed by a wash of white-hot rage. Her father had been so sure the *pretender* would never harm her mother, so delusional about the witch he thought would not dare to cross him. Although, given what had happened with Ajin's messages and the *pretender*'s interference, shouldn't he be thinking differently by now?

She beat back her anger and fear and tried to think what to do. Her mother had been looked after by the daughter of a couple that lived next door. She had volunteered to do so, and her parents had acquiesced. Ajin's father had agreed to pay the cost—one of the few times he showed any concern for her mother's welfare. There were lights on in the house, and no one about. It seemed safe enough that Ajin decided she had to chance it. But still she hesitated. Anyone could be watching from hiding, so it would be better to err on the side of caution. She would wait until dark to go to the neighbor's door. By then, no one would be paying much attention to a visitor.

She found shelter in the doorway of a building that was closed and waited impatiently for nightfall. When it arrived with sufficient darkness to mask her approach, she crossed the road to the cottage and knocked on the door. Kle'Ebin, the daughter who had cared for the former queen, answered. She gasped when she saw who was standing before her and took a step back.

"May I come in?" Ajin asked and, without waiting for an answer, moved inside, closing the door behind her.

"Doesn't make sense for me to stand around in the

open just now," she said, quickly scanning the interior. She walked into the kitchen, looking about. No one appeared to be there. Quickly, she washed the dirt off her hands and face. Another look as she turned. She heard no one moving about. It was just the girl. "Where is my mother?" she asked.

Kle'Ebin walked in from the living room, shaking her head. "I don't know. They took her two weeks ago, and she hasn't come back."

Ajin managed to stay calm. "Who took her?"

"Palace guards. Six of them." The girl was rooted in place, but her hands were shaking. "They just marched in, and when they came out again your mother was with them." She paused, her blue eyes bright with sudden tears. "I wanted to stop them. I wanted to ask what they were doing. But I was afraid."

"As you should have been. So, they took her and she hasn't come back?"

The girl nodded. "Some workmen came and boarded up the house a day or so later. They made it look abandoned, put up warning signs, made it clear no one was to go inside. And no one has. Not even me. And some of my clothes are in there."

"There have been no rumors about my mother?"

"None. What are you going to do?"

Ajin was already turning away, moving back toward the door. "Find her and bring her home."

She went out the door, closing it softly behind her. Kle'Ebin was terrified, but Ajin was pretty sure she was telling the truth. So the *pretender* had decided to keep her mother where she could do nothing to help Ajin or herself. Her mother would be a prisoner somewhere in the palace cellars, where the royals had locked away enemies and left them to rot since the beginning of the dynasty.

She felt sickened.

And she needed somewhere to go.

A glance across the road gave her the answer to the problem. Where was the last place anyone would look for her? In her mother's house, all boarded up and posted. She looked around and saw no one in the lane, so she moved over to the abandoned building and walked around to the backside. She found the rear entry boarded up, as well, but she had the barriers clear and the door open in less than five minutes.

It was cold inside, but the bed was still made and there were plenty of blankets in storage. She felt drained by the physical and emotional stresses of the day and craved sleep. She did not bother with washing up or eating. She did not bother to take off her clothes. She simply fell on the bed, pulled up the blankets to her chin, and fell asleep knowing she would be safe until morning.

She was wrong.

The beasts came for her sometime during the night, creeping through the house on soundless paws, crouching down in the manner of the wolves they so closely resembled. There were only four of them, but they were huge creatures—monsters born of some errant nightmare, mutations of man and beast. They slipped into her room and surrounded her, and it was only at the very last minute she sensed their presence and reached for her knives.

Too late.

They were on top of her before she could free her weapons, pinning her down and wrapping her tightly in the blanket, their hot animal breath on her face, growling and snarling. She saw them for a few seconds, flashes of fur and teeth and gimlet eyes, wolves save for their human arms and hands, with some mix of both species in their nightmare faces. Jaws snapped and teeth flashed, but they did not rend her, as she feared they might. After all, they had her pinned and did not need to do much more to secure her.

She fought back valiantly, driven by her anger and her fear, but it was no use. They were too strong and too many—even at only four—and she could find no way to break free.

So here was Ajin—who was always so prepared, so ready, so difficult to catch off guard—made a prisoner in less than a minute.

Still she fought as they lifted her up and wrapped ropes about her body. She fought, and then she screamed for help—a last desperate cry when she realized all was lost.

But a blow to the head silenced her, and she tumbled into a black nothingness.

# TWENTY-FOUR

---

"Ajin."

Her mother. She heard her voice as a whisper, reaching out to her from far away. In a dream, perhaps. But Ajin was locked in a black cocoon, and she did not think she could escape. She stirred within the darkness, but her limbs and body were limp and unresponsive. She thought she might be imagining her mother, but she wasn't sure. Her thoughts were sluggish and clouded. All her efforts at trying to regain some semblance of control were failing.

"Ajin, please."

She sighed; the sound of her mother's voice, speaking her name, was so wonderfully reassuring. But no, it couldn't be her mother. Her mother had been taken by the *pretender*'s soldiers and spirited away. This was no more than a dream, albeit a pleasant one.

Nevertheless, whether from need or out of habit, she answered. "Mama?"

Arms encircled her, and she was being lifted and cradled like her mother had cradled her as a child.

Her eyes opened slowly and she saw the arms holding her close and felt the press of a cheek against her own. She did not need to see the face of the person holding her to know who it was. Her familiarity after a lifetime of such embraces was undeniable, and she gave herself over to the comfort it offered. "Mama, you're safe!" she whispered.

Her mother's arms squeezed more tightly. "Oh, Ajin, why did you come back?"

Ajin shifted so she could see her mother's face. The older woman looked worn—haggard and pale—but her expression was calm. Ajin remembered the misfortune that had befallen her—the midnight attack by those wolf hybrids who had wrapped her in blankets and secured her with rope, and silenced her with a single blow when she had tried to cry out.

All of which brought her fully into the moment—which wasn't a dream at all, but a reality she had not expected. To be with her mother, even under the worst of circumstances, brought a momentary smile to her face. "Mama," she repeated. She took a steadying breath and exhaled sharply. "Mama, how long have you been here? Where are we? Are we in the palace cellars?"

Orestiana d'Amphere shook her head. "We are not in the palace. We are somewhere else, but I don't know where. This place, wherever it is, belongs to Agathien d'Amphere, your father's new wife. She is responsible for bringing me here, because she was afraid I would be seen and rescued by those still loyal to me if I was caged in the cellars of the palace. So here I am. But you—how did you end up here?"

"I was looking for you. Kle'Ebin told me you'd been

taken prisoner. Word of my return must have gotten back to the *pretender*, I suppose, so I was taken, too."

Her mother shook her head. "She has grown bold in your father's absence. She consolidates her power, keeping those who pledge their loyalty close while removing everyone else. Your father doesn't understand, but I think she intends to replace him on the throne. Replace us, too, now that she has imprisoned us. I do not think she intends to keep us here for more than a couple of days. After that, she will probably have us executed."

"Publicly? But everyone will know."

"I think she wants them to know. I think she wants to demonstrate her power."

"It won't work. Word will reach my father, and she'll lose everything."

"If he lives that long. But I think she has other plans."

Ajin stared in shock. "She must be insane! How does she expect to make all this happen? People won't stand for it."

Orestiana d'Amphere smiled. "I am afraid they will stand for more than you think, given their present situation. Starving, homeless, hopeless people are willing to listen to many things they would not consider in better times. They are willing to listen to lies—and to believe them. And Agathien is good at spreading lies."

Ajin straightened and stood, testing herself. Everything seemed to be in one piece. She patted her clothing—the same clothing she had worn on leaving the airship—searching for weapons. But even the throwing stars she had concealed were gone. She did not have a blade of any sort.

She glanced around. The chamber in which they were housed was a large, spare, stone-block cube, windowless and layered in shadows. A single torch burned inside their cell, but that was the extent of the light. The cell sat in the middle of the floor, unconnected to any of the walls of the cube. An excellent way, Ajin thought, to keep them under easy surveillance at all times. There would have to be a door leading out of the chamber, one they could use to escape were they in a position to go anywhere, but she could not detect it in the poor light.

"We're getting out of here," she announced anyway as she stalked toward the cell door.

Immediately there was a stirring in the shadows and a handful of the wolf creatures padded into view, fangs bared.

Ajin stopped where she was, and then backed away from the bars of the cage. "What are those things?" she asked.

Orestiana came to stand beside her. "I'm not sure. Agathien seems inordinately proud of them; she talks about them as her 'work.' Like she might have made them."

"How do you breed men with wolves?" Ajin shook her head in dismay. "I should have killed her long ago."

Her mother put her hand on Ajin's shoulder and squeezed. "What you should have done was stay with your father in the Four Lands."

Still watching the wolf-men as they retreated back into the shadows, Ajin permitted herself a quiet snort.

"My father sent me home. He claimed I had over-stepped my authority, and he punished me by sending me back."

"And you came?"

"It wasn't as if I was given a choice."

"You could have refused. You could have insisted! I know your father. He would have come around."

Ajin looked at her. "He didn't come around for you, did he? Once he found the *pretender*?" She stalked back over to the bed and sat down again. "He doesn't much care about either of us. He thinks we don't matter anymore. I did so much for him, and this is the way he repays me."

Her mother sat down beside her. "Tell me everything, Ajin. Everything that's happened."

So Ajin did, starting with her arrival in the Four Lands with the advance force and ending with her return home two days past. "I don't know about this machine the old man made, this weather-changing device, but some of those who accompanied me seem to think it can work. They are going to test it sometime in the next few days. Imagine what it would mean for the Skaar people if it did work!"

Her mother gave her a bleak look. "We've had hopes before, Ajin, but they all came to nothing. This winter is here to stay—and it will be the end of us if we do not find a new home. Your father is right about that."

"But the old man and his Rover friend have tested this device. Rocan told me. He watched Tindall use it to create a thunderstorm that put an end to a drought. Maybe it can end this winter, too, and change the weather back to how it was." Then she shook her head. "But that won't help *us*. By the time it happens—if it happens at all—we'll be dead and gone. We need to find a way out of here and get back to the ship. I have to think of something!"

But she despaired of being able to do so. They were in a situation where escape looked to be all but impossible, and time was running out. The *pretender* would not wait long before dispatching them. Ajin was somewhat surprised that her mother hadn't been killed already. It suggested that Agathien had plans for something very unpleasant.

They talked in hushed voices for a time, comforting and reassuring each other. And all the while, Ajin kept trying to think of a way to escape. She wondered if Dar might come once he realized where she had gone; he was headstrong and determined enough. The thought warmed her—but then he might end up imprisoned, too. She regretted now she had been so quick to leave him behind in the first place. Had he been with her—had there been two of them—she might not be in this situation.

But would she have ever found her mother? Would she have been able to find this cell, wherever it lay? It made her furious to think of the immense unfairness of the conundrum. What sort of choice was that to make, finding her mother by being locked away with her or staying free and losing her mother forever? Life was so cruel sometimes.

She was sharing her memories of coming to the Four Lands, her hopes of finding a new home, one still fresh and unspoiled, when a door at the far side of the room opened and a solitary figure stepped through. When the door closed again, the darkness returned and the figure disappeared, but Ajin could hear footsteps approaching.

Abruptly the *pretender* appeared, materializing out of the gloom, a pair of wolf-men moving to flank her. Ajin came to her feet, facing her enemy directly, daring her to come closer. Daring her, but helpless to make it happen.

Agathien d'Amphere was not what anyone would expect of a Skaar queen. She was not regal or threatening. She was not a forbidding presence in any way. She was small and slight and rather plain. So why her father had chosen this woman was a mystery that Ajin had never been able to solve. But it didn't matter; the deed was done. The *pretender* had seduced Cor d'Amphere, persuading him to cast aside his wife and former queen and take her instead as his new partner on the throne. She had changed Ajin's world in every way possible, and none of it had been for the better.

Now she stood there, looking smug and rather excited.

Ajin was too impatient and angry to wait on her. "Why are we still alive?" she demanded.

The *pretender* feigned shock. "Oh, my! How brutal you sound. How brutal you make *me* sound. Do you really think I would kill you and your mother while my husband is away and unable to prevent it? Wouldn't he be awfully angry when he came home and found out what I had done?"

"A charge of treason, a quick trial, and a public execution? You could have it over and done with and there would be nothing for him to do but accept it or cast you out. And he wouldn't do the latter, would he?"

"I'm not sure. I don't think I would want to chance it, though." The *pretender* thought about it a moment, then brightened. "Do you have any other ideas? This is getting interesting."

Ajin took her measure. "How about you just make us disappear, claim we ran off to find a better life? What could he do then? It would not be your fault if we left. He might search for us, but he would never find us. Not if you handled things correctly."

Agathien's smile was quick and dark. "I like that better, but I'm still not sure it would be satisfying enough. You've caused me considerable trouble, Ajin. You've cast doubt on me that my husband will not soon forget or easily dismiss. I think we need something more fitting for such despicable behavior."

She took a few steps closer, still keeping well out of arm's reach from Ajin and the confining bars of the cage. "You should have stayed in the Four Lands, Princess. Maybe you would have found a new life over there instead of coming home to end your present one. Foolish girl. Such a brave warrior—your father's pride and joy in spite of my efforts to discredit you— but so clueless about power."

Ajin knew when she was being baited and said nothing. Her mother was still sitting on the bed behind her, silent as well. Both were waiting to see how this was going to play out.

"We could make this easy," the queen said suddenly, looking as if she had suddenly been inspired. "I could give you poison, and you could drink it. Everything would be solved in a matter of minutes. Dead by your own hand, my place at my husband's side made secure, and all the loose ends tied up—what could be better?"

"I don't think either of us intends to make this easy for you," Orestiana said quietly, and Ajin smiled to herself.

"No, I didn't think you would." Agathien sighed deeply. "Nor do I think it would be satisfying enough for me. I want something more. I think maybe what I want most is to keep you both around. You might prove entertaining for those boring dark days when everything seems just a little too familiar. Doesn't that sound better?"

"Oh, keep us caged like dangerous pets you can visit every now and then?" Ajin snapped at her. "Please do. Sooner or later, caged animals find a way out."

Agathien looked perplexed. "Oh, no, I wouldn't want to keep you caged. That wouldn't be any fun. I want you to be free, but I would prefer you tame, too." She looked left and then right at the wolf-men who warded her. "Like they are."

Ajin made her lip curl. "My mother thinks you made these things."

The queen's smile was dazzling. "I did! Aren't they wonderful? I learned the skill from a witch in Arvania some years back, when I was studying necromancy and potions and mind control. Before I made my way here to claim your father's affections. That witch was a genius, full of all sorts of interesting ideas. She envisioned creating a whole new race of beings! I was her helper and student, and I was fascinated by her skill and foresight, eager to learn everything she knew. Eventually I did—all of it! Then I killed her. I mean, I couldn't let her stay around experimenting while I was carrying out my plans for becoming a queen. Besides, she was old and rather unstable, and I think maybe she was planning to kill *me*. But she was a little too slow."

"I would be quicker," Ajin said quietly.

The *pretender* shrugged. "Probably. If you were given the chance—which you won't be."

She sounded so pleased with herself that Ajin would have ripped down the bars and torn out her throat if she'd been stronger. With considerable effort, she forced herself to remain calm. "So you made these creatures to serve you. Does my father know?"

"Of course not! After all, one day I might decide to change him, too. It will be good practice for me to see how the formula works on the two of you first—a good indicator for how successfully it might work on him later."

"So you keep these things here?" Ajin's mother asked. "Do they live here?"

"Well, I can't have them staying in the palace or anywhere else they might be seen. But I let them go out at night to play. I have a few minders who keep them under control. The wolf-men are very loyal to me, but they do need to eat. So at night I let them hunt. A few go out and bring food back to the others. It's rather messy afterward, but their minders clean up." She paused. "Maybe you would like to know what they eat?"

Neither mother nor daughter spoke, but the *pre-*

*tender* carried on anyway. "Of course you would! How could you not? Well, my wolf-men are not so particular about what they eat, so long as it involves meat. They don't just *crave* meat; they *need* it, in order to survive. Were they without it for a time, they would begin to eat one another, you see."

Ajin was shaking her head, but Agathien did not stop. "They find it in the streets. The homeless. Men and women, yes . . . but children, especially. So tender; so delicious. And there are so many of them these days."

Orestiana d'Amphere retched and broke into sobs. In that moment, Ajin hated the *pretender* more than she had ever imagined possible. "You are the real beast, Agathien! Not your wolf-men."

The queen nodded. "I suppose I am. But I don't apologize. I think I have to be what I am in order to survive. In any case, now you know what I have planned for *you*. It will be fun having you both become my creatures. I can visit you every day without fear because the drink will change you completely. You won't remember anything about the way you were. You will become one with the pack, but you will be tame and obedient when you are around me. And I will feel so happy having you serve me!"

She began backing away, still talking. "I will let you think things over for a day or two. Enjoy each other's company while you can, and picture what life will be like once you belong to me body and soul. I cannot think of a better way of making you disappear without actually having to kill you or send you away.

Think about what eating a child will be like; you will get used to it quicker than you think."

She was almost out of view again, lost in the shadows. "Goodbye!"

Ajin walked up to the bars of the cage and spat in the direction of the *pretender*. She drew back just in time to avoid the claws of a wolf-man who lunged at her out of the black, hairy arm reaching through the bars, claws raking the air in front of her.

"You should be grateful I do not choose to feed *you* to them," the *pretender* called back from the door as she opened it. "They eat their prey while it is still alive, you know. I have watched them do it."

Then the door closed and she was gone, leaving Ajin and her mother to suffer with the knowledge of what was to be done to them.

*I won't let it happen,* Ajin thought as rage and fear warred within her. But she had no idea how she was going to prevent it.

# TWENTY-FIVE

◆

IT WAS ONE OF those perfect days. A day when the sun shines brightly, but the heat is not extreme. A day when everyone you encounter is pleasant and cheerful, and there is an expectation of good things coming your way in the not-so-distant future.

"Won't be long now," Lakodan remarked to the big man sitting next to him.

"Not long at all," Battenhyle answered. "Happy to be going back to Crackenrood?"

"Always. It's home. It's where we belong."

"That's the truth of it, isn't it?"

The Dwarf chieftain looked about at the bustling Federation camp, taking in dozens of small tableaus that made it eminently clear what sort of activity was occurring. Here men were bundling up various types of weapons—both ancient and modern, blades and flash rips alike. They sorted, wrapped, and stacked each set of items diligently before transferring them to wooden crates. Over there, various food supplies, tent posts and canvas coverings, cooking implements, blankets and bedrolls were being organized in similar fashion. And farther out, on the camp perimeter, horses were being divided into groups—some to haul the wagons, some to carry supplies, and a special few to allow the commanders and junior officers to ride.

The latter of which the Dwarves did not understand. Officers, they believed, were supposed to be leaders, and leaders should walk with the men they were leading.

Still, it was none of their business. When this pack decamped, the Dwarves would not be going with them. Finally, after well over a month, they were parting company. It was something the Dwarves had been anticipating since Belladrin Rish and the Federation commanders had reached a truce agreement with the Skaar.

"How do you suppose she managed it?" Lakodan asked his friend. Of late, the question had been bothering him. "Miss Belladrin."

Battenhyle glanced at him. "Of which miracle are we speaking? She seems to have managed quite a few."

"The truce between the Skaar and the Federation. How could she have accomplished such a thing, a young woman like that? I would not have thought it possible."

His friend shrugged. "Say what you like about her age, but you cannot deny she is accomplished."

"I understand. We are proof of her prowess, are we not? Did she not persuade us to come to the aid of our greatest enemy?" Lakodan looked off into the distance. "Still, I would have thought it would be more difficult with the Skaar. Why would they even listen to her, let alone enter into an agreement with someone who is little more than a scribe?"

"In title, perhaps. But you know her to be capable of almost anything by now, so don't be looking a gift horse in the mouth. She managed it, and the how of it doesn't really matter." Battenhyle paused, frowning. "But she did fail to find a way to return our Reveals."

Lakodan nodded. "At least the Federation could have offered us a fair price, not simply confiscate them. She wasn't so good in arranging for that, was she? I was surprised, given her success in helping us when Ketter Vause sought to violate the conscription agreement."

"She said those idiot commanders overruled her. They still see her as inexperienced, even after all she has accomplished. She cannot be expected to change their minds on everything."

"I know, I know. They want those Reveals for protection back in Arishaig." Lakodan refused to be placated. "But here's another thing, Old Bear. You have to wonder why the army is still packing up to fly back to Arishaig when the orders to decamp arrived days ago."

It had been the talk of the camp since Commander Aarcobin had returned. In a mere week after he had carried the treaty to Arishaig for ratification, he had returned with word that it had been approved and with orders for the army to decamp. Lakodan had overheard Commander Oberion remarking that this was the fastest the Coalition Council had approved anything save a pay raise for themselves, and that it almost seemed too good to be true. And yet still the army lingered.

"Well, it's hard to move an army of this size from

one place to the other, even with transports. Just the act of packing up all this equipment and supplies is daunting. They should take a lesson from the Dwarves. Pack light, travel light, no delay." Battenhyle shrugged. "Anyway, as I said, it is not our concern. We still have our mobile Reveals, even if they did confiscate the platform models. We were smart enough to keep those hidden. So we won't be leaving empty-handed."

They were quiet after that, sitting companionably, lost in their own thoughts, looking out from their perch on the back of an open wagon bed at the bustle taking place around them. But something about the whole business made Lakodan uneasy.

"Such industrious little ants," Battenhyle observed finally, chuckling.

Lakodan's frown deepened. "Better if their common sense did the same amount of work now and then."

"There's truth to that," a voice rumbled. The wagon lurched as Choten Benz climbed aboard behind them, using the spokes of a wheel to lift himself up into the bed, where he settled into place, resting his back against one of the side walls. "I'm troubled by all of this."

Lakodan glanced back at him. "Unusual for you, isn't it?"

Benz nodded. "Indeed. But these past few weeks have involved more than a few unusual events, and I am beginning to think we need to get to the heart of them before we return to Arishaig for good."

"That would be before *you* return to Arishaig," Lakodan pointed out with a laugh. "Old Bear and I are off for home."

Benz shrugged. "Just for the sake of argument, let's examine this a bit. It will pass the time, and it might help settle my concerns. What say you?"

The Dwarves shrugged and passed him the aleskin they had been sharing. "We've been discussing it ourselves, and there are a few troubling matters," Lakodan agreed. "For instance, if this truce is ratified, why is it taking so long to pack up and leave? And don't give me any crap about logistics; it doesn't take this long to decamp. Even the Skaar are mostly all cleared out. Any number of their units have already vanished, off to wherever they've chosen to go under the terms of this truce."

"Ah." Benz smiled. "*Crap* is the right word. But I was thinking about something else. What if this supposed truce is just a charade?"

Lakodan and Battenhyle exchanged a knowing look. "You think the Skaar might be planning a bit of treachery?"

Choten Benz cocked his head. "Well, we know they are capable of it. Everything about this whole business seems wrong. Right from the time the Federation army arrived on the Mermidon through the sneak attack, the assassination of Vause, and now this reliance on a truce almost no one has seen. So I'm asking myself. Who was there when the terms of the truce were arrived at?" He paused, giving them time to think. "A handful of Federation commanders, myself, and Belladrin Rish. But who actually spoke to the Skaar king to arrange the terms?"

Battenhyle and Lakodan exchanged a confused glance.

"Then I asked myself another question," the mercenary continued, as if not noticing the look. "Who was there when Vause was assassinated? Who intercepted the assassin and killed him?"

Battenhyle stiffened. "Wait a minute!" His bluff features had darkened. "What are you suggesting?"

"And who now finds herself substantially in charge of all the arrangements surrounding the army's departure for Arishaig? Who speaks for Ketter Vause and the wishes he seems to have voiced only to her regarding the terms of the truce and the efforts needed to secure it? Who makes all the suggestions about how to proceed? Belladrin Rish. How odd that she should find herself in a position of such power."

Battenhyle shook his head in disbelief. "I don't like what you are implying, Benz," he growled. "Miss Belladrin has done nothing but help the Dwarves since she talked us into coming here—even when it would have been easier to throw us to the wolves. Have you forgotten that she was the one to suggest we be placed in charge of the Reveals when the Skaar attacked us from the south and Vause was off chasing his tail? And now you think she might betray the Federation army? After all that's happened? After all she's gone through to keep us safe? For what reason? What does she have to gain?"

The other man shook his head. "We're just talking, Battenhyle. I am trying to reason this through because it bothers me. Can we do this, or must I seek help elsewhere?"

Lakodan shook his head. "Let him finish. I want to hear the rest. There is more, isn't there?"

Choten Benz nodded. "She was the one who spoke with the Skaar king—the only one. She claims she was able to set the truce in place because only she knew what Ketter Vause intended. So, in essence, we have only her word about that.

"Wait," he continued, holding up a hand to stop Battenhyle from interrupting. "Let me finish. She wasn't the one who suggested we use the Dwarves and the Reveals to save the army when the Skaar attacked the camp; that was me. She came to get you because I suggested it, and she knew the soldiers around her saw the value of doing so. And there's something else—something about the way Vause was killed. There were a dozen men guarding him that night, but not one saw this disgruntled soldier sneak into his tent. Not one! Nor does it appear they would have stopped him from escaping. It was Belladrin Rish who managed that trick."

He paused. "So I ask myself, who can get inside such heavily guarded quarters without being seen? Druids, I think. And Skaar. So this was no disgruntled soldier, no matter what anyone says. It was either that witch who tried to kill him once already, or a Skaar assassin. Now, if it was the latter—because the body was male and so could not have been the witch—how is it that Belladrin managed to kill him? How did she even manage to *see* him, when no one else did? And how does a young woman who is not familiar with weapons manage to kill him with a single knife thrust straight to the heart? Killing a man takes practice and experience—and I should know."

Battenhyle and Lakodan were silent, staring at him. "Are you suggesting *she* might be working with the Skaar?" the latter asked quietly.

"There is another possibility, one that seems more reasonable to me," Benz answered. "She might be one of them."

"That's nonsense!" Battenhyle made a dismissive gesture. "Ketter Vause must have investigated her when he took her on—and look at the responsibility he's given her! No, these are wild speculations, Benz. And it is entirely possible that striking down the assassin was due to nothing more than determination and luck. Who says the assassin remained invisible when he finished killing Vause and turned to leave? He could have revealed himself to her then. He could even have made a noise that brought her awake."

Lakodan shook his head. "I don't know. Benz might have a point. I don't like thinking of her as an enemy, but I find myself wondering."

"There's one thing more." Choten Benz leaned forward. "After Vause's assassination, I was summoned by Miss Rish and asked if I would stand with her when the Federation commanders confronted her. By itself, that was understandable; she was looking for an ally. But she was also very direct in suggesting it would be in my best interests to do so. When I suggested she was overly ambitious and playing her own game, she did not deny it."

Battenhyle was still shaking his head. "I still cannot bring myself to believe any of this is true. It just doesn't seem possible, given what we know about her. Given what we've seen of her conduct."

"If she is a Skaar spy, there is every reason to think we are still in danger of being attacked, perhaps somewhere during the journey home," Lakodan said to Choten Benz. "You might want to warn your fellow commanders."

"They are not my fellows," Benz growled dismissively. "I just happen to have been given a rank equal to theirs. A warning might be wise, but I think I have to confront Belladrin Rish first. I need to make sure of this. Then, if I still have doubts, I can speak with the other commanders."

He shook his head, rising to his feet and stretching before taking a last swig from the aleskin and handing it back to Battenhyle. "It's getting so you can't trust anyone around here."

Then he hopped down off the wagon and walked away.

It was nearing nightfall on the same day, the work crews giving up their labors to eat and sleep, but most indulging in a drink or two first. Belladrin Rish was at work at the Prime Minister's desk in order to prepare for their departure two days hence.

Each notation recorded which percentage of each unit would be flying home aboard the transports and which would travel afoot when it came time to depart. Some soldiers would be left behind to keep watch on what Skaar forces remained, still encamped on the other side of the Mermidon, but only a few. Most of the equipment, siege machines, flash rip cannons, and

Reveals that had been used against the Skaar would travel back aboard the transports. Only yesterday, she had broken the word to the Dwarves that their Reveals were to be confiscated.

She had been able to secure a written guarantee that the villagers of Crackenrood were to be awarded a fifty-year exemption from any further Federation conscription, but that had not been secured without argument. The agreement made by Ketter Vause, as Federation Prime Minister, and Battenhyle, as village headman, had been written down, she had pointed out to a bevy of reluctant commanders, and it was necessary they honor it. But perhaps, she had added quite deliberately, the Federation might keep the larger Reveals as a precaution against unexpected attacks. One never knew about the Skaar, after all. She was hoping, when she confronted Lakodan and Battenhyle, that they would be persuaded to accept the bargain and allow the Federation to keep the machines they already had in their possession as a preventive defense against the possibility of Skaar treachery. It was the sort of trade-off they would be quick to understand and agree to, and the ploy had worked. She had told them that she had objected on their behalf but been overruled. She was, after all, a young woman with no real standing in the hierarchy of the Federation army.

But she still hated lying to them.

And she hated having to organize the next part of Cor d'Amphere's plan even more. Much of what she had to do in preparation for the Skaar attack was already done, but the necessity of it bothered her.

Everything would have been simpler if Clizia Porse

hadn't insisted on trying to kill Tarsha Kaynin. Not only had she failed, but she had clearly sustained significant enough damage to prevent her from carrying out her promise to eliminate Cor d'Amphere. Belladrin knew this because there had been no word from either the Skaar or the Federation camps about the king's death—and there most certainly would have been if he were gone.

The struggle between the girl and the witch had been terrible. No one had borne witness to exactly what they had tried to do to each other, although Belladrin knew enough of each to deduce that massive amounts of magic had been employed. The tent in which Tarsha had been sleeping had been totally destroyed, and any number of nearby tents had been severely damaged. The guards she had placed on Tarsha had fled for their lives, and fire had consumed everything that remained.

That Tarsha was even still alive following her battle with Clizia was something of a miracle. For five days, the girl lay comatose and unresponsive in the Healer's tent, in spite of the best efforts of the Federation Healers to revive her. Her surface wounds and burns had been treated easily enough—though they were extensive—but there was interior damage they could discern but do nothing about. Rest and her own strong constitution would have to find a way to bring her back to herself—if such a way existed. And yet, incredibly, it seemed that it had.

Then, four days ago—while Belladrin was still waiting for word of the ratified treaty to come back from Arishaig—Tarsha had woken from her coma, and from there had recovered with such startling speed that she had left the Federation camp two days later, slipping quietly out in the night—perhaps worried that Clizia might return for her. And in the general jubilation over news of the ratified treaty and the army's imminent departure, which had preceded Tarsha's departure by mere hours, no one had seen her go. But if Clizia had similarly recovered and returned—keeping up her bargain with Belladrin in the process—then Belladrin had heard no such word. Cor d'Amphere, it seemed, was still alive. And her essential problem remained.

So now, amid everything else, she was making a last check on how she would execute her own departure. Secretly, she was planning to leave before Cor d'Amphere's plans to wipe out the entire advance force could come to fruition. That was not an event she had any desire to witness in person.

Her uncertainly about this matter was distracting her from her other work when, without warning, the tent flaps to her office parted and Choten Benz walked through. She turned to greet him, noting that his approach was both intense and determined. Whatever had brought him here, he had already decided on the result he was looking to achieve.

"Commander Benz," she greeted him, with a small bow of deference.

"Belladrin," he acknowledged, with no bow or attempt at courtesy. His greeting was brusque and direct. "We need to speak."

She motioned to a nearby chair and did not bother

to rise. This was to be a confrontation, and not a pleasant one.

Benz sat and immediately began speaking. "When I committed myself to supporting you and your efforts, I said I would do so as long as I did not discover you were lying to me. But now I believe you have been. So I am here to ask you a few questions, and you must answer them."

So here it was, she thought. He had decided she was something more than what she had presented herself to be. He might have even deduced who and what she really was. She was stunned and more than a little afraid, but there was nothing she could do but weather whatever storm he was about to create.

"Please ask me anything you wish," she told him, managing to keep her voice steady. "I will do my best to answer."

"Very well. I don't think you've been completely honest with me about everything that's happened with the Skaar, including how Ketter Vause died, so let's start with that. According to your story, the assassin got into the Prime Minister's private tent without anyone noticing—not even one of a dozen guards. Only you. Then you intercepted him—a trained soldier supposedly—and killed him with a single stroke. Yet no one can manage such a feat who hasn't been trained extensively in the use of blades."

He stopped, waiting on her. She gave him a puzzled look. "I was awake when he entered. He was not invisible, which I think is what you are suggesting. He was right there across from me. I was terrified. I watched him go into the Prime Minister's sleeping chamber.

Then I pulled myself together and went to stand just outside. I couldn't make myself move any further or do anything but wait. I couldn't even manage to call for help. I am ashamed of myself, but that was how frightened I was."

She paused, taking his measure. He was still listening and did not appear to have made any further judgments either way. "When he came back out, I reacted without thinking. An uncle I was close to served in the Federation army at one point, and he was an expert with knives. He taught me everything he knew." This was not true; her training had come at Skaar hands, but there was no easy way to disprove this version of things. "So I fell back on my training, and I plunged the knife I was carrying right into him as he passed me. He died instantly. And then I called for help. Are you satisfied?"

He wasn't, and she knew before asking that he wouldn't be. If he had doubts about that, he would have doubts about much more. So she let him ask his questions and pose his concerns, and she answered them one after another with explanations she had long since prepared, in case something like this happened. To be a Penetrator in the Skaar army was to be always ready to defend yourself, whether with words or weapons. She took her time with each suspicion, responding to it in her calmest voice, giving it the space it needed without ever sounding trapped or worried.

*It was just as I am explaining it,* her tone of voice indicated. *What you are hearing provides a believable, reliable answer to all your questions. Why would you ever doubt me? Think it through, and you will con-*

*clude that I am being honest and forthright on every level.*

But this was Choten Benz, who had spent a lifetime never trusting anyone too far, and never wholly believing even the most convincing of explanations. So when he had no more questions to ask—and when she had answered every single one he had presented with a solid response—he was still doubtful. And that was going to be trouble, because he was not one to keep quiet about his suspicions. A quiet word in one ear or another, and the whole camp would be buzzing about it before long, and her effectiveness would be broken.

"So what more would you have me do?" she asked. "Shall I resign my post and go home? Should I remove myself from the camp so you can rest easy? I have no other solution for you. I am not what you suspect, but call the guards, if you wish. Tell them to place me in irons."

He shook his head. "I am not yet ready for that; I am still making up my mind. But at least we have talked and you have given me something to think about. And just so you know, Battenhyle and Lakodan know of my concerns and they are bothered by some of what has happened, too. I am not alone in having doubts about you."

The Dwarves. So he had poisoned them against her, too. She masked a surge of fury behind a flippant response. "I am sure there are others, as well. It is the lot of women to be doubted about their competence and truthfulness—especially here in the Federation army. I have learned to live with it, and I expect to go on doing so. You may talk about this with whomever you like, and it will not bother me. But I think our friendship and any further alliance we might have enjoyed are over."

"Probably just as well," he said, rising. He looked down at her. "You are clever, Belladrin Rish. Maybe too much so. I will be watching you."

She stood with him. "Do what you think necessary, Choten Benz. I will do the same."

He turned away and moved toward the tent flaps, shaking his head. He was halfway there when she caught up to him, a sudden burst of wind arriving with shocking quickness. Her knife slammed into the base of his neck where it connected to his head, severing the spinal column and dropping him in his tracks.

He was dead before his body struck the ground.

Belladrin bent over him, breathing hard, furious at what he had compelled her to do. "If you don't trust someone," she whispered, bending close to his corpse, "you shouldn't turn your back on them."

# TWENTY-SIX

THE STRAKEN QUEEN'S SMALL company departed her fortress in Kraal Reach by the same means Drisker Arc had been brought there several days earlier—a coach constructed of bones bound with ligaments and chains and pulled by huge creatures that appeared to be a hybrid mix of oxen and bears. All six passengers were jammed together in the claustrophobic, bare interior, with three seated on each side. The air was uncomfortably close, the shades drawn, and the Druid was not happy about any of it. It would have been impossible to fit them all inside if the clawrake hadn't been able to change its size. Even so, there was nothing that could improve the conditions under which they were forced to travel—the darkness, the animal smells, and the hot, fetid stench of the slint's breath.

When it breathed on the Druid the first time, he thought he was going to pass out. But he caught the smirk on the Straken Queen's face and refused to give her the satisfaction. He wanted to ask for permission to conjure a flow of fresh air to help make the journey more bearable, but he knew it was pointless. She had decided on their means of travel and was familiar enough with her companions to know what it meant to be confined in a close space with them, so there was nothing for it but to endure their presence inside what he still viewed as a "rolling coffin" until they reached the borders of Brockenthrog Weir. Those of demon-kind she had chosen to bring wheezed and snarled and spit at one another and himself as the coach jounced and rattled across the rocks and hills of the waste-lands that marked the kingdom of Grianne-that-was.

He thought of her this way—*Grianne-that-was*—because this was how she struck him. There was lit-tle left of either the girl or the woman she had once been. Shedding her identity as the Ilse Witch when she became Ard Rhys of the Third Druid Order, it had seemed she might find peace. But consigned to the Forbidding years later—not once but twice—had been too much for her. Almost everything that had been human had been stripped from her. What remained was the shell of her former self: a ravaged husk that had survived years within the Forbidding, a dark and dominating presence that cared nothing for her past. And yet he knew from the bargain they had made that, deep inside, she still harbored a few small memories of when she had once found peace.

"Is this going to be a long journey?" he asked her at one point.

She shook her head. "Time and distance are un-certain in the Forbidding, and neither is reliable. That said, I posit a week of travel afoot after today's ride. I wouldn't trouble myself with counting days or hours, Druid. I would turn my thoughts to finding ways of staying alive and leave it at that."

"Could we not have flown in on dragons instead of traveling in this?" He gestured at the bone coach.

"All six of us? Each with our own dragon or in pairs? Use common sense, Druid. Do you not think it wiser to arrive by stealth rather than with trumpets blaring and fire roaring? I do. I chose accordingly." Her response was a low snarl. "Besides, dragons eat people, in case you had forgotten."

They said little after that, but rode in the bone coach for the entire day with only one brief stop for food and water and a bit of relief from their cramped quarters. For Drisker, the queen supplied cheese and bread. The others ate things that the Druid could not even make himself look at. Several of them were still moving as the demons consumed them.

The route of travel they followed was dismal when they set out and never improved. It was rocky and uneven the entire way, and the jarring of the coach was constant. While the other passengers remained reliably passive, the slint was constantly changing from one form to another, never staying the same for more than a few seconds—a dizzying kaleidoscope of monstrous creatures. And whatever it ate did not improve its breath. Drisker thought to nap, but such an effort proved impossible. No one wanted to speak or engage in any way that mattered. Even the Straken Queen sat in silence, a forbidding aura about her that indicated others should think strongly about following her example.

It was nightfall when their transport finally rumbled to a halt, and Drisker exited the coach with what he hoped was a not too obvious eagerness. Once outside, he was standing in not-quite-total darkness, staring out across a new landscape. Gone was the uneven, rock-studded carpet they had traveled across all day. Gone were the miles of hardpan and vast empty stretches of barren earth and broad skies packed with endless clouds. In their place, another daunting challenge revealed itself. The terrain ahead was wet and boggy and steaming like a cauldron, the swamp waters and marshes seething with wicked spurts and booming eruptions. The leaden sky leaked a constant, endless downpour through a gloom so thick that everything within it had the look of a mirage.

*Such madness in this world!* To go into this cauldron of roiling dark and claustrophobic invisibility seemed such an obvious mistake he could barely keep from shouting out his dismay.

"We walk from here," the queen advised him, standing at his elbow as she surveyed the terrain. "And yes, it is every bit as terrible as you might imagine. But it is also how we must go. The Iron Crèche sits back against cliffs too sheer and high to attempt to descend; entry that way is not practical. Entry this way is not much better. The Crèche is fronted by this swamp and its resident creatures and myriad hazards, all of which can kill you. While Trax and his Chule *know* the cliffs cannot be used as access, they believe the same of this swamp and so will not look for us to cross here—will not even think we would attempt such an impossible feat. A measure of protection lies in this belief that I do not intend to disturb. Just pay attention to what I say and do, and make your choices accordingly."

Without another word, she dismissed the driver and

the bone coach and began to walk into the miasma of what Drisker quickly perceived to be an endless array of unpleasant ways to end his life. Up until now, he had seen nothing of the creatures that she had warned were waiting there—creatures uninterested in anything but eating and sleeping, creatures devoid of the ability to reason, relying instead on instinct and experience. These were demons lacking any semblance of humanity, so predatory they would not hesitate to kill their own kind if they sensed a weakness. He knew of a few from Grianne's own writings in the Druid Histories: Furies, Conjulants, Spakes, Crustlings, and the like. Pack creatures that hunted and fed and mated together to survive and had no other purpose.

They were all in there, deep within the gloom and mist, waiting.

He gave a deep sigh and went to meet them.

As they walked, the sounds of life within Brockenthrog Weir rose all around them—a cacophony of howls, shrieks, and life-ending screams; a mix of muted huffs, snorts, and food-seeking grunts; a muddle of crunches, gasps, and resigned sighs signaling prey caught and predators feeding. The sounds blanketed the gloom. This was a world of fetid waterways with scattered islands grown over with sawgrass and reeds, of isolated wetland trees and barren atolls. Everything that hunted or was hunted hid within its midst. No human should ever venture into such a place.

The Straken Queen was prepared for this challenge, however. She took the lead immediately, casting a wide net of magic into the darkness ahead to ferret out the myriad, lurking dangers. She sought and found them, then paused long enough to send them slinking away before her companions attempted to advance. It was stop and go, advance and pause, and advance again, all that night. She wanted to complete their first leg of the journey by using the darkness and night sounds to mask their coming. After they were deep inside, they could risk travel by day. Whether this was true or not, Drisker wasn't sure. The Straken Queen was driven by her determination and conviction that nothing could stand against her, and it was Drisker Arc's hope that these attributes made her as close to invincible as it was possible to be.

They walked most of the night, Grianne Ohmsford leading the way. The others followed like predatory beasts, staying close, keeping quiet for the most part and not attempting to venture too far from the path they traveled. It was impossible for Drisker to determine what they knew of this place, or how much of it they had attempted to traverse before. Perhaps they had never come here and would not dare to do so now without her protection. He wondered again how she managed to maintain her leadership over them—how she had earned their grudging respect and loyalty. Even the most dangerous and unpredictable among them—and you could pick and choose which one that might be—showed a clear obedience.

Whenever the slint began shifting too wildly or straying too frequently from their party, its mistress brought it to heel with a single unidentifiable sound, and each time it was quick to heed. There was no pretense at asserting itself, no attempt at posturing or hesitating. It simply came, snapping back into line.

Drisker was aware of the others just behind him, close enough that he could feel their breath and hear the grinding of teeth and the scraping of clawed feet. He did not look back at them. What point would there be? To catch them in the act of attacking and dragging him down to feed upon? His life depended wholly on her—on the Straken Queen, their mistress—not on his own quickness and instinct and magic. His life was thoroughly in her hands. If she wanted him dead, he was already halfway there. If she wished him to live, these creatures would not go against her decision.

And all their fates would be determined when they reached the Iron Crèche and Vendra Trax.

Finally, at morning's first light—a pale, sooty imitation of dawn that barely registered its approach before it was simply there—she brought them to a patch of dry land within the watery morass and bid them sleep. She put Weka Dart at watch and slept herself, although Drisker could not help but feel she rested just below the surface of waking and was always aware of whatever was happening around her. He marveled at her endurance. She had walked all night without resting, and to the naked eye she was nothing more than a wizened crone, all bones and hard-stretched ancient flesh, shrunken down within herself and barely more than a corpse. But it was a deceptive appearance that clearly masked a vast inner core of strength.

He was exhausted as he rolled into his travel cloak, and he slept hard until she woke him.

He opened his eyes to muted daylight and looked

up at her. "We are leaving," she said quietly. "We are far enough into the morass that we can risk walking in daylight and still avoid the more dangerous stalkers that hunt at night. It is an apportionment of risk. I judge us to be deep enough into the weir now that the risk of daylight discovery is much smaller than the risk of night travel. Come, Druid. Quickly."

They set out again. It was impossible for Drisker to determine how long he had slept and how far into the new day his sleep had carried him. The others were already up and prowling about when he rose. The clawrake was gnawing on something red and bloody. Drisker quickly counted heads. All present and accounted for, so whatever the demon ate it was not a piece of any of its companions. Again, Grianne handed him bread and cheese and bitter ale with which to wash it down.

She smiled when she watched his expression on drinking the ale. "Not what you are used to, Druid?" she chided. She took back the aleskin and drank herself. "Mother's milk to we who are caged and forgotten by those who drink better. Keep walking."

He did. They all did. It was quieter during the day, as most of the hunters preferred to seek their prey at night. It was a world of shadow life here in this damp and dismal stretch—a world where creatures came awake during the darkness and slept when the light shone. Drisker had no idea what lived here; he had seen almost nothing of the residents, though he had heard them clearly enough. Some few were awake in the daytime, but mostly birds and bats and extremely large flying bugs, all of which revealed themselves in sudden bursts of movement. They lacked the color of the flying creatures of the Four Lands, being as muted as possible to better camouflage with their surroundings.

No color and wonder in this world, he thought to himself. No sense of anything good or kind or wondrous. Survival was a way of life, and death was never more than a snap of a predator's jaws away.

They walked for three more days and nights, only stopping to eat and sleep and once or twice to correct course. Drisker had no idea where they were or even in what direction they were traveling. There were no landmarks that he could distinguish and no differences in the terrain. But the Straken Queen always seemed to know where she was going.

She pushed them hard the entire way and set a demanding pace. Only once did she reveal what drove her. On seeing the exhausted look on Drisker's face, she bent close and whispered, "I am desperate to escape this place, Druid. I freely admit it. I loathe it and its creatures both. I want to return to the life from which I was taken!" She paused, breathing hard, her narrowed eyes like chips of flint. "You would do well to remember your promise."

Drisker didn't need to be reminded. He knew what he had promised, and he despaired again of being able to keep that promise. But he knew also, just as she did, that the quicker they reached Vendra Trax, the sooner they would find the missing darkwand and discover if it could save them both.

On the fourth day of their seemingly endless slog,

midway through the morning's march, the slint went mad.

It happened all at once and for no visible reason. One minute it was slouching along in silence and the next it was leaping into the air and shifting from one form to the next in what appeared to be an attempt to escape something the others could not see. Its thrashings were impossibly frenzied. Drisker, who had been closest to it when the transformations began, quickly stepped back, summoning his magic to form a protective shield. The clawrake began roaring in rage and fear, swelling in size until it was as big as all of them put together. Weka Dart and Styrik scattered into the undergrowth, seeking shelter.

Only Grianne Ohmsford stood her ground, but the perplexed look on her features revealed the depth of her confusion.

*"Haist'en qual epsit!"* she screamed at the convulsing slint.

But her words had no effect at all. It continued to shift with startling rapidity, thrashing as it did so like a creature possessed. Finally, she came at it with a flash of green light that enveloped it completely and put an end to its shape-shifting and wild careening and sent it crashing to the ground, half submerged in fetid water, half in heavy grasses. A sharp word and the clawrake was on top of it, using its superior size and strength to pin it in place while Grianne bent close and studied it warily.

"Borecasts," she whispered after a moment. "Two, at least. *Cash'tase omni'el pak, arivan'o,*" she said to the clawrake. "Hold him fast."

"What is it?" Drisker asked her, stepping close.

"Vile insects that penetrate through the ears and attack the sensory system. They can drive you mad in seconds and keep you mad until you kill yourself. Stand away."

She began to work a fresh magic on the slint, staying warily back as she muttered and gestured and caused crooked lightning to ignite at her fingertips and lance into the slint through its ears, eyes, throat, and nostrils. The unfortunate receiver of her ministrations jerked and howled and struggled unsuccessfully to escape as the magic worked its way through. Tendrils of steam leaked from its orifices, and tears streamed down its wretched face.

Then the borecasts emerged all at once from its mouth. Winged and ugly, armored and sleek, they seemed too large to be able to achieve the sort of penetration Grianne had suggested. Chased from their host, they sought an escape she was quick to deny them, catching them up in a web of her magic and crushing them in a series of sharp flashes.

Drisker flinched away from the stench of their dying and waited to see what would happen next. But Grianne simply signaled for the clawrake to keep hold and disappeared into the gloom. She was gone only briefly, and when she returned she was carrying a cluster of deep-purple weeds, thick and twisted and studded with bulbs. One by one she broke off the bulbs and handed them to each member of the company.

"Break it open," she instructed Drisker. "Rub the oil on your face and hands and arms. The smell is anathema to borecasts; they will keep their distance."

She shook her head, frowning. "I had thought bore-casts were only found farther north in the weir, but apparently they've moved."

They waited until she was satisfied that the slint was back to normal before continuing on, and the ex-perience did not repeat itself.

By now they had been walking for five days, and they were growing weary. The Straken Queen had allowed the pace to slow, but still she pressed them onward steadily. The thickness of the swamp air had increased, and rain had begun to fall again. By the end of the fifth day they were all drenched, and Drisker's companions were snarling and growling and snapping at one another—all save Grianne. For her, self-control seemed ingrained. While she was assertive and reti-cent by turns, she was never vengeful or deliberately cruel. She treated all of them the same and did not evi-dence anything more than frustration or disappoint-ment with any of them.

The clawrake tested her patience more frequently than the others. Its size and strength seemed to imbue it with a sense of entitlement. It was constantly testing the limits of the orders she issued and the boundar-ies she set. Once, it attacked and tore apart a swamp creature of some sort when it was hungry and then sat down and ate it without the slightest regard for the in-convenience it was causing the others. Another time, it disappeared for the better part of the day and re-fused to speak at all when it resurfaced toward night-fall. Grianne looked furious, but she held her tongue. Drisker wasn't sure how she managed it.

Drisker thought the clawrake a dangerous and

unpredictable menace that would eventually expose them all to a lethal situation, but Grianne seemed unconcerned about any threat it posed by its willful and reckless behavior, and simply resorted to a few sharp admonitions now and then to keep it in line. It was noticeable, however, that after she uttered those admonishments, the creature always fell right back into line with the others.

"We all listen to her when she speaks," Weka Dart whispered, noting Drisker's surprise on one occasion. "We obey her. Even the clawrake." His toothy smile surfaced. "She is our mistress, and we love her."

Drisker did not think *love* was quite the right word for it, yet on more than one occasion he caught each of them gazing at her with a kind of rapture in their eyes that was unmistakable. It made him wonder if some form of love was yet possible with these banished and forgotten creatures. He wondered if, in spite of everything, they were not still capable of the same feelings that those dwelling back in the Four Lands enjoyed. Surely any form of kindness or show of affection constituted love in the eyes and hearts of those who were lucky enough to experience it.

*Perhaps so,* he thought. *Do not be too quick to judge.*

On midday of the sixth day, they reached the Iron Crèche.

# TWENTY-SEVEN

───────────◆───────────

DRISKER ARC STOOD IN silence with the others and stared at the forbidding spectacle of the Iron Crèche. The Chule fortress sat atop a broad platform at the far end, set back against cliffs so sheer and high they disappeared into the mist canopying over the entire swamp. Solitary and so singular, it seemed a jagged mountain that had sprung from the earth in defiance of Brockenthrog Weir, resistant to rust and erosion, evidence of a power greater than everything surrounding it. This was no gleaming edifice, no testament to self-anointed glory or accomplishments. No flags flew and no parapets or gates or tower heights gleamed with polished metal adornments. Everything about this monstrous construction was flat black or smoke gray and streaked with odd striations that suggested cracks or splits in the metal, but which on closer examination were neither.

If there was any indication of wear in its vast metal plates, dominating battlements and towers, or massive gates and seals, the Druid saw no evidence of it. The Crèche sat solitary and indomitable amid the sweeping clusters of foliage and islands of grasses and reeds, lording over all for as far as the eye could see. It might as well be soundlessly shouting: *I am invincible and shall exist long after you are gone. If I chose to do so, I could crush you.*

Standing at least a mile off, Drisker nevertheless felt the weight of this monolith. Around him, the others were also reacting in their various ways to its overpowering presence. The slint had resumed rapidly shape-shifting. The moench had gone to ground— although where exactly amid the vast stretches of watery swamp, it was difficult to say. Weka Dart was clutching at the Straken Queen with a possessiveness that suggested he knew she was his only salvation in the face of such an overpowering presence.

*Haissst,* the clawrake hissed, drawing out the exclamation as it swelled protectively to increase its own presence.

Only Grianne Ohmsford gave no sign of what she was feeling. She just stared at the forbidding monolith, saying nothing and revealing nothing.

Drisker calmed himself by doing a quick assessment of how this beast of stone and metal was protected. Other than its dominating size and impenetrable appearance, everything around it for hundreds of yards on to the front and sides had been leveled, so no intruder could approach without being seen. A pair of huge iron gates could be seen from where they stood, the sole entry offered after one crossed acres of bog, which Drisker understood immediately would be riddled with sinkholes deep and wide enough to swallow them whole and predators living in the fetid waters, waiting hungrily.

The Druid took a deep breath and exhaled slowly, recognizing the impossibility of the task they had set themselves by coming here.

The Straken Queen gave them a few moments more to marvel at what they must conquer, then turned to the moench and said, "Time for you to prove your worth. Show us the way."

The sly, sharp features of the strange little creature brightened with cunning. After basking momentarily in the bright light of her approval, it cast a satisfied glance at Weka Dart before setting out along the uneven shoreline of the vast expanse of water that warded their destination.

The rain was still falling and they were soaked through, with no relief from the dampness in sight. They trudged along the water's edge with their shoulders hunched and their bodies shivering beneath their sodden clothing. They slogged through swamp foliage and fetid waters, stepping carefully as they went, aware of the hidden danger from quicksand and mud pits. The moench never hesitated, however, clearly knowing its way through this treacherous realm. Drisker wondered how that was possible. The moench must have been here before—and not for any brief period, but for an extended stay. Such familiarity was not acquired in a day, but over weeks and months and perhaps even years.

Grianne let it take them where it wished and did not question its choices. They island-hopped from one grassy atoll to the next, staying hidden as much as possible. The moench never hesitated, moving in a zigzag fashion through the swamp, uttering an odd chittering sound now and then as it directed them. They traveled a long way, and the daylight began to wane. Drisker found himself imagining how good it would feel to be dry again, how much he wanted to be out of the wet. It was a pervasive, dominating need, and eventually he had to cast it aside in order to focus on moving safely through the water and muck.

It was almost dark when they reached an island noticeably larger than most of the others, its surface crowded with willowy trees and spiky-leafed palms that clung together like siblings. Following the moench, they skirted the trees along the shores of the atoll until he finally found a space he liked and led them into their clustered midst. Once deep enough to be satisfied, he stopped. Glancing back at the Straken Queen, he pointed at a small open space ahead of them.

She nodded and gave the creature a smile of approval.

"I see nothing," Weka Dart groused.

"That is the idea," she responded and nodded to the moench. Styrik immediately reached downward into the earth covering the open space and lifted an iron ring, twisting it clockwise several times before stepping back. Slowly, the ground lifted away, revealing an opening in the island's ground.

"A tunnel that runs much deeper than this lake," she advised the others. "A vast warren of passageways, in fact. Built by Styrik's people—burrowing people—to allow them access to the Iron Crèche. They steal supplies and stores from the fortress, carrying away what they need, but never so much that it is evident to the

Chule. Resourceful, if dangerous thievery. This is how we must enter the Crèche. Needless to say, the Chule do not know these tunnels exist, so they will not be expecting us. It will be a lengthy, twisty journey and it will take time. It will feel confining to the point of claustrophobia, but you cannot allow it to affect you. If the moench can tolerate it, so can we."

She paused. "Also, do not become separated. If you do, you will be left behind. And in a maze of this size and complexity, even your bones will never be found. So stay close. Stay together. Stay silent. Now, come."

She nodded to the moench, which went down into the opening without hesitation. One by one, the others followed, with the Straken Queen going last in order to reseal the opening. As she did so, what little light remaining vanished, plunging the underground into total blackness, leaving them all blind to what surrounded them. But she quickly summoned a werelight and bid Drisker do the same, moving to the forefront of the company with the moench, then motioning for the slint and the clawrake to follow and placing Drisker and Weka Dart at the rear of the procession.

Once the order of the line was arranged to her satisfaction, they set out.

Drisker had endured more than a few ordeals over the course of his life—some life threatening, some just challenging—but never anything like what he experienced this night. Although the tunnels ran in all directions, splitting off from one another in endless succession, still it felt like he was in a tomb that had no beginning and no end and simply went on endlessly through a morass of suffocating gloom. The werelights helped, but they only illuminated their surroundings for a short distance and they offered a constant reminder of how tightly wrapped they were by the tunnel walls. None of this was improved by the way sounds were muffled and smells sharpened.

Then there was the cloying dampness and the harsh realization that a crack in these walls—however small—could bring the entire swamp pouring into their passageway and drown them in a matter of minutes. And every step of the way, there was evidence of how easily it could happen. Damp patches and splits in the earth, which were already leaking water to form puddles beneath their feet, mingled with the creaks and grindings of overstressed walls. Drisker tried to shut it away, but failed. He glanced now and then at the others and saw each of them looking about guardedly—save the moench, which was undoubtedly familiar with all this, and the Straken Queen, who seemed to have no fear of anything.

It was impossible to tell how far they walked or for how long—only that they were not progressing in a straight line but were angling this way and that. At a guess, the Druid imagined they traveled through the tunnels for at least several hours. By then, he knew, it would be dark outside and night would have settled in. It made him wonder if this would mark his end—if the end he had always envisioned for himself once he had borne witness to the fall of Paranor would come to pass here.

His mood was not improved when the crawling things appeared on the walls and ceilings. Insects, he could tell, although he could not be certain of their species. Some were large, and some small—and all were eagerly passing from one point to another with no apparent destination in mind. *Stay clear of them,* Grianne whispered back to those that followed her. *Do not touch them; do not let them touch you. Some are poisonous, and some have bites or stings that will immobilize you. Try to ignore them.*

*As if,* Drisker thought. They were all over the tunnel walls. Everywhere you looked, they were there. Ignoring them—especially knowing they could be life threatening—was asking more than he could manage. Instead, he kept his head lowered and his eyes on his booted feet, his tall frame hunched over and his arms and hands pulled close against him. He kept expecting these creatures to fall on him. He kept expecting the swamp to break through and pour over him. He kept expecting the walls to close about him in a vise that would crush the life out of him.

He kept waiting for his resolve and his courage to break like glass.

He kept waiting to die.

But none of it came to pass. His fears lingered but were not realized, and eventually the company reached the end of the maze and stood before a door set into a wall of stone. It was an abrupt conclusion to a seemingly endless slog and, other than the moench, no one was quite prepared for it. They stumbled to a halt, staring at the barrier as if uncertain what it meant.

"Is this the entry?" Drisker managed after long moments of silence.

Styrik muttered something unintelligible, and the

Straken Queen nodded at once. "This is *one* entry," she said, turning to face them. "There are others, but those are known to the Chule, who use them to bring in supplies. This is not one of those. This one was constructed in part by the builders of the Crèche. Some used it to attempt escapes. But only some. The moench found and finished it some years later."

She beckoned the others closer. "From here, we go into the cellars of the fortress. Likely there won't be anyone around, but we need to be cautious anyway. Remember, we still have to find what we came here to retrieve."

She repeated the words in different languages to those gathered and looked at each of them meaningfully as she did so, then turned back to the door. The moench was already working on a series of levers down near the threshold. When it pulled the last one, the door swung outward to admit them.

One by one, they stepped inside.

What they found, once through the doorway, was a small room with no windows or light. Grianne lit a werelight with her fingers and led them to a slab of stone that blended into the wall and was invisible until she triggered a release and it opened. On stepping clear, they found themselves in a huge hub servicing an array of passageways that ran off in all directions, their mouths darkened and depthless beyond the faint glow of the werelights.

After closing the stone slab behind her and watching as it disappeared into the chamber wall completely, Grianne turned to the moench, giving it a questioning look. The gimlet eyes fixed on her and a finger pointed to the first passage directly to their right. It was a match in size to one on their left and a third straight ahead, and Drisker realized these three were the main corridors to the cells and storage rooms, while the other, smaller corridors were for ancillary purposes.

The Straken Queen nodded to the moench and beckoned him ahead. As a group, they started forward. They walked in silence, their senses alert to any sounds that might indicate the presence of the Chule, but they heard nothing. Drisker waited until they had walked for some distance before moving up beside Grianne and leaning in.

"What are we doing?" he whispered.

She didn't bother to look at him. "We're going after the darkwand."

"But I thought you didn't know where it was."

A hint of a smile crossed her rough features. "Did you? Maybe you were mistaken. Be patient, Drisker."

The Druid stared at her in disbelief, but she moved ahead again, leaving him to ponder her words. Hadn't she already told him she didn't know where the staff could be found—that it had disappeared, and Vendra Trax claimed not to have possession of it? But if she did know where it could be located, why hadn't she told him? She was playing games with him, he sensed, and he did not know the rules.

What he did know was this: She was holding something critical back. But there was nothing to be done about it at this point. He had to continue on with her until the matter was resolved. He lowered his head, thinking about how badly this might turn out once he knew the truth. He listened to the footfalls of his companions echoing in the silence of these cellars—solitary, empty, and filled with dark promise.

They walked a long way, deep into the subterranean passageways of the Iron Crèche, and not once was there any sign of life. He should have felt better about this than he did. He should have been pleased they could navigate this warren so easily and safely, avoiding any encounter with those who would see them all dead in an instant. But this only made him more suspicious. The Straken Witch was a dominating and controlling ruler, protective of herself and her power, and that mindset infused everything she did. He understood that to survive in the insane world of the Forbidding and to protect herself against those who wished her dead, she had to be this way. But he was not one of those she should fear. He desired nothing more than the escape she sought for herself. So why was she so reticent to confide in him?

After what seemed an eternity of walking, constantly interrupted by sudden stops and cautious pauses, all of it through the bowels of a construct that felt as if it were waiting to crush them, they arrived at a pair of iron doors with no discernible seals or releases. The moench glanced at the witch and pointed at the barrier. Immediately she stepped forward, muttered a few words, made a quick beckoning motion, and watched as the doors swung open to admit them.

Once inside, they found themselves in a vast storage room filled with wooden crates and iron chests, all sealed and labeled in a language Drisker did not recognize. Drisker looked around and wondered again what they were doing. Was this where they would find the darkwand, hidden amid these stores?

"We rest here until tonight," Grianne Ohmsford announced. "Sleep if you can. It will be your last chance. I will give you something to eat. Make no noise. Do nothing to reveal our presence."

The slint and the clawrake wandered off into dark corners and made a noisy meal of the food she gave them. The moench conferred in whispers with the Straken Queen and then she gave it something to eat as well. Weka Dart watched his companions closely for a few moments, then wandered over to Drisker.

"She drugs them," he whispered. "She expects no help from them in finding what she seeks."

Drisker wasn't so sure Weka was seeing things correctly, but he nodded anyway. "She may have."

The Ulk Bog gestured at their surroundings, his wizened face crinkling further. "All this—this great fortress—was built by the Chule. Most of it in a time before Vendra Trax, most of it by his granduncle. It should not have been possible. It sits upon tons of rubble carried in by slaves that now lie beneath its weight, their purpose served. The Keep itself was ten years in the building, a place to which no one would ever wish to go. Such a place should not even exist."

"Yet here we are."

"Because she is misguided!" There was a manic quality to his whispered insistence. "We come here willingly. Foolishly! She doesn't know where the darkwand is. It isn't here! She's looked already! The Chule are ruthless and cruel. They threaten my mistress, seeking to cast her down, to see her destroyed. Vendra

Trax wants her throne. He wants everything she has, and he will keep after her until he has it! And now she has delivered herself into his hands. Can you not see it? For her to come here is madness!"

"Keep your voice down."

Weka Dart's eyes were furious now. "This is your fault! You are responsible for what is happening! It is because of you she is here—come to retrieve the black staff so she can leave our world and return to yours. She is bewitched by the idea, and it is a foolish hope!"

This was not true, of course, but Drisker saw no point in getting into an argument about it. Besides, it was not his idea that she escape the Forbidding; it was hers. *She* was the one who'd approached *him* at the Hadeshorn. She was the one who'd made the bargain with him. He had not come for her; he had been sent here against his will, and he had no wish to be here at all. It was not a place he would ever wish to come, no matter the reason.

He turned away from the Ulk Bog, no longer wishing to speak with him. The little creature glared at him a moment longer, then trudged off into a darkened corner and settled down, back to the wall, eyes glowing like coals. Drisker glanced over at him, took note of the rage and bitterness in those eyes, and looked away again. He chose a place out in the open and sat quietly, musing.

After a time, he noticed that the moench, the clawrake, and the slint were all asleep, while Weka continued to glare at him balefully.

A moment later, Grianne Ohmsford seated herself next to him. "You make enemies so easily," she chided.

"He thinks this is all my doing, that I came here to take you away. He won't ever forgive me for that."

She shrugged. "It doesn't matter what he will forgive or not forgive. All that matters is what you promised me." She paused. "I assume you haven't forgotten?"

Again, the reminder. But there was something about how she said it that troubled him—her tone of voice, her emphasis, something.

"Of course I remember. You needn't keep asking." He faced her. "Now tell me. Do you or do you not know where the darkwand is?"

Her smile was quick, grim, and not entirely reassuring. "The moench knows. And if it lies, it doesn't matter. The darkwand is in Vendra Trax's chambers. The moench thinks to guide us there tomorrow, when Vendra Trax is out, but I am not inclined to wait so long. What the moench does not know is that I have my own guides in this place, and they can lead me to Vendra's chamber without him."

"Guides? What guides?"

"The ones who came before us. The ones who live in the walls."

Drisker stared. *What?*

"The Forbidding, Drisker Arc, is not like the Four Lands. Or any other place. It is unique, and within its confines life takes different forms than what you are accustomed to. So tonight, we sleep. But not so long as the others will. You and I have something else to do."

"Which is?"

"We will leave this chamber and go to where the

darkwand is concealed. We will find it, reclaim it, and come back again before morning. According to my dreams, this is the key. That the staff will come to you and me alone. We are the ones who can do this."

"But what of Vendra himself? Won't he be in his chambers at this hour?"

"Yes, but asleep. I can easily enchant a sleeping Chule." She glared at him. "Never assume there is something I cannot do, Drisker Arc. That would be a mistake. I can do anything I want to!"

He did not doubt she believed that. And it might even be true. "So these wraiths will guide us? Why?"

"Because I am almost one of them—not yet become what they are, but well on the way. They are kin to me, and what I ask, they will grant."

"How? Will they provide us with a map? Show us a path?"

She shook her head slowly. "They live within the walls of the Iron Crèche, Drisker Arc. Tonight, they will bring us into the walls with them."

# TWENTY-EIGHT

◆

DRISKER SLEPT, AND HIS sleep was deep and dark. Lack of comfort was not a consideration—nor lack of privacy or quiet, warmth or any sense of reassurance. Exhaustion dominated him, dragging him under quickly and holding him down so that interruptions could not intrude for the time he had been given to rest. It was not until hands seized him and shook him awake with surprising roughness that he woke to find himself staring into the depthless eyes of the Straken Queen.

"Time to go," she whispered as she released her grip.

He rose, coming awake quickly—anxious now, and more alert than it had seemed possible on waking from such an all-consuming sleep. He stood with her in the near darkness, the only light a faint glow from her fingertips as she guided him through those sleeping around them to stand before the blank surface of the rear wall. None of the others woke.

"I drugged all but Weka Dart," she whispered once more, confirming the Ulk Bog's suspicion. "This task is for us alone. The dreams revealed as much."

He searched the room and, after long moments, found the glint of the Ulk Bog's eyes in the darkness, staring up at him, watching. He nodded faintly, not even sure if the other could see him. Conflicted as he was, Weka Dart would help his mistress in her efforts right until the end of either one or the other.

Grianne laid one glowing hand on the wall and closed her eyes, doing whatever she did to contact her spirits. Long minutes passed and nothing happened. Drisker grew restless and began to shift from one foot to the other. The Straken Queen reached out to him with her free hand and placed it on his arm, cautioning him to remain silent. Drisker nodded, but what was taking so long? He did not want to ask, even though he wanted to know. The uncertainty was working on him, but he stiffened his resolve and held back his words.

Then he caught a glimpse of what looked to be a shiver in the stone of the wall, as if it were becoming liquid. A moment later a figure emerged—human in shape, but featureless: a wraith given human form but stripped of any definition or color. It bled through the wall and stood before them. A second followed and then a third. They did not speak. How could they, given they had no mouths? But while no audible communication took place, it seemed as if something was passing between Grianne Ohmsford and the wraiths—another form of communication suggested by her change of expression and gestures, to which the ghosts of the dead responded in kind.

"Let them take your hands, Druid," the Straken Queen ordered.

One of them reached for his hands and Drisker gave them willingly, forcing himself to remain unresponsive even when the chill of the creature's touch would have otherwise made him jump in shock. Icy, it was. Such cold!

"We go into the walls," she whispered again. "Do not resist. Do not fight against what you feel. Let yourself be led."

Drisker forced himself to relax, trying not to think of the stone as a material that could easily smash his body to bits, but to see it as the liquid it had appeared to be for the wraiths. His minder slid into the stone, which instantly softened for him, giving him easy access.

Drisker went with the creature, and it was as if he were being pulled through a screen—or perhaps a sieve—separating his body into a million tiny fragments. He closed his eyes as he felt it happening, not wanting to see what it would do to him. *Just let it happen.* He did so, holding his courage and his trust together even as his body came apart.

It took everything he had not to react to what he was experiencing—every bit of courage and faith in the word of the Straken Queen. It felt as if skin and ligaments, cartilage and sinew, blood and brain were disintegrating under the force of his entry into the wall. Then all of him was inside. He risked a quick peek through the slits of his eyelids and quickly sealed them again. The world beyond was a blank. Those who dwelled within the walls were gone. The Straken Queen was gone, as was everything he might have recognized. There was only the cold pressure of his guide's hands holding his, and nothing else.

Time slowed to a crawl, or perhaps it raced away so quickly he could not track it. Then again, perhaps it ceased completely. All he knew was the lack of anything familiar pressing in around him, investing him with chilling certainty that this was the end. Drisker felt a sudden urge to scream and quickly tamped it down. Screaming would do him no good. Only perseverance would save him now.

He concentrated on responding to the steady pull of his guide's hands, feeling their roughness and strength, all of his senses centered on the presence of those hands—on the lifeline they offered, on the promise they would see him clear and safe again.

The feeling that his body was under attack lessened as he proceeded, and he began to adjust to the unpleasantness. In fact, after a time, the feeling began to seem natural, a part of who and what he was. He had endured, and by doing so managed to reduce the experience to something approaching normal.

No words were spoken nor thoughts exchanged as they progressed. Save for the hands leading him steadily on, Drisker was alone. But he was thinking now, reasoning, rationalizing, positing what might happen when they reached their destination. His hopes for escape had climbed a notch, and now a way out no longer seemed quite so impossible.

If they could reach the chambers of Vendra Trax . . .

If they could gain possession of the elusive darkwand . . .

The wall pressed in on him—not with stone and mortar but with doubts and fears.

Then the tearing, stripping, and fragmenting of his body and mind began anew. He passed out of the confines of the wall and back into the fetid swamp air of the Iron Crèche, free again of his imprisonment and gulping air without impediment.

He felt the hands of the wall dweller release his own, giving him his freedom, and he blinked in the near darkness and saw the gnarled form of the Straken Queen standing nearby, searching the room. Barred windows warded it, and only a single door provided entry. It was a bedchamber, but it was empty. Drisker cast a wary glance at the bed, which was nothing more than a huge stone slab with a pile of straw atop it— devoid of mattress, sheets, pillows, or blankets. It made him wonder. Were they even in the right place? And if they were, then why wasn't Vendra there, too?

Uneasiness stirred.

"These are his chambers," Grianne whispered exultantly, as if reading his mind. "According to the moench, the darkwand is hidden here!"

"So where is Vendra?" Drisker whispered back.

She just shrugged. "Elsewhere, apparently."

"He should be sleeping."

"Who knows what a Chule does at night? But it doesn't matter. The room is empty, and we are here!" From the almost manic glitter in her eyes, he could tell she was too caught up in the fulfillment of a long-desired dream to trouble about the details.

But those details troubled him.

Darkness filled the room, and only the dim glow

at Grianne's fingertips provided any light. Drisker watched her a moment as she stood listening to the silence and decided they were indeed alone.

Then he saw their three guides pass back into the walls. Grianne ignored their departure, moving deeper into the chamber, beckoning him to follow. Ahead, curtains parted to reveal another chamber, this one a room filled with armor and weapons and various forms of battle gear—and still no Vendra Trax. In one corner stood an armored warrior bearing a huge spear, an apparent decoration. The Druid and the queen navigated the maze to a far wall, and from there to a corner of the chamber in which a cabinet stood. Grianne opened the cabinet door and Drisker peered inside. Scrolls and maps and bound documents of all shapes and sizes filled the space.

"Perhaps in this cabinet," Grianne said quietly.

She removed the scrolls, one after another, clearing out the cabinet to study the empty space, running her fingers over its wooden sides, bottom and top. When she was done, she pulled back, a puzzled look on her face. "Nothing." She shook her head. "I must be missing something." She looked at him. "Can you sense where it is?"

Drisker wasn't sure he could sense anything in this foreign world, but he studied the cabinet and then the scrolls. *Something* . . . He bent down, moving the scrolls about slowly. Here, within the scrolls. *Something hidden* . . . He sensed it rather than saw it—felt it the way you feel another's presence when you have not witnessed their actual coming.

He knelt amid the scrolls and began to work his

way through them, running his fingers over their smooth surfaces, feeling up inside the rolls and down along the spines. One by one, he went through them. Then, just as he was beginning to think he had made a mistake, his fingers encountered a small indentation in the wooden boll around which a large scroll was bound with leather thongs. He fingered the indent carefully, noting the obvious give to its surface, and he immediately became wary.

"What is it?" the Straken Queen asked eagerly, bending close.

He shook his head. "Something more than a scroll. There is a trigger carved into its surface. I don't know what it does."

"Press it."

"But if we're wrong . . ."

*"Press it!"* she hissed. "We don't have the luxury of being cautious!"

He did so, and the room exploded with light—a huge sunburst of fiery illumination that seemed to ignite rather than simply appear. Drisker and Grianne both shrank from its brilliance, and suddenly the armored warrior was moving, coming to life as if woken from sleep, swinging about to face the intruders, assuming a fighting stance as it began a slow advance.

"A trap!" Grianne growled in her low, dangerous voice. "The moench lied!" Her expression was one of rage and frustration. "Leave this to me, Druid."

She let the armored figure get to within a few feet of her, then cast the spell she had been preparing. It encircled the creature and froze it in place. One step, another, and then it ceased all movement.

She stepped away, glancing over at Drisker.

"What was the point of that?" he asked. "That statue wasn't much of a threat."

"It wasn't supposed to be." She spit out the words as if she found the taste of them foul. "Activating it simply gave warning to Vendra Trax that we are here. Now he will come for us."

In the storage room where the others still slept, Weka Dart was awake. He did not trust sleep in a place like this. This whole fortress was a trap waiting to be sprung. He did not trust any part of it. In particular, he was suspicious of the moench. Before his mistress had drugged it, it had kept looking toward the door, watching and waiting. It seemed clear enough to the Ulk Bog, but what should he do about it? His instincts told him to run, but *where*? His mistress and the Druid were still gone, and how would he find them in this stone-and-iron maze?

So he sat there in a darkened corner, seething inside. He hated the moench. He always had. Had never trusted it, never thought she should listen to it, never wanted it anywhere near her. But the Straken Queen was fixed on her course, so he had been forced to endure its presence. Coming here as they had was madness, and it was all due to the presence of the Druid. The Druid would take his mistress away and Weka Dart would be left behind. He would be abandoned.

All they needed was the staff.

Though first, of course, they had to find it . . .

His thoughts shifted, one after another.

He should flee.

He should stay.

He should warn the others.

He should remain very still.

Hiding was what he did best. He searched for a better place to conceal himself . . .

Then it was too late to do anything. Outside the storage room, there was movement, furtive and muffled. He looked about quickly. *Hide! Now!* He saw the moench moving toward the door to open it. *Stop him! Too late!* He scrambled up, still little more than a shadow, and disappeared into a crate of cloaks and shoes deep in the chamber.

No sooner had he tucked himself away than the storage room doors burst open and the Chule poured in. Lean, ragged creatures with elongated limbs and barked bodies, they were as tough as the cordwood they resembled. They carried knives and spears and blades of all sorts, and there were a lot of them. Too many. They swarmed over the clawrake and the slint and bore them to the floor of the chamber, slashing and stabbing wildly. The clawrake roared and threw them off. The slint became a thing of such monstrous appearance that his attackers shrank from him. The struggle surged back and forth amid the crates and barrels of stores, and for a time it was an equal match.

But the Straken Queen's companions were outnumbered, and in time both began to falter. The slint died first, its shape-shifting efforts slowing until at last it collapsed, a mass of blood and torn limbs. The clawrake lasted longer, its huge body dominating the smaller Chule and forcing them back. But there were too many of them, and eventually it weakened enough that they were able to pull it down and begin to dismember it while it struggled futilely to rise.

When they were dead, a huge shadow darkened the entry and stood watching. The halls outside blazed now with a fiery illumination cast by dozens of torches, backlighting Vendra Trax as he looked around at the carnage. From his hiding place, Weka Dart could see the moench rushing up to him and throwing itself at his feet in supplication. *Traitor. Lickspittle!* The Ulk Bog hated it and wanted it dead, yet he could do nothing but watch and wait.

"Where is she?" Vendra Trax demanded, nudging the moench with the toe of his boot.

"Gone, master," the moench whispered, cringing away. "She was supposed to stay here until morning, as we had agreed, but she drugged me and then vanished with the Druid. I do not know where she might be."

"Which says something about your usefulness, doesn't it?"

"I brought them to you, master! I brought them here, just as I promised!"

The vile creature sounded frantic, Weka Dart thought with satisfaction. Good, let the traitor squirm a bit. Let it beg.

"You were told to stay awake and keep watch until I arrived," the leader of the Chule said. "You were told to keep them here until I did. Was that so difficult? Was it asking too much?"

"No, master, no. I . . . should have done better. I will do better next time. Just take me into the Crèche and let me serve you. You will see soon enough!"

Vendra Trax bent down, his huge frame towering over the moench, draping it in shadow. Massive hands reached down to gather it up as if it were a toy. "I don't think I want to see any more of you," he hissed.

And he tore the moench apart and flung the pieces to his Chule followers, who devoured them eagerly.

He stood then, looking about, and Weka Dart was certain he would search the room and find him. But a moment later the Chule Lord jerked his head about, as if he had heard something. Sharp teeth appeared behind jaws that opened in a wide smile.

"I believe I know where they are," he called to the others. "Let's collect them and finish this."

He was gone quickly, his Chule with him, and Weka Dart was left alone to wonder what would become of him.

"He was expecting us. He knew we were coming. It was the moench. It had to have been. Styrik was the only one who knew of the details of our coming—the one who provided us with entry and told me where the darkwand could be found."

The Straken Queen's fury was cool and collected, but there was a dark rage lurking beneath it. Drisker looked around hurriedly. "Then why isn't Trax here with his Chule, waiting for us?"

She considered. "Because he expected us to still be back in that storeroom with the others. That is where the trap is closing. As I said, the moench didn't know of my plans to use the wall dwellers. We have to hurry! The darkwand *must* be here somewhere!"

The truth burst upon him as brilliantly as the spell

that had activated the warrior. "Grianne!" Drisker shouted, bringing her about quickly. "There's no point searching. The darkwand isn't here. Don't you see? Trax used the staff as bait to trap you! We have to leave right now. We will be caught and killed if we waste any more time. If the waking of the armored automaton was a signal, Trax will be here in moments!"

"No!" she screamed in undisguised rage. "I need the darkwand! We both need it, Druid, or we will be trapped in this monstrous world forever!"

He shook his head. "No, we won't. You aren't listening to me! The darkwand isn't here. And it hasn't been in years!"

She stared at him in shock and disbelief. "What did you say?"

And with that, the hallways beyond the Chule Lord's chambers erupted with the pounding of booted feet and cries of battle lust, and there was no time left to talk about anything.

Grianne acted at once. Using guttural words and intricate gestures to summon magic, she cast a locking spell on the door, freezing it in place. Then she seized Drisker's arm and pulled him close, her fingers iron clamps, her face twisted in fury.

"The darkwand isn't here?" she repeated, her face inches from his. "You're certain of this? How can you possibly know? No, wait, you do know, don't you? My visions of the future, they told the truth. This is why you are here. Do you know where it is? Tell me, Druid!"

Drisker glanced toward the door, where fists

pounded and shouts of rage rose. "I don't know where it is, but I know how to find it."

She released him and gave him a long look. "You had better be sure. Your life depends on it. Do you understand me?" He nodded, because he was sure. All the little nagging doubts and inconsistencies that had been troubling him suddenly made perfect sense. "Very well. We will leave this place on your promise you can find the darkwand. You are right enough about our choosing to stay. It would be foolish. They knew we were coming. Those we left in the storeroom are likely dead by now."

Drisker experienced a sinking sensation in the pit of his stomach. Not Weka Dart. Weka Dart had to be alive.

Grianne beckoned hurriedly. "We go back the same way we came; we have no choice. The Chule will be blocking the hallways outside. Quickly, now! The wall dwellers are returning. Hold tight to the hands of the one who guides you and remember your courage."

Then their wraith companions were back, collecting them as they would children, linking to them hand in hand, and bleeding into the walls once more.

# TWENTY-NINE

SHEA OHMSFORD STOOD TO one side of the workers, watching as they carried the sacks of chemicals and casks of water to the staging area on the aft deck of the *Behemoth*, one load after another. It was not an easy job. Each sack weighed more than a hundred pounds and each cask more than five hundred. A single man could manage the former if possessed of sufficient strength—as most were—but three or four were required to muscle each of the latter up from where they were lashed to the masts and risers at various places. Meanwhile, Tindall stood aft by Annabelle, yelling out instructions and warnings in an ever-increasing frenzy.

*Watch that step, man! Keep your grip secure; if you drop it the staves will give way and the water be lost! What do you think you are doing, idiot? Those materials are precious! Irreplaceable! Worth more than your fingers, dolt!*

And so on and so forth—a constant assault on the senses and patience of men for whom such admonitions were neither welcomed nor needed. Tindall quickly became the target of any number of dark looks and more than a few muttered oaths. Shea would not have stood for it, had he been one of them, and eventually he wandered over to where Tindall was holding forth and stood next to him in silence, hoping his proximity alone might help quell the old man. When that failed, he waited for a moment when most of the beleaguered Rovers were out of hearing and leaned in.

"They are doing the best they can, you know."

Tindall wheeled on him. "You mind your own business, young whippersnapper! This doesn't concern you."

"Have they dropped a single sack or broken a single cask?"

"No, but only because I am here to make sure they know not to."

The boy shrugged. "Perhaps shouting at grown men who do heavy lifting and know well enough by now of your concerns does nothing but make their work more difficult."

It was the fourth day since their arrival in Skaarsland, and work on Annabelle had been proceeding apace. The weather had been quite good on the first day—less overcast, cold, and snowy than it had been, the wind steady and persistent but offering the promise of an opportunity to launch the *Behemoth*, bearing the fully charged Annabelle aloft, where she could work her chemical magic. Tindall alone knew how to create the mixture of materials that was needed to achieve their purpose, and Shea was well aware that the old man would have preferred to manage the entire process alone. But he lacked the necessary strength, so was forced to stand aside and let the more able Rovers do what he could not. And he compensated for his obvious frustration by excoriating them endlessly while they worked.

A poor decision to the boy's way of thinking, but Tindall was clearly not in the mood for reason.

"You fail to understand what is at stake!" the old man practically shouted at him. "One false step, one careless moment, one single misstep, and we could lose the chemicals we hauled all this way, with no simple way to replace them. Then what?"

"Maybe a word of encouragement would serve as well as your constant shouting and threats; that's all I'm saying. Just give them a little praise for the work they're doing, because they're doing it for you."

Tindall glared at him and gave an audible *hurrumph* in response, and Shea abandoned the attempt. Best to let matters sort themselves out. When the oldster was this cranky, he was not fit to be around. During their weeks of travel, the boy had gotten to know Tindall well enough to determine how best to react to whatever sour mood he happened to be in. He could read him as well as anyone—and perhaps better, thanks to his life on the streets—enabling him to decide how hard to press and how quickly to back off. Tindall was irritable by nature, but mostly he was concerned for his creation. After a lifetime of inventing, he had been constantly thwarted by the Federation in his efforts to put his inventions to good use, so he had no intention of letting anything like that happen now.

Coming to Skaarsland to employ Annabelle was a clear risk—and one that Rocan was still not happy about. Tindall, while not doubting Annabelle, was nevertheless every bit as concerned that matters be handled in the right way, and that every precaution be taken to assure that nothing went awry. The Rovers—crew and family alike—found the old man amusing and insufferable by turns. But whatever mood they were in, they were not the type to tolerate being berated for very long. So Shea was worried that things might get out of hand. What a fifteen-year-old boy was supposed to do to prevent this from happening was not something he cared to speculate on. All he could manage were small steps in that direction, carefully chosen and cautiously taken.

But on this occasion, to his surprise, he found he had achieved a small victory. Tindall had stopped his excoriations and begun shouting out encouragements, just as Shea had recommended. The men shook their heads at the old man's attitude, but started smiling, too. When he glanced over at Shea, still standing off to one side, Tindall gave a small shrug of his bony shoulders as if to say, *See? Are you satisfied now?*

Shea had the grace to nod and smile.

Seconds later, Seelah was at his elbow. Seelah, according to Rocan, did not much like the cold. But here she was, nuzzling up against him, purring loudly and wrapping herself about him before sliding away and then coming back again, just as he thought her gone for good.

"Stop teasing me!" he said, vaguely irritated but at the same time rather pleased. "Why are you topside anyway when you hate the cold so much?"

She gave no response (she never did, save to Rocan,

who could understand her odd mewling), choosing instead to study the boy with those impossibly beautiful golden eyes. Then she wrapped herself about him again and squeezed gently—a gesture he did not entirely understand—before sliding away and disappearing for good.

He waited a long time for her to return, but when she failed to do so he walked forward and stood at the bow.

After a time, his thoughts drifted to Drisker Arc, and he found himself wondering—not for the first time—how the Druid was doing in his efforts to help stabilize the upheaval in the Four Lands. This led, in turn, to thoughts of Tarsha Kaynin and memories of their brief time together at the Rover village of Aperex. She confused him, but he liked her. She was smart and capable, and he wished she were still here. He wondered how she was now, off with her brother and the grandfather, trying to do something about that witch and finding a way to halt a Skaar attack on the Federation.

He wondered when he would see her again.

He wondered suddenly if he ever would.

So much about all their fates was in doubt that it was impossible to know how things would turn out. It was all he could do to see a way forward, let alone imagine the results of getting there. He was by nature a positive person, but there were limits. And feeling his life spinning out of control—his direction confused and ever-changing, his goals as distant as his home and his friends—was not helping. Not that Rocan was not a friend once more, but it wasn't the same since he had lost the other's trust. Everyone else was something of a stranger. He would like to think this would change, but for that to happen he would need more time than he was likely to get.

Just this morning, he had heard Tindall talking with Rocan and Darcon Leah about testing Annabelle that afternoon. Everyone felt that any sort of further delay would be a mistake, now that they were moored in Skaarsland and highly vulnerable to any sort of attack. Best that they get on with their experiment before they were discovered. Yet Dar insisted they could not leave until Ajin d'Amphere had returned from the city. He seemed convinced she would do so, but she had been gone for four days now, and even the Blade was beginning to look worried. Shea had noticed his furtive conversations with the Elven prince.

Something, he sensed, had gone wrong.

Within the home city of the Skaar, deep inside whatever complex the *pretender* conducted her experiments, Ajin d'Amphere was growing discouraged. It was the third day that she had been imprisoned with her mother, and there was no sign of any rescue coming. Not that there was any reason to expect one, but she had hoped that perhaps Dar Leah would come for her the way she would have come for him. Yes, she had told him she wanted to go alone and that he must give her time and space to do what she needed, but she had somehow thought he might put all that aside and come for her anyway. It was what she would have done for him, she kept telling herself, so why wouldn't he do the same for her? She knew with certainty now how much he loved her.

Ah, how that conviction burned in her! It had taken so long for him to admit it, to convince him they should be together. Odd, how it had been so evident to her right from the beginning—right from their first meeting. Right from the moment she had seen him spring over the side of his airship and come to the rescue of the foolish Druids her soldiers were attempting to kill. He had fought his way to the woman even when the man was lost, snatched her up, and carried her to safety in spite of the odds.

He had been so determined, such a force of nature. He had been magnificent.

And she had known in an instant that he was absolutely right for her. She could not let him go now.

Yet after all they had been through, had *he* given up on *her*?

She was sitting with her mother in the cell, staring out into the blackness of the room, eyes sufficiently adjusted to the darkness that she could make out the furtive movements of the wolf-kind prowling about near the far walls. Humans made into hybrid wolf creatures, made slaves, stripped of their will and their freedom and their identities: This was what the *pretender* would make of Ajin and Orestiana. This was the fate she would force upon them. *You will live to serve me. You will become two more of my pets, my creatures, and you will live out your lives in my company, watching as I rule Skaarsland. Maybe I will see to it that your father joins you and I will rule alone, a better queen than he has ever been a king. Would you not find that amusing, your little family bonding together as my creatures, my pets, my servants? Would you not appreciate the irony of it?*

Ajin would have ripped her heart out if she could have reached her, but the *pretender* was careful not to come too close to the cage that imprisoned them. She was careful, too, to keep a pair of the wolf-kind close at hand. She knew what her stepdaughter would like to do to her, but she came to Ajin anyway. The taunting and teasing pleased her; she wanted her prisoners to know their fate. And she wanted to enjoy herself while she waited for them to break down and beg for mercy.

Which, Ajin knew, would never happen.

Even so, her threats to slip the poison into their food and drink had persuaded them to stop eating and drinking entirely. They had gone without any form of sustenance now for two full days—and counting. Three times each day, food and drink were brought to them by the wolf-kind, and they left both untouched. Ajin and her mother had made a pact. They would die before they let the *pretender* make them her slaves.

But time and lack of nourishment were wearing them down. And when they were sufficiently drained of strength, the *pretender* would simply walk into their cage, have the wolf-kind hold them down, and pour the poison into their mouths. She had told them as much. She would have her victory, one way or the other.

Oh, to have a blade in her hand! One only, and a chance to fling it through the bars to end her stepmother's evil life! One momentary opportunity; it was all she dreamed about now, all she yearned for. But she knew it would never happen.

Sometimes, she cried. She did so silently and when Orestiana was sleeping, so she could not see. These were not tears of pity or fear or despair, for she had not shed those since she was a little girl. These were tears of frustration at her inability to do anything but wait for the inevitable.

She was crying now as her mother slept beside her. They slept more now as their bodies weakened. Her mother cried, as well. She had seen the tracks of her tears, the stains on the bedding. Ajin was hallucinating, too. She had caught glimpses of Dar in the darkness several times, furtively crossing to free her—his familiar crooked smile, his lean features, his black blade drawn and ready. Precious moments that did nothing more than generate false hopes. He was never there. And she felt more and more certain by now that he never would be.

She gave in to her tears for a bit longer, then steadied herself. Nothing was ever accomplished by weeping. What she needed to do—as she had needed to do all along—was to find a way to lure the *pretender* close enough to kill her.

More time passed. She could not tell how much because there was nothing by which to measure its passage. But at some point the door to the chamber opened, and the *pretender* appeared out of the gloom. She smiled as if greeting an old friend while glancing at first one and then the other of her prisoners in silent contemplation.

"You are not eating," she observed. "Nor drinking.

How foolish of you. All you are doing is prolonging your fate."

Ajin glared at her, saying nothing. Her mother stirred behind her, coming awake slowly and blinking into the dim light given off by the pair of flameless torches that offered what small illumination there was. "Ajin?" she asked uncertainly.

"Hush, Mama," Ajin said quickly. "We have company."

Her mother saw the *pretender* and shook her head. "I don't see anyone."

Agathien d'Amphere snorted. "Very brave. Very droll. Aren't you two a pair? But you change nothing by your refusal to accept your fate. You should stop being so stubborn and relent. Once it is done, you will remember nothing of this life. You will be free to begin your new life as my pets. You will even come to like it."

"We will never cooperate with you," Ajin said, "not even if we feel our lives slipping away. Should you try to force us, we will kill ourselves. We have already discussed it, and we know how it can be accomplished. You will not be able to stop us."

She was lying, of course, but it might give the *pretender* pause. And anything that caused her discomfort was a victory. Perhaps Agathien might even enter the cage and put herself within reach. It was not impossible.

But the *pretender* only shrugged. "I grow tired of this game. I think it is time to end it. I will give you another day—perhaps two—then I will see this business finished. Think on that, why don't you?"

And then she was gone.

Aboard the *Behemoth*, Dar Leah and Brecon Elessedil were deep in conversation. They had moved away from Annabelle—and away from the strident admonitions of Tindall—to the bow of the vessel, where they could be alone. They had been standing together all morning while the work was being carried out, discussing what precautions ought to be taken to protect the vessel and its precious cargo while the latter was put to use. They were aware they could remain hidden in this cove for only so long. They were even more aware that the weather was worsening.

It had begun to change the day before—a deepening of the cold, a sharper bite to the wind, and a thickening of the cloud cover, sealing away the island and those on it. The window of opportunity for using Annabelle effectively was closing. They had heard Tindall and Rocan discussing it, both concerned that if they delayed much longer, all chance of employing the machine would be gone.

But just now the Blade and the Elven prince were discussing another chance that might be lost.

"She should be back by now," Dar insisted for what must have been the twentieth time. It was the fourth day since Ajin had left to go into the city and search for her mother.

Brecon nodded. "Agreed. But what she was attempting might have taken her longer than she hoped. And she told you to wait."

"I've waited too long already. What if something happened to her?"

"It doesn't help that you are so smitten with her, does it?" his friend pressed.

The highlander grimaced. "You know it is more than that. In spite of all the obstacles and arguments, she completes me in a way no one else ever has. Some things cannot be reasoned away, and what draws me to her—what binds us together—is one of them."

Brecon shook his head in dismay. "If you say so. You had better decide then and stop agonizing. What will you do, wait one more day or go after her now?"

Darcon Leah considered, even though he already knew the answer. "I will go now. Right now, before I lose any chance of finding her."

His friend smiled. "Well, then, wait here a moment."

He started away, and Dar called after him. "What are you doing?"

"Coming with you, of course."

Dar shook his head at once. "I don't think so, Brec. I don't want you risking yourself."

"I didn't ask your permission."

"I can do this alone," the highlander insisted.

"Alone? Oh, really? And how will you find your beloved?"

"I don't know. Somehow, I will. I will search until I find her."

Brecon actually laughed. "How very inefficient when your best friend possesses the means of finding her right away. Let me get the Elfstones, and we will find her together."

The Blade smiled in spite of himself as he watched the Elf disappear below.

# THIRTY

THE JOURNEY BACK THROUGH the walls of the Iron Crèche was every bit as challenging as the one going in. Once again, it was facilitated by the wall dwellers, who took them by the hands and gave them the capacity to pass through the stone. Drisker still could not imagine how this was happening and could only barely tolerate the sensation of coming apart as the walls closed about him. Yet he pushed ahead through the mental barrier and fought back against his fears and doubts.

How this was affecting Grianne Ohmsford he had no way of knowing. She had said nothing about it on the way in and was an invisible presence within the walls on their journey back. Although he was struggling mightily to keep his composure intact, he assumed she must be tolerating it much better than he was. And her strength of will was forged in iron. She was impervious to so much of what the Forbidding would throw against her because she had lived in this prison for centuries. It made him shudder to think of what she had gone through and what it must have required of her to survive. It was unimaginable. He was not at all sure he could have done it. He was not sure he could do so now.

But he came through the walls unscathed and emerged back into the storeroom to discover the carnage that awaited. Blood and body parts were strewn everywhere. A sizable chunk of the clawrake was still recognizable, but little else. Some of the pieces were partially eaten, with teeth marks still evident. Drisker thought he might gag but managed to control it, closing his eyes momentarily and holding his breath.

When he opened his eyes again, the wall dwellers had disappeared, and the Straken Queen was across the room near the door. "Chule cannibals!" she hissed in fury. "Trapped and killed them all. But wait. Maybe not all." She sniffed the air. "Weka Dart!" she called out. "Come out!"

The little Ulk Bog emerged from behind a stack of supplies, staring at her in shock and despair, and Drisker felt a surge of relief. "I didn't do it, mistress. It wasn't my fault. I would never betray you! But I could not stop this from happening. I couldn't do anything but hide!"

His voice was breaking; its frantic tone had gone shrill by the end of his disclaimer. The Straken Queen went to him and bent down, taking him by his shoulders. "There, there, little one. I do not blame you. No one blames you. Of course you would never betray me. It was the moench, wasn't it?"

Weka Dart nodded at once. "He brought us here deliberately. It was all done so the Chule could kill you. The clawrake and the slint fought back, but there were too many. Then Vendra Trax killed the moench, as well, because he was displeased that it had failed to keep you in this room. He has gone to search for you and the Druid."

He glanced quickly at Drisker, his look ugly. "This is all your fault!"

"Hush, Weka Dart," the Straken Queen admonished. "This was my doing."

The Ulk Bog sneered openly. "But *he* was the one who caused all this to happen by leading you to think there was a magic that could help you leave the Forbidding! And leave me!"

Drisker turned to face him directly. "Then I guess you will be happy to know you were right. The darkwand wasn't anywhere to be found."

"Of course it wasn't!" Weka Dart was working himself up to a barely contained fury.

"And you even told me it wasn't here."

"I did! I warned you!" Weka Dart was right on the edge of breaking down. "I told you there was nothing to find! I told you this search was a waste of time . . ."

Suddenly he stopped talking, realizing he had said too much.

Grianne realized it, too. "You told Drisker the darkwand wasn't here?" Her voice became tight, and her eyes narrowed. "How did you know this, little Ulk Bog?"

"I . . . I didn't mean it that way. I just meant I was pretty sure." He was wincing as if in pain, his gestures frantic. He wheeled on Drisker. "This Druid has me all confused, using his tricks and twisting my words. You should leave him here!"

The Straken Queen stepped close to him, peered

into his frightened eyes, and reached down to squeeze his shoulder. She squeezed it so hard it dropped him to his knees, crying out in pain. "Are you afraid, Weka? Don't be. No one gets left behind. We stay together. We have to get out of here and go back to where we came from. To Kraal Reach. All of us." She turned to Drisker. "Am I right about our destination, Druid?"

He nodded. "I think so."

She turned back to Weka Dart. "Let's test your memory. What did I ask you to do before we left home?"

"Memorize our path . . . in so we could find our . . . way out again." He was crying softly.

"And did you do this?"

He nodded, grimacing at Drisker so that all his sharp teeth were revealed. "I know the way."

"I'm sure you do. I think you know quite a lot about things—a lot of things you've carefully kept to yourself. But we'll talk about that later."

Grianne turned to Drisker Arc. "I asked him to memorize our way into the Crèche so if we lost Styrik, we would be able to find our way out. He won't cross me now, but we must go. Vendra Trax and his Chule will be after us soon enough."

They moved to the door leading out of the storeroom, stopping to listen for what might be waiting beyond. Both could hear the sounds of movement and voices—not necessarily right outside, but close enough that once they emerged, they would be seen.

Drisker felt Weka Dart pressing in between them. "They will stop us!"

"They will try," the Straken Queen corrected. "But they will fail. Drisker Arc, are you ready?"

He raised his hands, where the blue Druid Fire burned at his fingertips. He gave her a small nod. "I will stand with you until we are either free or dead. It's odd, but I never thought this would end any other way. Not once since I found out where I was."

She gave him a surprisingly warm smile and a look of appreciation that revealed some small part of the woman she had once been. Then she eased open the storage room door and they stepped outside.

There was no one about. Weka Dart moved to the forefront, leading the way back. Drisker Arc stayed directly behind him, watching his movements. He had deduced the Ulk Bog's secret too late to change the outcome here. But now that he understood what the little man had done, he was not about to give him a chance to flee. A reckoning would come once they arrived back at Kraal Reach.

Down the hallway they went, sliding along the wall. Most of the voices were behind them, and the way forward was empty for as far as they could see. Drisker held the Druid Fire poised, ready to strike down those who might attempt to stop them. He felt oddly at peace with himself. It was the anticipation that was the worst. This moment felt seminal to him—a chance to redeem his decision to withdraw from the Druid order and his position as High Druid when he should have tried to forestall the destruction that followed. He could not have explained why, only that he felt it to be true.

They reached a place in the corridor where it

branched. To Drisker's consternation, sounds of life were coming from the way Weka Dart was indicating they must go. Druid and queen exchanged a knowing glance, and Grianne motioned for the Ulk Bog to get behind her. Slowly they advanced. She did not rush their approach, but gave it time, and indeed the volume of voices slowly lessened and died away until there was only their own muffled breath.

*They've gone,* Drisker thought.

They continued on, their backs pressed against the walls, the glow of torches ahead a flickering of light in an otherwise dark tunnel.

It all ended in an instant. There was a warning shout, then a rush of bodies hurtled toward them. The Chule—lithe, rawboned, swift, and sure—barreled out of the dark, the fire from the torches glinting off their blades.

Simultaneously, blue fire discharged from the fingers of both Druid and queen and slammed into the attackers. Half went down for good and the other half were thrown back and left gasping. Grianne stepped forward, her aged face a mask of fury as she dispatched those who had survived with what appeared to be no effort at all. The trio rushed on almost recklessly now, no longer holding back, the way forward momentarily clear. From behind, shouts and the pounding of booted feet rose in a din. Weka Dart was back in front, leading the way, as heedless as his companions. None of them knew what waited ahead, only that they must get clear of this fortress to have any chance at all of surviving. Passageways came and went—a blur of deep gloom brightened sporadically by patches of smoky torchlight, an endless progression of darkened corridors. Here and there, a clutch of Chule stood against them, only to go down under the Druid magic.

Once, a blade caught Drisker a glancing blow, but his adrenaline was surging and he felt nothing from the cut. He glanced at his side. Bleeding, but not badly. He rushed on, ignoring it.

There was no sense of time passing, no real recognition of how far they had come, and then abruptly they found themselves back where they had gained entry to the fortress. Weka Dart fumbled with the locks, seeking to release them. It seemed the worst was behind them. They were on the verge of escaping.

A whooshing sound was all it took to cast all their hopes away. Chain-link nets crashed down on them, dragging them to the floor. Only Weka Dart evaded the chains, too close to the door to be caught in their grip. Drisker felt the weight of the chains as he would the weight of his fate at the hands of his would-be captors. Vendra Trax was there—with a dozen of his Chule at his side—a huge, monstrous figure bearing an iron mace. His voice rang out amid the clash of the chains and the shouts of his men.

"Tighten them down! Pin them fast! I don't want them escaping again! I want to watch them struggle as we cut them apart!"

Drisker couldn't tell what the Straken Queen was doing, but he had summoned an acid that was already eating through the iron links. He watched the chains fall apart and was on his feet. Huge hands swung the mace in a deadly arc, but he blocked the blow with iron of his own—his arms like bars that could deflect any weapon. The Chule Lord stumbled back. Others took his place, and the Druid—become in those few seconds a berserker—destroyed them in a single sweep. Black robes flying out behind him, he launched himself into those that remained, bearing them to the floor, dispatching them one after the other. Strike, block, roll, and defend anew. He was back on his feet quickly, fighting with every bit of strength that remained to him—barely aware of what he was doing, just acting on instinct and need and emotion.

Something struck him from behind and drove him to the stone floor. He struck hard, headfirst, and was left dazed, pulling himself up on hands and knees.

Vendra Trax stood over him, his mace lifting to strike.

"Trax!" Grianne Ohmsford screamed in fury.

The Chule Lord turned instinctively to protect himself and found her standing less than five feet away. She, too, had gotten free of the chains. She faced him as if she might spring atop him, crouched low, gathered. Her face was a mask of pitiless rage, contorted and filled with a lifetime of fury brought forward for this moment.

Her hands were on fire; the flames licked up and down her arms as if feeding on her skin.

When she thrust her arms at him, the fire raced down her limbs as water might run from a faucet, surged free from her body, and engulfed the Chule Lord. In what could have been no more than a few seconds, he was burning from head to foot, a human torch welded in place by the death that had claimed him.

In a few seconds more, he was turned to ash. All about him, his Chule minions lay dead.

"Ulk Bog!" his queen said quietly. She pointed. "The locks."

In moments the door was open and the three companions were through the opening and into the tunnels beyond—back beneath the lake surrounding the fortress island, back into the damp and darkness. There were no longer any sounds of pursuit, but Drisker did not for a moment think the chase was over. Other of the Chule might come after them—if not through these tunnels, then across the lands beyond. They would hunt them down if only because penetrating their defenses and entering their fortress was reason enough to see them all put to the blade, if not in revenge for their dead leader. Unless finding Vendra's body took the heart out of them. But none of them would know how they might react until it happened.

Those fleeing moved as swiftly as the dim werelight at the fingertips of the Druid and the Straken Queen would allow, listening to one another's heavy breathing. Their journey was long and empty of everything but the sounds of their flight. No one talked. There was nothing to say, after all. Until they secured their freedom at the other end of the tunnels, there were no further decisions to be made and no reason to waste breath they would need later. Drisker found himself thinking of Tarsha and realized he had not made contact with her in days. He did not know where she was or what she was about. He had no idea if she was in danger. He had promised he would see her safe, and if he were to find freedom at last through an escape from the Forbidding, he would need to do so at once.

He was conscious of a throbbing in his side where the blade had cut him. He reached down for the wound and winced at the pain his touch brought. There was no blood, but the ache was intense nevertheless. He gritted his teeth against it and ran on.

Eventually, they reached the end of the tunnel maze at the other side of the swamp and emerged once more into the gray gloom aboveground. It was no longer night, but the clouds seemed to scrape the earth, and the mist was a thin rain that soon had them soaked. A quick search revealed that their pursuers had not yet found them. For the moment, they were alone.

"We must walk on a bit longer," Grianne informed the Druid, "but I assure you that we will not have to leave the same way we came in."

Drisker said nothing. He did not much care how they departed this foul place as long as they got out. And the sooner, the better.

They set off on foot and walked for a time before the Straken Queen noticed that Drisker was struggling. She stopped immediately and bent to examine him. "You've been hurt. Take off your cloak and tunic. Let me have a look."

He did not argue; the pain in his side was intense and unrelenting by now. He stripped off the clothing covering it, and Grianne bent close. "Ugh! Your wound has become infected, Drisker Arc. The blade was fouled with poison. You should have said something earlier."

She straightened and looked around. "We'll have to stop while I treat this." She pointed. "Over there, within that patch of scrub trees, should be a good enough choice for our concealment."

She led him into the crooked trees and found a patch of solid ground on which to lay him down. Weka Dart followed, looking irritated and anxious, but she had no time for him. When Drisker lay prone, she knelt beside him and carefully placed her hands on the wound so that they covered it completely.

"Stay still. I'm going to use the wishsong on it."

He lay quiet beneath her touch as she began to hum and then to sing in a voice that better belonged to a less ruined creature. Yet as she called forth her magic, years of her damaged life seemed to fall away. For the time she sang, she was transformed into another person entirely—younger and softer and less sharp-edged, unburdened from her years and memories of travail and sorrow. She sang in a steady cadence, the words indiscernible—if indeed they were words at all—the power of the magic flowing from her fingers into his body. The pain in his side lessened and then dropped away almost completely. His transformation was nothing short of a miracle. His relief left him feeling as if he were reborn into the world.

When she had finished, she continued to kneel beside him, her head bent, her eyes tightly closed. It seemed that she was recovering from her use of the wishsong, as if it had taken something from her and left her bereft. When she lifted her head and he saw her face again, he realized that all that the magic had given her had been whisked away. She was again whom she had been.

"Do not look at me," she whispered. She was crying, and she wiped furtively at the tears. "I cannot help myself. The wishsong gives me back a little of my old self when I use it to help rather than to hurt. Such moments are few, and each time I treasure them. The effect is only momentary; the magic cannot hold beyond the using. It never has, and it never will. My life's direction is determined by how I have lived it."

She shook her head, her lips forming a bitter scowl. "Would that I had lived it better." She glanced over at a watchful Weka Dart. "He needs to rest," she said, nodding at the Druid. "His healing requires it. He fought bravely back there in the Iron Crèche. He saved us all. We will sleep here for a few hours before continuing on."

She turned back to Drisker. "Understand, you are not yet made well. The poison went deep inside you. In a better place and time, we would let you rest for days and not hours, but hours are all we have, so we must make what use of them we can. Sleep, now. I will wake you when we need to go on."

He held up his hand to stop her. "Wait. Let me speak with Weka Dart first. Just the two of us alone. I think it might help."

She shrugged. "He has already given himself away. I don't see what talking will achieve before returning to Kraal Reach. This is where you believe he has hidden the darkwand, isn't it?"

Drisker nodded. "Let me speak with him anyway.

I think I might be able to persuade him to help us retrieve the staff willingly."

She rose without another word and walked off into the darkness. "Weka!" she called to the figure huddled to one side. "Go speak with Drisker. Now."

The Ulk Bog slouched over to where the Druid lay and stood looking down at him. "What do you want?"

"Where is the darkwand?"

The little man spat. "I should have let you die!"

"Maybe. But you didn't. So listen carefully. You can't lie about this; she will see right through you. She's already realized the truth. You stole the darkwand from the Chule to stop her from using it a long time ago. You stole it to keep her from leaving the Forbidding. You've kept it hidden away all these years. She knows this, and you have to make things right. You have to go to her and admit what you did, tell her you are sorry, and beg her forgiveness, or there is no hope for you."

The Ulk Bog shook his wizened head. "If I give her the staff, she will leave. She will go back into her old world with you, and I will be left behind. I would rather die! I won't do it."

"You have to. If you don't, you will be killing her."

"I will be killing myself, you mean!"

"No, you will be killing her. She will die if you refuse to let her go. Can you not see this?"

The Ulk Bog snarled at him. "I would never hurt her! Never! You will kill her by taking her back into your world. She almost died there before!"

"At the hands of demons from the Forbidding. At the hands of Tael Riverine. And how long will she live if she remains here? You told me yourself she has enemies everywhere, working to rid themselves of her. She is old and she weakens, don't you see? In the Four Lands, she can go back to her old life as a Faerie creature, an aeriad. This is what she longs for. Will you deny her what she wants most when it is within your power to give it to her? I cannot believe it of you."

"I will protect her!"

"You will *try* to protect her, but you will fail. And how will you feel when she's gone and you have only yourself to blame?"

They stared at each other for several long minutes, considering the arguments and the choices that might result. Drisker felt himself growing drowsy from the healing efforts Grianne had employed on his behalf. He had to end this.

"I will make you a promise," he said quietly. He waited for the Ulk Bog to look at him directly. "If you do as I ask, I will insist she bring you back with us if it is possible. I don't know that it is—I don't even know if she can take me—but I will tell her she must take you if she takes me."

Weka Dart shook his head. "She will never forgive me. She will leave me no matter what you say."

"I will try to prevent that from happening." He sighed wearily. "What else can you do but return the staff? If you don't do what I said, she will find a way to force you to tell her where it is, and she will certainly never forgive you then. You've done a terrible thing. You have betrayed her with your selfishness. So make it right. Go to her and offer your help. Then there is at least a chance of forgiveness."

Weka Dart rose, shaking his head. "I will think about it. But I promise nothing,"

He walked away without another word. Drisker watched him go, wondering if anything he had said had made a difference. When Grianne wandered back over a few moments later, he was trying to rise, to tell her he was rested enough that they could continue their efforts to flee this place, but without a word she pushed him down. A quick word of magic passed her lips and he was asleep.

# THIRTY-ONE

THE SUNRISE WAS FIERY in the eastern sky when the Federation camp began to stir, full of expectations for their last full day before the journey home. But those expectations were not the same for everyone—and particularly not for Belladrin Rish. As she woke, having barely slept, a mix of concerns and hard truths preoccupied her. One phase of her life would be ending and another beginning. One way or the other, she would be leaving Belladrin Rish behind by day's end. And while she harbored few regrets about leaving, she had a raft of doubts about where she was headed.

No Clizia-related miracle had occurred to hasten Cor d'Amphere's death. And on top of that, she had been forced to kill Choten Benz to prevent him from exposing her further. She had managed to hide the body in a trunk filled with clothes that had belonged to Ketter Vause, then ordered the trunk removed to the storage area for supplies, materials, and weapons designated for return to Arishaig. This had bought her perhaps three or four days, but before long the smell would give the game away and Benz's body would be discovered. Time was running out, and nothing was coming to pass as Belladrin had hoped.

But she was a Skaar Penetrator and was never entirely at a loss for ways out of trouble. Her reluctance about going through with Cor d'Amphere's plans to destroy the Federation army had not changed. She was living with too much guilt already to want to take on more—especially now that she must add in Choten Benz who, after all, had stood by her on more than one occasion in the past and for whom she had harbored some admiration.

But what could she do to change it? Thanks to Clizia Porse's ineptitude and poor judgment, Cor d'Amphere was still alive. And if she did not go through with her part of the plan, the Skaar king would kill off the remainder of her family and hunt her down. And she knew only too well how persistent he could be in eliminating those who had betrayed or disappointed him.

She would miss the Dwarves, Lakodan and Battenhyle. They were good men and—had things been different—she would have preferred to consider them friends. She liked the former's gruff demeanor and tough resilience, and the latter's warm charm and easy, straightforward way of seeing the world. But her obligations to Cor d'Amphere would never permit friendships with the people she was betraying, and her life would never give her another moment's peace until she was free of the Skaar king—which she was determined she would be once this was over. You could not serve two masters in this world, no matter who you were, and she was done with it.

So today she would begin the journey that would take her to a better place. She would disappear when the fire and iron descended, slipping away like the ghost she saw herself to be, gone into oblivion and eventually forgotten by all. The Skaar king would think her dead, and she would do her best to see that—as far as he was concerned—she really would be. She would leave the camp and its inhabitants before they were eradicated and hasten to the small airship she had managed to commandeer. She would send a warning to her family of what was coming before fleeing to her new life. Where that life might be she couldn't be sure, but she would find it.

Today she would begin to find peace and comfort in her own, real skin, and all the charades and pretenses and dissembling would be left behind.

But there remained one unpleasant task for her to undertake. Choten Benz had nearly undone all her plans before she had killed him, and he had shared his suspicions about her with the Dwarves, which meant there remained a loose end that must be tied up. She regretted what that meant more than she could say— and if it was just her own life at stake, she might have willingly sacrificed it for their freedom. But it was the life of her family in the balance, and that was a sacrifice she could not make.

She regretted, too, losing Benz as an ally. He was the only member of the Federation hierarchy who had stood by her instead of against her. Even if his choice to ally himself with her was driven by personal ambition, he had helped her immeasurably in her confrontations with Commanders Aarcobin and Messit.

If only he had left well enough alone and just done as she suggested, he would still be alive. But in the end he had pushed a little too hard.

She rose, washed and dressed, thought about eating, then decided against it. Instead she summoned her aide from the adjoining chamber.

"Daemount," she greeted him when he slipped through the tent flaps. "Please summon Lieutenant Commander Oberion and ask him to attend me."

Her aide nodded wordlessly and disappeared back outside her chamber. She stood looking after him for a moment, feeling sick at what she was about to do.

She had genuinely liked those Dwarves, and they did not deserve the fate to which she was about to consign them.

Lakodan and Battenhyle were helping their men finish packing their supplies and weapons so they could set out for home by midday when Lieutenant Commander Oberion approached them. Lakodan, always the more intuitive of the pair, saw at once from the officer's young face the promise of something unpleasant. He glanced at his companion, who was still unaware of the man approaching, and nudged him gently. "Trouble," he whispered.

Battenhyle turned, looked, and said nothing.

"Good morning," Oberion said, in a tone that suggested he found it anything but. "I have a message from my superiors. They have decided they need both of you to come with us as far as the walls of Arishaig in order to protect against unexpected attacks on our journey home."

Both Dwarves stared at him. "Attacks on your transports?" Lakodan asked in disbelief.

"Attacks from whom?" Battenhyle added quickly.

The lieutenant commander shook his head. "The Skaar, I guess. We need someone more familiar with employing the Reveals if an attack should occur. Our men are trained, but they are not as experienced as you. The rest of your men can continue on their way; all we need are the two of you. You will be free to go once we are safely back in Arishaig."

"Do they think the Skaar will attempt to attack us?" Battenhyle pressed. "Even with the truce in place?"

Oberion rubbed his face with his hand. "I couldn't say. Perhaps. I wasn't consulted or informed until just a few minutes ago, but I was told to say that if you failed to come with us, you risked losing your protection against conscription. I know it is your decision, but for what it is worth I think you had better comply."

"So, another promise proved false," Lakodan sneered. "The Federation makes a habit of it."

"What does Miss Rish say to this?" his companion asked. "Did she argue against this nonsense?"

"I couldn't say; I wasn't there when the conversation took place. She was simply relaying orders. But perhaps what happened to Commander Benz has put them all on edge."

The Dwarves exchanged a furtive glance. "Choten Benz?" Lakodan asked quickly.

The young officer nodded. "It looks like he might have deserted; no one has been able to locate him all morning."

Lakodan frowned. He knew Benz, and the man

wasn't one to desert; he took his duties seriously. But beyond that, he went missing the morning after he confronted Belladrin Rish about his suspicions? No, this had all the earmarks of something else entirely.

He was about to say as much when Battenhyle grabbed his arm and shook his head. "If you need us, we will come with you," he told Oberion. "Please inform the commanders, will you?"

The lieutenant commander was only too happy to do so, nodding his thanks and scurrying off. The Dwarves stood silently and watched him go, then Lakodan said, "What's going on?"

"I think our friendship with Miss Rish is over." Battenhyle turned to him and lowered his voice. "You and I already had doubts when Benz came to us yesterday. He said he was going to speak to her—*confront* her, in fact."

Lakodan nodded. "And it didn't end well for him."

"So it seems. But what if he said something to her about speaking with us? Now she has to dispose of us, as well—not knowing, of course, how much we were told or what sort of danger we now present. If she's done all the things that Benz believed possible, she would not chance it."

Lakodan rubbed his huge hands together vigorously, then threw up his arms in disgust. "Why not just kill us and be done with it?"

Battenhyle shook his head, then looked at him speculatively for a moment. "What if she doesn't need to?"

His friend stared back at him, frowning. "What are you thinking?"

"What were we telling ourselves yesterday about another surprise attack on the Federation—one that would succeed because it would come when the camp was most exposed? If you were the Skaar king, what would be the optimal time to launch such an attack?"

"On the way back to Arishaig? Use their warships to blow the Federation right out of the sky?"

"If they attacked then, the Federation warships would be able to fight back and the Skaar would have lost their greatest advantage."

"You mean their ability to become invisible?"

"Exactly. Wouldn't it be smarter to strike while the airships are still on the ground and the Federation soldiers are preoccupied with moving aboard?"

Lakodan nodded slowly. "You think they intend to attack tomorrow?"

"Yes, at the moment right before we lift off. That's when I would do it. From the ground and from the air both. If they really do intend an attack."

"But how can we know?"

"As matters stand, we can't. Not until it happens. So maybe a little preparation might be a good idea. And we can warn Oberion, at least."

"He won't believe us."

Battenhyle nodded. "Who knows? He might. Why don't we find out?"

Belladrin Rish was packing her travel bag—a small, easily carried backpack filled with a little bit of clothing and some food and water—when Battenhyle walked into her chambers. She turned at once, surprised to find him there and angry that he had walked in unannounced.

"Blessings on you, Miss Belladrin," the Dwarf greeted her cheerfully.

"And on you, Elder." She gave him an appraising look. "Usually, men don't walk into a lady's chambers without asking permission, but in your case, I will make an exception. How can I help you?"

"Well, I have a problem I must solve, and it involves you. Would you be willing to help me?"

"Always. What sort of problem could you have that would involve me?" She was suddenly uneasy. "Does this have to do with you and Lakodan accompanying us until we reach Arishaig?"

"Orders given by you, I am told—and therein lies the problem. You have done so much for us and for the Federation while acting as a personal adviser to the unfortunate Ketter Vause, but the circumstances surrounding your help are troubling. Let's review. Only you seem to know what the former Prime Minister intended. When the Federation delegation traveled to the Skaar king after Vause's death, only you were present when the conversation with the Skaar king took place and the terms of the truce were reached. Only you were taken into the Prime Minister's confidence about that mysterious letter he left. Only you were there to kill the Prime Minister's assassin. So much of what has transpired is based on information known only to you, or to those who are dead. Do you see?"

She forced her features to remain expressionless. "What I see is a man who has worked too hard and fought too well to be speaking such nonsense. How could I have managed everything of which you seem to be accusing me? I was nothing more than an assistant to the Prime Minister. I did not make policy; I was not consulted on any of his decisions. Think about it. How could I have done what you suggest and not been caught out?"

Battenhyle skipped right past her question. "Consider the circumstances surrounding the Prime Minister's assassination. Ketter Vause was killed in his sleep by a disgruntled soldier, you say. A common soldier who bypassed numerous guards to reach the Prime Minister's sleeping chamber? And then almost escaped until you happened to kill him? How did you manage it? You must have been the luckiest person alive. Killing a trained assassin with a single thrust is extremely difficult—especially for a young woman who, as you've said, was nothing more than an assistant."

She held his gaze, but she was beginning to feel trapped. "I was lucky, Elder. I acted without thinking because I was afraid for my life. I've had some experience with blades, yes; my brother was in the army. Nor have I lived a sheltered life. I have had to learn to look out for myself."

Battenhyle shrugged, his bluff face untroubled. "Maybe. But then there's the matter of Choten Benz. Missing, presumed deserted in the night, not long after he expressed to Lakodan and myself the same concerns I have just voiced to you? He even said he was going to confront you about it. I have known Choten Benz a long time, and he is not the type to abandon his duties without giving word to anyone, no matter how unpleasant. Is it possible he came to see you about his concerns and you saw him as a threat and killed him? And now you have arranged for us to accompany you to Arishaig. Why? Keeping us close? Are you worried there might be a breach of a truce you negotiated?"

"Am I wrong to worry? The Skaar have attacked us before when we did not expect it. Is it so unlikely that they might do so again?"

"Not so unlikely," the Dwarf agreed. "Just the opposite, I think. The attack is already planned, is it not? I believe you orchestrated that, too. You suggested that most of the heavy equipment be sent on ahead, along with the warships; those are already gone. What remains behind are the transports and the bulk of the army. And you suggested this as well, I've learned. Your advice is far-reaching and perhaps self-serving. When will this attack happen, do you suppose?"

"I think you should go now." She felt herself grow angry and knew she was starting to lose control. "You rant and you insinuate, and you have nothing to support your theories but supposition! I reject all of it, and I want you gone. Now!"

Battenhyle kept staring at her. "The attack won't happen at all, Miss Rish, because Lakodan and Lieutenant Commander Oberion and I found the damage to the diapson crystals and parse tubes of the transports and repaired it. I imagine that was what brought down the airships when the advance force was destroyed as well, wasn't it? Do you remember what happened when the last Federation advance force was destroyed? Their airships were sabotaged, and all those within them died. Those left on the ground were cut to pieces. Isn't that right? But it won't happen this time."

"You found . . ." Belladrin Rish saw her plans for the future catch fire and burn. Everything she had been planning had turned to ash. Still, she fought to keep control. "So, I was right to think there might be an attack and you would be needed. That doesn't mean I am involved."

"Belladrin!" he snapped, any attempt at maintaining formalities cast aside. "Stop lying. Your lies reveal you for who and what you are. We found Choten Benz while searching the storeroom for items to be transported, jammed into a trunk of clothing, with a knife wound in the back of his neck. And—" He paused. "—you were seen dragging him there."

She felt the blood drain from her face. "But there was no one . . ." she started to say, then caught herself. Too late. Too late! She tried to cover her slip anyway. "No one could have seen me because I was never there."

But Battenhyle just shook his head. "That ship has sailed, Belladrin. You are Skaar, then? All this time, you have been serving the Skaar and undermining the Federation. When they try you in Arishaig, you are not likely to receive much mercy."

"I do not have to . . ."

"So why don't you do something to make amends? Now that the Federation is prepared, another battle will leave hundreds more dead—on both sides. But you have a truce in place. The Skaar have secured the land north of the Mermidon. Is that not enough? Can your king not accept this as a reasonable settlement?

There are too many of us, Miss Belladrin—far too many for the Skaar to believe they can conquer us all. Once the Elves are involved—and the Dwarves—your people will be annihilated. You simply don't have the numbers. So put an end to all this. Go tell your king to hold to the treaty. This war is over."

She stared at him, weighing her options. He was right; so much of what lay ahead involved further loss of life. And to what end? She was sick of it. All of it. She wanted it all to be over, but could see no way out save one.

"You would free me to return and speak on your behalf?" She had to ask; she knew that further pretense was not possible. Battenhyle and Lakodan and Oberion had made up their minds about her. "Why should I agree?"

"If you refuse my offer, then we will send word to your king that you have betrayed him and come over to our side. Either way, you will be removed from any further involvement in this war. Which do you choose?"

She saw Lakodan and Lieutenant Commander Oberion step through the flaps. Listening from outside all this time, she realized. She shook her head wearily. All of her machinations and scheming had been revealed. Everything she had worked for had come to nothing. What was the point in continuing to pretend? So, they wanted her to return to Cor d'Amphere and tell him it was pointless to continue. Confront him with the truth and hope for the best. His plans were revealed, and the Federation was prepared to stop him. His attack would fail. His soldiers would fight and die for nothing.

"This man you would send me back to—this king of the Skaar—does not accept explanations of the sort you suggest, Elder," she said. "He will likely have me drawn and quartered and attack you anyway."

Battenhyle shrugged. "At least we will be fully prepared for him if he does. And executing you here is an option none of us particularly care to employ. You are well regarded by our soldiers, and knowing we had harbored a spy in our midst would be detrimental to morale." He glanced over his shoulder at his companions. "Am I not right?"

Both nodded, Lakodan with a scowl and Lieutenant Commander Oberion with a sad look that demonstrated the depth of his disappointment.

She nodded back. "Then I accept your offer. But I am surprised you trust me to do what you asked." She paused, forcing a smile. "What's to keep me from just flying away, once you give me a ship?"

"Who said we would give you a ship?" Oberion snapped. "You can find your own way back. And if you should wander off in the wrong direction, you will be hunted by both Skaar and Federation forces. I will see to it personally, and any freedom you think you might enjoy will not last for long."

She considered, sighed, and nodded wearily. "Then I accept your offer. Is there anything in particular you want me to say?"

"You know him better than we do," Battenhyle said. "What we are doing is taking a calculated risk. If you are successful, the war is finished. No attack is mounted, no lives are lost. You are most persuasive when you want to be, Miss Belladrin. I think you will find a way."

"Pack what you need, and we will provide a lift across the Mermidon," Oberion said. "After that, you are on your own. You are free to go anywhere you wish."

She might have laughed under other circumstances. She almost did. Free to go? It was unlikely she would be allowed to go anywhere once Cor d'Amphere had her in hand. And her plans for the safety of her family were dashed to bits. They would all be executed along with her, victims of a man for whom forgiveness and mercy were strangers. A failure must be punished, and a life of service ended when the service could no longer be rendered. Unless . . .

"I will leave at once," she told them, and she turned away to finish packing.

When finished, she followed Oberion to the airfield and a waiting two-man, stowed her pack behind the cockpit, and climbed inside. She would not return to Cor d'Amphere as she had said she would. She would not attempt to persuade him of anything, as such an attempt would never succeed. Instead, once deposited on the north bank of the Mermidon, she would disappear into the far reaches of the mountains west, settling into some little community where she would never be found. She could not go home, because she had no real home after so many years in service to the king. She would not even have a family anymore—not after everything that transpired today. She had sacrificed everything for years to protect them, shedding her youth and her innocence in equal measure, engaging in acts of which she had never thought herself capable. She was a good person with a good heart, yet how many lives had been lost because of what she had done? Maybe it was time to end it all, even if it also meant the deaths of those she cared for most.

She could not bear to think on it for more than a few moments. She hated herself, hated that she was being selfish and cowardly, but she intended to salvage what she could. And all that seemed possible was saving herself.

Yet once airborne, she began to have second thoughts. She had given her word to at least attempt to persuade Cor d'Amphere to give up his plans for attacking the Federation command. They had released her because she had given her word when they could have held her prisoner, taken her back to Arishaig, and executed her. She had escaped with her life in exchange for a single act of redemption, thanks to Battenhyle and Lakodan, who had been her friends. Even after they had revealed her as an enemy, they had given her a chance. In truth, they had been the only real friends she had ever had.

So she abandoned her plans for an immediate escape, deciding she would go to the Skaar king after all. She felt a twinge of fear at the thought of facing the king, but a clear sense of relief, too. She would keep her promise, and no one could fault her for not trying, even if she failed. The attack on the Federation was scheduled to take place tomorrow, but now that it had been uncovered and the explosives disabled, she had more than enough time left to keep her promise to the Dwarves and Oberion. A direct appeal to Cor d'Amphere's common sense, and then it would be over and done with and she could vanish like mist in a wind.

Once landed and left on her own, she set off for the Skaar camp. Her resolve tightened as she came up to the perimeter, but she stopped there still within the forest. Finding a secluded space, she curled up in a ball and went to sleep, waiting until nightfall. She found it hard to sleep, knowing what was coming, but she did the best she could until twilight descended, napping on and off, thinking back on her life the way one does. She was not of this country, but she had grown to love it, and perhaps she could yet become a part of it. Perhaps one day, she would even return to find Battenhyle and Lakodan, go back to Crackenrood and surprise them. Perhaps she would even end up living there.

No. It was a dream, all of it. She knew the truth by now. Which was why she had decided on a fallback plan.

When it was dark she made her way into the heart of the camp—moving stealthily to avoid any chance of detection. She found the king's tent, and made certain he was alone before slipping inside. She found him staring into space, looking old and worn. She stared at him for long minutes before interrupting.

"Your Majesty," she said.

His head lifted. "What are you doing here? I told you to remain in the Federation camp."

His words were angry and threatening. It was as she had said to Battenhyle. He would never listen to her, and her efforts to persuade him would come to naught.

Even so, she said, "The plan has failed. They have discovered the damage done to their airships and righted it. They suspect what you intend. An attack now would be a disaster for the Skaar."

He stared at her. "And who are you to make such a pronouncement? I am the one who will decide what needs to be done! How is it that they discovered our sabotage of their transports anyway? You were to make certain they did not! *And* you have disobeyed me by coming here."

"I thought you should know how matters stand. And I have been thinking. Can we not simply stay where we are and begin building a new home? We have possession of the entire Northland. We have a truce in place with the Federation. We *will* be left alone and allowed to settle if we give up our plans to attack them. This will save many lives—on our side as well as theirs." Her sigh was deep and weary. "Do you not grow tired of all this? Of the constant wars, of the endless struggles? Should we not return home for the rest of our people and bring them here while there is still time?"

He laughed abruptly—a raw, mocking laugh. "You know nothing, Belladrin—or whatever your name is today. You are a spy who does my bidding and you are never to question me! You think they will let us live in peace as neighbors? How foolish you are. They are going to be our enemies forever, and I have to crush them while they are weakened and off balance."

"I am only trying to ask questions you should be . . ."

He lurched to his feet, enraged. "I should kill you and your entire family and rid the world of your presence! You were useful enough when you were younger, but you are starting to become troublesome. Perhaps you need a lesson on who rules and who serves. It might even be enjoyable for you—take your mind off your failure and your cowardice."

He lurched toward her, and she took a quick step back. Always, she had been afraid in his presence, and she was afraid now. She spied the decanter and glass on a table nearby. Cor d'Amphere had been drinking, and the effects were showing. She had seen him like this a few times before. When he was this way, he would not allow himself to be persuaded to anything.

As she had suspected, there was only one way to keep her promise to Battenhyle and Lakodan—only one way, and it would cost her everything.

She let him come up to her, waited for him to reach for her, then slipped free the dagger sheathed in her belt behind her back, took a firm grip, and struck. The force of her blow carried the weight of the conviction that she could bear no more from this man, fueled by a toxic combination of loathing, desperation, and fury. She drove the blade into his chest so hard that she buried it up to the hilt. *This is for me and my family. This is for Kol'Dre. This is for all the times and ways you used me. This is for all I have suffered. This is for the life you have stolen from me.* The king gasped, his legs buckling as he dropped to his knees and then to the floor of the tent. He lay there, one hand trying unsuccessfully to pull out the blade.

She knelt beside him, looking into his shocked eyes.

"I am free of you," she whispered. "But at what further cost to me?"

She watched his breathing slow and then stop altogether.

What she had once dispatched Clizia Porse to do she had ended up doing herself. There would be no attack on the Federation now. There would be no war, no bloodshed, no loss of life. At least not until a decision could be reached on how to proceed now that their king was gone. A message would have to be sent home to ascertain who would now rule. Because whatever else happened, the Skaar people would no longer be ruled by Cor d'Amphere.

And for her? What would there be for her?

She smiled, shook her head, and rose. It was impossible to say just yet. She still had a chance at the life she had planned for herself—a life free of Cor d'Amphere's domination. She had only to begin the journey that would set her on that path.

She moved to the rear of the tent, cut a slit in the fabric, slipped through soundlessly, and disappeared into the night.

# THIRTY-TWO

◆

IF CLIZIA PORSE HAD thought her sickness after banishing Drisker Arc was bad, her illness after her battle with Tarsha Kaynin was ten times worse. Even though she had not used the Stiehl to put an end to the girl, she was still drained and nauseous. Not knowing what else to do, she had fled back to Winstrom and the Jachyra—whose level of disobedience to her commands she had not even bothered to ascertain in the face of wounds both physical and mental.

She might have survived the encounter, but she was wondering if it had been worth it.

This time, she tried everything to improve her condition, using both healing magic and medicines to fight back. She cleaned and bandaged her wounds. She applied poultices and wraps. She tried rest and limited exercise, baths and a hot room turned steam bath by wood fires that burned in dampened iron grates. She employed fresh doses of healing magic to mend and cure. She then resorted to waiting it out when all else failed—a forced march through nightmares when she slept and hallucination when she awoke.

The effects were bad enough that, at several points, she had resigned herself to dying.

Once again, she lost track of the passage of time, but her worst fears were not realized, and slowly her wounds—both physical and magical—began to knit. Which meant, in turn, that she would soon have to discover whether Tarsha Kaynin had also survived their encounter. If she had, then Clizia was confronted by two obvious choices. She could search out and kill Tarsha Kaynin—and really kill her, this time—before the girl got to her first. Or she could eliminate the Skaar king, Cor d'Amphere, as she had promised Belladrin Rish, in order to prove her value to the Federation—for her need for that alliance had still not diminished.

Still, she would do better forgetting about the king for now and focusing her efforts instead on the greater danger Tarsha Kaynin would present if she were still alive. Better to determine if that threat was real first. This girl was not some irritant to be pushed aside. She was a wielder of powerful magic—an Ohmsford descendant and bearer of the wishsong. If she became any more proficient in its use than she already was, she would be fully capable of defeating Clizia. Especially if Clizia continued to be so weakened by the use of her own magic.

Tarsha Kaynin had to be eliminated, and quickly.

After locating the Jachyra and reasserting her dominance once again—fortunately, it looked like the creature had at least been more circumspect about its kills this time around—the old woman stared out the window of her cottage and into the night. Witch light played off the swamp waters and filtered through the trees. Night sounds filled the countryside air, signaling the start of a sordid dance between predators and prey.

*Tarsha Kaynin, where are you? How can I find you, little girl?*

And suddenly, she knew.

Tarsha Kaynin had returned to Emberen, where she was trying hard not to think about Drisker Arc. She had arrived in Emberen a week earlier, after she had woken at last from her coma and left the Federation camp. How long she had been in that coma she could not have said, but at some point she had woken long enough to use the wishsong to begin her healing, and after that, everything had progressed swiftly. And once she felt strong enough, she chose to slip away without notice to anyone.

She felt vulnerable amid the Federation soldiers—out of place and exposed. She knew she would do better back in Emberen with Flinc and Fade and perhaps Drisker, should he have managed to escape the Forbidding by now. She also felt certain that she had damaged Clizia sufficiently that her enemy would not be coming for her again right away. Clizia, too, would need time to heal, and Tarsha had sensed a weakness in her enemy that had not been there before.

But now that she was back in Emberen, she was growing increasingly anxious while waiting for Drisker to contact her. She spent a portion of every day reading the Druid's books of magic in an effort to find an alternative to the darkwand that might free him from the Forbidding, but so far she had located nothing useful. She was fully aware of how much danger the Druid was in and how little control he had over his life until he recovered the darkwand. That he might not be successful in his efforts was not something she would let herself consider. He *would* recover it, no matter what it took. He would ally himself with Grianne Ohmsford so that, when she summoned the staff's magic, he would be transported back into the Four Lands. Then he could stand beside Tarsha when she again faced Clizia Porse.

Which was another concern. She had not heard anything from the witch, either. This was good, but it only meant postponing the inevitable. The witch would come again at some point, enraged at how Tarsha had managed to stand against her, furious at the damage that had been done to her, and Tarsha would have to face her—Drisker or no Drisker. Revenge was a powerful motivator, and Clizia was not immune to its call. Tarsha would have help from the forest imp and the moor cat, but not the sort of help that Drisker could offer. Still, she was resigned to the fact that she could change nothing of what was going to happen. Especially where Drisker was concerned.

Because Drisker had not come to her in dreams for almost two weeks, and she was beginning to wonder what had happened to him.

She devoted a portion of each afternoon to sitting at Tavo's gravesite and reading to him. She liked the sense of closeness it gave her; she liked thinking he might somehow be hearing her. Usually, Flinc sat with her, keeping her company, listening to her read. But on one such day, he grew restless and began to complain.

"I'm rather bored with all this sitting around. I have a headache. Maybe we should take a walk down to the stream to watch the beavers build their dam. Now, there's a worthy task. There is an effort to admire for the work and the skill that goes into it. Much more so than what you are doing. And look at your hands! Filthy! You keep digging at the boy's grave, soiling your pretty fingers. Why do you do that, lovely Tarsha? Is this a habit you cannot break? Maybe it would help if I put gloves on your hands. At least it would help keep your hands clean. Did I mention how hungry I am? Aren't you hungry? Can't we have something to eat? Just a little something . . ."

On and on until she thought she would scream. She would have preferred the company of Fade, but the big moor cat was off keeping watch. Flinc, on the other hand, had nothing better to do than sit with her. But usually he did so quietly and uncomplainingly. She had suggested he read with her more than once, but the forest imp was quick to point out that this wasn't the sort of thing his people did.

She would have liked to know exactly what they did do, other than sit around commenting on other people's efforts, but she doubted she would get a forthright answer. Flinc was not the sort to discuss his life. She knew next to nothing about his people—not even how long they had been around, or how many they were, or what sorts of powers they possessed as descendants of an ancient Faerie folk. Everything they talked about was of the here and now.

After a time, she grew tired trying to read over his incessant complaints and sat back on her heels to stare off into the forest. The shadows cast by the great old-growth giants were lengthening as the day began to wane, and the sun to drop into the horizon. Flinc was still nearby, but he had gone silent. She found herself thinking once more of Drisker, wondering if there was a way for her to reach out to *him*—to project her astral self to him as he did to her. But she didn't know how to do it, and so was reduced to waiting. Her sense of helplessness troubled her. She then thought about Shea Ohmsford and the others aboard the *Behemoth*, somewhere off in Skaarsland—either already arrived at or close to reaching their destination. She wondered about the machine they had taken with them, the marvelous invention that perhaps could change the weather.

And by doing so, maybe change the course of history.

Her thoughts drifted to all that had happened since she had first come to Drisker's cottage, then without warning she was crying. It happened regularly and all at once these days—a grieving process she could not control and knew she must work through. Losing Tavo had all but destroyed her. Losing him after finding him again. Losing him after so much had happened to bring them back together.

And losing him this time for good.

She was crying hard, and Flinc was at her side, a hand on her shoulder. For once he was not saying anything. He was offering reassurance simply by being close enough to touch her, to let her know he was there.

She reached up to put her hand over his and cried

herself out with nearly silent sobs, head bent to hide her tears.

Hidden from her, as a result, was the war shrike sitting high in a nearby tree, watching.

Five days earlier, Clizia had decided to summon and dispatch shrikes she commanded into the Four Lands to hunt for Tarsha, concentrating her efforts on the areas where she suspected the girl might be found. It wasn't that much of a stretch to think she would return either to Paranor or to the Westland—the two parts of the country with which she was most familiar—but she started first with the Federation encampment. Once she discovered the girl was no longer there, Clizia went back to her first impulse and sent her birds into the Westland and to Paranor. If they could not find the girl there, she would expand the search to other regions. But she needn't have worried. The seventeenth shrike to return brought the news she was seeking. Tarsha was living once more in Drisker's cottage in the Westland village of Emberen—a place both familiar and comforting for a young girl who had lost everything.

But maybe her choice of a safe haven was something more as well. Was it too much to believe she might have gone back there to find the Druid's books of magic and perhaps unearth a spell or conjuring that might allow her to help Drisker return to the Four Lands?

She knew at once this was exactly what the girl was doing. Unable to help her mentor in any other way, she would seek his books and find within their pages a magic that would give him a path back home. Whatever else happened, Clizia knew she could not allow this to happen. Twice, she had rid herself of Drisker and thought him gone for good. She had failed the first time, and she had no intention of failing again. She had no idea if a way existed to bring the Druid back, but she knew immediately she must go to Emberen and make certain it didn't happen.

It might be that Tarsha was only waiting for him to find his own way back, but she couldn't risk the girl's interference. Her intelligence and her magic were too dangerous. If the girl were silenced for good—as Clizia had thought she had managed to do at Cleeg Hold and again at the Federation camp—any risk of her helping Drisker Arc or interfering with Clizia's plans would be eliminated. Clizia did not underestimate the danger of confronting Tarsha yet again, or the chances of failure, but she was convinced that her abilities and her magic were superior to Tarsha's—at least for the present.

Besides, she had no intention of handling the matter herself. She had already faced the girl several times, and each time had not only failed but also risked herself needlessly. She could not risk using the Stiehl, and if she could not rely on the best weapon she possessed, why should she tempt fate yet again? No, Tarsha Kaynin was too dangerous. So instead of confronting her directly, she would send the Jachyra. Whatever risk Tarsha might present to her, she could be no match for the demon. The Jachyra would tear her to pieces.

Once that was decided, Clizia could rest easy. With

no help from the girl, Drisker would be well and truly trapped in the Forbidding for all time—or for as long as it took for something else to kill him. That was the nature of life in that world; everything that lived there was lethal in one way or another. No matter the Druid's skills and determination, sooner or later he would make a mistake or be caught off guard or simply overpowered.

Tarsha Kaynin was his only chance to escape, so Clizia needed to snuff her out like a candle. Then she would be able to continue her efforts to rebuild the Druid order with herself as High Druid, and Paranor would be open to her again, the Guardian of the Keep resigned to her presence as the last of the Druids. She would form the alliances she needed and begin the task of assembling her followers and consolidating her power base and her control over the magic she knew was her rightful inheritance.

She called back and dismissed all the war shrikes but the one who had found Tarsha and prepared it to lead the Jachyra to its prey. But at the last minute, she had second thoughts about her decision to send her pet alone. Tarsha had proven resilient every time Clizia had thought to finish her in the past. Why did she think it would be different this time, even with the demonkind as her weapon? No, the only way to be sure was to go witness the girl's death herself—as dangerous as this might prove to be. She must accompany her pet to make certain it did what it had been told to. She would allow the Jachyra to do the killing, but she must be there when it happened if she wanted to make certain.

If she ever expected to enjoy peace of mind on the matter again. If she ever expected to not always wonder if she were mistaken in her belief that the girl was gone for good.

The decision made, she called the Jachyra to her and prepared to set out for the village of Emberen. At the last minute, she pulled the Stiehl from its hiding place and tucked it into her robes. Just in case.

# THIRTY-THREE

◆

When Grianne Ohmsford shook Drisker Arc awake again, it was as if no time had passed. But it clearly had since it was daylight now—or as close to daylight as it ever got in the Forbidding—the skies clouded and gray across a sunless sky, the landscape an empty, mist-shrouded expanse, the larger world sullen and silent. He lay in his cloak without moving after he had muttered a response and the shaking had stopped, his waking a slow and somewhat tenuous process. The warmth within his cocoon and a deep lethargy inhabiting his limbs made it difficult for him to decide that moving at all was necessary. When he looked around, he heard the Ulk Bog snoring loudly and found the Straken Queen kneeling next to him.

Her eyes fixed on his. "Are you better today?"

And he realized he was. He didn't believe it at first, but his body was free of pain and his wound was no longer inflamed. Grianne Ohmsford's powerful wish-song magic had managed to restore him.

He took a deep breath and exhaled. "I think I am."

He sat up and decided he was indeed feeling stronger. He waited a moment longer then stood, letting the normal feeling of waking flood through him. *Better!* He allowed himself a smile of satisfaction and relief. Grianne was standing next to him, smiling back crookedly.

"You *are* better," she said quietly. "And you will need to be. We still have a day's journey ahead. Are you ready? Can I depend on you?"

He nodded. "I'm as eager to leave this land as you are."

"Then I'll wake the Ulk Bog and we'll get started. The Chule and their allies may still be hunting us."

They paused for a hasty breakfast, and then they were on their way, a ragged procession of three fugitives in a land where everything was hunting them.

The country they passed through was still swampland, and so they moved furtively, paying close attention not only to anything that might be tracking them but to anything in the fetid waters, be it enemy or predator. But nothing showed itself, and Drisker allowed himself to think of escape once more. He pictured returning to the Four Lands, being reunited with Tarsha Kaynin. He would see Clizia Porse eliminated and the Four Lands set right again. Grianne Ohmsford would be returned to her former safehold and reunited with Mother Tanequil. He imagined this and much more, and his thoughts buoyed him as he traveled.

There was little talk. There was nothing much to say, anyway. Drisker knew the overriding need was to get through this wasteland and put themselves beyond the reach of their pursuers. They had to return to Kraal Reach and retrieve the darkwand, wherever Weka had secreted it. And then Grianne and he would discover if the staff really would provide them with the escape they hungered for—if it could indeed transport both of them out of the Forbidding. He suspected Weka Dart might be left behind, the darkwand's magic unable to break him free of the prison to which his kind had been consigned for so long, and he knew the Ulk Bog would come to accept this. After all, he had been left behind before when Grianne had escaped, and he understood the rules that might forbid his release. He would have to find comfort in knowing his sacrifice had helped return his mistress to the life she had been yearning for. The Ulk Bog was a survivor. Look at the way his arm had regenerated itself. He would manage.

They walked only a short time—perhaps a little more than an hour—until they came to an open stretch of relatively flat, dry terrain, backed up against a solitary cluster of large boulders. There Grianne brought them to a halt, looking pleased. "At last! Now we can summon our transport."

"What transport?" Drisker asked with a frown. There was no way her bone coach could make it through this bog, despite this stretch of dry ground.

"One you yourself suggested, Ard-Rhys-That-Was," she answered, almost playfully. "After all, we no longer need to worry about preserving the secrecy of our approach."

She motioned them back toward the boulders, which formed a sort of makeshift shelter. When she decided they were sufficiently tucked away, she spread her arms and called out into the windy, gray void overhead. She finished in a bone-chilling howl and immediately began murmuring in a voice so low and indistinct as to be barely audible. Her hands moved in accompaniment to the rise and fall of her voice, and the air about them turned suddenly as black as a starless, moonless night.

Drisker stared. *What is she doing?*

He could feel the magic rising, the spell she had cast working its will, the space about them charged with the stench of its raw power. Weka Dart shrank against him, pressing close. The Ulk Bog was terrified, and perhaps Drisker should have been terrified, too, but he did not understand yet what was about to happen. Weka Dart, apparently, did.

"What is it?" the Druid whispered, but the Ulk Bog simply cringed against him more insistently.

Then an explosion of light filled the weir and a rain of fiery light-shards descended, spreading out all around the Straken Queen. She was instantly encapsulated, bound, and held fast by summoned protections as a shriek rent the darkness and something so massive it defied belief descended from out of the skies to land before her.

Drisker peered through half-blinded eyes to see what it was.

A dragon!

A dragon so massive that it dwarfed everything about it. It was so terrifying with its spikes and horned ridges and teeth and claws that it left even Drisker searching for a way to escape. But the creature was looking at him and at Weka Dart and the witch that had summoned it, yellow eyes aglow and head lowered to where it was face-to-face with all three, and there was no possible avoidance. Just by its presence, it *commanded* them to look.

Somehow Drisker held his ground, eyes fixed on the monster. Then Grianne was moving forward to place a hand on its massive snout, letting it rest there, inches from teeth that could shred her in an instant. The great body—glistening with moisture that steamed off its bulk—rippled in response. It was in her thrall, and yet Drisker sensed it would require only a moment's distraction—just a small movement or sound—to shatter the connection. And he found himself holding his breath against such a frightening possibility.

"*Cho'disen'ra, olst dragent.*" She spoke the words clearly enough in the deep silence to be heard by the others. "*Kase'ta roi coous.*"

The dragon responded with a sudden nod—a quick sharp movement of its head as it knelt before her.

"The *Crush'ton dragent* is ready now," she called over her shoulder. "Mount her from just behind her wings, once she unfolds them. Do not hesitate once you begin. Hesitation breeds doubts, and you do not want this one doubting you."

"We are expected to *ride* this dragon?" Drisker asked in disbelief. "I thought you said riding dragons was a bad idea because they tended to eat their riders."

"This one might not, now that I hold sway over her."

Drisker was not reassured. "Is there no other way for us to reach our goal?"

Grianne never took her eyes off the dragon as she answered. "There are other ways, but I do not intend to take them. I have no desire to remain in this bog—

and in this place—any longer than necessary. And this beautiful creature will hasten our journey home."

"Perhaps it would be better simply to walk faster?" Weka Dart ventured, his voice quavering.

"Do not be foolish, Ulk Bog. Climb on now, as I ordered you to do, or leave and go your own way. Make your choice."

Drisker was already moving. There was nothing to be gained by delay or doubt at this point. He had to believe Grianne Ohmsford would do the best she could to keep them alive. He had to believe that the dragon would give them the best chance of surviving those that hunted them.

He reached the dragon's side and found himself facing a wall of black scales that defied any attempt to ascend. "Wait, Druid," the Straken Queen called to him.

A moment later, a wing unfolded from the massive body to form a ramp to the dragon's back. Seeing what was intended, Drisker walked over to the lowered wingtip and scrambled up. Weka Dart followed, and finally Grianne herself. The wings were of a roughened texture, but lacked the protective scales of the rest of the dragon's body, so climbing them was relatively easy, even though it left them feeling a bit graceless.

Once aboard, they settled themselves in place, Grianne farthest forward to act as principal rider, the other two seated just behind.

"Watch yourself," the Straken Queen warned. "Those scales can shred your skin." She glanced over her shoulder at them. "Do not waste your time looking for handholds. There are none. You will not fall, in any case. You cannot. The magic will hold you fast no matter what maneuvers the dragon performs. Remember that. Do not panic if she dips or dives or even worse. You will not fall."

"This beast isn't even real, is it?" Drisker asked suddenly, realizing the truth. "It's just a product of your magic."

"It is real enough, Druid. Magic is real, after all; you should know that. When I created a dragon, I created a genuine dragon, with thoughts and feelings and instincts of her own. So do not think of her as anything but what she appears to be. Our enemies will find it wise to see her that way, too."

Then they were lifting off, rising into the night sky, climbing through a low ceiling of clouds and mist where a wash of rain immediately began to soak them. The rain made it difficult to see anything, but then what was there to see? Drisker told himself to do as the Straken Queen had suggested and ride this creature formed of her magic. That she could make such a thing—that her power was so immense—told him that, whatever anyone might say, there had never been a more accomplished Druid.

They rode silently through the day, heads lowered against the steady fall of the rain and press of wind, feeling the dragon shimmy and undulate with the movement of its great wings. What the country below them was like they could only imagine, because they could not see any of it. They were wrapped about by mist. After a time, Drisker simply gave himself over to the rocking movements of the dragon and the slow, steady passage of time.

Finally, the skies ahead began to clear, and the world of the Forbidding—blasted and empty and barren—revealed itself anew, laid out below them in ragged detail. Stretches of rocky hills, swathes of empty wasteland, and now and again a creature moving far below. It was a familiar sight by now, but much more welcome than ever before. While nothing specific was recognizable and Drisker was unsure of exactly where they were, his expectations were undeniable. They could not be far from their destination.

"We're here," Grianne announced suddenly—a pronouncement so abrupt it startled the Druid. But when he looked ahead, he could spy the tall spires of Kraal Reach silhouetted against the skyline.

As they drew closer, the dragon began to descend, carrying them down onto an open patch of terrain that fronted the fortress gates, settling with such gentleness that they might have been riding a feather floating to the ground. Once landed, the dragon steadied itself, keeping its balance as it lowered one wing so that the extended tip touched the ground.

Neither Drisker nor Weka Dart waited a single second before sliding down that wing to solid ground, moving quickly away from the monstrosity that had served as their conveyance. A moment later the Straken Queen was beside them, her worn features alight with an inner joy that Drisker guessed must come from her satisfaction at having used such powerful magic so successfully. She stood beside them for long moments, looking back at her creation appreciatively, then motioned it away. Without any hesitation, the dragon rose back into the sky and disappeared into the mist.

"Took me two years to discover how to create it," she told them in a voice that was distant and rife with fond memories. "Such a wonder! Such a joy to ride."

Drisker might have questioned such an assessment, but he chose simply to nod.

The gates to the fortress swung open as they approached, and a bevy of guards and servants hurried out to meet them and escort them into the keep. It was an odd greeting. None of those arriving said a thing—not a word of welcome, no astonishment over the dragon—and it wasn't hard to deduce that what bound these people to their queen was not fondness or respect but fear and self-preservation.

*No wonder she wants out of this world,* Drisker thought once again.

Once inside, Grianne wasted no time. Dismissing her escort and others who tried to approach, she ordered Drisker and Weka Dart to follow her to her quarters. Once they were inside, she closed and locked the door, then seized the latter by his throat.

"I should kill you, little Ulk Bog," she hissed softly, teeth bared.

"Mistress, please, no!" He could barely get the words out, her grip was so tight. "Forgive me! Don't you see? I did it to protect you! I did it to keep you here so you would be safe!"

"You did it to keep me here; that much is true. But you were thinking of yourself. I would have left here years ago if I had gained possession of the staff, if you had turned it over to me!"

"You would have abandoned me! I would have been left alone!"

She tightened her fingers, and he began to choke. "You made a choice you had no right to make. The choice to stay or go was mine, and you stole it from me. You are a thief! You are a liar and a coward! You have betrayed me, and I should kill you here and now and be rid of you!"

It appeared to Drisker, standing off to one side, that this was exactly what she was intending to do. "Grianne!" he called out sharply. "The darkwand!"

She gave him a threatening look and abruptly released Weka, practically throwing him from her. "Yes, the darkwand. That, treacherous little man, is why I won't kill you. That, and the fact that you have otherwise served me long and well." She gestured angrily at the closed door. "Retrieve the staff and bring it to me. Do it now. No . . . wait!"

She walked over to him and helped him to his feet. "Hear me well. Whatever happens now, I will not harm you once you bring me the staff. Once I have it in my hands, the fact that you hid it will be forgotten. But . . ."

Again she seized him and dragged him close. "Do not think to run. Do not think to escape. Do not think to do anything other than what I have asked you to do. If you disobey me now, your life is forfeit. Do you understand?"

"Yes, mistress," her minion answered, his gaze lowered.

She released him a second time, and he went out the door hurriedly, closing it behind him. "Should I go with him?" Drisker asked.

She glared. "No. Half of me wishes he would make an attempt to escape. Then I would have an excuse to sate the anger that consumes me. What he did . . . What he dared to visit on me . . ."

The cold light in her eyes was enough to tell the Druid to let the matter be, and he simply nodded. If Weka Dart was foolish enough to create any further obstacles to Grianne's departure, she would hunt him down and dispatch him, even if it took her the rest of her life.

The minutes came and went—too many of them, Drisker thought—and still the Ulk Bog did not return. Twice, as they waited, Drisker thought to say something to the Straken Queen—to suggest they go looking to be sure Weka Dart was coming back. But the rigid set of her body was evidence of the rage boiling inside her, so Drisker held his tongue. She would see if Weka Dart was still loyal, and woe be to him if he should decide to run.

Finally, the door opened again, and the little Ulk Bog reappeared bearing a long, thick wooden staff as black as darkest night, its length gnarled and worn and riven with carved runes. He came over to her, but then stopped while still ten feet away and turned to Drisker.

"What of your promise, Straken?"

Drisker nodded and turned to face Grianne. "When I spoke with Weka the other night, I told him to confess the truth to you. I told him you would understand and forgive him. I also promised we would try to take him with us when we left the Forbidding."

"You had no right to promise anything!"

"I had every right!" he snapped back in reply. "I am trapped here, too. I want out of the Forbidding every bit as much as you do, so I saw no harm in making the promise. Weka loves you, and I think he feels he must be with you if he is to survive. Besides, leaving him here alone, without your protection, is likely a death sentence. What harm if we try to grant his wish?"

She gave him a long, considering look. "What harm? You meddle in business you know nothing about, Drisker Arc. You think you might be doing the right thing, but you might be doing just the opposite. Still . . ."

She shook her head, and he sensed there was something dark she was holding back. He felt a chill run down his neck but tried to pretend he was mistaken. "It's done," he said. "I can't undo it."

"Then I won't ask you to," she promised. "You did what you were supposed to do—what my visions told me you would do. You found the darkwand. Take it from the Ulk Bog and hand it to me. Fulfill the vision as I saw it."

He walked over to the cringing Weka Dart and held out his hand. The bearer of the staff gave him a long, malicious look and handed him the darkwand without a word. Then Drisker, in turn, walked over to the Straken Queen and passed the staff to her.

She hefted it in both hands, and the look on her

face revealed a yearning for something she had once thought lost forever.

"Better," she whispered, almost to herself.

That night, after a dinner empty of conversation and rife with expectation for what was to come, Drisker returned to his room to wait for morning. In an odd gesture of forgiveness, Grianne allowed Weka Dart to eat with them. It would have been difficult to say whether or not this helped soothe the Ulk Bog's damaged feelings about what was to come, but he must have recognized it for what it was nevertheless.

But there was no forgiveness for Drisker Arc in the Ulk Bog's eyes and silences. What little he said and showed of his feelings did nothing to suggest his mind had been changed about his feelings for the Druid. If anything, the anger that clearly showed in the glances he cast in Drisker's direction demonstrated that no lessening of blame was in the offing.

The meal was endless and marked by harsh silence and cold looks, punctuated by a few words and an occasional exchange of hopefulness between the Straken Queen and the Druid. So when Drisker reached his sleeping chambers, he was quick to lock his door and cast a spell that would warn him if the locks were tampered with while he slept.

He sat down then with paper and penned a letter to Tarsha, taking his time, choosing his words carefully, looking off into the dark and into an uncertain future as often as not, but fully engaged. The letter was needed as a precaution, and while he hoped there would be no need for it, he was realistic enough to know that it might be required nevertheless.

When he had finished it, he sealed it with candle and wax, then tucked it into his tunic and went off to bed.

# THIRTY-FOUR

◆

THE FOLLOWING MORNING, GRIANNE directed them through the cavernous halls of her fortress and out the gates to where the rolling coffin waited. She spent no time at all looking over her shoulder at the home she was leaving. She spared no words of parting to those she passed. Whatever attachment she had felt for Kraal Reach was over and done with. In her mind, she was already gone from it.

The coach would convey them to the place she had chosen to engage the magic of the darkwand. She wanted it to happen in private, so only the three of them and a driver set out, the Straken Queen having determined from whatever source of divination she relied upon that there was no longer any real danger of pursuit. She was back in her own country, she pointed out, and the Chule seldom ventured outside of Brockenthrog Weir. Vendra Trax was dead, and in all likelihood they were already engaged in electing a new leader—a process that usually involved blades and blood. Rather like everything that happened in the Forbidding, this, too, was a case of survival of the fittest.

They rode in silence the entire way. Grianne spent her time looking out the windows of the coach, ignoring her companions, become a gray presence dwelling in a place best avoided by everyone else. Weka Dart was having nothing to do with anyone, either, slumped in one corner of his seat, asleep almost as soon as they started to move. Drisker might have been willing to converse had anyone shown even the slightest inclination to do so, but since no one seemed interested, he remained silent. In his head, wheels were spinning. He was thinking of what he might do when he arrived back in the Four Lands—where he would begin the work that needed doing, how he would go about finding first Tarsha and then Clizia Porse. He wondered about the *Behemoth* and her passengers and crew. He wondered about the impending war between the Skaar and the Federation.

So much work awaited his return; it tired him merely to think of it. But the prospect of what he might accomplish energized him at the same time.

He was anxious to get home.

It was only toward the end of the journey that he broke his silence, reminded of the letter to Tarsha that he had tucked in his tunic. He turned to Grianne.

"If I don't make it back," he began.

Grianne frowned. "Losing faith already, Druid?" she mocked him.

He refused to let her goad him, but instead talked right over her. "You must promise me something. If the darkwand transports you back to the Four Lands without me, you must find Tarsha. She will likely be residing in my former house, in a village called Emberen. You must go to her, give her a letter I have written, and help her to defeat Clizia Porse. For my part in your escape, you must grant me this, at least."

She raised an eyebrow. "Did I not already grant you the means of saving your land from the invaders? And now you would ask for more?"

"For your freedom? I would think you would allow me almost anything. You must promise me this, Grianne."

She paused for a moment, then took the letter he was holding out to her. "Very well, Druid. If you do not make it back, I will go to the girl."

And Drisker felt some of the tension go out of him.

They traveled for less than thirty minutes more to the chosen site. All three passengers climbed out of the coach, stretching cramped limbs and looking about at a forested stretch riven with gullies and studded with boulders. Grianne spoke quietly to the driver, then left him with the coach and led the other two into the trees a short distance before bringing them to a halt and turning back to speak to them.

"I have something to say to both of you, and you will not like it. You can consider it a judgment of sorts on all of us, if such things exist. What it is, in any case, is a dark and terrible truth." She looked at Weka Dart. "I fear you will not be able to come with me when I leave."

The Ulk Bog was dumbstruck, his face contorting into a mask of terror. "Mistress!" he managed, that single word a clear plea that she might retract what she had just said.

"Save for your poor behavior in hiding the darkwand from me, you have been a loyal friend and helper always," his queen continued. "Whenever I needed aid, it was always you I could turn to. That you failed me this once has nothing to do with what I have just told you. It is not something I would ever wish on you, little Ulk Bog. It is not something I ever hoped might happen or even thought could—until I gave serious thought to what it is we are attempting."

"Then you aren't entirely sure?" Drisker pressed, sensing the matter wasn't entirely decided.

"Until we try, we can never know anything for sure. But reason and rational thinking suggest my conclusion is right. Consider. The darkwand was created to help Pen Ohmsford come into the Forbidding and bring me out. It was a corrective magic, a magic designed not to contravene or subvert, but to set right. I did not belong in the Forbidding; I was a creature of the Four Lands. The purpose of the magic was to restore the balance. That is true now as well, but only for you and me. We are creatures brought over to a place in which we do not belong. The darkwand will take us out because the magic will work to right an obvious wrong."

She paused. "But you, Weka, are a creature of the Forbidding, and carrying you over to the Four Lands—no matter how right the reasons or how genuine the need—is a clear violation of the rules of the Forbidding, which do not permit any who belong here to go free. It is the fate decreed by circumstances of your birth and events that took place eons ago. It is neither fair nor deserved, but it is fact."

The Ulk Bog wheeled on Drisker. "This is your fault! You lied to me! You tricked me into giving my mistress the staff, and now she will abandon me!"

"I did *not* lie to you," the Druid emphasized. "Nor was it my intention to trick you. I knew nothing of what the staff's limitations might be. It seemed reasonable to think it could convey you out of here if we wanted you with us. But Grianne may be right. The magic may not allow for it. I am sorry."

"Sorry?" the Ulk Bog screeched. "Oh, such misery do I see on your face! Such sorrow!" His fists were clenched. "That makes everything all right, does it? Just a whim of fate, but not your fault?"

"We will try our best," Grianne said, motioning him back. "We *will* link you to us and attempt to take you with us, as Drisker promised we would. But you need to know what might happen. It would be unfair to say nothing and see you left behind with no explanation. Do you see?"

Weka Dart looked at her for a moment and then looked away. "I see well enough," he said coldly.

His words were ominous, and Drisker felt a sudden need to use the darkwand as quickly as possible. Grianne seemed to have the same thought and ordered them both to stand close to her. "Put your hands on the staff," she commanded.

They did so, and the Druid and the Ulk Bog locked gazes. "You won't take her without me!" the latter hissed. "I won't allow it!"

"Hush!" Grianne cautioned. "No more talk."

She began to summon the magic. They clung to the staff in the manner of drowning sailors clinging to a lifeline. Grianne said nothing more to either of them, concentrating on conjuring. Little was required. The runes carved into the darkwand's surface began to glow and then abruptly burst into bits of flaming light as though the staff itself were afire. But there was no actual burning, nor was there any pain for either Drisker or the Straken Queen, as both kept a tight hold.

It was not so for the Ulk Bog, however, who screamed and wrenched his hand away, burns evident all over his skin. "It isn't working!" he gasped. "It won't let me keep hold of it!"

"Then hold on to me!" Grianne ordered.

But when Weka attempted to do so, the glow from the staff was already beginning to enclose her and he experienced the same scalding and again was forced to let go.

"You cannot leave the Forbidding, Weka Dart!" the Straken Queen said quickly. "I warned you this might happen. Step away and let us go!"

But the Ulk Bog was beyond any reasoning or recognition—and especially any intention of accepting what was clearly inevitable. His face contorted into a mask of desperation, his rage so intense the heat of it was coming off his body. "You did this!" he screamed at Drisker Arc. "But if I cannot leave, neither can you!"

Drisker saw the attack coming but could not act quickly enough to prevent it. Pulling a dagger from somewhere within his clothing, the Ulk Bog drove the blade into Drisker's stomach and chest three times in rapid succession, and the third time he left it buried there.

Grievously wounded, the Druid dropped to one knee. With one hand clinging to the darkwand, he wrenched the blade free and cast it away.

There was blood everywhere. He looked at Grianne. "Leave me," he gasped, feeling the cold of his own death rushing through him. "Help Tarsha . . ."

"Help her yourself!" the Straken Queen snapped, her face gone white, her anguish evident. She kicked a flushed wild-eyed Weka Dart out of the way. "You fool!" she spat at him. "You had no reason! None!"

She wrapped one arm about Drisker, holding him up. "Do not let go. Your Tarsha is waiting for you."

A moment later the glow sharpened and expanded to enclose them both. Everything around them disappeared, the gray world of the Forbidding diminishing behind the wall of the staff's magic. Drisker felt the unexpected weight of its fiery light settle on him, crushing him, smothering him, shutting off the air he struggled to breathe.

Then he was enveloped in darkness and the weight pressing down on him lifted away.

When the magic's power faded and the fiery light surrounding her disappeared, Grianne Ohmsford found herself standing alone. She breathed clean air she had thought she would never breathe again. She closed her eyes against a brightness that had been denied her for so long, she could no longer bear it. She kept her eyes closed, waiting for them to adjust to this new intensity. She gripped the darkwand tightly as she did so, seeking reassurance, leaning on it for balance, the strength gone out of her.

Finally, she opened her eyes again, blinked against the light, squinted to protect them, and looked around for her companions.

Drisker Arc lay sprawled on the ground beside her, looking up at the sky. She knelt beside him at once, one hand reaching out quietly to touch his cheek, then pass in front of his eyes, and over his mouth. Nothing. She felt for a pulse, then sat back. Drisker Arc was gone, his great heart stilled.

She stared at him a moment longer, and then she looked around for Weka Dart. Just to be sure. But he was nowhere to be found.

Using the darkwand, she lowered herself back to her feet, remembering the letter Drisker had given her. She carried it now, tucked away in a pocket beneath her blouse.

Kept safe, in case the worst happened.

And the worst had.

But she could keep her promise and find Tarsha Kaynin. She could help her stand against Clizia Porse. She could let her know the awful truth about her mentor's passing. She could give her the note and try to make her understand.

All these she could do, and the promise she had made to Drisker Arc would be kept.

She looked around again. She had wished for the magic to convey her to the Westland village of Emberen, where the Druid made his home and the girl might be found. Off to one side, she could see the roofs of a village amid a wide stretch of forestland. She was in the Westland, unless she missed her guess.

She wrapped Drisker's body in his cloak and fastened the garment in place using its ties and his belt. Knowing what was needed, she set off to begin her new life.

# THIRTY-FIVE

◆

DARCON LEAH AND BRECON Elessedil left the *Behemoth* by flit immediately after making their decision to go after Ajin. The day was already half gone, the light from the sun a weak glow in the sky overhead, masked behind heavy clouds. They flew upriver until they were perhaps a mile from the *Behemoth* before finding a small clearing in which to land. Then, concealed within a stand of trees, Dar waited as his friend extracted the Elfstones from their pouch, clasped them tightly in his fist, stretched out his arm, and pointed them in the general direction of the still-distant city.

Brecon closed his eyes, concentrating on Ajin's face and waiting for the magic to come alive. It did not take long. Almost immediately the stones began to emit their brilliant-blue glow, brightening the gloom. Brecon's eyes opened again, and together the Elf and the Blade watched the intensity increase until a jagged blue streak shot into the trees toward the Skaar city, working its way over the rough winter terrain— over drifts of snow and icy ground, past trees painted white with frost, and hills and ridgelines barren and stark. The light continued on over the white-capped landscape until it reached its destination—a city turned grim with cold and bitter winds and a never-ending winter. Walls and parapets, towers and battlements, capstones and gates—all had become victims of the cold and lack of sun. Into the city the beacon raced, through clusters of frigid, dark buildings, down streets shadowed and empty, past the huddled bundles in doorways and alcoves that were all that remained of the people who had frozen in the night—or even the night before—and had yet to be collected by the corpse gatherers to be buried or burned.

The vision was stark and raw and frightening, and both suddenly understood just why the Skaar had been so desperate for a new home. Dar flinched away in spite of himself, his fears for the Skaar princess already spiking simply from witnessing the grimness of the world into which she had disappeared.

The beacon continued on, heedless of the despairing vision it was portraying, intent on finding the person that Brecon's image had shown it. It moved to an even more derelict portion of the city, where warehouses clustered like prisons, dark and deserted-looking. Here no one moved through the streets—not even at midday on the broadest of avenues. It was abandoned and forsaken, a barren wasteland of dead industry.

Then the light angled sharply toward a particularly grim monstrosity, passing through heavy metal doors and down into a cellar in which only a single light burned. Vast and cavernous, it had an abandoned look to it at first glance, but then shadows began to move and the watchers could see monsters that were half men, half wolves lurking against the walls, slinking about like scavengers, huge and ferocious.

And then . . . Dar gasped. A barred cell stood in the exact center of the chamber—a cage in which two women huddled together. Their arms were wrapped about each other and the looks on their faces revealed the extent of their weakened condition.

"Ajin!" Dar gasped in shock.

For it was indeed the Skaar princess with a woman he did not know, but whose resemblance to the princess was unmistakable and whom he immediately knew to be her mother. In seconds, it all became clear to him. Ajin had overreached or been betrayed. Ajin's stepmother had taken both women prisoner and shut them away in this monster-infested building to be dealt with later in ways he did not care to contemplate. This was why she had not returned.

The blue light held the vision fast for a few seconds longer, then disappeared, leaving the watchers cloaked in gloom once more.

"What *were* those things?" Brecon asked, his horror at having seen the wolf-men twisting his features in a grimace.

Dar didn't know. He only knew that Ajin—the enemy he had once thought he might have to kill and the woman he had now, against all odds, grown to love—was in terrible danger, and it was up to him to rescue her. She would be waiting for him, knowing he would come for her, but time was slipping away quickly. He could not forget the despair he had seen in her face, the trapped look in her eyes.

He gave his friend a hard look. "We can't afford to take the time to walk in, Brec. We have to use the flit, whether they see us or not."

Brecon nodded his agreement, already returning the Elfstones to their pouch and stuffing them back in his tunic. He pulled his cloak more tightly about him. Snow was beginning to fall again. "Let's hurry."

They climbed back into their small airship and lifted off. The pair had already informed Rocan Arneas of their intentions, and to his credit the Rover leader had not objected. Engaged in helping his fellows and Tindall prepare the weather machine, he had not had the time or energy to argue. And he could see clearly enough the determination reflected in the Blade's eyes. He asked only that they watch out for themselves, because he didn't have the men to come searching for them, and to remember they intended to employ Annabelle later that day. A swift journey in and back again would be advisable. They would wait if they could, but if their purpose in coming to Skaarsland was placed in jeopardy or their efforts to achieve their goals were put at unnecessary risk, they would have to leave them behind.

Dar and Brecon understood, but the former was too distraught by Ajin's continuing absence to be deterred and the latter refused to let his friend undertake this journey alone.

Now they flew inland rapidly, with Dar at the controls. Fearful and angry, his need to do *something* demanded he not sit idly by but rather take action. So he would not settle for being a passenger when he could be a pilot. Brecon understood and was quick to step aside.

They encountered no other airships on their way in, and saw no patrols or work parties on the ground. The snow was falling harder by then, their vision obscured beyond a few yards and the danger of flying into something substantially increased. Dar kept the flit well off the ground while still staying in sight of the treetops they were passing over. They flew in silence, their concentration entirely on keeping watch. Ahead, the world was a filmy white vision materializing out of snowfall and rising mist.

When the walls of the city finally appeared, Dar steered away automatically to avoid being seen by watchers on the parapets. He took them in a slow circle that kept their destination in sight, but only barely. He was looking for an entry point where they might approach on foot and gain access without being stopped. But it was Brecon, with his sharp Elven eyesight, who found what they were looking for and pointed it out.

"There, where the wall is crumbling, by that tower."

Indeed, much of the city was breaking apart, and the walls in particular. Decay and instability had beset the city with the debilitating onslaught of the endless winter, and efforts to shore up the damage had apparently been abandoned. Dar took their small craft down into an open space still back within the trees, keeping one eye on their newfound access to the city as he did so. Once landed, they climbed out and stood looking at the bits and pieces of the wall they could see through the snowfall. From where they were standing, the city appeared dead.

Brecon took out the Elfstones and again summoned their magic. It appeared instantly, flying into the snow and mist, through the walls and along the streets and byways to the by-now-familiar warehouse where Ajin and her mother were being held. They did not need to look further once they had determined it was not all that far from where they stood. It sat at the backside of the city a short distance from the walls, surrounded by similar buildings—all of them dark and apparently abandoned.

The Elf and the Blade exchanged a look. "How do we do this?" Brecon asked.

Dar shook his head. "We go there, we get inside, we find a way through or past those wolf-things, and we free Ajin and her mother." He paused. "I will take the lead. If something happens to you, your mother will never forgive me."

"You say that like a threat!" Brecon laughed. "I can take care of myself—even if my training isn't as thorough as yours."

"Your training isn't the issue. Lack of experience is. Anyway, try to stay safe, will you?" He looked toward the city. "We need to hurry."

They set out through the woods and were soon close to a section of the wall not far from the tower they had marked out as their guidepost. Skirting through the last of the trees, they arrived at a point just across from the crumbling part of the wall Brecon had spied earlier. A gap had opened that was partially repaired with timbers set crosswise. The repair would keep out a large animal, but not much of anything else—and certainly not two determined men.

Dar nodded to Brecon and led the way to the gap. Farther down, a sentry stood staring out into the weather, his cloaked form barely visible through the falling snow. He never glanced their way as they squirmed through the opening and into the city. *Fortune favors the bold,* Dar thought as they stood just inside the barrier and looked ahead toward the dark shapes of the buildings. They made their way from one patch of shadows to another, from one concealment to the next, all the while watching for passersby or sentries. They found some of the former and none of the latter. Those few they did find were frightened, furtive creatures, ragged and worn, creeping through the back streets in search of food and shelter. The city had been built to house thousands, but now the dead were everywhere, their bodies sprawled in failed shelters, abandoned or simply lost.

Dar was appalled. From the look of the populace, all the able-bodied men and women must have gone with the king into the Four Lands.

They used the Elfstones twice more to find the building they had been shown, and quickly located it. They stood outside its walls, with the front doors directly across from them, and studied it. There were other, smaller doors on the sides of the building, but no windows anywhere that weren't shuttered or blacked out by boards nailed tightly in place. No light from within was visible.

They risked one final look using the Elfstones so

they could track Ajin and her mother once they were inside. The Blue Elfstone's light took them through the heavily barred front doors to an interior corridor and another door, which in turn took them down heavy wooden steps and into the cellar that housed the prisoners. Nothing about their situation had changed. Nothing suggested there would be any way to free them without fighting an uncertain number of prowling wolf-men.

"The new queen should be there, too," Dar muttered once the light had flared and disappeared. "Why aren't we seeing her?"

"We would see her if she was there," Brecon said. "The Elfstones would show us. She must be somewhere else." He smiled. "That might help."

Dar doubted anything would help at this point. "Doesn't look like there is any clever way to do this, does it?"

His friend shook his head. "Break the locks on the front doors and go in, just as you said. Are you sure about this? Maybe we should try to get help. Ajin's a Skaar princess and her mother a former queen. They must still be popular with some in the city."

"But with whom?" Dar shook his head. "We have no idea whom to ask. We know no one in this place."

"You do know that once we've done this, the city watch—or possibly whatever army remains—will come after us. We may be jeopardizing everything Tindall and Rocan are attempting with their machine."

"But they said they were doing it today. The weather is getting worse, and they can't risk waiting. Anyway, even if a search is mounted, it won't matter. No one will know where to look. The others are far enough away they won't be found. Not for a while."

"You hope."

Dar's smile was tight and swift. "I don't have anything else to fall back on. Besides, I can't leave Ajin in that cage."

Brecon pocketed the Elfstones, then thought better of it and brought them out again. "If there's magic involved, the Stones will help protect us. Your blade, too. Once we're inside, we need to find out—as quickly as we can—what those creatures are."

"They don't look natural," the Blade agreed. "Not like anything I've ever seen. Stay ready, Brec."

He started to unsheathe the Sword of Leah, then hesitated. Instead he reached into his pocket and brought out a packet, unwrapping it swiftly. Brecon stared down at a lump of gray material—not quite clay, but similar. "What's that?"

"Rocan gave it to me. He said it might be useful. Shea used it to free Tindall from his cell in Assidian Deep. Let's try it on that door."

They crossed through the heavy snowfall like ghosts, crystalline flakes gathering on their heads and shoulders as they hunched within their cloaks. In moments they were standing before the front doors of the building where Ajin was imprisoned. The heavy doors were metal-clad, and the locks were formidable. Brecon shook his head. "I don't know."

Dar nodded wordlessly. "Let's see what it can do. It can't hurt."

He extracted a wad of the material and slapped

it on the cover plate that shielded the locking mechanism, forcing as much as he could through a wide keyhole entry. The lock was ancient and primitive, a relic of another time, but it was effective enough. No one without the key could ever get inside the building without breaking down the housing and getting at the works it protected.

Once he was satisfied with his efforts, he spit on the clay and stepped back, watching as it flared and burned with a fiery incandescence. Within seconds, the locking mechanism was completely melted away and the lock freed. Dar pulled the door open slowly, attempting to avoid any sound. He was mostly successful. They stepped inside quickly and pulled it shut behind them.

"No one about," Dar whispered, looking around in the gloom.

Brecon nodded, indicating the way forward. There was an odd brightness emanating from the ceiling, almost a witch light, and it provided just enough illumination for them to see. They started ahead, moving cautiously, listening for any sound, watching for any movement. Even though it seemed apparent there was nothing hiding, they took no chances. Dar had to fight to hold himself back, desperately worried for Ajin, afraid that any delay would mean they would arrive too late to help her. But he had been in situations like this before and was experienced enough to know not to rush.

They came to the cellar door and found it was locked, too. Dar never hesitated. With a quick look over to his friend, he put more of the clay on the locking mechanism, spit on it, and stepped back. Once more, the clay flared and the metal melted away. Dar tightened his grip on his blade as it did so, then grasped the handles, pulled the door open, and rushed through, with Brecon a step behind.

The cage and its prisoners could be seen where the vision from the Elfstones had said it would be, with Ajin and her mother crouched within. Both looked up instantly, startled by the sudden intrusion. Their rescuers were already charging down the steps, rushing to get to them, when Ajin came to her feet and rushed over to the bars, her face drawn and worn, but bright with relief.

But Brecon had realized what Dar had not, and he reached out to slow his friend. "Where are the wolf-men?"

Indeed, they had disappeared. Of all those creatures they had seen in the vision, not one remained in view. Dar slowed in response to Brecon's question, searching the shadows, the corners, the walls. No wolf-men. Something was wrong. A trap? How could it be? No one knew they were coming. This was something else.

Then his eyes met Ajin's, and everything else was forgotten. Her smile was brilliant.

She reached through the bars to take his hands. "I knew you would come!"

"I should have come sooner. I've been worried for days, but I just kept thinking how you insisted on doing this alone and I didn't want to interfere." He took in the sunken cheeks and disheveled clothing. "Are you all right? Are you hurt?"

She shook her head. "Not hurt. Just hungry and thirsty. I'm also angry and embarrassed that I let this happen." She turned to the older woman. "This is my mother, Dar. Orestiana d'Amphere."

"So, you did find her." He gave a nod and a smile in the former queen's direction. Ajin's mother looked as if she could barely hold her head up, but she smiled back.

"We stopped eating and drinking a few days ago," Ajin continued, pressing against the bars of the cage. "We had to. My father traded my mother for a *witch*. She made the creatures that guard us—by feeding them a potion that turns them from humans into these hybrid monsters. She threatened to do it to us. She said she would put the potion in our food and drink, and we would never know when it would happen. So we quit taking anything she offered." Her face darkened. "I will make sure *she* takes something when I find her again!"

"She made those wolf-creatures?" Brecon asked in disbelief.

Ajin sighed, her exhaustion apparent. "Can you get us out of here?"

Dar drew out what remained of the clay, peeled off a hunk, and pressed it against the lock on the cell door, working it into the keyhole. "Where is she, anyway? And what happened to those wolf-things? We saw them when we were using the Elfstones to find you, but now they've disappeared."

"Dar," Brecon said quietly from behind.

The Blade ignored him, spit on the clay, and

watched it seethe, flare up, and melt the lock. "That should do it."

"Dar," Brecon repeated a little more loudly.

The highlander was tugging at the door, dragging it open. "In a minute."

Ajin had gone back for her mother and was helping her to her feet. Orestiana d'Amphere was pale and drawn, but game. She tottered toward the cell door, and with every step her strength appeared to return.

"Young man," she greeted Dar as she reached him. She took his hand in hers. "I am forever in your debt. My daughter had faith in you, and it was well placed."

Dar turned away, embarrassed, and looked back at Brecon, who was standing much closer than before. "She's worn down, Brec. We have to . . ."

He trailed off. There were wolf-men all around them. They had come out of the darkness from who knew where and were closing on the prisoners and their rescuers. Their eyes burned a deep gold and their bodies were huge and muscled beneath leathery hide. They began to snarl and growl, revealing rows of teeth and long pink tongues.

Brecon's sword was already drawn.

"They look hungry," Dar replied. "What do you suggest?"

"This was your idea. *You* suggest something!"

The Sword of Leah was still sheathed. "Get back inside the cage."

"What?" the Elf exclaimed in disbelief.

"I'm finished with that cage!" Ajin snapped.

"Look at how many there are," Dar pointed out, his eyes shifting from one wolf-man to the next as he stepped inside the cage. Their advance had slowed, but he knew it wouldn't stop. "There're too many for us to break past all of them—especially with Ajin's mother to consider. But inside the cage we have a chance. If they break through, only one of them can come through the opening at a time. There isn't space for more. Two of us can hold them off."

"Three," Ajin corrected, having already moved her mother safely back before snatching Dar's long knife from his belt. "This is my fight, too."

Brecon glanced around, then quickly followed them into the cage. Dar closed the barred door and used several blocks of his clay to fuse it in place, melting its iron frame into the doorjamb. No one spoke because no one wanted to think about where this was all leading. Sooner or later, the wolf-men would break through. Sooner or later, the door would give way. They might stop most of their attackers, but it was unlikely they would stop them all.

Dar drew out the Sword of Leah and placed himself squarely in front of the cell door bars. He wished now he had thought earlier of a way to summon help from the airship. But help would never reach them in time anyway.

The monsters surrounded the cage, reaching their arms inside to grasp at the prisoners. Dar gave them a moment, then struck out. Two arms fell away, severed. Another creature staggered back, mortally wounded by a quick lunge from Brecon. Ajin stayed back, waiting for her chance, keeping one eye on her mother. "We had better think of something else if we ever want to get out of here."

There was no hint of levity in her voice, no indication of bravado. She knew how serious their situation was. They were all going to die here, one way or another, if they could not get past the wolf-men.

"Try using the Elfstones," Dar suggested to Brecon.

The Elven prince sheathed his sword and retrieved the blue stones. Holding them out, he willed them to throw back their assailants, to break apart the ring that encircled them. The Elfstones flared, their blue light blinding in the near darkness, causing a handful of the wolf-men to shield their eyes and fall back, but nothing further happened. Which meant, Dar knew at once, that whatever the beast-men were, they were not capable of using magic.

"Can the stones do anything else?" Ajin asked quickly. She took a quick slice at a beast's extended arm and the arm withdrew swiftly, a gash opening near the wrist.

Brecon shook his head, shoving the stones back in his pocket and taking up his sword once more. Assailants and defenders shifted warily, feinting with lunges and withdrawing swiftly, each side seeking to gain an advantage.

"What is this?" a voice called out sharply.

Dar peered into the gloom. A shadowy figure had appeared and was moving toward them. A quick gesture of one slender arm and the wolf-men gave way obediently. It was a woman who approached, a tight expression on her face. She was small and slight and plain-looking—nothing special about her, nothing threatening. Save for the clothing she wore, she did not appear to be anyone important. But Dar knew at once who she was.

*As if things couldn't get any worse.*

She came right up to them. "I see you have visitors, Princess. But visitors aren't allowed. You know that." A smile appeared. "Those are the rules, I'm afraid. Now they will have to share your unhappy circumstances. I hope they brought their own food and water. But if not, I have some of both for them. Oh, but what's this? The door into your cage is stuck, isn't it? How did that happen? But never mind. What's stuck can be unstuck."

She spoke to the creatures about her, and several disappeared back into the gloom. When they were gone, she looked again at Ajin. "What were you trying to do, summon help? There is no help to be found. There is only the help that I offer. Why don't you end this nonsense?"

"Why don't you step inside this cage, Agathien, and I will!"

"So bitter. Why do you persist in this refusal to accept your fate? I think perhaps it is time we put a stop to your pointless acts of defiance. Once my wolf-men are inside the cage, I will have them hold you all down and feed you the potion I mentioned, the one that will make you more compliant. You and your mother *and* your friends. Then you will belong to me, and things will be exactly how they were meant to be."

Dar was measuring the distance to where she stood, trying to decide if he could throw a knife through the bars with enough accuracy and force to dispatch her. He didn't think so. The hand that had strayed to the blade he kept strapped to the small of his back moved away. It was too risky. He would only get one chance, and he couldn't afford to waste it.

Agathien d'Amphere was looking at him. "I might decide to keep *you* around for a while," she said. "I can easily imagine the fun you and I could have. Fun you've already had with Ajin, perhaps? Well, it would be better with me. And if not, I have different potions to help. One takes away your will to resist. Another takes all your memories. You would do whatever I asked of you and find nothing wrong with doing so. Sound interesting?"

Her wolf-men returned with long iron pry bars, which they fitted in place to free up the door that Dar had fused. Two other creatures had found spears, clearly intended to keep the prisoners back from the cell entry while their fellows rushed inside.

"I think, after this is done, I will dispatch your father, too, Princess. He troubles me with his foolish wars and constant absences. I would be a better queen if I were rid of him." She glanced at the wolf-men with the iron bars. "Break it open."

The pry bars went to work, and the metal at the fused points began to groan and crack. In moments, the wolf-men would be inside. Agathien d'Amphere had stepped back to watch, too far back now for Dar to use the knife. He had missed whatever small chance he might have had.

Their end seemed inevitable.

But Dar, admittedly grasping at straws as he frantically tried to come up with a plan, had a sudden thought. It seemed so wild at first he discounted it, but then he wondered if just maybe . . .

He turned to Brecon. "Take out the Elfstones," he said quietly.

"What?" Brecon shook his head in confusion. "But the magic doesn't work on these creatures."

"Maybe it does. Just don't use it to attack them. Use it to project images of who they once were."

"What are you talking about? I don't *know* who they once were, so how can I summon the magic to reveal it? And why would I? What good would it do?"

His voice was verging on desperation, and the Blade grabbed hold of him and pulled him close.

"Brecon, just listen. Closely. What if you imagine men and women standing out there, instead of monsters? They were human once; that's all that matters. So don't worry about specifics. Just imagine their general look and the Elfstones might do the rest. Let the magic reveal who they used to be. Let it show them what has been stolen from them. Let's give them a good look at what they've lost."

Brecon quickly saw what Dar was trying to do and extracted the Elfstones and held them out, summoning their magic. At the entry of the cage, the door was giving way. Dar moved over to block the way in, the Sword of Leah held ready. If his gamble using the Elfstones failed, the wolf-creatures would be inside and on top of them.

He felt Ajin move up beside him. He saw the glint of her long knife in the pale light of the single torch. "I love you," he whispered.

"I know," she replied.

"This might be beyond me," Brecon called out from behind them. "I can't seem to make the Elfstones do anything! I can't feel any . . ."

Then abruptly the magic exploded through the cage bars and filled the darkness. Shaggy heads jerked in surprise, and hungry yellow eyes blinked and widened. Then the wolf-men fell back in shock.

An array of men and women confronted them, features slowly sharpening. Mewling and whining filled the darkness, recognition reflected in the eyes of those watching. Memories returned with shocking suddenness, and the horrified wolf-creatures stretched out their arms to embrace the people before them. But their arms passed through the visions uselessly and could not capture what they sought. To further emphasize what had been done to them, Brecon altered the vision ever so slightly, to portray the moments when their individual transformations had taken place. And in each one, Agathien d'Amphere was present, reveling in the changes she had visited on them, celebrating the damage she had wrought.

The wolf-men went mad, leaping and shrieking in recognition, lost in a mix of horror, rage, and desperate need. For a moment, Dar was certain they were going to vent their frustration on the four trapped within the cage, but then he realized he was mistaken. It was toward the *pretender* they chose to turn, remembering that she was to blame for what had happened to them. As their eyes fixed on her and she realized what they intended, she turned and raced for the stairs leading up from the cellar.

But flight was pointless; her wolf-men were far too

quick. They caught her before she was halfway there and took her down. In seconds, her screams ceased, and her body was reduced to scraps of flesh and bone.

Dar pushed Ajin through the partially open cage door, motioning for Brecon to follow, whispering to the Elf to keep the images in place. Then he went back and swept Orestiana d'Amphere into his arms and carried her out to join the other two. They crossed to the stairway at a cautious but steady pace, trying not to look at what remained of the *pretender*. Her pets were already beginning to eat bits and pieces of her off the floor, and to lick up her blood.

Ajin, to Dar's surprise, gagged and quickly looked away.

In minutes, they were up the stairs and into the corridor that had brought them inside. Dar fused the cellar door and then, once they were down the hallway and back outside, the huge metal-clads as well. The sealing of the doors might not hold the wolf-men prisoner for long, but it would slow them down enough for Ajin to send soldiers to end their unfortunate lives.

Already, in spite of the hour, a crowd was gathering, drawn by the sounds of the struggle within the warehouse. Shouts and cries began to sound at the sight of Ajin and her mother—voices of people who recognized the princess and welcomed her return. Apparently no word of her exile had reached the home city as yet. Apparently no report of her father's dismissal had come, either. To those gathered, Ajin d'Amphere, princess of the Skaar nation, was officially home.

Dar realized the implications immediately. Once a few announcements were made and soldiers still loyal to the princess assembled, she would be able to assume control of the city. Her popularity at home had not diminished, and her presence was a reassurance to the people in this deepest of winters. Ajin brought hope and the promise of something better to come.

Dar hoped they were right.

# THIRTY-SIX

THE WEATHER WAS WORSENING. Huge banks of darkening clouds were building against the horizon to the north, their masses roiling and fusing like waves on a windblown ocean. Where before there had been glimpses of light from the seldom-seen sun far above the clouds' hazy ceiling, now there was an absence of everything but the faintest illumination south. The wind had gusted from gentle or even brisk to a point where it could only be called harsh—its bite bitter and freezing with sharp gusts that now and then threatened to knock the crew members over.

Yet still they worked, determined to finish so that the contents mixed in the belly of Annabelle could be launched and sent skyward to change the destiny of a ruined world. No time remained; the readings both Tindall and Rocan had taken earlier were in agreement as to what was coming: They were in for a storm of unusual proportions and indeterminate length. If a test was to be made, it must happen now or wait another five to seven days.

Shea Ohmsford stood to one side as the Rover crew worked under the direction of Rocan and the old man.

The boy had wrapped himself in his heaviest cloak, having added a neck scarf and gloves and tied his hood tightly in place. Even so, he was freezing in the face of the wind's bitterness. It had stopped snowing for a while, but now the snow returned and the world disappeared in a thick blanket of white flakes. Banks of it were forming against the railings and deck walls, pinned in place by the unrelenting wind. A coating of white frost had formed on the northernmost surfaces of the masts and hull, giving the *Behemoth* the look of a ghost ship.

And the sounds! Shades! The boy had never heard howling of this magnitude—a scream that rose and fell but never ceased entirely. At first it was audible as little more than a low, insistent wail, but as the strength of the storm built and the force of the wind increased, the sound strengthened into a roar that might have signaled the end of the world. Shea wanted it to stop but could only grit his teeth and endure it.

"The devil's breath, right enough," shouted Sartren, his blocky form little more than a shadow in the blowing snow. "Makes one think the sun will never show itself again."

Shea squinted to make him out. "Are we almost ready? Is she primed?"

A deep laugh. "How would I know? I am but a poor seaman with a blood tie to this vessel's skipper. I do what I am told, and it's not for me to know such things."

"What does Rocan say?"

Another laugh. "Rocan says much. Over and over, he says it. 'Get back to work!' he says. I am more sick of those words by now than I have ever been of anything!"

Then off he walked into the haze and disappeared. Shea thought to move closer to the workmen, but he had found comfort in a makeshift windbreak formed by stacked supplies and did not much want to give up its shelter. He remained where he was, willing the work to be finished and the moment to arrive when the *Behemoth* would rise into the clouds. He spent the time thinking back to all that had brought him here—right from the moment he had first encountered the grandfather in Arishaig in the company of that insufferable girl.

The girl who was Tarsha Kaynin, and the grandfather who was Drisker Arc.

His thoughts shifted abruptly, and he wished he knew where they were and how much success they were having back in the Four Lands. Then he wondered if he would ever find out. Times like this made him feel like the world was closing down and his life ending.

He warmed himself with a memory of Tarsha and the kiss. He hadn't much cared for her at first, with her pushy manner and know-it-all attitude. He hadn't liked the way she treated him as excess baggage. But that was in the past and seemed a long time ago. He missed her and wished she were there to talk to.

What he got instead was a visit from Rocan Arneas, who somehow found him huddled back between the crates in the whiteout of the storm. The Rover came out of nowhere and bent close.

"How are you holding up?" he asked, with a smile

on his face. "Bad as I've ever seen, this weather—and it's not likely to improve anytime soon. But we have to work with what we have, and a blow can't be allowed to stop us."

Shea shook his head in puzzlement. "I don't see why we can't give this storm a few days to blow itself out. Give yourself and Annabelle a chance to do what she was meant to do and not risk doing it for nothing!"

"Time flies, Shea, and we have to act now. I didn't tell the others—not even Tindall—but I will tell you, if you give your word to say nothing." He waited for the boy to nod. "We were seen."

Shea stared. "Seen? By whom?"

"Some fishermen passing along the shoreline a few days back. It doesn't mean they reported it or even gave it a second thought, but we can't be sure. So we have to do what's needed with Annabelle, storm or no storm, then set sail for home."

"How can you think to accomplish anything in this wind?"

Rocan shrugged. "Not sure. We'll prepare Annabelle and wait for our chance. It will come."

He was gone again before the boy could think of anything further to say, and the snow and gloom closed about him. Shea's thoughts then turned instead to Ajin, Dar Leah, and the Elven prince. The Skaar princess had been absent from the airship for days, and now the two men had gone after her. He found himself worrying for their safety, wondering if they might get caught. Wondering if Ajin had been caught already. It was a possibility he could not ignore. It had been foolish for any of them to go into the city in the first place.

But there was nothing to be done about it—not with the preparations aboard the *Behemoth* in full swing and the weather continuing its decline from barely reasonable to full-bore insanity.

Fresh activity drew his attention away from his musings and brought him out of his shelter. The workers had climbed down off the ladders and platforms that allowed them to work on Annabelle and were gathered about her base. A handful had started rolling casks of the mixture Tindall had prepared a few days earlier to where they could be loaded into Annabelle once they had ascended high enough to allow a scattering of the mix into the clouds. It would have been nice to be able to send the airship aloft and let the dissemination of the mix happen without human assistance, but the weather had made that impossible and now Rocan and Tindall were arguing over who should carry out the job.

"Rocan, you cannot manage this without me!" the old man insisted. "I am the only one who understands how the mixture must be dispensed—the amounts, the texture, the temperature, all of it. I have to be there!"

But Rocan was already shaking his head. "None of that matters once the casks are aboard and the airship is launched. All that is needed is to complete the preparations before we ascend. I can handle the mechanics if you just tell me what is needed."

"It's too complicated! Too many variables!"

They were shouting at each other, but the wind was still drowning them out. Shea could see the heat in their faces brightening as they argued. He moved closer, wanting to hear everything.

"You make this sound impossible for anyone but you to do, which is patently ridiculous," Rocan snapped. "Do you have any idea how hard it will be to dispense the mix and do all these other things you're saying need doing?"

Tindall straightened. "Look at the weather, Rocan. Anyone who goes up now is at serious risk. I'm an old man. I've lived my life. If anything goes wrong, I want to finish it knowing I didn't waste the lives of others. You have to stay here to carry on should I fail."

"I could go," Shea offered suddenly. His cap had blown off and his hair was sopping wet, hanging down in his face and giving him a ragged look. He brushed a few strands away quickly. "I'm not afraid of storms."

Both wheeled on him together and, using more words than necessary, shouted his suggestion down. Shea backed off, stung and irritated at the abruptness of his dismissal.

"We have to go up right now!" Rocan had returned to arguing, seizing the front of Tindall's cloak and yanking him close. "We are positioned exactly right for the wind to carry us southeast over the island and farther onto the mainland if needed. Stop arguing with me and let me do this!"

"Unhand me, please," the old man ordered angrily. Rocan released him at once. "This is my invention, my machine, and my mixture. Whether you accept it or not, my skills are vital, and it is my duty to employ them. You'll serve best by staying right here on the ground and doing what's needed to make sure I stay safe."

Rocan stared at him for a long moment, then shrugged. "A noble offer of self-sacrifice, but no. We'll go together. We started that way and we will finish that way. No more arguing. The matter is settled. Climb on."

"Wait!" Shea called out. "Let me go, too!"

Rocan looked furious. "I thought we'd covered this."

"I know how Annabelle works. Tindall taught me. He also taught me all about what might go wrong and how to fix it. I am small and agile, and I do not panic. You *know* this."

"Shea, I cannot . . ."

"Tindall also taught me how to fly the airship. He explained its workings and how to make sure nothing gets out of balance. You need to let me go with you! I am here for a reason. The grandfather—the *Druid*—said so."

Rocan shook his head. "You seem determined, but this is the ultimate folly!"

"Look how I've lived my life! I'm a street kid. I have been on my own since I was big enough to run away from the orphanage. I have managed well enough, and I doubt there is much that could happen that I wouldn't be prepared for. Tindall will be with me. He can advise me without having to leave his work with Annabelle."

"As he could just as easily advise me. You ask for something I cannot give. You argue well, but permission is denied."

"I am not asking permission. I am telling you what I intend to do."

Suddenly Tindall was in front of him. He placed his hands on Shea's shoulders. "You are a brave and capable lad; no one would ever suggest anything else. And I have seen what you can do. Rescuing me from Assidian Deep was an astonishing accomplishment. And you stood with Rocan and me on more than one occasion when you knew you were putting your life at risk. I think the world of you, Shea Ohmsford. I want you to know that."

Then he embraced Shea and whispered into his ear. "I have something for you. Hide it well; keep it to yourself. If something should happen to me, you decide who should have it. The Skaar people, I think, would be best, but the decision will be yours."

He reached down and shoved a clutch of papers into the gap in the front of the coat Shea was wearing. "I trust you, Shea. You are quicker and smarter and better suited than even Rocan. Read my notes. All of them. I think you will know what they are for. But listen to me. Rocan is right about one thing. You are not coming with us."

He released Shea and started toward Annabelle. "Let's get on with it," he said to Rocan.

Rocan took Shea by his shoulder and moved him away. "Sartren," he called. "Take Shea in hand. I don't want him doing something foolish."

"I was thinking to go with you and Tindall," his cousin said. "You will need someone familiar with taking the controls while you assist Tindall."

"No. I want you to manage things down here in my absence. Someone reliable needs to stay behind, and you are the man I trust the most. Aberst and Kiftain will be help enough. Either can fly the airship."

Then he was climbing aboard, anxious to get into the air and test Annabelle's abilities. The casks were all filled and ready for use, save a dozen that were being held in reserve aboard ship. Tindall was quick to join him, the two glaring at each other momentarily and then turning their attention to preparing Annabelle. A mechanical device would siphon the mix out of the casks and into the belly of a sprayer through a series of snake-like hoses, which in turn would pump the mix to the crow's nest on the mainmast, where a nozzle would release it to seed the clouds. But the thunderheads that waited overhead were churning violently, dark and threatening, and now the sound of distant thunder was audible, as well.

"This is foolhardy," one of his cousins called up to him.

"Come down out of there!" another urged. "Wait for the skies to clear a bit."

A chorus of Rover voices quickly joined in agreement, offering various warnings about the weather and the risk they were taking of being swept right out of the sky. Rocan knew they were right. The winds were too strong; even a ship as big as the *Behemoth* would find it difficult to maneuver in such weather.

He felt his opportunity slipping away, but he could not let this slip though his fingers if there was even the smallest chance of success. He and Tindall had worked too long and fought too hard to give up on their creation now.

"Ready *Behemoth* for liftoff!" he shouted to his crew. "All of you get aboard!"

Silence and blank looks. Sartren stared at him. "Are you serious, Rocan? You want *all* of us to go with you?"

He was screaming out the words as the wind threatened to drown them out, blowing them about like leaves and whisking them away.

Rocan seized him by his shoulders. "Do I have the best crew that ever sailed the skies of the Four Lands or not?" he demanded. "Do I have men of courage and strength and belief in their abilities to overcome any obstacle or not? Tell me, Sartren, because we need to do this."

"But the risk of falling out of . . ."

"Tell me!"

Sartren stared at him for a long moment and then turned to the crew. "You heard the captain, Rovers! Family, all! Jump to! Ready the ship! It's a good day to fly right down into the netherworld and back out again, and so we shall!"

Galvanized by the force of his orders, the crew moved quickly to obey. They clambered aboard in a rush and moved to their stations. Rocan set a modicum of sail only, powering up the diapson crystals to provide lift and thrust, tightening the rigging and the stays to the parse tubes. Men and women scrambled about, and the weather seemed to respond by growing even more fierce and threatening. The winds quickened further, and the darkness increased as thunder rolled closer. And now—*now*—the skies filled with lightning. Jagged streaks of it crackled and flashed, opening jagged splits across the darkness overhead.

Rocan impulsively embraced Tindall. "You and me, old man. It will take two to make the siphon perform as it must—two to operate the pumps and measure the amount of mix they must release. It will be me in the crow's nest and you on the controls." He grinned fiercely. "This is our day. This is what we have worked for, and by all the shades that roam the earth, we will seize this opportunity and see the success we deserve!"

Tindall hugged him back, unable to speak, tears in his eyes.

Rocan turned back to Sartren, who was standing now in the pilot box, ready to lift off. "Wake Seelah. She's sleeping below in my cabin. Tell her I said I was sorry to leave so quickly, but I'll make it up to her. Tell her to watch over Shea until I get back. I want him protected. Do it now. Quickly!'

It was a last-second decision, an impulsive choice, in recognition of the danger they would be facing and into which he did not choose to place the boy. He had no knowledge of what would happen, but he loved the boy in spite of everything that had happened, and he was determined to keep him safe.

Seelah appeared, jumped off the airship, and went to stand by Shea. She gave Rocan a long, steady look, her cat eyes gleaming as she hesitated. Without speaking, the Rover made an abrupt, dismissive gesture. Lingering a second longer, the shape-shifter guided the boy away from the departing airship and walked him back beneath the overhanging boughs of a giant spruce.

Then she turned and looked at him once more, and he could read the anguish and disappointment in her eyes.

"Well done!" he called, gave her a tight-lipped nod, and turned away.

The *Behemoth* rose slowly into the darkness, and almost immediately the wind began to buffet the airship as waves would an untethered buoy. Huge gusts slammed into her side, and when Sartren attempted to turn into the wind to better absorb the blows, the wind shifted—almost as if sensing the efforts being made to thwart its power. Slowly, the *Behemoth* overcame blanketing snow and darkness, climbing toward the clouds in fits and starts as the wind continued to hammer against her, the resulting jolts requiring the crew to attach safety lines and brace themselves as best they could. Ascension was a horrifically slow process. Time crawled, and the fierce weather continued to pound them.

Yet still the airship struggled to rise, its floundering bulk able to withstand the force of the wind's powerful blows, but so cumbersome that steering was out of the question. But as fate would have it, direction didn't matter. Gaining height was what would determine success or failure—what would allow for Annabelle's efforts to produce the desired result and change the destructive weather besieging Skaarsland.

*If we can just get above the clouds,* Rocan thought.

They were in the teeth of the storm then, and it was chewing on them with a vengeance. Caught in its jaws, it was all the airship could do to maintain its slow rise. Rigging came down in clusters. Masts threatened to break in two, and the topmast and spars aft gave way with a violent snapping that could be heard all the way forward. Casks, crates, and bins broke loose from their rope stays and tumbled over the side. Pieces of railing shattered and went flying like spears. Yet still the ship held together, and its crew crouched and braced and fought to hold their places as the weather attempted to rip them away.

Lightning flashed in the distance, closer now.

*We cannot take much more!*

Rocan glanced skyward. There was a hint of brightness leaking through the clouds, little more than a crack in the sky; their goal was beckoning. The Rover leader yelled to Tindall to prepare the spraying apparatus and then snatched up the hose and nozzle and began climbing the rigging to reach the crow's nest.

But he knew at once he was in trouble. The power of the wind hammered at him with terrifying force, throwing him sideways against the ropes. Without a safety line to secure him until he reached the top, it took everything he had not to fall. Abruptly, the *Behemoth* shot skyward, caught in an updraft. It happened so quickly Rocan hardly had time to catch his breath before they were above the clouds and into open skies flooded with sunshine. Yet even here, the wind was so fierce the rigging rattled and shook from the insistent buffeting, and so cold that within seconds the dampness that had soaked him through was hardening his clothing.

"We need to start spraying!" he yelled down to Tindall as he finally reached the crow's nest and climbed inside the railing.

But his words were lost in the roar of the wind, and he was forced to gesture until Tindall glanced up and recognized what he was asking. The old man made a quick gesture in reply and threw some levers on Annabelle before giving a thumbs-up.

His safety lines secured, Rocan moved to the railing and directed the spray into the clouds below. Fighting against the constant buffeting of the wind, he worked the mix methodically across the dark expanse, the cold so intense it froze the moisture that layered his hands and face and turned it into a painful second skin. Ignoring his agony, he and Tindall emptied the contents of one cask, then two . . .

But suddenly the *Behemoth* began to sink.

*What's happening?* Rocan thought in shock.

Whatever it was, no one aboard the *Behemoth* seemed to be able to do anything about it. Crew members raced to adjust sails and shift to find fresh wind, but still they continued to fall back toward the clouds and finally into them. Slowly, the sunlight faded and the darkness closed about once more. Storm clouds previously heavy with snow and rain were now shedding sleet. Rocan did not stop working, recognizing his efforts were in jeopardy. Bursts of lightning cut through the darkness all about them, and he heard the booming of the thunder draw closer until both were right on top of them. He crouched down protectively as the storm worsened, realizing the wind was becoming too strong for him to remain upright.

*I've got to get down from here!*

It was his last thought before everything peaked in a single moment of unexpected fury. An instant later a bolt of lightning struck the mainmast and the crow's nest exploded. The structure didn't just blow into pieces; it incinerated, taking Rocan with it. Only the contents of the casks survived the conflagration, tumbling away to the decks below.

The lightning then continued to travel down the length of the mast to the *Behemoth*'s deck and ignited Annabelle. Metal shards flew out in all directions, and half the airship's crew was killed instantly—Sartren, standing in the pilot box, among them. As the decking began to burn, all of the casks held back in reserve fell victim to the intense heat and blew apart, sending the burning airship into a slow spin. One by one, the casks flew off into the storm, shattering as they did so, becoming flaming brands that pierced the storm clouds and filled them with chemicals—very much in the way that Tindall had envisioned they would, but on a much grander and more intense scale.

By now, all aboard the *Behemoth* were dead, and the massive transport was falling earthward in burning, broken pieces. But suddenly an ear-shattering scream—seemingly come out of nowhere—rose above the conflagration, violent and piercing. And in its wake, a chain reaction took place, erupting into and shattering the storm. Everywhere, the remnants of the chemicals infusing the air exploded anew—forming massive starbursts that infiltrated clouds and air and wind. The effect was monumental and dramatic; the skies for miles seemed to shudder under the force behind the scream's power.

And then the skies across Skaarsland, though still layered with ragged strips of storm clouds, began to clear for the first time in decades.

Far below, Shea Ohmsford stood by helplessly, watching as huge flashes of lightning split the clouds and drew down thunder—watching as a single massive strike ignited the mainmast and incinerated the crow's nest and its solitary occupant, then traveled the length of the mast to destroy the *Behemoth* and all aboard. Debris was raining down all about him—all across the inlet to where its waters disappeared into the gloom, back toward the ocean that had carried them in. He crawled from under the tree and stood looking up at the destruction, heedless of any danger the falling pieces of the *Behemoth* posed.

Beside him, Seelah was on her feet, head thrown back, long hair streaming out behind her in the wind, beautiful face upturned.

Shea Ohmsford followed her gaze skyward, stunned.

What had just happened?

They were gone. All of them. The airship *Behemoth,* Annabelle, the chemical mix she had been created to dispense, and all the men and women who had ridden with them into the storm. Even the old man; even Tindall. All gone. He couldn't believe it. Everything they had done had been for nothing. Tindall's machine hadn't worked. The chemicals hadn't mixed the right way or spread far enough. His friends were dead and Annabelle was destroyed. Nothing they had sacrificed would make the slightest difference. The weather hadn't been changed, the invasion by the Skaar would continue, the Four Lands would be overrun, and his homeland would be broken under the weight of a relentless assault . . .

He stared skyward in a desperate effort to find something—anything—that would suggest he was wrong. *Not all of them,* he begged whatever gods and fates there were in this life. *Not every last one.*

It was too much to bear. The scream broke from him as if it had been trapped within him all his life—as if the sheer agony of what he had just witnessed had finally released it. The sound was more a howl than anything: a wrenching cry torn from his very heart. The force of it exceeded anything he had ever thought himself capable of. It exploded out of him with such force that the recoil sent him staggering backward, a puppet jerked by manipulative strings, and the sound seemed to shatter the world. Seelah caught him before he struck the ground and hugged him tightly—holding him protectively, keeping him safe. Her arms were reassuring, but the look in her amber eyes was one of wonder.

Overhead, something incredible was happening. The clouds—infused with the mixture from Annabelle and the *Behemoth*—were igniting, a wave of chemical explosions breaking apart the storm so thoroughly that it was already little more than a splattering of droplets and a few distant rolls of fading thunder. The pervasive gloom was giving way to an unfamiliar light as the sun appeared and shone down.

Shea Ohmsford gasped. He had not caught a glimpse of the sun since he had arrived in Skaarsland, yet now it was revealed—and its appearance was the best proof possible that Tindall's belief in Annabelle's capabilities had not been misplaced. The old man *had* performed a miracle. With Rocan and his Rover clan to help him, he had managed to change the weather, and bring back the warmth that had been absent for years—which the boy was just now beginning to feel against his skin.

But, no. It had been more than that. He had done something, too. His voice—his unbidden, violent scream—had given fresh power to what was happening. He knew it instinctively—knew it as surely as he realized he had released a magic he had not known he possessed. It was an impossibility, yet he had no other explanation. The magic of an Ohmsford heir? Was he, in truth, a member of that family in more than just name? Did he, like Tarsha, possess the fabled wishsong? He could not quite believe it, but he could not make himself ignore what his instincts told him was true.

All at once, he remembered Rocan's embrace as the Rover ordered Seelah to keep watch over him. He remembered Tindall shoving a wad of papers into his coat for safekeeping, entrusting him to do what was needed if anything happened.

Asking him to keep them safe.

Shea sank to his knees and began to cry, the weight of everything that had happened too much for him. Seelah cuddled him against her, nuzzling him gently. The boy buried his face in her shoulder, sobbing uncontrollably. He was not sure how much time passed as they remained locked together, and eventually he fell asleep.

But just before he fully slept, while he was still conscious of being cradled in her arms, he was aware of Seelah bending close and nuzzling his hair before kissing him once on his cheek as she lowered him to the ground and her warmth went away.

He did not hear the flit as it landed behind him. He did not hear Dar, Brecon, and Ajin d'Amphere approach.

When they lifted him to his feet and embraced him, he looked around for Seelah, remembering. But she was nowhere to be found.

# THIRTY-SEVEN

◆

TARSHA KAYNIN WAS SITTING on the porch of Drisker's cottage, basking in the warmth of the sunshine, allowing the day to pass at its own pace. She had been reading for most of the morning, perusing documents her mentor had written early in his service as head of the Fifth Druid Order. From what she could determine, he had only been serving as Ard Rhys for a few months when he penned these documents, so disillusionment and frustration had not yet set in. During these early days he had written regularly, recording discoveries from experiments and research while still making entries on current Druid activities in the fabled Druid Histories.

She was doing this primarily to help pass the time but also in the faint hope she might find something to help Drisker in the event the darkwand failed to free him. She was trying not to worry needlessly, but was beginning to grow steadily more concerned as time passed and her mentor failed to show. It was a leap of faith to think he would actually be able to escape his imprisonment and return. There were so many obstacles preventing it, and countless reasons he might fail.

Yet no matter the odds Drisker Arc faced, she would be patient. She would not question or doubt, and she would not give up on him.

She was much recovered from her terrible battle with Clizia, her health recovered and her self-confidence returned. This did not mean she was reassured of her ability to overcome any further attacks, only that she knew she could stand up to the witch. When Clizia came again—which she was certain to do, if Tarsha did not go to her first—they would at least be meeting as equals.

It was noon on a sunshine-filled day at the cusp of winter's end and spring's beginning. The snow of weeks past was only a memory, the bitter cold gone, and the long dark days become steadily brighter. There was an undeniable freshness to the air, a blend of scents from flowers and new grasses carried on the breeze. Overhead, the leaves of the deciduous old growth shivered and rippled, and their movement caused a small whisper in the stillness of the day—the sound soothing and reassuring. Birds flew from branch to branch, gathering discarded bits and pieces of the forest for nest building, courting potential mates, and seeking tender worms and bugs.

Tarsha paid no attention. She was aware of all of it, but otherwise occupied, deeply immersed in her reading. As a result, she did not hear or even sense Flinc approach. He stopped at her elbow.

"You seem very much at your ease on this beautiful day, gentle Tarsha," he said quietly.

"You mean unaware, don't you, since I failed to notice your coming? But it was you who assured me I was safe. No one and nothing could get to me without you warning me, correct?"

"It is true I have arranged to have you warded so you will know if you are threatened. But readiness is a habit that will always serve you well when danger remains so close at hand."

She raised her head and looked at him. Wrinkled, worn, nearly hairless save for a topknot tuft of gray and a bit of fluff about the ears and chin, he seemed a child's caricature of a Faerie creature. Yet his looks were deceptive and his manner a ruse.

"Is there cause for me to be wary?"

"You know there is."

"Does she come, then?"

"No, not yet. That time has not arrived. When it does, it will not find us unprepared. I have set a watch, and nothing will allow her to evade it."

*Clizia Porse.* No word of her had surfaced since their battle in the Federation camp, and yet sooner or later the witch would discover she was alive and come searching, if only for revenge.

But especially if she learned that Tarsha was still trying to help Drisker return from the prison in which she had trapped him.

"When Clizia comes," she began, pausing to look directly into the forest imp's aged eyes, "will you please reconsider placing yourself in harm's way? I understand your reasons for doing so, and I am flattered you would think me so valuable, but I am afraid for you. I do not want to lose you again. You and Fade must let me stand up to her alone."

Flinc nodded patiently. "I do not intend to interfere

if she is alone. But if she brings others to help, then Fade and I will step in to balance the scales."

He was referring to the thing that Clizia had likely freed from the Forbidding to take Drisker's place in the Four Lands. "Remember." Flinc was bending close. "She has tried several times to kill you and twice almost succeeded. Beware risking it a third time, Tarsha-of-the-magic-that-sings. Beware a risk taken one time too many."

Twice she had almost died. Once at Cleeg Hold and once in the Federation camp battle. She thought momentarily of Parlindru's rule of three. It had been a while since she had called it to mind.

*Three times shall you love, but while all three will be true only one will endure.*

*Three times shall you die but each death will see you rise anew and live to go on.*

*Three times shall you have a chance to make a difference in the lives of others and three times will you do so. But one time only will you change the world, as well.*

So, apparently, she had another life to give. A third encounter in which she could die, yet rise again. But how could she be sure? How was she supposed to decide which instances fulfilled the requirements of having lived and then been reborn? It felt as if she had died a dozen times in the past few months, so which were the three that mattered? And how many had she loved, in some way or other? More than three, she believed. Her parents, her brother, Drisker, even Flinc, for starters. Her family was all gone. Would the one that endured be Drisker Arc? Or someone else entirely?

What really mystified her was how she would have any chance at all to make a difference in the world. What did that mean? Had she found even a single way to do this thus far? Had she made a difference of any sort in the lives of others? She supposed so. But how would she know which of those would somehow change the world?

It was confusing and frustrating, trying to sort out its meaning. But that was the nature of prophecies of the future. You could never know when they would come to pass until they did. She could do nothing about what Parlindru had predicted no matter what she decided. Her fate was written, if the seer was accurate in her foretelling, and knowing that the rule of three would apply did nothing to clarify what she must look for or what she must do to prepare herself.

She gave Flinc a reassuring smile. "I promise you I will do whatever I can to stay safe. But we both know I cannot avoid Clizia Porse forever. She does not forgive those she believes have betrayed or challenged her, and I have done both. I must be prepared to face her at least once more, Flinc."

"Avoidance is perhaps preferable to confrontation where the witch is concerned. I should know. I have faced her down and seen the power she wields—and the hatred that drives her. You are strong, pretty Tarsha, but the witch is deeply evil and lacks a moral center. She is a dark force of nature."

They left it there, for there was nothing more to be said and nothing more Tarsha cared to hear. She knew what Clizia Porse was. More, she believed, than did the forest imp. More than she wished.

She went back to reading. When she looked up again, he was gone.

Overhead, the sun shone bright in the sky, and the warmth blanketed her comfortingly. After a few minutes, she dozed.

She woke again when Flinc shook her shoulder gently and whispered in her ear, "Wake up, Tarsha. Leave your dreams behind."

She blinked, and her eyes opened to find him bending close. "What is it?" she asked sleepily.

The forest imp managed a wan smile. "She comes."

Tarsha took a moment to process what he was talking about, then managed an uncertain nod. "Now?" she asked. "Are you sure of this?"

"She is less than an hour away. She was seen approaching Emberen by a fling-wing flying to the south. The description fits; there is no mistaking her for anyone else." He paused. "Especially considering what accompanies her. For she does not come alone."

Tarsha sat up, rubbing the last of the sleep from her eyes. So it was here: the time she had been anticipating. Somehow, she knew instinctively this would be the final time she would face Clizia Porse. She was not afraid, but she was unsure of herself. She had been drained by their last battle, and she had not tested herself to see if she was fully healed. Now she would be tested in a way that would allow for no mistakes and no failure. Because there was only one possible end to the confrontation. Once it was over, either the witch would be dead, or she would. There was no other viable option.

She took several deep breaths and stared out into the trees, gathering her courage and resolve about her like armor. *Clizia.* She remembered finding Tavo dead on that cliff ledge fronting Cleeg Hold, and all her grief came back to her in a rush. After all she had done to help him come to terms with the madness that had consumed him for so long, after everything she had gone through to get him back again, after everything it had taken to reassure her brother, the last of her family, that she had always loved him . . .

The witch had snatched it all away.

*Clizia Porse. How I hate you!*

"What sort of creature does she bring with her?" she asked Flinc, coming to her feet.

"A Jachyra. A demon-kind. Very dangerous. One of them killed the Druid Allanon."

She now recalled this, but it didn't matter. She brushed it aside. "It will not kill me."

"No, it most certainly will not." Flinc's features were calm, but his words were hard. "Fade and I will see to that."

"I asked you not to . . ."

"Not to interfere when you faced the witch," he interrupted her quickly. "But the Jachyra is a different matter entirely. A balancing of the scales is needed, and those who have sworn to protect you will see to it that this happens."

She saw her own determination mirrored in the forest imp's eyes and realized nothing she could say would change his mind. She nodded her agreement. "Thank you, Flinc."

"All will be well, Tarsha. You will see."

His pronouncement made, he turned and disappeared into the trees, leaving her alone to await what was coming.

Her thoughts again drifted to the past—to all the terrible losses she had suffered, to all the frightening close calls she had survived, and to those who had stood with her through the worst of everything. She felt a deep sense of gratitude sweep through her, born of the realization that so much of what we can endure depends on the support of others. She was grateful all over again to have Flinc and Fade standing with her. A forest imp and a moor cat—not what she had expected, but invaluable nonetheless. She only wished Drisker could have been here, too, inflicting on Clizia Porse a little of the suffering she had inflicted on him. Maybe he would still arrive in time. It could come to pass, given the nature of all that had happened to her.

She wondered again if she was up to this fight—if she retained enough of her magic to overcome a mage so much more experienced and powerful than she was. How much of her magic had she expended over the past weeks—in support of Tavo, Drisker, and the others? How much strength had she lost and not yet regained? It was impossible to know, of course. She felt as strong as ever. She felt fully recovered.

She would be whatever she had to be and survive whatever she was called upon to face.

Then she stood up to wait, staring off into the forest, marking the small quick movements of the ground animals amid the grasses and ferns, enjoying the bursts of sudden flight of the birds through the trees. None of them knew what was about to happen to her, and none of them cared. She envied the simplicity of their lives, wondering what it would be like to have everything reduced to such basics.

She closed her eyes, seeking her calm center, trying to quiet and ready herself. There was no way to plan for what would happen, and no further preparations to be made. She had only a single weapon: her wishsong. It would save her if she could manage to use it in the right way and if she kept from panicking. If she failed to use it wisely she would be lost.

She sensed movement and opened her eyes. The clearing before her was empty; the movement had come from back in the trees. She waited for the source to reveal itself. Clouds passed over the sun, and the day darkened as if in recognition of what was coming. Tarsha felt her throat tighten and took a deep breath. The heavy brush directly across from her shivered as something pushed forward, and all the birdsong, which moments earlier had filled the day with bright music, went silent.

Slowly a nightmarish form emerged, easing its way out of the foliage into the newly formed shadows, crouched down on all fours. Tarsha knew at once it was something born of the Forbidding, for there was nothing that looked this foul living in the Four Lands. It was lean and spidery, but at the same time huge— sinew and muscle wrapped about its lean frame, while its claws and teeth were those of a predator and all out of proportion with the rest of its body.

The remains of a rabbit hung from its jaws, which were chewing, chewing steadily, slowly devouring its kill. Tarsha watched, repulsed. So this was a Jachyra. A single word called itself to mind as she studied it.

*Loathsome.*

The Jachyra did not see Tarsha at first, but when it did it stopped where it was, finished its meal, and swallowed it while regarding her with eyes the color of swamp water. And then it brayed. The sound it made was horrific and seemed to penetrate her entire body, leaving her shivering. But she stood her ground, summoning her magic. This thing meant to test her, and she sensed it would test her as nothing else had. But she would be ready; she would not give way.

The Jachyra dropped into a full crouch, gathering itself, its attention now fully fixed on her. She waited, her magic ready—a low, dangerous humming that reverberated all the way through her. She was forming it into something massive—something that would slam into this monster and send it all the way back into the Forbidding with a single strike.

Suddenly the Jachyra threw back its head and emitted another heart-shattering bray, then charged. It was so fast she almost failed to act quickly enough. But act she did—her magic exploding from her lips in a song of iron that slammed into the beast and threw it back into the shadows from which it had first emerged.

Then, silence.

She waited on it to reappear, but it did not. She stepped down off the cottage porch and went to find it. She was wary, but she was not afraid. She had sensed what this monster would try to do to her, and she told herself she could withstand it. Whatever drove the Jachyra to try to kill her, it would not be enough.

Overhead, sunlight passed through the clouds, and she felt a fresh surge of confidence.

When her enemy reemerged, catapulting from the trees in a slashing blur of claws and teeth, it was not from where she had flung it but from farther to her left, which caught her off guard. A rush of uncertainty gripped her. The reek of the Jachyra's body preceded it in a nauseating wave, leaving her inexplicably paralyzed. The creature's speed had doubled. It was fast— incredibly fast. A nightmarish blend of teeth and claws, size and power.

But Fade was faster still.

The moor cat shot out of nowhere, a blur of gray fury, hammering into the Jachyra with such force it sent them both rolling across the clearing, teeth and claws biting and ripping. Tarsha's thoughts raced to catch up with what she was witnessing. *Fade! Lying in wait. Coming to my aid. And Flinc will be close as well.* A burst of exhilaration flooded through her. The forest imp had said they would balance the scales if Clizia brought the Jachyra, and indeed they were trying.

The combatants broke apart, facing each other. The Jachyra was more cautious now and infinitely more dangerous, as it quickly showed. It flung itself at the moor cat, dodged a swipe of one huge paw, then caught Fade and flung her away. Fade weighed eight hundred pounds, and the Jachyra swatted her aside as if she were no more than a feather. The moor cat tumbled over and over but came back to her feet, meeting the Jachyra's fresh attack with a counter-rush of her own.

The struggle was even at first, the combatants a match—each as determined as the other to prevail. But while Fade's strength was prodigious, the Jachyra's endurance was seemingly endless. Instead of growing tired as the fight progressed, it seemed to get stronger. Tarsha tried to help, striking out at the creature when the opportunity presented itself, but she was hampered by the way the two were so often locked together and by the Jachyra's quickness, which caused her to miss her target over and over.

Frustrated and afraid for Fade, she screamed out to draw the Jachyra's attention, hoping to turn it toward her. But the Jachyra was fully focused on the moor cat, and it was as if Tarsha didn't even exist. Try as she might, she could not find a way to change what was happening.

Fade was weakening.

But Flinc was nearby, and now he showed his mettle. Standing at the forest's edge, small and seemingly insignificant, he made a series of gestures that summoned a buzzing cloud of insects from the forest. Tarsha stared. Hornets—thousands of them. They swarmed above the forest imp for long moments, and then he called out to Fade and the moor cat broke clear of the Jachyra. Instantly, the hornets were on top of the demon, stinging it over and over—a swarming shadow that engulfed it entirely. The Jachyra howled in fury, tearing its tormentors from the air and crushing them, falling to the ground and rolling over and over to rid himself of their stinging.

Tarsha thought to take advantage by striking now, but she worried that anything she might do that involved serious force would likely kill all the hornets, as well. So she hesitated and then it was too late. When the hornets were finally driven off, the Jachyra side-stepped another attempt at a strike and quickly moved to resume the battle with Fade. But it was the forest imp the demon found waiting, standing no more than a dozen feet away.

The Jachyra hesitated, clearly knowing there had to be something more to this creature than met the eye. By now, it was a mess—its leathery body studded with hornet stings and deeply clawed by Fade. Even so, it showed no sign of giving up.

After a quick appraisal of this new opponent, the Jachyra barreled across the short distance that separated them, again avoiding Tarsha's belated strike. Claws outstretched, it tore into Flinc—only to find he wasn't there. Instead, a tree stump suddenly materialized, the imp's glamour lifted, and the Jachyra flew into it headfirst. The scream it emitted on slamming into the stump could have woken the dead—and it quickly appeared that it had. Dozens of wraiths swarmed out of the woods and bore down, completely covering it. There were enough of them that the Jachyra disappeared for long moments, the wraiths a heaving, writhing mass atop the creature they had thrown themselves upon.

*Yes,* Tarsha cheered silently. *Suffocate it!*

But it was not to be. All too soon the Jachyra discovered the wraiths possessed no weight or substance, and it broke free. Tarsha saw it pull loose and instantly used the wishsong to pick it up and throw it back into the forest.

Tarsha felt a twinge of hope. *Stay there! Crawl off and be done with this!*

Then she heard Clizia's voice from somewhere close at hand: "You waste your time, foolish girl."

A quick scan of the area revealed no sign of the witch. She was still in hiding, not yet ready to reveal herself physically. Tarsha was suddenly furious. "Come out and face me, Clizia!" she screamed.

But it was the Jachyra that responded, rushing from the forest to slam into Flinc with such force that the little imp went flying onto the cottage porch twenty feet away, where he lay limp and unmoving. Fade tried to help, but she was too late. The Jachyra catapulted away, safe from her rush, then attacked from the side, snatching up the moor cat as if she weighed nothing and throwing her a dozen feet. Fade clawed at the air, trying to right herself and failing, then struck the hard ground with an audible gasp to lie motionless in a ragged heap.

*So strong! How could anything be so strong?*

Now Tarsha stood alone, and the Jachyra turned to face her once more. This same creature had put an end to Allanon and even proved a match for the Weapons Master Garet Jax. *Shades*, she begged the silence, *help me find the strength I need!*

The Jachyra attacked—a swift and terrible blur as it tore across the clearing to reach her. But when it caught her, it found only an empty image. Tarsha wasn't there, having used her magic to create an illusion. Instead, she was standing off to one side—a trick she had remembered while watching Flinc—waiting for her chance. Her attacker wheeled back frantically, but she was already using her voice, shaping her wish-song into a weight that bore down on it with terrible force, crushing it against the earth. It wasn't enough. The Jachyra threw off her efforts and rose once more—a relentless berserker, its hatred a poison that drove it to the point of insanity, able to submerge the pain of its wounds and any hint of weakness beneath its driving need to put an end to anything it viewed as a threat.

And it had long since decided that Tarsha was just such a threat.

Tarsha used the wishsong and threw the monster away again, but again it came at her. And again. When it came a third time with no sign of the attacks slowing, she began to despair. She was doing all she knew to overcome this monster, and it wasn't enough. She had to think of something else. She had to find another way.

*Wham!* One powerful glancing blow across the face sent her sprawling. Bruised and bloodied and now dazed as well, she struggled back to her feet to fend off her attacker. But for all that she was using her magic against it like a hammer, it was having little effect. Some supernatural resilience allowed it to shrug off her most savage strikes—the worst she could manage—while remaining just as strong.

*Find another way!*

But what way was there? What could she do that would stop it for good?

The Jachyra came at her again. She cut its legs out from under it, pinned its arms to its sides, rolled it in hardening mud and buried it six feet beneath the earth and stone, and still it rose to attack again. She tried to break its bones, blind it, smother it, wrench its head from its shoulders, inflict any of a dozen other disabling injuries, and all of them failed. Her head was throbbing from the blow it had struck her, and she was bleeding from wounds she was barely aware of receiving.

Slowly, her strength was ebbing away. She was going to lose this battle. A glimpse over to Flinc and then to Fade showed their still-limp bodies. Perhaps they were dead. Perhaps she was destined to join them.

Then a heavy blow struck her from behind and she was thrown into the dirt, choking and gasping for air. A terrible refusal screamed at her from within. *I cannot let this happen!*

But could she prevent it?

# THIRTY-EIGHT

LONG MOMENTS SHROUDED IN an unnatural silence passed as Tarsha Kaynin lay gasping for breath, still not quite sure what had happened. She was still struggling to breathe—not so much from the exertion of the battle she had fought or the wounds she had sustained as from the shock of being caught off guard.

"Finding yourself a bit overmatched?" a familiar voice teased.

Tarsha closed her eyes in weariness and frustration. *Clizia Porse.*

She had almost forgotten about the witch in her focus on the Jachyra. But of course Clizia had never been far away, even while the battle was being fought. She had been there, watching—waiting to see how it would end so she could react accordingly.

And now Tarsha was under threat yet again, and with no resources on which to rely save her wits and cunning. She pushed herself up on one elbow, but a booted foot quickly pushed her back down again.

Clizia stood over her, looking down speculatively. "I think it best if you stay where you are. You look very tired, Tarsha. That was an impressive display of magic you used to try and put an end to my pet. Not that I would have cared all that much if you had succeeded. I will have to kill it anyway, sooner or later. Really, it has caused me no end of trouble."

Tarsha did not respond. Had she survived one devastating struggle only to end up facing one that would be even worse? How could she save herself from Clizia? Her strength was exhausted; her magic was drained. She was barely maintaining consciousness; her attention even now wandering to Fade and Flinc, both of whom she realized were also at risk. If they were even still alive.

"You might be wondering if I intend to offer you yet another chance to defend yourself," Clizia said brightly. "After all, you have proven yourself an astonishingly adept opponent. But the answer is no. I cannot risk giving you any further chances. I wrongly presumed you dead before—along with your half-mad brother—but some mistakes can be corrected, and this is one."

A sense of futility washed through Tarsha, but she tamped it down and did what she could to husband her strength. She might not have much magic left to rely on, but she would make good use of what remained. She would have to play for time, to stall for as long as she could, hoping she could come up with some sort of plan. She knew how crazy that sounded, but she had survived worse. Besides, Parlindru's prophecy had said she was destined to die three times and yet survive. She had survived two deaths already at Clizia's hands; perhaps she could survive this one, too.

"Drisker has returned from the Forbidding, you

know," she lied. "He might already be on his way here."

The witch laughed. "Do you really believe that? And even if he does return, he won't be the same person he was. No one who returns from there is ever the same."

"How would you know?" Tarsha gave the words a biting edge. "It isn't as if you've ever been there and come back. But Drisker Arc has returned from banishment once already—from Paranor when you sent the Druid's Keep into limbo."

Clizia scoffed. "Drisker Arc is a failed Druid! Besides, what makes you think he's even alive? He's not equipped to survive the Forbidding. By now he's likely dead. Believing he might somehow come back and save you is foolishness. This is my time, Tarsha Kaynin!"

Then something odd happened. Earlier, in the aftermath of the battle with the Jachyra, the world had gone unnaturally still. But such stillness cannot last, and soon enough the familiar sounds of the forest returned—the rustling of the ground animals, the songs of the winged fliers, the whisper of the wind and the stirring of the leaves at its touch. So now, as clouds passed across the sun and dimmed the light around the girl and the witch for a second time and all the familiar sounds died away again, it was immediately noticeable to both. And both paused and looked up.

"Your time is over, Clizia Porse."

A new voice spoke—deep and ragged—sounding of suffering and weariness but also of an indomitable determination. Clizia wheeled about to find the speaker, and from her prone position Tarsha peered up, as well. An ancient crone stood at the edge of the clearing, hunched and crooked, worn and beaten down until she appeared no more than a skeletal creature, barely possessed of flesh and blood. She looked exhausted as she leaned for support on a rune-carved black staff.

Clizia laughed, but the sound carried a hint of uncertainty. "Who are you, old woman, to threaten me? I'll snuff you as I would a candle!"

The newcomer shuffled forward a few steps, drawing herself up slightly and taking on a different look—one far less vulnerable. "I am a messenger, come from a distant land, to give you warning. Drisker Arc intended to do so in my place, but he was unavoidably detained. You should know that he saved my life, however, and I owe him a debt. And like you, I repay my debts—whatever it might require. Do you not know me?"

Tarsha saw it first—recognized it before Clizia—and felt a ripple of excitement course through her. "Grianne Ohmsford!"

Clizia stiffened. "Noooo!" She drew the word out, as if to emphasize her certainty. "It can't be! She was consigned to the Forbidding centuries ago. What sort of charade is this?" She made a commanding gesture toward the newcomer. "Who are you really?"

The old woman transformed so quickly it was as if she had become someone else entirely. From a ragged crone she turned into a figure of such presence that Clizia took a step back. The years and the ravages fell away, replaced by strength and certainty.

"I had thought to kill you myself, but I think your fate belongs to another," she said softly. "Step away from the girl. Now."

Clizia Porse saw the truth then, and she was quick to act. She pretended to do as she had been ordered, turning sideways to hide the hand that slipped into her pocket to retrieve the Stiehl. She would *have* to risk the consequences of using it. Shifting slightly back toward Grianne, she whipped the Stiehl toward her, propelling it by magic so fast it was little more than a blur—a killing strike that would put an end to this creature once and for all. But Grianne Ohmsford blocked the attack, deflecting the blade effortlessly so that it spun away into the trees, writhing and twisting as it disappeared.

"Step away!" Grianne repeated.

This time, the witch did as she was told, staring in disbelief, stunned by what was happening. Tarsha looked from one to the other with a deep sense of wonder at how quickly things had turned around.

"Rise, Tarsha Kaynin, and face me." Tarsha climbed back to her feet and stood waiting. "Are you strong enough to face this creature and give account of yourself? If not, say so now."

Tarsha did not need to think about it. This was all she wanted—a chance to face Clizia Porse, one-on-one. This was what she needed to do to avenge her brother, what she had been seeking from the moment she had held his lifeless form in her arms on the cliffs of Cleeg Hold. She owed this to Tavo. She owed it to Drisker and so many others. She owed it to herself.

But Clizia had ideas of her own. She made a frantic

gesture at the Jachyra, which had been momentarily forgotten, and two words broke from her lips in a piercing shriek as her skeletal arm thrust at her enemy.

"Kill her!"

Instantly the demon launched itself at Grianne. All this time, it had been waiting, held in check while its mistress toyed with its original prey. Now it was eager to release the bloodlust that raged inside it.

Tarsha flinched in horror. *Do not let this happen!*

But Grianne just waited patiently as the Jachyra came for her. Only when it was close did she release her wishsong—her voice a weapon of such power that it could almost be seen as it left her lips, the magic crystallizing the air and turning it into millions of razor-sharp fragments that flew into the Jachyra much as a flash rip's discharge might have.

Tarsha gasped at what happened next. Grianne's magic stopped the Jachyra in its tracks, lifted it off the ground, and held it pinned there. Her magic was sustained and fury-driven and more inexorable than what any living creature could possibly withstand. For heart-stopping seconds the Jachyra hung helplessly, writhing and braying in dismay. And then it simply exploded into pieces and was gone.

In the aftermath of the Jachyra's demise, Grianne Ohmsord sank to the ground and stayed there, slumped over, the black staff lying next to her. It did not appear as if she had been injured, only that the strength had been leached from her body and left her drained. Tarsha rushed to her side and knelt next to her. Immediately Grianne's hand rose, and she placed her fingers against the girl's lips in what was clearly meant to be a warning.

"Say nothing," she whispered. Her eyes locked on Tarsha's. "That took more out of me than I had expected, thanks to the magic I had to expend to escape the Forbidding." Her smile was tight and bitter. "I am not what I once was."

Tarsha shifted her body to block Grianne's words from Clizia Porse. Again, those piercing eyes found her own. "You must face your enemy on your own, Tarsha Kaynin. Drisker had faith in you, and I, too, believe you can do this. I am not going to be able to protect you further. I need time to recover, and there is no time left."

The girl glanced behind her to where Clizia stood watching. The witch's ancient face still reflected her shock at the ease with which Grianne had dispatched her pet, but the shock was fading, replaced by cunning. She had realized what was happening to her enemy and was seeing a path to victory. She would be quick to recognize that only Tarsha now stood in her way.

Grianne's hand felt light as it slipped over Tarsha's. "Be strong. Be what the Druid saw you to be. Save us both."

Tarsha rose and turned to face Clizia, resolved anew to end this once and for all. She was strengthened by her determination and by her trust in her heritage. She was the bearer of the wishsong, the heir to the Ohmsford legacy, and the child of a history that stretched backward in time almost three thousand years.

"Things not working out quite the way you had hoped?" the witch teased. "Lost your champion, did you?"

Tarsha took a deep breath and shook her head. "I am my own champion."

The depth of meaning in her words, the boldness of her claim, did not escape Clizia. A hesitation—a tiny hint of uncertainty—surfaced in her expression. "If you wish, you may beg me for forgiveness, and I will grant it. It is not yet too late for you to join me in rebuilding the Druid order."

Tarsha Kaynin dismissed the offer out of hand. She was remembering how Tavo had died, how merciless the witch had been once she disabled her brother and had him lying at her feet. She remembered how Clizia had betrayed the Druid order and allowed all of them to die as a result. She recalled how her enemy's Druid magic—power gone wrong and turned dark— had been used to send Drisker Arc into limbo, leaving him trapped inside Paranor. And then been used again to see him banished from the Four Lands to be trapped inside the Forbidding. She was thinking of all the harm this evil old woman had done—and all of it to serve her own self-interests, with no concern at all for the cost to others.

She hated Clizia Porse, and she was not going to let her live any longer. No more machinations and cruel manipulations of others' lives. No further time spent spreading hatred and misery among the peoples of the Four Lands.

It ended here. It ended now. It ended with her.

Clizia must have sensed at much, because she instantly launched an attack that slammed into Tarsha and would have destroyed her instantly had she not been prepared. But prepared she was, shields already raised and defenses already formed. The attack shattered against her protective wall, and Tarsha stood unharmed.

In spite of itching to launch a counterattack, she stood waiting—baiting, challenging the witch, demonstrating her confidence in herself and her certainty that Clizia was no longer a threat. Clizia attacked again, this time with iron shards and wooden barbs that filled the air with singing death. They sped toward the girl, propelled by a deathwind, driven by the old woman's hatred and frustration.

The projectiles struck the defensive wall Tarsha had formed and were absorbed instantly. She felt their force, experienced their sting, and still she did not falter. It was almost as if her body welcomed the magic into her, converting it for her own use, finding it not threatening but sustaining. Tarsha had crossed a line she could not identify and had not realized was there, but it revealed in no uncertain terms that she was no longer the student of the magic she had been born with, but its mistress.

And perhaps more revealing even than that, she was indeed the equal of Clizia Porse.

Still, the battle was not over, the victory not yet secured. Clizia remained dangerous—perhaps more so in her growing desperation. Seeing that the direct attacks were failing to work, she turned to something else.

"Little witch!" she screamed—perhaps in simple

fury but perhaps in an effort to tighten her own resolve. "You think yourself a match for me? You are nothing but the failed dream of a failed wizard and your own worthless hopes!"

Words and gestures ensued—frantic arm waving and weaving hands and expressions that promised terrible pain. It was almost comical, and hard to credit that it would amount to anything more than hot air and wasted effort. But within seconds Tarsha felt something working. It started as a nudging from somewhere deep inside and quickly began to spread all through her. She fought back, but she could not slow the process down. Quickly, it overwhelmed her defenses and became so painful she screamed in response. It was as if hot irons were pressing against her body from within. She felt herself begin to burn all over, intolerable pain ratcheting through her until all her efforts at resistance were overcome.

She dropped to her knees. She was dying; she could feel it. She was drowning in pain, consumed from the inside out, her organs eaten away, her blood vessels bursting, her life sliding into an abyss from which there was no return.

She could hear the sound of Clizia's voice, laughing and taunting. She could feel the witch's hands wrenching at her heart and lungs, trying to yank them free of her body. Everything was spinning about—the whole of the world whirling madly—and she was beginning to fall.

Then an understanding came to her, and she grabbed hold of it and held on tight.

*Do not fight that which threatens to steal all hope; embrace it and make it your own.*

Drisker's words, spoken long ago, back when he was first training her and had told her that sometimes what you couldn't overcome by force you could co-opt with acceptance. This was one such time; she was certain of it. Clizia could not have gotten inside of her, could not have broken through her defenses so easily. This was an illusion only, planted by the witch and allowed free rein by Tarsha's own mind.

*Clizia, I am finished with you!*

Tarsha opened herself fully to the burning, the iron, the pain, and let herself move through and past it. And there, at the end, was Clizia Porse, poised to strike a killing blow, prepared to send her to join her brother in the netherworld.

Gathering herself in response, she struck the witch first, her own magic white-hot and deadly accurate. A single, iron-wrapped lance of wishsong power, formed and dispatched so swiftly it was on top of Clizia before she knew it was coming. She saw the danger in the last moments of her life, and then the lance penetrated—piercing her, shredding her, stealing away her last breath, her last heartbeat, her final thought, her life.

She died on her feet, and the magic infecting Tarsha fell away.

Tarsha dropped to one knee, head bent, breathing rapidly as Grianne knelt beside her. One slender arm came about her body, and the girl was aware suddenly that she was shaking all over. The arm tightened reassuringly. "It's finished," the other woman whispered.

Tarsha shook her head doubtfully, not yet able to accept that it really was, still caught up in the battle she had fought.

"Listen to me, Tarsha Kaynin." Grianne drew her up so that she met the other's steady gaze. "You fought the battle you were born to fight, and you prevailed. Clizia Porse is gone, and she is not coming back. But there is more that you must see."

Tarsha flinched, feeling a sudden surge of dread fill her. "What is it?"

But Grianne merely helped her to her feet and guided her away from the battle site and into the trees. She saw almost at once the body lying amid the grasses, wrapped in a gray robe, carefully covered.

"Your friend—your mentor and protector, Drisker Arc. We fought side by side to escape the Forbidding, but the effort cost him his life. He is gone."

Tarsha Kaynin stared at the old woman, wanting to deny what she was hearing, to tell her she was mistaken, but what she saw in those ancient eyes told her it was true.

It seemed as if the world collapsed on her then—as if she were suddenly buried beneath everything she had experienced since she had first gone to the Druid all those weeks ago. She moved woodenly to kneel beside the still form, to reach out tentatively and touch it. Then the tears came in a flood, hot and unwelcome, and she began to cry as if she would never stop.

# THIRTY-NINE

◆

WHEN TARSHA HAD CRIED herself out, Grianne raised her to her feet once more and positioned her so they were facing each other directly. "He died at the hand of an Ulk Bog, a demon who thought Drisker had betrayed him, even though he was only trying to help. We were all trying to escape the Forbidding. Drisker found the darkwand; he saved me, Tarsha. He freed me when I thought nothing ever would. I could not save his life, but I brought him back with me anyway. Back to the Four Lands, back to where he belonged. He asked me to come to you, to help you stand against Clizia Porse."

She smiled, and suddenly she was a younger woman, a less worn and world-weary creature, and Tarsha thought she could see something of the girl she had once been.

"But you never needed me to help you. You only needed yourself." She took Tarsha's hands in her own. "I had always believed the darkwand would permit only the Druid and myself to cross back. As an Ohmsford, I could access passage. As my charge, the Druid could accompany me. The Ulk Bog could not, because he was a prisoner of the Forbidding and could never be set free. Nor was I entirely certain about Drisker, yet I was determined to try. And I succeeded."

"I always thought he would return," Tarsha said. "I always believed he would find a way."

"He was strong," Grianne agreed, "but it was his time. He knew it. I regret I could not save him. I regret I could not save the unfortunate creature who killed him; Weka Dart was loyal to me for so long; but reason failed him, and madness drove him to take the Druid's life. My wishsong has saved others who were badly injured, but it failed me this time. The Druid's injuries were too grievous, and my magic was already engaged with the darkwand and could not be turned. Yet I had made him a promise. If he failed to come back to you, I would find you and protect you in his place. I decided he should come with me, even if his life was over. He deserved that much from me."

Tarsha was weeping again. "He did so much for me. He tried to save my brother. He did save me. He cared for the Four Lands, and he was the sole reason so much of what went wrong was set right again. I wish he could be here to see the rest made right, as well."

The other woman nodded. "He may be seeing it anyway, from where he now dwells. One day, he might come to you to speak about it. Until then, honor his memory."

They rose and walked together to see to Fade and Flinc. A bit of joy surfaced inside Tarsha when she found both beginning to stir. The moor cat's injuries were not so severe they could not be treated with the wishsong's magic, so Grianne acted immediately to do so. The forest imp, too, was sitting up by then, looking thoroughly befuddled as he caught sight of her. "I remember you," he said to Grianne. "You probably don't remember me, but we crossed paths a long time ago—so long ago I can't remember exactly when it was. Yet here you are. How is that possible?"

They sat together then and Grianne explained again what had befallen Drisker Arc. She described how Drisker had gone with her to retrieve the darkwand, and how together they had come back to find it at Kraal Reach. She described his death at the hands of Weka Dart. She took her time and did not rush her explanation. It seemed to Tarsha that she gave them what peace of mind and solace she could.

By the time she had finished, Fade was sleeping next to her, exhausted. The magic of the wishsong seemed to have helped her, and the depth of her sleep was a clear indication she was healing. Flinc was gone. He had slipped away, and Tarsha hadn't even noticed. He had not explained how he and the Ilse Witch had crossed paths, but she knew he would do so one day.

Because Grianne had brought Drisker's body back with her, the two women decided to bury him next to Tavo. As they finished, the day was waning, the sun sliding west into the trees, casting their long shadows across the graves of Drisker and her brother. Tarsha wasn't sure if it was right, but she thought she would stay here for a while. She would grieve and wait for news of the *Behemoth* and her friends. She would try to heal, although at that moment she wasn't at all sure she ever would.

"Do something for me, please," the older woman asked. "Find the Stiehl. Then retrieve the darkwand from where I left it and search what remains of Clizia Porse for any other talismans of magic. Bring them all to me."

Tarsha did so, finding a scrye orb in the witch's pocket, but nothing else of note. She carried it all back to Grianne and laid it at her feet. The old woman glanced at the objects, then reached into her pocket and brought out a second scrye orb. "I took it from Drisker Arc, after he was gone."

Tarsha said nothing for a moment and then sat down beside her. "What will you do with them?" she asked.

A slow smile lit the other's seamed features. "Nothing. I will ask you to keep them here. Hide them where you think best, and when the time is right—and you will know when it is—bring them out again. But they cannot stay with me. Now then, I need to ask a favor of you," she said.

Tarsha smiled back. "Whatever I can do, I will. I owe you my life. Tell me what you want."

"I want you to take me home."

Grianne saw the confusion in the girl's eyes as she tried to make sense of what she was being asked. What home could Grianne mean? Surely not the Forbidding she had finally managed to escape. Her only real home had been lost when she was stolen as a child and made into the Ilse Witch. Since then, Grianne had never really had a home. But she had found peace and purpose in another place and life—in the mountains of the Klu and the valley of the Inkrim, in the company of the aeriads and in service to the strange entity known as Mother Tanequil.

It was there, she told the girl, that she wished to return. Back to that life and the joy it had given her. Back to the only comfort and tranquility she had ever known. Take her there, and Tarsha would be granting her a favor of such immense proportions there were no words to adequately describe what it would mean.

After a few days' rest, during which they talked to each other at length and kept company with the recovering Fade and the enigmatic Flinc, they boarded Tarsha's two-man and set out for the distant north. The day mirrored their mood and their expectations—bright and cheerful and welcoming. Grianne felt a mix of excitement and intense anticipation she had not known for longer than she could remember. Here was the goal she had set for herself when wrongly swept back into the Forbidding by the Ellcrys all those years ago. Here was the dream that had never died but lived on as a live coal within ashes of despair, burning with hope.

They flew north into the Streleheim, swung down below the River Lethe and then northeast along the borders of the Charnals until they reached the broad spreading waters of the Lazareen and the Rock Troll city of Taupo Rough. It was a journey that required the better part of a week to complete, but it gave the girl and the old woman time to talk further about their lives and how they had been shaped by history and been impacted by forces beyond their control. For her part, Grianne was pleased to be able to open up to someone for the first time since her imprisonment.

She liked Tarsha, and she understood what the girl did not as yet—that she was the linchpin for the future of the Druids and Paranor. Once Grianne had returned to Mother Tanequil, Tarsha would become the last of the Druids. It wasn't a sentence, but it was a responsibility she would have to face.

But for now she was content to tell her story and let Tarsha tell hers, and they both did so willingly and without reservation, opening up as two old friends might after a long absence. For Grianne, it was a final chance to tell someone who could understand what it had been like for her to lose and find so many different lives over the course of centuries. For Tarsha, it seemed to help unburden the guilt and sadness she carried for the loss of her family and so many of her friends and companions.

The time and the journey both passed away, and on the sixth day they found themselves flying into the Charnals and, more specifically, into the Klu. They passed through the towering peaks of the sprawling mountain range without incident, the good weather and mood helping to speed them along.

By sunset's approach, they had arrived at the Inkrim and were setting down before the ruins of the ancient city of Stridegate. Once there had been a people called the Urdas living here—creatures of another time that considered the ruins sacred and worshipped the ghosts of their ancestors. But they were all gone, and no one remained to challenge the intruders.

"We have only a short distance to go now," Grianne informed her companion. "I would like to do so today, before dark."

She caught the flash of regret on the girl's young face and moved quickly to embrace her. She would not have done so before—in her old life, inside the Forbidding—but the change in her on being free again was so complete that even intimacy had become possible again.

"I will miss you," she told Tarsha, hugging her. "I will think of you always as family. But I cannot wait any longer. It is almost as if I know that, by waiting, I will lose whatever chance I have of getting back what was stolen from me."

The girl nodded. "I know. I understand. We can go now."

They walked through the ruins, the sun sinking west, lingering on the horizon, its warm glow falling across their shoulders, its light showing them the way. Soon enough they came to the crevasse that eons ago had split the earth apart and left a forested island at its center, where the tanequil had taken root. A footbridge of stones that were interlinked and seemed to float on the air gave access to the island. They crossed the narrow bridge and stood together at their destination.

"I wish I could come with you," Tarsha told her. "I feel so close to you—as if you were my mother, and I'd found you again. I don't want to lose you."

Grianne placed her aged hands on the girl's shoulders. "You have your whole life ahead of you, Tarsha. This place is not for you. One day, maybe, but much still awaits you in your own life, and much remains to be done. I think you will find others to replace those you have lost. What was it Parlindru told you? Three times shall you love another, but only one of those loves will endure. Your family and your mentor are gone, but I think there is another love still out there, waiting for you."

She reached into her pocket and brought out a small leather pouch. "This is for you. I found it in Drisker Arc's possession after he died. He would have wanted it to come to you. You are now the one to whom it belongs."

She handed it to the girl, who accepted it reluctantly. "Open it," Grianne told her.

Tarsha did so, and the Black Elfstone dropped into her palm, gleaming onyx fire in the fading light.

"What am I to do with it?" the girl asked, genuinely confused.

"Indeed," Grianne said, smiling. "Now, then. I have one thing more for you." She reached into the same pocket and produced an envelope. "This, too, is from Drisker. He would not tell me what it was he had written, and I did not presume to look. You will do so when you are ready. Or you will leave it unread, if that is your wish. The choice is up to you." She handed over the envelope. "Take it and keep it for later."

Then she gave Tarsha a final hug and turned away. "Go back across the bridge and wait for me to come to you. I will do so, one way or the other." Only steps away, she turned and looked back. "Goodbye, Tarsha Kaynin. Be well. Be strong. And be at peace."

She disappeared into the trees, her eyes on the way forward, her long journey almost at an end.

———

Tarsha crossed back over the stone bridge to the ruins of Stridegate and sat down to wait. The sun had set, taking the light with it, and the clear skies were filling with stars and a moon that issued their own white brightness. The world around her was mostly silent, but she was aware of night birds and small ground animals that flew and darted through the ancient stones of the fallen city. She watched the island of the tanequil for any indication of Grianne's promised return but saw nothing.

She looked at the envelope several times more before putting it away for good. She was not ready for what might have been Drisker's final thoughts. She was not ready to imagine his voice speaking them. She would need to grieve further, and to heal more completely.

Eventually, she fell asleep sitting up.

When she woke, she was aware of another presence. When she looked, she could not find it. But she was not mistaken in what she had sensed; she knew that much.

—Tarsha. I am here—

She straightened at once, knowing it was Grianne. "Are you all right?"

—Perfect. I am perfect! Go home now—

"I don't know if I want to. I don't know if I can."

—You can do anything you set your mind to, Tarsha Kaynin. Anything at all. Go home—

And then her voice went silent. Tarsha felt the void her departure left, the sudden feeling of being alone. She waited, but nothing more came.

Grianne Ohmsford was gone for good.

She waited for her tears to stop and her emotions to settle before rising. This was what Grianne wanted—what she had been searching for, hoping for, desperate to find again after so many years. No one had the right to feel sad because she had finally found it—especially Tarsha.

She rose then, walked back through the ruins to her two-man, climbed aboard with no thought of eating or sleeping, and flew home.

# FORTY

FAR TO THE SOUTH in the Dwarf village of Cracken-rood, Lakodan and Battenhyle were sitting on Batten-hyle's front porch with their feet up, sharing a pitcher of ale and discussing the events of the last few weeks. They had returned to Crackenrood with the rest of their little company of Dwarves ten days ago, and the simple pleasure of being back among their own people had not yet worn off.

After Belladrin Rish had been sent back to the Skaar, the Federation had dug in for the expected attack, but it had never come. The return home to Arishaig had been delayed for another week until scouting reports confirmed that the Skaar army had decamped. Further investigation revealed that the invaders had gone from the Four Lands entirely.

The war with the Skaar was apparently over.

The Dwarves had exchanged a knowing glance when Oberion advised them of this unexpected change in matters. "What do you think?" Lakodan asked his friend.

Battenhyle shrugged. "We know her to be a resourceful young lady. Perhaps we should try to think better of her."

"I wouldn't be that optimistic," Lakodan growled, looking very deliberately at the lieutenant commander. "I'd keep a wary eye to the north, were I you."

Over the next few days, Oberion took the precaution of dispatching scouts all up and down the Mermidon's north shores. Then he sent flits to scan the entirety of the surrounding countryside. Neither effort produced anything; there was no sign of the Skaar. Once he was sufficiently persuaded that the invaders were truly gone, he released the Dwarves from any further service, telling them he now felt the Federation could manage on its own and promising he would see to it that the agreement regarding the conscription exemption was honored.

He wished them well, and they wished him the same—even though he did not return the Reveals. But as Battenhyle remarked later to Lakodan, "Not everything works out the way we think it should in this world."

The Dwarves were in a good mood when they set out, and even took time to say goodbye to various members of the Federation army with whom they had become friendly. The issues that separated their countries were created by politicians, and most saw no point in any of it. Most believed politics did more to hurt than to help in creating good relations between their peoples.

"One day, there will be a genuine understanding between us," Battenhyle told his old friend now, as the two sipped their ale. "All this conscription nonsense will stop, and we'll be friends."

Lakodan shook his head. "It will never happen."

"Oh, I think it will. The law of averages says, sooner or later, our chieftains and their Prime Ministers and Coalition Council will be of a similar mindset. We might not live to see it, but others will."

A brief silence followed before Lakodan said quietly, "I wonder what happened to her? If her king was sufficiently displeased with her failure to carry out his plans, wouldn't he have had her executed?"

Battenhyle looked at him speculatively. "Do you think maybe she was successful in persuading him not to?"

"As you said, she was a very resourceful young woman."

"Do you think we will ever find out the truth?"

Lakodan laughed. "Do you really want to?" Then he laughed harder still.

Sometimes, you just get lucky. It happened that way with Belladrin Rish. She slipped out of Cor d'Amphere's private chambers after ending his life and no one saw her go. Reenergized by what she recognized as an unbelievable stroke of good fortune, she took a risk and commandeered an airship while the inhabitants of the camp were engaged in other pursuits, then boarded and flew far enough off that she could watch the Skaar camp unobserved—just to make sure they would not attack the Federation in retaliation for their king's death. Because, if they did, she felt compelled to warn the Dwarves.

But instead, to her relief, the Skaar struck camp over the next two days and moved to a more distant location, where they seemed intent on going into hiding while they presumably dispatched a messenger back to Skaarsland to inform the queen of her husband's death.

Knowing she had bought the Federation what time she could, Belladrin boarded her airship and departed.

She was through with being anyone's pawn. There would be no more bowing to the needs and dictates of the Skaar throne. No more playing at being someone she wasn't.

Still, she had no idea what she was going to do or where she was going to go. She had come to love this new land, but she had not seen enough of it yet to know if she wanted to remain here or go home. And now that she had a ship and all the time in the world on her hands, there was no need to rush the decision. She would stay far away from Paranor in the event that Clizia still lived, but she would love to see the Elven nation, and Rainbow Lake. There were wonders aplenty to explore, and time to do it—even if she would occasionally be keeping quiet tabs on the Skaar.

Maybe, eventually, she would go visit the Dwarves in Crackenrood. She liked them in spite of their having exposed her. Admired them, really. It would be fun to see them again, spend a little time talking everything over. Lakodan and Battenhyle. Just a quick visit. Just a few days.

Wouldn't they be surprised!

She smiled at the prospect.

Dar Leah, Brecon Elessedil, and Shea Ohmsford had stayed on in Skaarsland for Ajin's coronation, which had been delayed until the Skaar army had returned from the Four Lands to their remade world and been given time to reunite with family and comrades. The advisers to the throne—those old men and women whose duty it was to guide the Skaarsland rulers in carrying out their obligations and making their decisions—would have held the coronation the minute word came of the king's death, anxious to have the matter settled. But Ajin, who was to be their queen, had more on her mind than orchestrating a quick conclusion to the question of succession. She thought it highly improper to proceed until all of her people were reunited in their homeland—especially those comrades she had once led on the field of battle and who would have considered it a betrayal if they were not included.

It was an excruciating time for Dar—a time of deep misgiving. Ajin was ensconced in the royal palace, which was now her new home, while her guests were placed in a distant wing. Gone were the days and nights the two had spent together, their liaison forbidden by the prospective queen's advisers on what they saw as very sound grounds. The people wanted to see their queen fully focused on her investiture, they said. The people did not want to imagine her sleeping with an outlander, or considering his needs ahead of those of her people. Best they stay apart until after the coronation, and then the matter of living conditions could be reviewed.

Very sound grounds, they repeated.

And Ajin, to Dar's chagrin, went along with this nonsense.

"Don't rush things," she said to him when they were alone. "Give this time. We have time to spare, and I need to work on convincing them of the importance of accepting our relationship. Let them have their few weeks while I make them understand I am not going to tolerate anyone's interference in making decisions that are mine alone to make. If they think they will be able to control my life, they haven't been paying close attention for the last twenty years."

But Dar didn't like it. In spite of her promises, he was not reassured. He didn't like being away from her, and he didn't like where he believed this was heading.

"What's to say they won't continue to take this stand even after you are crowned? They won't give up on forcing you into what they think is best for you, and I'm not it. They will seek to make you a better match. They will string you along until everything you and I have is buried by time and separation. Don't do this, Ajin."

But she did, and he was left with the option of seeing her only when she could manage to slip away. Which, he quickly discovered, was infrequently. The advisers and their preparations for her coronation kept her occupied almost the entire time.

"I know something of coronations and their protocols," Brecon tried to explain. "I was raised in the Elven court, so I am very familiar with how these things work. And rules and prohibitions are the name of the game. Remember, appearances are everything. Nothing must seem out of place or untoward, even if it feels unnatural to you. But Ajin loves you. She would never abandon you, and she would never attempt to replace you. You have to see that, Dar. Use your common sense!"

But Dar wasn't interested in common sense or patience or anything else that would further his separation from Ajin. He began to worry as her absences grew longer and the time remaining until the coronation grew closer. Somehow, he knew, she *was* going to be taken away from him. He had always thought it would happen in battle; that she would die by the sword. That was bad enough. But this? This was much worse. It was all dark expectations and nagging uncertainties. It was death by small cuts.

He chaffed and he worried. He spent as much time as he could trying to persuade himself that matters would work out as Brecon believed, while at the same time finding reasons why they wouldn't. He considered ways he could stop Ajin from falling victim to the manipulations and wiles of her advisers and their allies. Wild, crazy plans formed—harebrained schemes and impossible happenings—all of them involving either spiriting Ajin away by night, or demanding she give up the throne so there could be no one else controlling their future.

All of it was impossible, and all of it was hopeless. It always came down to the same reality. The past was over, and the future was taking them in different directions. Ajin had agreed to assume the throne because her people wanted her to and she knew it would be wrong to turn her back on them. Her mother, too, had spent long hours convincing her of the importance of recognizing her duty to her country. Dar had been there for some of it, and he had not objected or tried to argue her out of it. It wasn't his place to do so. If she wanted this, he had to stand aside and let her have it.

He had to support her—even if it was destroying him to do so.

On the night before her coronation, she came to his bedchamber, stealing away from her mother and her well-meaning caretakers to throw herself into his arms and tell him anew how much she loved him. But right away, he was on his guard. Trust was no longer an issue. Necessity now governed everything, and his ideas of what constituted the right course of action were no longer the same as hers.

So even as he hugged her back, pressing her against him with such ferocity he feared she might cry out, he resolved that no matter what she said or did, he would not do anything to stand in her way.

"I missed you," she breathed into his ear.

"Not as much as I missed you."

"I would have come sooner if I could have."

"I know. Are you ready for tomorrow?"

She nodded, her head against his shoulder. "I am. Will you be there to watch me?"

He was stunned. He moved her away and stared at her. "Why wouldn't I be?"

"Because we won't be together when it happens.

Because I am required to stand apart from everyone during the ceremony, to demonstrate my strength and resilience as the future queen. The protocol is clear; I cannot be allowed to appear as if I need help from anyone."

He shook his head. "That's nonsense! Everyone needs help from someone at some time. And queen or not, no one ever stands completely alone. I am so sick of this pretense—all this insistence of following rules and keeping you shut away as if you might break if I were to hold you in public! I want you to tell these so-called advisers that all this is over the moment the coronation is complete."

She glared at him. "Don't make demands! And don't presume to tell me what I must or must not do! That makes you just another adviser. If you cared for me, you wouldn't even suggest it!"

"Well, I love you and I *am* suggesting it. In fact, I am insisting on it. If we really love each other, we have to stop pretending nothing is happening." He paused. "Unless, of course, you've changed your mind."

"I haven't changed my mind, but I am beginning to wonder if you've lost yours. Things aren't the same as they were when we were fighting for our lives. Then we were just trying to survive. Now we're trying to find our way to the life we always thought that struggle would give us. So don't downplay the importance of what we are doing."

He shook his head. "But I don't *understand* what we're doing! I see us fighting still, only now it's with people who should be trying to help us. Why do you keep making excuses for what they are doing to us?"

She exhaled sharply. "You know what your problem is? You have no patience and not the foggiest idea how to massage difficult situations. I told you I would need time to make this happen, and that nothing has changed between us. But allowing that to happen while not diminishing my advisers and my mother isn't all that easy."

"Apparently."

"Now you're just being mean. My mother knows how important you are to me. She has spoken to the royal advisers countless times already about how much she and I both owe you, and how you saved both our lives. I have spent time doing this as well, working to build you up and make them see what a good man you are. I am starting to see some cracks in the wall. But you have to understand that protocol and appearances mean a great deal to these people, and they rely on the members of the royal family to conduct themselves with respect and wisdom. My father disappointed them, so I cannot. They need order. They crave reassurance. I have to give them this, or my future rule will mean nothing."

"Perhaps you've made a wrong choice, then!" he snapped, forgetting the promise he had made himself.

Immediately he regretted the words as Ajin stared at him, hurt. "Ajin, no, I didn't mean . . ."

"But you said it, didn't you?" Her eyes flashed and she stepped back from him. "I had meant this evening to end differently, but I don't think that's going to happen now." She paused, then added, "I want you to consider carefully what you've just said to me. I want you to consider how much you are willing to tolerate in order to remain together. Because more will be asked of you, and more will be required. I will love you forever, but not if you can't accept this."

"Ajin!"

He reached for her, but she stepped away. "Sleep well, Dar. And think about what I've said."

A few further steps, and she was through the door and gone.

He spent a sleepless night, thinking about how matters stood between them and how it felt like they had drifted into a dark place. Come morning, he dressed in something of a daze before joining Shea and Brecon. Wordlessly, they ate breakfast, then the three made their way to their reserved viewing area while the coronation took place. Dar was aware of his companions glancing over from time to time, and he knew they were aware that something was wrong. How could they not be? He wore the evidence of it on his face.

The coronation began at midday and lasted for hours. Dar remembered almost nothing of the details afterward—only the pageantry with its colors and flags, its trumpets and drums, and its sea of rapt faces filled with awe. He was close enough to Ajin to see the happiness reflected in her smile and in the exuberant waving of her hands. She seemed fully invested in what was happening, and she did not once glance his way.

Afterward, there were greetings exchanged in a long line of notables before an adjournment to the royal dining hall for an evening meal. But Dar was not hungry. He was numb and devastated. When it came to his turn in the reception line, Ajin offered him her hand to kiss and gave him a wink. Nothing more. Nothing special. Nothing reassuring. Then he was moving on to other dignitaries.

What he knew then quite suddenly—and what he had failed to realize before—was that he was wrong for her. He might have been her match when they fought side by side against imminent disasters, but this was something else. This was the hereafter, and she needed someone who could better fulfill the part of a court-trained and educated consort. He would never be that person, and he knew it.

It was a stunning, harsh reality, but staying in Skaarsland would eventually lead to something ugly growing between them. She deserved to be queen, and she would be a good one. She was strong and able and determined. He would only hold her back; he would always be a hindrance. His service to the Druids had only trained him for one thing—to serve as Blade to the High Druid: a position that no longer existed. Ajin would not accompany him back to the Four Lands, and he could not imagine staying here with her, knowing how useless it would make him feel.

Halfway through the dinner celebration, he got to his feet and said to Brecon and Shea, "We're leaving."

They stared at him, then rose wordlessly and followed him toward the exit. When they had reached it, he brought them to a sudden halt. "No. I have to say goodbye to her."

The Elven prince shook his head. "You mean good night, don't you?"

Dar shook his head. "I don't belong here. This all

feels wrong to me. Go on to bed. I will speak with her and then join you. In the morning, we will fly back to the Four Lands. I will ask for the use of an airship, and we'll go home."

"Are you sure . . . ?" Shea started to ask, then stopped when he saw the look on the highlander's face.

"This is nonsense, you know," Brecon said, unable to contain himself. "You are making the worst mistake of all time! Whatever is bothering you, find a way to work it out."

But Dar just turned and walked back into the dining hall, moving toward the head table and Ajin. As he neared, he saw her talking with a young Captain of the Guard he had noticed her with earlier and slowed. Then he stopped, just as she noticed him approaching. He stood there, not knowing what to do, then gave her a wave and pointed toward the door. She beckoned him to her, but he shook his head, turned around, and left the room.

Really, how much more convincing did he require to reassure himself that he was doing the right thing?

He was making a poor attempt at sleep when she came to him for the second night running and crawled into bed next to him. Without thinking, he took her into his arms, and they kissed. For a long time. And for those moments, he was transported back to when there were no obstacles to how they felt about each other.

Finally, she whispered. "I'm sorry I left you alone. I was trying to do the right thing, and I ruined it."

He kissed her nose. "You did what you had to. I understand that. I was just feeling sorry for myself."

She was quiet for a moment. "You know I care nothing for that captain you were glaring at. I care nothing for anyone but you. Please do not think anything else, Dar."

"I don't," he lied. "I was just tired and not feeling well, so I came to bed."

"Can we talk about all this tomorrow?" she whispered. "Can we leave it for then? I want to feel close to you tonight. I want to feel how much we love each other and nothing else. Can we do that?"

He found they could.

But even so, he had not changed his mind about their future and what he had resolved to do.

# FORTY-ONE

TARSHA DECIDED SHE WOULD stay at Drisker's cottage. No one else would claim it if she didn't, and it was as close to a real home as anywhere else. She was like Grianne Ohmsford in that way. She had lost everything while still young, but had found this cottage a place where she could be at peace, protected against the world. She had always assumed she would stay for good, but that Drisker would be here with her. Even with her mentor's death, his cottage still spoke to her, so she would forsake any other plans and remain.

She had the company she wanted in the moor cat and the forest imp. Fade was always there, seldom for more than moments at a time, but at least once every day nevertheless. Her silent passage through the forests surrounding the cottage gave reassurance that a sentry was keeping watch. Flinc, too, picked up with her right where he had left off with Drisker—teasing, questioning, offering unasked-for advice and what passed for sage wisdom—which she found both heartening and entertaining. She liked listening to him talk about the old days: days so far in the past the Four Lands had not yet come into being. He was quite old, she discovered—so ancient that the time of his earliest ancestors predated both the Druids and the Ohmsfords. He never revealed exactly how long he had been alive, but she got the impression he might have been there when the Faerie folk of light and dark fought their war and the Forbidding was created.

She thought now and then of Grianne Ohmsford, safely returned to the home she had sought for so long, become again an aeriad in the service of Mother Tanequil. She was a Faerie creature now, endowed with new purpose and freedom from the horrors of the Forbidding. That she was happy to be living a free-flowing life was unmistakable. Tarsha had heard it in her voice; she had sensed it from the tone and inflection and lilt of each word. The Ilse Witch was gone forever, and the Straken Queen was no more. What remained was just an ordinary woman, unburdened and at peace.

The days passed leisurely and without incident, and slowly the raw edge of Tarsha's memories softened sufficiently she no longer cried thinking of them. Life in the Four Lands seemed to have settled. There had been no word of war breaking out, but news traveled slowly to Emberen, and she found the pace suited her. Still, eventually word reached even this remote outpost. The Skaar, it seemed, had departed, their war with the Federation over. But why and how they gave up so completely, she might never know—at least not until the crew of the *Behemoth* returned.

She looked for them at first, and then stopped. Why bother? They would come when they could. They would come when they had accomplished what they had set out to do or they would not come at all. The latter was possible, but her faith in Shea Ohmsford, the Blade, Brecon, and the others who had gone with them was strong enough to make her believe they would overcome whatever odds they faced. The only uncertainty was the performance of the odd machine the old man Tindall had invented. But it was what they had to work with, and the best chance they had for resetting the weather and putting an end to the Skaar invasion. Still, maybe the Skaar's departure alone was a signal of the mission's success, because what else might have induced them to leave?

Then, one day, months after her return from the tanequil, three figures walked up the road from Emberen and into her yard. She knew them before they reached her—knew them even sooner than she could see their faces clearly, she would insist later.

*Shea Ohmsford, Darcon Leah, and Brecon Elessedil!*

She leapt out of her rocker and charged down the cottage steps to meet them, yelling with unrestrained glee. She hugged them all and kissed their cheeks, not bothering to wipe away her tears of joy as she did so. She was so happy to see them again she could not stop smiling.

She took them up on the porch, sat them down, and poured them glasses of ale. "Tell me everything," she urged impatiently.

"You first," Shea insisted. "What's happened here? We know the war with the Skaar is over, but not much else. Tell us about yourself."

Tarsha shook her head despairingly. "There's so

much. Not all of it good. Drisker is dead." The minute the words were out of her mouth she began to cry. After regaining control of herself, she added, "But so is Clizia Porse." And she told them all about Drisker's banishment into the Forbidding, and her battles with Clizia, and the demon Clizia had brought out of the Forbidding in exchange for Drisker. And then about Grianne's fate, and the bond they had formed.

By the end of her story, they were all shaking their heads in wonder.

"We lost Rocan and Tindall," Shea said. "And the *Behemoth* was struck by lightning while trying to use Annabelle and exploded. The entire Rover crew was killed."

"Annabelle was destroyed," Brecon continued, "but her demise was the trigger that brought about a new spring, so there's a new beginning for the Skaar. They have a home again where they can grow crops and live off the land. Everything's changed. Shea, tell them what the old man did."

The boy looked embarrassed. "He left plans and writings with me that explained how Annabelle was built and how the chemicals could be mixed and used to seed the clouds. I don't know if he sensed he might not be coming back when he saw that storm coming, but he must have thought it was a good idea to leave some sort of record. He wanted the plans to go to the Skaar people—it was so awful over there—so I gave them to Ajin. I thought she would know who might put them to the best use should the weather turn bad again."

"Tell her the rest," Dar urged gently. "You can't

be hiding things at this point. Not from her." Tarsha turned to look at Shea questioningly. The boy hesitated, perhaps searching for the words, and the Blade cocked an eyebrow in disapproval. "As it happened, Shea had a great deal to do with how everything turned out. Tell her."

Shea shrugged and blushed—a response that caused Tarsha to raise an eyebrow. "Yes, tell me."

The boy rolled his eyes. "All right, all right. You know how I've said I didn't think I was any part of the Ohmsford bloodline? I was orphaned early, and I never knew my parents or my history. I always thought that even if I was an Ohmsford it didn't matter; I didn't inherit the wishsong. There's never been any evidence of my possessing it."

Tarsha took his wrist and held tightly. "But now you think maybe you do? Is that what you're trying to say?"

Shea gave another shrug and nodded. "There's no 'maybe' about it. When lightning struck the *Behemoth* and blew her . . ." He stopped, suddenly unable to continue. Everyone waited as he gathered himself. ". . . blew her and everyone aboard to pieces, I was watching it happen from the ground with Seelah. I didn't do anything for a few moments; I guess it hadn't sunk in yet. But when it did, I screamed. I don't know where it came from. It didn't sound like a real scream; it was something much louder and more violent. It just burst out of me. But when it did . . . well, it caused the whole sky surrounding the remains of the ship and Annabelle and everything else to just explode. It was the chemicals—the mix the machine used to spray the clouds. It was like I started a chain reaction that went across the sky for miles in all directions, shoving back the clouds, the cold, and the winter. I could feel this power radiating out of me, this . . . this *magic,* I guess. I don't know why it happened then and not before; it was the stress and horror of what was happening, I suppose. But I don't have any other way to explain it. I'm still trying to get used to the idea."

"So the change in the weather was due not just to Tindall and his chemicals, but to your scream, too? You think it was the wishsong?"

"I know it was. But it was not like your wishsong or the grandfather's magic. This was something different. Something really scary." Shea shook his head again. "I don't know what to do about it. Will it happen again? Can I find a way to control it? Is there something I should know that you can tell me?"

"He wants you to teach him how to manage it," Brecon finished for him, with a grin.

Tarsha was immediately reminded of Tavo. She had wanted to teach her brother how to control his magic, but she had failed him. Now she was being offered a second chance.

"What of Seelah?" she asked suddenly. "What became of her? She must have been devastated losing Rocan that way. You told me how close they were."

"She disappeared," Shea said quietly, and the way he said it told her not to ask anything more just then.

"Shea Ohmsford," she said instead, very deliberately using his full name. "I don't want you to worry about using this newfound magic—wishsong or whatever it may be. I promise I will do my very best to teach you."

The boy laughed. "Then I promise I will do my very best to pay attention."

It took them considerable time and effort to finish their explanations. But time was something they had, and they were in no hurry. For the first time that any of them could remember, there was no immediate threat to the Four Lands or themselves, and they could be at ease.

"Where is Ajin?" Tarsha asked finally. By then, the light had started to fade and the sun to slide west in the afternoon sky. She was beginning to think about food and sleep.

Brecon shook his head and Shea looked down at his hands. Darcon Leah cleared his throat. "A messenger from the Skaar army returned home while we were still there, and she learned her father had been assassinated in his own tent during the standoff with the Federation. They didn't seem to know by whom, and were reluctant to attack the Federation again without their king and commander. So Ajin ordered the whole Skaar army to return, and when it did, she was welcomed back by her soldiers. Moreover, her people begged her to become queen and she accepted. So she gave us her airship and sent us home."

"But I thought you and she . . ." Tarsha began, but the sadness in Dar's eyes stopped her.

"It's funny," he said, in a voice full of regret. "In the beginning, when we first met, I tried everything I could think of to persuade her that we weren't meant to be together. When I finally changed my mind, it was too late."

"You don't know that," she told him. "She might still come."

He shook his head, permitting himself a rueful grin. "I don't think so. Her people want her to rule, and she knew it was the right thing to do, so she embraced her duty. Besides, she was always meant to be queen. She will be perfect at it."

Tarsha fed them after that, the four of them sitting around the little table in the dining area, talking further, speculating on the future, just taking advantage of being together at least once more. Eventually, they ran out of things to say and the silences grew longer and more awkward. She asked them to stay the night and perhaps another day, but she knew they would leave soon. Brecon would go back to his family, and the other two would go to wherever they now believed their homes to be. It made her sad to think they might never see one another again, but she knew it was inevitable.

But they all did stay on another day, and then Brecon and Dar departed, both bound for the Elven capital city. They asked Shea to come with them, suggesting he might enjoy a short visit to the Elven nation, but the boy declined, arguing he needed help from Tarsha to manage his magic and should not put that off.

"Thanks for letting me stay—apart from helping me with the magic," he confessed to Tarsha when they were alone. "I don't really have anywhere to go now that Rocan is dead. I think the Rovers would take me in if I asked, but it wouldn't be the same. All my friends were on the *Behemoth*."

"I know. And I am so sorry about what happened to them."

"You probably have plans of your own, and they probably don't include me hanging around, but it would just be for a little while." He gave her one of his familiar crooked grins. "You know, until I get a firm grip on . . . well, whatever it is I need to get a firm grip on."

She put a comforting hand on his shoulder. "I have no plans, and you can stay as long as you like." She said it warmly, understanding only too well the feeling of having no place to call your own.

He nodded his thanks, then looked suddenly embarrassed. "Also, this might sound weird, but . . . I missed you. I know we didn't start off as friends, but I feel like maybe we could be friends now."

She almost laughed at how hard he was trying not to sound desperate, but managed to keep a straight face.

"Shea, I think we are way past the *could be* stage. You and I *are* friends. And I meant what I said. You can stay as long as you wish."

"Well, that's . . . I can't tell you how much . . . really, I won't be in the way, you just tell me if I . . ." He trailed off, gathering himself. "Thanks, Tarsha."

This time she did laugh. But she hugged him once more, and gave him another kiss.

# FORTY-TWO

———————————————◆———————————————

AFTER LEAVING TARSHA AND Shea in Emberen, Dar Leah accompanied Brecon to Arborlon for what he intended to be a week and ended up being more like a month. They hunted and fished, worked in the Gardens of Life, and ate and drank lavishly. They walked the woods and talked at length about everything that had happened since the Blade had come to the Elven city to persuade his friend to help find Tarsha Kaynin. The Elfstones were back in their old place of concealment—the new king's sleeping chambers—with no one the wiser. Neither the Elf nor the Borderman saw any point in poking that hornet's nest—especially since Brecon's oldest brother was now king and the two had never been particularly close.

And, well . . . some things are best left untold.

They did spend time with Brecon's mother, who made a point of thanking Dar profusely for seeing her son home safely. Both Brecon and he insisted they had never been in any particular danger, and the entire voyage east over the waters of the Tiderace had been nothing more than a grand adventure. Neither mentioned the Skaar or their encounter with the *pretender.*

Neither mentioned Ajin d'Amphere.

Except when they were alone; then Ajin's name came up all the time. Brecon knew how his friend felt about the Skaar princess and kept insisting that maybe Dar's decision to leave Skaarsland was made too hastily and out of a misplaced concern for her future as queen of the Skaar nation.

"Even though Ajin is queen, that shouldn't be an impediment to being with her. You helped save Skaarsland, after all. Surely the people would make an exception for you. And besides, when has Ajin not gotten exactly what she wanted?"

Dar shook his head. "It isn't Ajin's place to make such a decision. There are rules and traditions when it comes to marrying into royalty. We were never more than lovers, Brecon. I have no royal blood and I am not a Skaar, in any case. We argued this out. Her advisers have told her any relationship with me would be a mistake. She says she can change their minds, that she can find a way, but in the meantime, what happens to her life and mine? I just don't see how this can work out the way we want it to. Royal consorts can't be commoners—especially ones who come from another part of the world."

"But she loves you. She always has. And who's to say the Skaar wouldn't love you, too? Or at least respect you enough to realize what you mean to her? Besides, you just left her. You didn't even say goodbye; you just flew out of there the morning after the coronation. You need to go back and see how things stand. You need to put things right between you."

"Trust me, things are as right as they will ever be. Let her have her life. Let her have a chance to see what matters now that she is queen. If I go back now, I will just be a reminder of what she can't make happen."

Brecon found this line of reasoning infuriating nonsense and said so. But by the time Dar left for home, intending to go back to his family in the Highlands, the Elven prince had given up the argument and simply told him not to stay away so long before coming back for another visit. If he did, Brecon would be forced to come drag him back by force.

So Dar Leah went home to his parents and siblings, giving them news of the fall of Paranor and the demise of the Druids, then providing them with details of the Skaar and the war that had never come about, saying nothing of Ajin. He could not make himself speak of her to them, although he couldn't have said exactly why. Perhaps it was his feeling that what had happened between Ajin and himself was private, and should be kept that way. Besides, it hurt too much to do anything else. In spite of his stoic acceptance of their separation, he thought about her all the time. And although he tried not to, he found himself wishing he had made a different choice.

He missed Shea Ohmsford, too, but he knew the boy belonged with Tarsha Kaynin for now. One day, he would go back to Tarsha and find out if Shea was still there or had moved on. He was inclined to bet on the former.

After a little more than a month with his family, he

grew restless. Making his excuses, he left for the hunting cabin he had helped build as a boy, deciding he wanted to be off by himself for a while to think about his future. His time as a Druid Blade was finished, and he was not now sure where to go or what to do. So, basically, he settled on doing nothing and waiting to see what came along.

He waited weeks, and then one fine summer day—a slow, lazy, warm day when life feels so good it seems nothing can improve it—he walked back to his cabin after a long hike and found a familiar figure sitting on the steps, waiting.

It was Ajin.

His heart quickened, and he found himself slowing down almost without realizing it. *Impossible,* he thought at once. He was imagining it. This was someone else. It *had* to be someone else. He wanted to believe it was Ajin, but his mind and his eyes were conspiring to trick him. It couldn't be her.

Yet as he drew closer, he saw it was. The same blond hair cropped short and teased into ringlets, the same clear blue eyes, the same exquisite features and maddeningly confident look.

He walked up to her, shaking his head while he gathered his thoughts. "It really is you!"

She shrugged, not bothering to rise to greet him, just sitting there, staring back, a faint grin on her lips. But still, he could see the uncertainty behind her eyes. Perhaps she wasn't as confident of her reception here as she was pretending—and that very hesitation sent a wave of tenderness flooding through him.

"Aren't we the star-crossed pair?" she said. "We just keep bumping into each other."

"How did you find me?"

"Hard work, that. Brecon pointed the way to your home. Your family was very helpful once they knew who I was. They were a little surprised, though. It seems you had never mentioned me."

He could hear the hurt in her voice, and shook his head. "I couldn't talk about you with them. It was too painful."

"Are your memories of me that bad?" she teased, though her voice was tight.

He laughed in spite of himself. "Well, they're haunting, anyway. I've thought about you every single day since I left."

"Have you?" Her smile was firmer now, dazzling to his eyes. "You certainly didn't suggest it by running off immediately following my coronation. One last night of passion and out the door?"

When she smiled like that, everything else disappeared, and his attempt at staying calm vanished in a tumble of emotions. He took a deep breath. "Is that why you're here? To chastise me?"

"Maybe. You deserve it. But I came for something else."

"What would that be?"

"Oh, various things. A bit of curiosity. A bit of impulsiveness." She paused. "But I mostly just wanted to see how you were."

"How long are you staying?"

"That depends." She got to her feet and walked up to him. "I've been doing good work, Dar. I've been a better queen than I expected I would be. My mother thinks I am exactly right for the position, and my people agree. Everyone is happy—except for me. And I'm the one who matters. I should be enjoying the challenges; I am provided with the sorts of opportunities I enjoy—working with people, understanding their problems, figuring out how to solve them. But something is missing, and I think you know what it is." Her gaze locked on his. "You."

She paused, reflecting. "I know my counselors said we couldn't wed, that people wouldn't accept it. So I told them I'd resign, turn in my crown, and wish them well. Unless, of course, they changed their minds about allowing us to be together. They've had sufficient time to see how well I was doing and to realize what it would mean if I abdicated. Too many people rely on me; too many appreciate the way I have conducted myself as ruler. Things are so much better now than before I came back. With the winter gone, the milder weather has resurfaced, and life is returning to normal. Our scientists have begun building more machines like the one Tindall invented. Soon enough, we will have dozens of Annabelles to rely on should the weather choose to change back again."

She paused. "In any case, Skaarsland is settled enough for the moment that it can do without me for a bit. I decided to take some time to see what I could do about my own unsettled feelings. I thought perhaps reaching an accord with you would help correct that. I didn't much care for the way we left things between us—especially after I found you chose to just disappear rather than try to work them out."

She shrugged. "So, here I am."

"Here you are," he repeated.

She placed her hands on his shoulders. "I want you to come back with me, Darcon Leah. You know as well as I do we belong together—no matter the obstacles, no matter what others think. I believe we can work things out. That is . . ." She looked uncertain again. ". . . if that is what you still want?"

He shook his head in disbelief. "I've never wanted anything else. But I don't see that anything has changed, Ajin. You're queen, and you can't partner with a commoner—especially an outlander. And if we can't be together in every sense, where does that leave us? We would both be miserable. It's why I chose to just disappear. I saw myself as an obstacle, and I didn't want to be that. And I love you too much not to share your life."

She looked amused. "I said much the same things to my advisers on announcing why I was giving up the throne. I don't need someone to help me rule. I don't need a king." She gave his shoulders a hard squeeze. "What I do need is Paranor's Blade to be my personal defender, there at my side every hour of every day, protecting me and keeping me safe." She raised her hands to cup his face. "Who is there can do that better than you?"

"Ajin . . ."

"Who better, Darcon Leah?"

He smiled. "No one."

"This is what I told them. This is what I made them understand. What difference does it make if we are something more than Skaarsland queen and Blade?

We are meant to be life partners. We are meant to be together always. And my advisers have come to accept I won't tolerate not having you with me. For now, that is enough. A marriage and a wedding will come with time."

Being so close to her was making him dizzy, and it was hard to find words. She was offering him everything he had always wanted.

"So, again, here I am." She moved closer. "What do you have here that would be better than being with me? Tell me that you honestly prefer living out here in the wilderness, counting pinecones for entertainment. If you can convince me there is anything at all to keep you here, I will say goodbye right now. Otherwise, you will come home with me. Together, we will face my advisers and anyone else who thinks we don't belong together, and together we will convince them that they are wrong." She moved right up against him. "Tell me, do you still want me?"

"Always."

"And how *much* do you want me?"

"A lot."

Her eyes locked on his as she kissed him. "And how much is that, my brave but often muddleheaded Blade? How much?"

He started to answer, but her hand came up quickly to cover his mouth. "No. Don't tell me. Show me."

Then she kissed him again, and he took her into his arms and his life once more.

# FORTY-THREE

---

SEVERAL MONTHS AFTER SHEA Ohmsford moved in with her, Tarsha Kaynin remembered the letter that Drisker had written. She had tucked it away in a drawer, thinking to read it when she felt more able to hear his voice in her head, then had simply forgotten about it. Now, sufficiently recovered from the shock of her mentor's death and the terrible knowledge that he was gone forever, she recalled it and decided it was time to take it out and read it. Shea was off in the woods somewhere with Flinc, practicing his tracking skills. He had been working so hard on mastering his use of the wishsong that she had decided he needed a break for the day. So she was all alone until late afternoon with no demands on her time, and there was no reason to wait any longer.

She sat down on the porch, untied the leather binding strap, and unrolled a single sheet of paper. She read it through, then read it again before setting it aside and staring off into the trees.

*Three times shall you have a chance to make a difference in the lives of others and three times shall you do so. But one time you shall change the world.*

Parlindru.

The rule of three.

She recalled, as best as she could, how each of the three might have come to pass, but her reasoning felt flawed. Some fulfillments seemed clear, while others felt uncertain. But she felt a need to list them.

How many times had she died and come back to life? Surely more than three. Once, when Tavo tried to stab her with the Stiehl, while under the sway of Clizia Porse, but had found only an image created by Drisker. Again when Clizia caught her off guard at Cleeg Hold and knocked her over the cliffside into a canyon hundreds of feet deep. And most recently here, in Emberen, again facing Clizia. She had escaped all three, but it still seemed as if there must have been more.

And then Parlindru had told her she would love three times, but only one of the three would last. There was Drisker and Tavo, that was two, and now both were dead, so that had come true. But who was the third? Flinc? She did like the little forest imp, but love him—on any level? Maybe Brecon, then. She had been very attracted to him. Would he come back into her life?

Then she paused when she came to Shea. Was the street boy from Varfleet someone she could love? She shook her head, refusing even to consider it. She was in no way ready to let herself think about the possibility of Shea Ohmsford as her one true love. It was simply too strange.

Which left the third prophecy in Parlindru's rule of three.

She would make a difference in the lives of others three times, and once when she did she would change the world.

She hadn't given it much thought—certainly not as much as the other two—possibly because there was no way she could imagine such a thing and possibly because it did not even seem real. What could she possibly do to change a life?

But now, here it was, clearly set forth in Drisker's letter—the prophecy she had been wondering about, and perhaps the last to go unfulfilled. She could not mistake it for anything other than what it was. She balled up her fists and squeezed her eyes shut in frustration and dismay. She did not want this. She wanted no part of it. But she knew she could not avoid it or ignore it or shove it off on someone else. Only she could make the choice.

And she *would* change the world, whatever she decided.

She sat waiting for Shea to return, and the wait was a long one. She drank several glasses of ale and ate lunch, still sitting on the porch. She thought to walk a bit but couldn't muster the energy. She felt oddly drained; it was as if the knowledge of the charge she had been given had sapped her strength.

*Shades! What am I supposed to do?*

It was dark when Shea returned, appearing abruptly out of the shadows, moving into the moonlight and crossing the yard to sit down beside her. For a moment, neither spoke.

"That forest imp knows a whole lot about tracking," he announced, giving her a look. "And about hiding in plain sight. And about leaving no tracks, and finding trails others have thought to hide." He glanced over. "Has he really been alive since the time of Faerie?"

Tarsha shrugged. "He says so. That doesn't make it true."

"But who's going to call him on it, right?" The boy stretched his legs, then he glanced over at her and paused. "What's wrong?"

"Nothing. Just thinking."

"Maybe. But you're thinking about something that's wrong. What is it?"

She looked back. He was so intuitive, so sharp. She liked that about him. "Why do you ask?"

He looked astounded. "Maybe because I'm your friend and care about you? Maybe because you look like you've been sitting there all afternoon, and I was hoping maybe you were waiting on me to talk about it?"

"Maybe I was."

"Then let's talk. What's wrong? Something is; I can tell that much."

She stared at him a moment, taken aback at the ease with which he read her mood. Then she nodded. "All right. Before he died, Drisker wrote a letter and gave it to Grianne Ohmsford and asked her to see that I received it if he didn't return. She delivered it, but I put it in a drawer, intending to read it when I felt more distanced from the pain of losing Drisker. Then I forgot about it. Today I remembered."

The boy nodded, waiting on her.

"I have to go back to Paranor," she said. "I've been

asked to do something, but I don't think I can decide whether to do it or not without going there. Will you be all right without me?"

"Wait! What? You're not going to tell me what was in the letter? You can't do that!"

She gave him a look. "It involves me, not you. I will only be gone a few days. Will you be all right?"

"I'll be just fine, because I'm going with you."

"This has to be my decision, not—"

"I don't care about your decision!" he shouted. "I'm going with you!" He took a deep breath, steadying himself. "Rocan left me behind when he took Annabelle and the *Behemoth* and all his relatives and friends into that storm, and none of them came back. Then Seelah left me, as well. I don't know what you're up to, but I'm not going to be left behind again—not for any reason. I won't interfere with your decision, whatever it is. I just want to be sure nothing happens to you. This can't be so difficult for you to understand, can it?"

Then quickly he held up one hand as she tried to talk. "No, listen! You need company, just in case. What if things go wrong and you're all alone? Then what?"

"They won't go wrong."

"Oh, sure. You can see the future, right? You can tell what's going to happen? Just forget it! I'm coming, and that's the end of it."

"You're angry."

"I'm not . . ." He broke off. "Okay, maybe I am. But you hurt my feelings when you said you don't need me. Besides, I don't believe it. You do need me. I'm your friend. Probably your best friend . . . and maybe I'll be more than that, one day."

"Oh?" She grinned. "You've been letting your imagination run wild again, haven't you?"

He shrugged. "I like you. A lot. And I think maybe you like me, too."

"Maybe. Just don't get carried away."

"I'm fifteen years old. You're only three years older than me."

"Four." She got up. "I'm going to bed. We can talk about this in the morning."

But she had no intention of doing any such thing. Bright and early—before the sun was up and while night's shadows still draped the forest and the darkness was deeply hushed—she rose, dressed, grabbed the canvas bag she had packed the night before, and slipped from her bedroom. She passed silently through the living room and went out the front door. She was going alone, no matter what he thought.

"What took you so long?" Shea said, emerging from the shadows packed and ready to go. It brought her up short. How did he know what she was going to do? She shook her head at him. You had to admire his persistence. When that boy made up his mind, he followed through. And sometimes you had to accept the inevitable with as much grace as you could muster.

She smiled and nodded. "Sorry to be late. Let's go."

They flew east for three days to reach Paranor, spending the first night under a clear sky in the Streleheim, wrapped in blankets and pointing out shooting stars. There was a certain comfort to having Shea with her,

Tarsha had to admit—a certain relief in not being alone. She had thought it better to do this by herself, but she realized quickly enough she had been mistaken. For something like this, it was better to have company—to have a witness, someone to question any choice she made.

That might not be a bad idea at all.

They reached their destination late on the third day, landing close to the walls of the Druid's Keep, its bulk a huge dark presence in the fading light. It had aged already, as if standing empty for even those few months had allowed the forest to alter it dramatically. Weeds and vines grew up against the stones of its massive walls. Cracks had even begun to appear— a stark contrast with the seeming immutability Tarsha remembered from before. With no one inhabiting the Keep, it looked to have become a relic of a different age. It looked as if it were sleeping, and the Guardian sleeping with it. All these years it had stood there— the home of the Druids, and a symbol of the magic they wielded. A powerful guarantee that the Four Lands would be warded against the dark things of their world.

And now it was fading.

"Creepy," Shea declared. "Do we have to go inside?"

Tarsha shook her head. "No. We can stay out here."

Leaving him where he was, she walked closer, listening for the whispering sounds of the Guardian, but there were none. Paranor was quiet. It was a living entity—created of ancient magic and imbued with the power to exist eternally—and yet it seemed devoid of life.

Shea came up beside her. "Are you going to tell me about the letter now?"

She nodded. "The letter was written when Drisker . . ." She stopped abruptly, a tear sliding down her cheek. "I'll just read it to you."

She pulled it from her backpack and began:

Tarsha.

If you are reading this, then I am not coming back. This means you are the last Druid. To you falls the responsibility of forming a new Druid order—of curating the magic of the Four Lands, of protecting her from dark conjurings and darker artifacts that might threaten her, of opening Paranor and making it your home.

Druids past would say it is your duty, but I disagree. The decision is yours, and yours alone.

I could not do any of this successfully when I was Ard Rhys, and I do not suggest you will be able to do any better. But you have to decide. The words written below will send Paranor back into a limbo existence and she will disappear from the Four Lands until summoned again, and the Druid order will die with me. Or should you change your mind, you can take up the mantle that I failed to bear and use the Black Elfstone to bring her back again. I cannot tell you what to do. I can only tell you to do what feels right.

The choice is given to you and to you alone. Choose well.

She finished and put the letter away again. Shea was staring at her when she looked up, astonishment reflected in his young features. "What are you going to do?"

She shook her head. "I don't know. I came here to try to find out. I thought it might help if I was present when I made the decision."

Random thoughts assailed her. How the Shade of Allanon had ordered a reluctant Drisker to ordain her as his successor at the shores of the Hadeshorn so that she would be prepared to take up the Druid mantle. How when she entered Paranor in search of a way to bring her mentor out of the Forbidding, the Guardian of the Keep had confronted her, but instead of attacking her, had bowed. Did she not have an obligation to honor those acknowledgments? Could she refuse the responsibilities that had so clearly been bestowed on her?

And what of the artifacts that Grianne Ohmsford had left in her care: the darkwand, the Stiehl, and the two scrye orbs? Could she simply leave them in their hiding place as if no care or usage was required of them? Could she pretend that all of Paranor's magic was better off left untouched and forgotten?

Could she walk away, even knowing it was what she wanted to do?

"This all seems wrong!" Shea exclaimed. "It's unfair to ask one person to make such a choice—and especially you. You've been through enough. I don't care what the grandfather says. It shouldn't have to be you."

"But apparently it is."

She told him then of Parlindru and the rule of three. She skipped the details on the other two prophecies and concentrated her explanation on the one saying she would change the lives of others three times, but once she would change the world.

"Don't you see?" she asked quietly. "Whichever choice I make, I will be changing the world. The course of events resulting from my choice will depend heavily on whether or not there are Druids and magic. If I do as Allanon expected me to do, I will be adding to a line of magic users that has lasted almost three thousand years. It is the Druids who have fostered and sustained magic, and the Druids who have managed it so that its uses are wise ones. So if I become a new Druid, I will be committing to sustaining magic as a presence in the Four Lands. If I step away, significant amounts of magic will be lost and perhaps it will die out entirely. So which choice is better? Are we better off with magic in the world or not? Just look at what happened because Tindall decided to build a machine that changes the weather. We have a new science now. Perhaps this is what the Races are meant to rely on. Perhaps magic has run its course. Maybe the world is better off without it."

The boy started to say something but stopped himself when she continued talking.

"But how will we find our way without magic after we have relied on it for so long? Magic has protected us. Magic has allowed us to evolve—to bring that new science to life. And what happened in Skaarsland would not have happened had science and your magic not combined. So are we to abandon it? The Elves won't. Magic has always had a purpose for them, even before the Great Wars. How will they be affected? What will they do as a consequence of having something no one else has? Will they disappear as they did before? Will they be driven from the Four Lands because they have power no one else does? If all that remains is rogue magic and stray artifacts, what will this do to the Races?"

She slumped to the ground, staring at Paranor's walls as the shadows closed about. "I'm being asked to decide the future without knowing anything at all about what will happen once I do. I'm being asked to intuit what is right for *all* the Races. But how can I know this?"

Shea dropped down beside her. "You can't. No one can. All you can do is what the grandfather told you. Choose the way that feels right and hope for the best."

Tarsha nodded wordlessly, overwhelmed by the challenge, afraid of what would happen no matter what choice she made. What if the future was less a choice between science or magic, but a balance? What if both were needed, to move forward together, much as Shea had proved in Skaarsland?

The boy moved closer to her and put his arm around her shoulders. "You know what? I think whatever choice you make will be the right one. And no matter what you decide, I will support you. That's what friends do, and we're friends, aren't we? Look at how much help you've given me with my wishsong. Now maybe it's my turn to do something to help you."

She reached up and placed her hand over his and felt him lean his head against her. They sat in silence as the sun disappeared, taking the last of its light with it. Together, they watched the stars appear.

Together, they tried to imagine the future.

Read on for an excerpt from

# CHILD
# OF
# LIGHT

## BY TERRY BROOKS

◆

From the brilliant mind behind
the Shannara saga comes the first book
in an electrifying new fantasy series
about a human girl struggling
to find her place in a magical world
she never even knew existed.

Enjoy this sneak peek!

WE BREAK OUT AT midnight, just as we agreed. Like ghosts risen from our graves to reclaim the lives that were stolen from us, we flee.

We are quick and we are fast, one following the other, staying in order the way Tommy has taught us, pretending it's just a drill, knowing it isn't. No one speaks, no one whispers; no one makes any sound they can avoid. There are no mistakes because there can be no mistakes. Others who have tried to escape this facility before have all made at least one mistake. And all are dead.

*Courage,* I tell myself. I am desperate to get free. We all are. *Don't think. Just go!*

There are fifteen of us—too many for what we are attempting. But once someone is in, it is impossible to decide later that they are out—unless of course you are willing to kill them to keep them from talking. I couldn't do that. None of us could. We're just kids. Ordinary kids in other circumstances; something else now. But still, just kids, not killers. Not yet, anyway. None of us has killed anyone—except maybe JoJo. He says he has, but we can't be sure about what he has or hasn't done. He's big on talk, but you can usually tell when someone is padding the truth, making himself appear to be something he isn't. We all thought that was what he was doing.

But still we wonder.

We started out as a group of eight: Tommy, Malik, Barris and Breck, Wince, JoJo, Khoury, and me. That would have been enough if together we possessed the skills and knowledge that are needed. But we need more to make this escape happen, as we find out quickly enough once we begin to talk our way through the plan. So we are forced to bring in other kids. It is easy enough to choose the ones we are looking for. All we have to do is keep our eyes and ears open until we discover the handful we need. There are only about 330 of us in the camp. I don't know if other camps exist.

Still, I assume there must be more. Given this one's purpose, there'd pretty much have to be. It's simple mathematics. Our captors number in the hundreds. We call them Goblins—though in truth we have no idea who or what they really are, save not Human. Piggish faces, warped and twisted limbs, bodies much larger than those of Humans, skin hanging loose in gray mottled folds, voices that communicate as often with grunts and snorts as with words. They are despicable creatures that transcend our worst nightmares. The kids in the prison are here to serve them. We are brought here from all over and raised in captivity. Our lives are predetermined. Someone is needed to maintain and operate the hydroponic farms and weapons factories. But the Goblins require something else from us in payment for their services as our jailors. Goblins are carnivores and require fresh meat, so prisoners offer a ready source of both food *and* labor.

Our fates as prisoners are fixed. From the moment we arrive, all of us must work to maintain or repair the prison and grounds or be eaten. The disabled, weak, and injured kids are dispatched early. Those who remain healthy and able-bodied are allowed to grow until they are deemed adults and then sent to the reproductive pens, the work farms, and the factories. Unless, as sometimes happens, overpopulation of the prison requires a culling. Then the healthy are eaten, too. Our numbers are never allowed to fluctuate far. If too many die, new kids take their place. Where do the Goblins find them? Where did they find any of us? How are we chosen? No one knows. I don't know what I am doing here, and this seems to be true for the others as well.

The one common denominator we all share is that no one seems to miss us. Some of us are orphans. Others had families—gone now? I wonder if it is the same in the other camps, the ones we never see. Is it different for them? I don't know; I have no way of knowing. I just hope it isn't something worse.

All of us are between the ages of ten and twenty. Adults and little kids are kept elsewhere; we don't know where. Kids like us are designated as worker bees until we are determined to be old enough for transport to the reproductive pens. There we are paired off and forced to make babies. Once you spend enough time in the pens to renew the population, you are shipped out to work the farms and factories. If you are unable to reproduce or work, you are retired. That's what it is called—*retired*. A euphemism for *executed*. Put down because you no longer serve any useful purpose. Disposed of because, if you can't work and you can't reproduce, you are just taking up space. Sometimes they keep you for other reasons—but not often and not for long. And not for pets. Goblins don't have pets. Just those monstrous things they call Ronks, and those are used primarily for hunting. You can imagine what sort of hunting, right?

I am nineteen years of age, as best as I can tell, but the Goblins don't know it. I look very young for my age. Luck of the draw. Because in another year, maybe less, they'll quit caring how I look. They will send me to the pens anyway. I have already made myself a promise. I won't make babies for them. I will die first.

The fifteen of us trying to break free have agreed about what is going to happen. There are only two possibilities. *All of us will get out or none of us will.* If it is the latter, there is no point in wondering about your future. If it's the former, we will be hunted like animals—because, like I say, that is how the Goblins see us.

We go out of our cellblock in two groups—one of seven, one of eight—using lockpicks I have fashioned during the weeks of planning, opening all the doors we can to allow others to do what they want so long as they understand they are not to follow us. Some try anyway because they see it as their only chance, but JoJo discourages them as only JoJo can. What happens to them after that, I don't know. I can't stop to think about it because when you are on the run you don't have time to think about anything but what's going to happen if you are caught.

Once clear of the cells, we take out the night guards who patrol the walkways—a process carried out by Tommy and Malik using makeshift knives one of our group has fashioned from stolen pieces of shop metal. Their efforts are quick and silent, and the blood on their clothes marks a rite of passage. We race down the stairs to the cellars and through the storage areas. The Goblins don't see us; they don't hear us. Guards standing watch outside the doors of the compounds have no idea yet what is happening inside. Why would they even think about it? You don't think much about your animals once they are safely penned in for the night. You just lock them in and come back for them in the morning. Escape? To what end? Even if we get out, where will we go? We will be missed quickly enough during the morning count; we will be hunted down and brought back. Most will be made an example of. I have seen what that means; they assemble everyone to watch. It isn't something you are likely to forget. It takes a long time to die when you are systematically dismembered. It serves as a useful deterrent to further escape attempts.

Except that sometimes even that isn't enough. When survival means you live in a cage and are reduced to the life of an imprisoned animal, a chance at freedom is worth any risk.

The tunnel we crawl through is actually an old drainage pipe. It is only used during the flooding periods, and we aren't in one now. Finding the pipe was a rare piece of luck. At first we figured we'd have to climb over or tunnel under the prison walls, using rope ladders for the former or endless digging for the latter. But Wince found the opening to the pipe by accident one day while mopping the cellar floors. It lay behind an iron lid fastened to the stone block wall, but he could tell the lid was meant to open and close and he figured out how to do it. Next time he was sent down he carried lockpicks concealed in the soles of his shoes. It took him only minutes to release the seal on the lid. Once he got that far he wriggled his way inside (being every bit as supple and stretchy as a desert cat) and found a hatch that opened into the pipe. Not long after that, he was moved from mopping floors to organizing storerooms, but he still risked everything to slip away and unseal the hatch, crawl inside, and follow it both ways, discovering that one direction took you to what appeared to be a very deep spill pit and the other to beyond the walls and a way out onto the wastelands.

It was Tommy who decided this is how we would escape. A grate seals the far end, but that is hardly enough to stop us if we can make a substance that will melt and break the lock. A big problem without access to chemical corrosives, but then Khoury surprised me by saying she could provide what we needed from the dissolvent she works with in the labs. What was left was to figure out when we would go and how we would survive once we were outside the walls. How big are the wastelands? How many miles would we have to walk to cross them? No one knows. We were all either born in prison or brought here from other places, and we don't know where anything is. But

Tommy found a way onto the roof one day on the pretense of checking for damage after a storm, and his report was deeply troubling. There is nothing but open ground and scrub brush for as far as the eye can see.

No one knows for sure what is out there. How are we supposed to stay alive knowing so little?

But Tommy had an answer for this just as he did for everything. He is the son of survivalists, after all, and he knows how to stay alive in any environment. He knows where to find food and water. He knows how to hunt and camp and hide so we can't be found—how to create a false trail and conceal his tracks. You can't learn how to do all that unless you've done it, and he has. Unlike the rest save for me, he lived free until he was in his teens, when a Goblin patrol caught his family in the open and took them prisoner. Tommy was brought here. He doesn't know what happened to his parents—he never saw them again—but Tommy is a survivor; we all know that. We chose him as our leader because he is our best chance for staying alive.

Tommy chose me first for his escape plan because I know something of the larger world—although not as much as I pretend—and because I have made it clear that I am determined not to be left behind. We are attracted to each other, and we share confidences. Together—to the extent such things are possible behind prison walls—we make a good team.

Others were added to our little team as time passed. Carefully added. We are a diverse group, united by a common goal but fully aware of the risk we are running.

Girls and boys are housed together in indiscriminate fashion save for one rule: Opposite sexes are never allowed to share the same cell. Reproduction is tightly controlled, and forbidden altogether where we are. Tommy's cellmate is Malik; mine is Khoury—which is one of the reasons she ended up coming with us. But twin sisters are housed on one side of JoJo's cell, and he got to know them pretty well. It was his suggestion we bring them along. Barris and Breck are twins, even though they don't look very much alike. Breck is a chameleon, Barris unchanging. Breck knows how to make things out of scraps and leavings others would never think to bother with. She can fashion clothes, boots, gloves, and hats to protect against the sun, because exposure poses a definite risk if you are caught out in it for too long. Barris is wise and centered and a good source of advice. She always knows what needs to be asked and answered, and someone like that can do a lot of good when you are on the run.

Malik is big and strong, and there was never any question about including him. He is able to lift and haul like a machine. Nothing seems to be beyond him. Incongruously, he is one of the more docile and obedient of us. He is quiet most of the time, seldom chooses to speak—just sits there listening. He latched onto Tommy early, follows him about like a pet dog, and does whatever Tommy asks of him. This can prove to be a problem if Tommy isn't smart about the influence he wields over Malik, but he is careful never to abuse it. After all, it is important to have someone who possesses that size and strength on your side. Still, if Malik ever switches his allegiance or decides Tommy has betrayed him in some way, there will be problems.

We crawl through the drainage pipe in single file, Tommy in the lead, Khoury right behind so she can use the substance she has stolen from the camp stores to break down the metal of the locks and allow us to get out once we reach the grate. We go in single file, same as before, no talking, and no sounds at all. We crawl in darkness, eyes as adjusted to the black as they can be, everyone keeping their heads down. It seems to take much longer to reach the grate than is actually possible, and the feeling of being trapped is pervasive. But no one loses heart or breaks down. Everyone stays in control.

On reaching the drain cover, Khoury moves to the forefront and uncaps the melting substance and pours it on the locks. Steam, a hissing sound, and a sharp, pungent stench ensue. It takes three applications, but finally the locks fall apart and the grate comes free. Malik is there to grab it so it doesn't make any sound when it starts to tumble away, gripping it with both hands as he leans out to lower it into the scrub-choked ditch outside. He goes out after it, then reaches back to help the other kids climb down the steep, slippery sides of the ditch.

In moments we are all in the clear. We stand as a group at the bottom of the ditch and say our good-byes. Our core group of eight will go one way. The second group of add-ons will go the other. There is no particular reason for the choices of direction. But Tommy's thinking is that we will stand a better chance if we split up and reduce our numbers. Common sense. It is easier to track larger groups. Once we are far enough away from the prison, we will all split up again. If we are lucky, most of us will make it out. We will have our chances, each one of us. But I know it won't be enough. Because each of us fully believes that he or she will survive, while common sense says that some of us won't.

I go with Tommy, Malik, JoJo, Barris and Breck, Wince, and Khoury. We go left; the others go right. None of us has the slightest idea in what direction we are traveling or what lies ahead. It doesn't matter, so long as it takes us as far away from the prison as possible before we have to surface onto the flats. The night is cloudless, and moon- and starlight brighten the terrain. Once we crawl out of the ditch we will be exposed. It is bad enough that we will be tracked by the Ronks; worse still if natural light reveals us clearly enough that the Goblins' long-range weapons can bring us down. The Goblins have carriers, too. They will use those to try to find us quickly, crisscrossing the flats until they stumble over us. Luck will prove valuable, if fickle. But foot pursuit using the Ronks doesn't require luck, only patience.

A sudden terrible thought presses in on me, driving straight past my determination. *This is suicidal.* I don't want to think it, but I do. It is a wicked whisper inside my head, a dark promise that foretells my future with sly certainty. I have been fooling myself into thinking escape is possible. It is not. I am going to die.

As if in response to this invasive conviction, everything goes to hell a minute later. Shouts rise up from the other direction—from the direction in which the other group went—sharp and clear, deep-throated and guttural. Goblins. Screams follow and weapons fire reverberates. Spitfires: the nickname given to the long-barreled automatic weapons used by the Goblins, spewing projectiles in sustained or single bursts. There are growls and snarls from the Ronks, and the screams increase. Frantic activity. Desperate pleas rise out of the madness. Our friends, begging. A few final, awful sounds of dying and then silence once more.

They are all gone. All seven of them, caught and killed. I know it is so. I know it as surely as I know we will be next.

Tommy scrambles out of the ditch and looks around. Sees something and beckons us out. We follow him up in a mad rush. Distant vehicle lights shine in the darkness, revealing movement: Ronks. Impossible to mistake them for anything else—hunched shoulders, burly and shaggy bodies, all of them tearing at the remains of our friends. They are a long way off, but it feels like they are already on top of us. The others in my group start out, but I cannot move.

"Auris!" Tommy grabs my arm and drags me away. *Forget them. They're gone.*

Does he speak the words or do I think them instead? Doesn't matter, does it? It is what it is.

We run. I'm not sure toward what, if anything, but I do know why. Escape requires movement, and we are moving fast and hard. Ahead there is a building, low and squat. Tommy heads for it, and we follow. Is there safety to be found? Does Tommy know something we don't? Did he know this building was here and is that why he insists on running toward it?

Tommy, the survivalist, trying to keep us alive. I have to believe that.

I glance back once. The lights of the pursuing vehicles are moving, swinging about in our direction. Coming for us.

We reach the building and find a pair of wide doors opening into it. They are heavily locked. Khoury uses her substance once more, but there isn't all that much left. The metal sizzles and steams, but the lock holds. Malik shoves forward abruptly, seizes the locks in both hands, and yanks hard while twisting—once, twice. The lock separates and the door opens.

We rush inside. Black as darkest night, but light from the moon and stars illuminates four vehicles, all of them similar to the ones coming for us. We clamber into the closest—all but Tommy, who is doing something under the hood. Then he is aboard and in the driver's seat and we are off, bursting out of the building with a surge of power, tires spinning and then gaining traction, racing wildly across the flats.

"Which way?" he yells, as confused by the dark, featureless look of the landscape as the rest of us.

No one answers, because no one knows what to say. Except . . . maybe I do. I have the oddest feeling that I know just which way we should go. Maybe I am crazy but my certainty tugs hard at me.

"That way!" I shout suddenly. And maybe Tommy is crazy, too, because he follows my lead without hesitation, swinging the vehicle in the direction I am pointing.

Behind us, we find three vehicles giving pursuit, Goblins in each, their spitfires flashing. Hunkered down for protection, we hear the sound of multiple charges pinging off the armored shell of our sturdy machine. We have no weapons save for a few hand-made knives. But JoJo rummages around inside a footlocker in the rear of the vehicle's interior and yanks out a pair of long-barreled spitfires. He grins in wild abandon as he flings open a top hatch and rises up to fire at our pursuers. I can't see the results, can't determine the consequences. JoJo drops back down.

We hit a series of rough spots that throw us all over. Another barrage of weapons fire strikes our vehicle, bouncing off the armor and flying away into nowhere. Except for one that doesn't. That one penetrates through a crack in a vent behind the driver, flying about like a guided missile gone rogue. It stops only after it slams into the back of Tommy's head.

Just like that, he is dead.

The shock freezes us all in place, until JoJo screams, "Grab the steering!"

Tommy is slumped over the controls. Malik lifts him away, settling him onto his lap and clasping his friend's lifeless body like a parent would a child, whispering to him. JoJo vaults over the seats and takes Tommy's place. He fumbles about for a few precious moments that cost us speed and distance from our pursuers, and then figures it out. Our vehicle lurches forward with a fresh surge of power, widening our lead anew. I am already thinking about what we have lost. Without Tommy, we have no survivalist knowledge, no steady voice of command, and no leadership to guide us.

Suddenly I am incensed. At fate for depriving us so pointlessly, at the Goblins for being the animals they are, at life in general for its quixotic nature, and mostly at myself for just sitting there. I snatch up the spitfire that JoJo has abandoned and poke my head through the hatch. My hair flies out in a dark stream as I sight down the barrel and start firing in sharp bursts. Whatever sort of ammunition we are using, it is deadly. The spitfire's charges streak in fiery lines to their target—the front windshield of the closest pursuer—and the driver's head explodes. The vehicle veers away, tumbles end-over-end, and bursts into flames.

*One down, two to go.*

I am newly confident now, emboldened, the bloodlust rushing through me red-hot as I take aim at the tires of the second Goblin vehicle, thinking to take it out as well. How did I learn to shoot like this? I don't remember ever having used a weapon that wasn't a blade, but the spitfire feels oddly natural, familiar. Instinctively I know that if I hold down on the trigger, the spitfire will release six short bursts—which is what happened with the first vehicle. If I press and release, it will send a single rocket with six times the punch. I test my instincts by taking aim at the tires and pressing once on the trigger. A rocket streaks out, but the tires hold. I try again. Still nothing. Bullets fly all around me and I duck down. The tires are tougher. I will have to go back to attacking the windshield.

No one tries to take my place in the top hatch. All of them are cheering me on, surprised and grateful that I know how to use the weapon. Flush with excitement, I rise up and open fire once more—this time with a quick release aimed at the windshield. The charge strikes with such force that the glass explodes into fragments. I keep firing. The vehicle catches fire, veers away, and is gone.

More cheers and shouts of appreciation and encouragement. I duck down again, grinning madly. I have a purpose now. I have a use. I have a way to vent my rage. I am elated enough to think we are going to escape after all, that we will get out of this mess and find help.

We are flying across the flats, JoJo doing the best he can to keep us away from the deep ruts and cracks in the hardpan that can slow us down, his face intense. Everything is happening so quickly, but it feels just the opposite; time is all but stopped and we are frozen in place. I check the spitfire, unsure of its load, then cast it aside and take up the other one. A moment to take a deep breath, and I prepare to lift myself back through the hatch for another go at the last pursuer.

But suddenly JoJo looks in the side mirror and grunts in fury. "Something happening back there! Hold on!"

I poke my head and shoulders out of the hatch for a quick look, spitfire extended. Our pursuer is almost on top of us, a fiery charge exploding out of a port above its heavy front bumper. The charge slams into our carrier's rear end and everything goes up in fire and smoke and screams. The entire back shield disappears, and I am thrown halfway out of the hatch and onto the roof.

An instant later the Goblins hit us with a second charge, and our vehicle shudders, lurches, hits a crevice or rut or rough patch, and takes flight. When it comes down again, it is listing heavily and I am flying through the air. Somehow I manage to hold on to the spitfire when the carrier and I part ways—when I am separated from the others entirely—clutching it as if it might give me wings so I can fly to safety. I pinwheel through the air, everything a jumble, then land with a shock so severe I am sure I have broken every bone in my body.

I slide into blackness and everything disappears.